PRAISE FOR THE SPLIT WORLDS

"Newman's return to the Split Worlds series (after *All Is Fair*) is a triumphant merger of Victorian values with modern magic; her fantastical romp through another world takes on class and gender dynamics."
—*Library Journal* **on** *A Little Knowledge*

"If you've yet to encounter this magical series (now available in new editions), you're in for a treat... If you like urban fantasy, regency flair, dark magic, darker fae foes, family feuds, and, most of all, tea, this is the series for you."

—**B&N Sci-Fi & Fantasy**

"Newman brings an intriguing mix of modern world, Victorian/Regency England, and faery in her Split Worlds series, and this third volume brings a strong resolution to the conflicts between the worlds established in the first two volumes."

—*Locus* **magazine**

"A modern fantasy that playfully mixes magic and interesting characters into an intriguing mystery."

—*Kirkus Reviews*

"Newman renders the Split Worlds with verve and an infectious sense of fun, and presents in Cathy a strong and personable heroine."

—*The Guardian*

"Emma Newman has built a modern fantasy world with such élan and authority her ideas of why and how the seemingly irrational world of Fairy works should be stolen by every other writer in the field. Her characters are complex and troubled, courageous at times and foolhardy. This book of wonders is first rate."

—**Bill Willingham, Eisner A~~~~~ ~~~~ ~~~er**
and creato~~~~~~~~~~~~~~~~~~~~~~~~ns

"Emma Newman has created a ~~~~~~~~~~~~~~~ ~e
that charming is not safe. *Betw~~~~~~~~~~~~~~~ ~s

beneath the glamour of the social Season. Learning to be a young lady has never seemed so dangerous."

—Mary Robinette Kowal, Hugo Award winner and author of *Glamour in Glass*

"With a feather-light touch, Emma Newman has crafted a very English fantasy, one brilliantly realised and quite delightful, weaving magic, mystery and parallel worlds together with ease. Newman may well be one of our brightest stars, The Split Worlds: *Between Two Thorns* is just the beginning of a remarkable journey."

—Adam Christopher, author of *Empire State* and *Seven Wonders*

"*Between Two Thorns* is magical, exciting, and clever. It manages to conjure a world that feels completely natural but also mysterious, sometimes dangerous, sometimes funny, combining several different kinds of urban fantasy into one story, and capturing a lovely sense of modern Britishness that is reminiscent of other fantastic British fantasy. I'm eagerly awaiting the sequel!"

—Fantasy Faction

"This novel draws you in from the very first, tempting you with magical creatures set against present day Bath. I tried only reading one chapter just to test the writing style, etc but found myself, a few hours later, having read a vast amount of the book… It sits beautifully within my favourite type of fantasy novel, fairy tale within the present day."

—SF Crowsnest on *Between Two Thorns*

"An enchanting novel from Emma Newman, an urban fantasy that has no sign of tattooed women in leather pants. A headstrong scion and an investigator discover dark doings in the outwardly genteel world of Bath's secret mirror city."

—SF Signal

"Once you start this magical book, you won't be going anywhere until you finish it. Absolutely brilliant."

—Geek Syndicate on *Between Two Thorns*

all good things

THE SPLIT WORLDS
BOOK FIVE

EMMA
NEWMAN

DIVERSIONBOOKS

Also by Emma Newman

The Split Worlds Series
Between Two Thorns
Any Other Name
All is Fair
A Little Knowledge

Diversion Books
A Division of Diversion Publishing Corp.
443 Park Avenue South, Suite 1008
New York, New York 10016
www.DiversionBooks.com

This is a work of fiction. Names, characters, places and incidents either are the
product of the author's imagination or are used fictitiously. Any resemblance to
actual persons, living or dead, events or locales is entirely coincidental.

For more information, email info@diversionbooks.com

First Diversion Books edition June 2017.
Print ISBN: 978-1-68230-616-1
eBook ISBN: 978-1-68230-617-8

For the shining ones who donned their best garb
and entered the Split Worlds via the mundane city of Bath
on the 7th of May, 2016, and for the incredible souls
who helped to weave that magical day around them.

1

The sickly scent of burning irises made Cathy's eyes sting. But she wasn't done yet. It had been a large bouquet and there was a lot of rage to vent.

"He said he loved me." She plucked a petal and tossed it into the flames. "He did not." Another soon followed it. "He made me think I had consented." The penultimate petal was pulled off. "I. Did. Not. Consent." After ripping the last petal away from the stalk, she watched it curl and combust before throwing in the rest of the stem.

There were three flowers left in the tissue paper. Mrs Morrison, Sam's housekeeper, had cooed over them when she'd brought them to the living room, all smiles and delight. It had taken what little energy Cathy had left in her to accept them calmly and not just splurge her emotions all over the poor woman. If Sam had been there, she was certain that he'd have turned the florist away and paid them to never return.

Tired, spent, and aware she'd wallowed enough, Cathy snatched up the last three blooms. "Fuck. William. Iris," she said with each one thrown into the blaze. The tissue paper, along with the unopened card, soon followed.

"He's such a dick," she muttered. What did he think a bunch of bloody flowers was going to achieve? Surely even he knew that no Iris magic would survive past the boundary of Lord Iron's estate? Did he honestly believe a bouquet would make her regret leaving him? Idiot.

Cathy frowned into the flames. No. Will was many things—she drew in a sharp breath at the messy torrent of images and memory flashes that hit her then—but he was not stupid. He wasn't trying to make her feel anything emotional. He was sending her a message: *I know exactly where you are.*

She'd known that would be the case. No doubt he and Lord Iris had felt Sam breaking all the magic they'd forced upon her. And it wasn't like Sam could hide away, given the fact that his bizarre inheritance had made it into the national press. He was the only person Cathy knew of who was a big deal in all the worlds. Finding his home would have been a trivial matter.

Shivering despite the fire, Cathy pulled the fluffy blanket off the back of the sofa and wrapped it around herself. The assumption that she'd be with Lord Iron was an obvious one; there was literally nowhere else in any of the worlds where she could be safe. She'd simply exchanged one gilded cage for another.

The tears seemed to have no end, even though she'd been crying on and off for the whole week since she'd fled. Swearing beneath her breath, Cathy fished another tissue from the box and wiped her face. All she had done was cry and watch TV. She'd curled in a ball in the corner of the huge sofa, trying to keep an emotional tsunami at bay with *Adventure Time* and *Battlestar Galactica*, all the while knowing she should be doing something. There were too many people dependent on her, too many people who needed her help, for her to disappear in such a cowardly manner. But the truth was: she had no idea what to do. If she left the house, she had no doubt that Will would pounce on her. It felt like she was a mouse cowering in a hole with a cat waiting outside. With Lord Iris's plans for a child, she knew Will would have the most powerful magic at his disposal. If he got hold of her again, she'd never be able to escape.

The fear of being under his control again and the genuine lack of any other safe place to go were utterly paralysing. She had bolted as soon as Max had revealed the magic Will had cast upon her, thinking of nothing but getting away from him and making her mind and her heart her own again. But what was the use of this clarity if it rendered her useless?

Having no idea what to do next left her traitorous mind free to ruminate. How many times had she replayed that last morning with

Will when he'd placed that choker around her neck? He'd collared her like a dog, reducing her willpower to that of a puppy. Sometimes it made her physically sick. She'd lost weight. Even now, when she was free of that damned magic, he was dominating her thoughts.

A groan slipped from her as she pressed the sides of her head. She didn't want to haunt Sam's house like a lost soul but she was too afraid to leave. There had to be someone she could contact, something she could *do*.

Scanning a list of allies in her mind took a depressingly short amount of time. Margritte was in exile, as was her former governess, Natasha Rainer (Cathy would never forgive Tom for that). She wasn't sure where Charlotte was now, having fled just after Bertrand had been arrested by the Arbiter, so all she could do was hope Charlotte was at least safe somewhere in the Nether, far away from the Society that had failed her, along with her children.

The only potentially sympathetic person Cathy could think of was Lucy, her sister-in-law. They hadn't spoken properly in weeks, though. The others had wanted to keep Lucy out of their feminist group, for fear of Tom finding out. Considering what he did to Natasha, it was probably just as well. It wouldn't be fair to suck Lucy into anything now. Any hint she'd received contact and both Tom and Will would put terrible pressure on her to reveal anything the two of them had said.

Cathy nibbled at her thumbnail. Perhaps if she found some way to send Lucy a message, without magic—without even touching the note—she'd be able to make contact without it being detected. Without someone in the Nether, there was no way she could help the people she'd left behind. Surely it was worth the risk?

A knock on the living room door made her jolt. "Come in."

Sam's other houseguest peered round the door cautiously, as if concerned a wild fox might be in the room. Her long, dark blonde hair was tied into two long braided pigtails, making her look like someone from a pre-Raphaelite painting. It took Cathy a moment to remember her name. *Beatrice*, that was it. They'd been introduced shortly after she'd arrived but Cathy had been in such a terrible state Beatrice had avoided her.

"Sam's out," Cathy said, thinking she was looking for him. "I don't know when he'll be back."

"Are you still crying all the time?"

Cathy blinked at her. And she thought *she* was bad at people stuff. "Did you want something?"

"I want to talk to you. But if you're still crying, I'll come back later." Beatrice paused, her lip slightly curled. "You've been doing that for days. Is there something wrong with you?"

"I haven't been crying every minute!"

Beatrice raised an eyebrow. "I have sampled your behaviour twenty-six times over the past five days. You were crying every time."

"You…you what?"

"Why have you been behaving this way?"

"Something really bad has happened to me."

"And is crying improving the situation?"

Cathy scowled at her, trying to fathom the strange woman's intent. The words sounded like she was being deliberately cruel but the way she said them didn't match that at all. The tone was of a genuine question. Before she could think of something to say, Beatrice asked, "Did someone die?"

"No. I was betrayed, all right? Is that a good enough reason to be upset for you?"

The retort didn't seem to lessen Beatrice's concentration. "Was it a man who betrayed you?" Cathy could only nod. The frown lifted from the strange woman's face as her eyes brightened with understanding. "This makes sense. Someone you loved, no?"

"*Thought* I loved."

"He said he loved you, yes?" Another nod, this time mirrored by Beatrice. "I know this pain. When I was betrayed by the man I loved more than anyone and anything in the worlds, I cried just as much."

Cathy blew her nose again, the tears having stopped, thankfully. "What did you do?"

Beatrice's smile glittered. "I killed him, took his power and destroyed everything he held dear."

For the first time in a week, a flicker of hope stirred in Cathy's heart. "Come and sit down," she said. "I think we should get to know each other better."

• • •

Will leaned against the car, exhausted. He'd barely slept for days and his eyes felt like he'd rubbed sand into them. The wind was bitterly cold, promising another snow flurry soon. He was supposed to be supporting his brother in Oxenford, at a ball that had already started, not lurking in Cheshire behaving like a criminal. He was desperate, and with good cause: Lord Iris had demanded that he retrieve his wife and Will was certain that if he didn't succeed soon, his patron's patience would soon come to an end.

"Cathy," he whispered beneath his breath. "Why do you have to be so damn difficult?"

"We've confirmed that Lord Iron has left the estate, your Grace," Carter said, still unable to look him in the eye since the woman he was charged to protect had been stolen away. "We're ready to move in when we have your permission."

Will looked at the mansion in the distance, nothing more than a collection of lit windows in the winter darkness. He'd told his men that Cathy had been kidnapped by Lord Iron, who'd been obsessed with her. He wished he believed his own lie. It would be so much easier to bear if that was the real explanation, and although he didn't know why Cathy had left him, he had his suspicions.

All he knew with certainty was that the Arbiter from Bath— the one who'd gone rogue and tried to prosecute his father—had collected her from the house seven days before. She'd been at her sister's wedding earlier that day and everything had seemed perfect. She was loving and affectionate and…compliant.

He pulled his scarf tighter around his neck as he thought of the choker. He'd had to do it. There was no way he could have continued to let that damn Poppy magic make her destroy everything, but the memory of putting it around her neck haunted him. He'd stooped as low as the Rosas. He'd resorted to controlling her.

She must have found out what the choker did. The Arbiter probably told her. It was easy to imagine her rage; he'd felt it himself, when he'd learned of the Rosa Charm acting upon him. The Charm that resulted in the illegitimate child now growing in Amelia's womb. It still made him feel ill.

Much as it all sickened him, Will couldn't fathom any other way to have handled her behaviour and keep his Patroon happy. Cathy simply didn't understand the pressure he was under. He just wanted to explain, to somehow make her see that he'd had no choice. To talk it through with her and come to some sort of accord that would bring her home with him. If he could just get her out of that damn house, away from Lord Iron, perhaps he could persuade her to give him a second chance. Surely she wasn't going to run away from all the other things she cared so much about?

And if she couldn't be persuaded… He clenched his teeth. Was he prepared to go beyond persuasion, taking her free will completely, to do what he must? Could he live with himself?

"Your Grace?"

"Do it," Will said, his gaze still locked on the mansion. "Be quick. And remember, Lord Iron might have tricked her into believing all sorts of things. About me. She may not want to leave."

He watched Carter's jaw set and his back straighten. "Whatever he's done to the Duchess, I'll bring her back to you, your Grace. We'll make sure she's safe again."

Will nodded, feeling the deceit wrap itself around him, choking him almost. "None of our Charms or artefacts will work within the boundary of the estate, remember. You may have to…a Doll Charm won't work, so…"

"I understand," Carter said, and gave a curt bow before going over to the other men waiting nearby.

All four of them were dressed in modern black clothing in stark contrast to the white tie that Will wore beneath his coat. As soon as they were done here and Cathy was back at home, he would go to Oxenford and support his brother.

Will watched the men pull balaclavas down over their faces and shuddered. They would terrify Cathy but there was nothing to be done about it. No doubt Lord Iron used mundane security cameras and the last thing he needed was anyone traced to him. No glamours, no Charms, no magic at all. He could only hope that Carter's superior training would be sufficient.

The men slid down the ditch by the side of the road and were soon out of sight. Will got back into the car and let his head rest against the back of the seat. In a few hours, all would be well.

2

"I'm back!" Rupert called as he entered the office. "I brought jelly snakes."

Max grabbed his cane and started to hobble over. Kay glanced up at Rupert, gave a brief nod, then went back to whatever she was doing with the computer. The gargoyle, who was currently lying on the floor next to Kay like an oversized house cat, didn't even look up.

"Bloody hell, what do I need to bring with me to get a hello? Turkish Delight? Crack?" Rupert dumped the large paper bag on his desk and shrugged off his coat. "It's snowing, by the way."

"Ooooh!" Kay leaped out of her chair and dashed to the window. Being on the top floor of Cambridge House, a lot of Bath's city centre could be seen below. "Oh, it looks beautiful!"

Rupert fished out a long green jelly snake and bit its head off. "If cold wet stuff that overstays its welcome is your sort of thing, I suppose. Ah, Max. Jelly snake?"

"There's a problem. I've been trying to get in touch with you."

"I was busy."

"I was trying to get hold of you too," Kay said from the window. "I finished the database and the modified app is in beta but I need sign-off on the extra functionality. Where were you? It's been days."

"Busy," Rupert said, chewing on the green jelly as he sat on the desk. "Ya know, Sorcerer stuff."

"Sir, about that problem."

Rupert sighed. "Go on, you go first. But I'm warning you now, I won't care and it won't be as important as what I've got to tell you."

"George Reticulata-Iris is free and living in the Nether as if nothing has happened."

Rupert just stared at him, chewing. Max waited for a response long enough for Rupert to shrug. "I'm waiting to hear the problem."

"Oh, bloody hell, Rupert," Kay said, turning from the snowy view. "You know what that bastard did, and that Max busted him—I talked to you about it!"

Rupert's lips smacked together as he worked on the latest mouthful. "If the Patroon decided not to chuck him out, what're we gonna do? I can't go and get medieval on his ass. We have to make them think Ekstrand is still the Sorcerer of Wessex. If I go there and pass myself off as a totally-not-dodgy replacement, then that woman will hear of it and then we're buggered."

"It isn't right!" the gargoyle snarled. "That Iris kidnapped dozens of people over hundreds of years! He just posted them off to Lord Iris without a second thought for their families or—"

"Look," Rupert held up his hands and a half-eaten snake. "George Reticulata-Iris is a grade-A fucknoodle, I get that. But we've got to accept that with things the way they are, we can't get all the wins we want."

"Then what's the point of doing any of this?" Kay snapped. "You're never here, and you don't back us up. It's all very well having these Sniffers all over the city, but we only have one Arbiter. The rest of the Fae-touched are going to look at what happened to George Iris and think it's worth taking more risks—and you know what? They're right! You're supposed to protect people, Rupert! Do some bloody protecting!"

Rupert tossed the snake onto the desk, giving Kay a furious glare. "The fuck? You've been here like five minutes and you think you know how to do all this better than me? I've been doing this for hundreds of years!"

"Yeah, with loads of staff and actual power!" Kay said as the gargoyle started to growl at Rupert. "Now you've only got the people in this room and poor bloody Bob, who's barely keeping it together! It's not enough! Stop acting like it is. A boy was almost taken by a

Buttercup yesterday, and two days ago the Lavandulas were up to something at Lansdown School—which is a Peonia anchor property, in case you didn't know—and now the whole place has been closed off with this bomb scare nonsense! Where were you?"

"Hang on," Rupert said. "Who the fuck is Bob?"

"Robert Amesbury. The man who helped me crack the Iris case," Max said. "One of his victims, indirectly. Even if he was in a fit state to help us, he isn't suitable for active field work."

"Oh, yeah, I remember now." Rupert nodded to himself and then looked at Kay. "Yeah, all right, you've got a point."

"Thank you."

The gargoyle stopped growling.

"But I haven't been sitting on my arse. I've been busy too. And I may not be dealing with the puppets, but I am fixing the bigger problem: *that* woman who killed all the other Sorcerers. Once we've dealt with her, I can wade in on whatever case you want, I can flick Patroon balls again, whatever you need. But until she's dealt with— preferably dead—my hands are tied."

"We don't even know why she killed them all," Max said.

"As long as she doesn't get another chance to kill me, I don't really give a flying fuck about her motivations," Rupert said, resuming his attack on the jelly snake. "But I've finished what I've been working on and now I need you." He waved the last of the snake in Max's direction.

"So we're just supposed to forget about George Iris?" the gargoyle said with a snarl. "After all he did?"

"Get this job done, and then I'll make the Iris Patroon break George Iris and chuck him into Mundanus with nothing more than the skin on his back. Okay? It's just a matter of…priorities."

"We can't ignore everything else," Max said. "The puppets are getting bolder by the day. I've shut down the Second Sons, but in Aquae Sulis the Master of Ceremonies is already suspicious. If he and his sister feel confident enough to shut down a mundane school with a bomb scare, they're going to do worse very soon."

"A bomb scare?" Rupert raised an eyebrow. "Doesn't sound like a puppet tactic to me."

"There's a bomb from the Second World War that's been found in the grounds, apparently," Kay said. "Some builders found it during renovation work. But the day before it was reported, we picked up a massive spike of Lavandula magic there, so we think they might have been involved. We don't know why, though."

"The Peonias must have pissed them off," Rupert said, disinterested.

"And you should know that Londinium is unstable," Max said. "The Viola Patroon expelled Bertrand Persificola-Viola from the Nether in disgrace, and the Violas are one of the wealthiest allies of the Duke. And the Duchess has left him."

"And I should care about this because...?"

"Because unofficially Londinium is now within your jurisdiction, along with the rest of the Heptarchy," Max said. "Instability in the Nether usually results in more risk-taking as the puppets try to gain the backing of their patron to mount a coup."

Rupert scratched the stubble on his chin. "Still not as important as this. I don't want you working on anything else, Max, not until that woman is dealt with."

He reached into his pocket as the gargoyle stalked forwards. "There are people being used like machines in the basement of the Agency's headquarters," it said in its gravelly voice. "We need to get them out. And Cathy said—"

"Do I need to say this again with like pictures or something?" Rupert shouted. "I have zero fucks to give about anything except this." He pulled out a new gadget from his inside pocket. It was smooth black plastic and the size of a small cigar tube. "This will find that woman if she's anywhere on this island. If she crosses the sea, it's a problem. So you need to go find her fast."

"And then do what?" the gargoyle asked. "She has weird hybrid magic. She could turn us inside-out or something."

"I'm working on that part, and I'm nearly done," Rupert replied. "I just need an exact location. It's legwork, that's all. It feeds info to your phone and Kay's database too. She'll be able to track where you are and support from here." He noticed Kay roll her eyes. "What?"

"I'd like to do more in the field," she said. "I know it's not safe, so we need to find a way to fully protect me. We'll need it in the future, right? Once this project is done with?" At Rupert's blank expression, she sighed. "We need an alternative because you can't make more Arbiters."

"What makes you think that?"

"Ethics and consent."

"Shit, can we deal with one thing at a time?" Rupert tossed the gadget to Max. On closer inspection, Max could see a row of ten tiny lights running up the side of the device, currently greyed out.

"They change colour when you get closer," Rupert said. "You'll get more info on your phone app, but you have to keep that thing on you for it to work, okay? It's got all the clever stuff inside. She's somewhere in the north-west of England as far as I can tell. Start in Manchester. There aren't any puppets there, so she might have chosen that for a base."

"Rupert, I'm serious," Kay said. "We need an alternative, then we can recruit faster."

"Yeah, yeah. But you're not going out into the field."

"Why not?"

"Because I need an apprentice." He stuffed the last piece of the jelly snake into his mouth. "And I want it to be you."

3

Cathy scooped up the remnants of iris leaves from the hearth and chucked them into the fire. "So how do you know Sam?"

"I came to commission some ironwork from him," Beatrice replied, padding barefoot over to the armchair farthest from the fire. "He offered to let me stay while he works on it. And you?"

"Oh, that's a long story." She didn't know what to say about it, given that it involved the Fae and a Sorcerer.

"He told me it had something to do with Exilium, but not the details."

"So…you know about all of that stuff, then?" When Beatrice nodded, Cathy sat on the sofa. "Sam and I got tangled up with a Sorcerer who chucked both of us into Exilium to do his dirty work. I made sure Sam didn't get royally screwed over by the Fae, and Sam…" She looked at the flames, trying to work out the best way to put it. "Sam became one of the few people I trust."

"Was it Rupert of Mercia?"

"No, Ekstrand, from Bath. What an arsehole he was. Do you know everything about Exilium and Mundanus and…?"

"Yes. I used to work for a Sorcerer."

Perhaps that had made her social skills atrophy. Cathy wished she had as good an excuse. "I'm from the Nether. I just left it. Again."

Beatrice leaned forwards, her gaze focused so intently on her that Cathy had to look away into the fire. "Tell me more."

"Why do you want to know?"

"I think we may have something in common."

Cathy hesitated. Could Beatrice have been sent by the Irises? No, she was already here when she'd arrived, and no one had any idea she'd left Will at that point. For Sam to let her stay suggested that he trusted her. She took a breath, wondering whether to just shut the conversation down, when there was a scream from the kitchen.

"Mrs M?" Cathy called from the door. "Are you okay?"

Mrs M's red face poked into the hallway. "Sorry, pet, there was a spider the size of a bloody dinner plate in the pantry. Just caught me off guard, that's all."

Cathy smiled and went back into the living room. Beatrice didn't even look concerned. "Spider," Cathy said. "Mrs M hates them."

"Tell me about why you left the Nether."

"The first or the second time?"

"Both."

Once Cathy started, it was hard to stop. It was so rare that she could talk to anyone about what she'd done. She didn't name her family or her patron and Beatrice didn't ask for those details. She was a good listener, and it helped to talk about something she felt proud of. But as Cathy went on, describing the forced marriage and the husband she didn't name, it got harder. The shame crept in, bringing with it the fear that she wasn't ever going to be free. What kind of feminist activist was she, hiding in a man's house, hiding behind his power from another man? "Why are you so interested in me?"

"Lord Iron protects you unlike any other. Why? What is it about you that made him take you in?"

Cathy pulled a cushion close, needing something to hide behind. "I think I remind him of his wife. That's all." When Beatrice continued to stare, she added, "I was trying to change Society. In the Nether, I mean. I was trying to make it better for women. And I failed."

"Is that why you ran away?"

"Wow, you really don't dress things up, do you?" Cathy sighed. "I ran away because of the betrayal. But even before then I was losing hope anything could ever change there. I just can't see a way to do it, not when all the men who hold the power have no reason or inclination to share it. Nothing ever changes in the Nether.

Short of burning the whole bloody place down—which is literally impossible—I can't see what could ever make it better."

Beatrice's unexpected smile was broad. "You're so angry."

"I am so far beyond angry I don't even know what to call it."

Beatrice tilted her head, evidently considering something, when a movement at the window drew Cathy's attention. It had got dark some time ago and she hadn't closed the curtains, being out of the habit of doing so herself. Nervous of the way Beatrice was staring at her, Cathy crossed the room and looked out. Perhaps it was just an owl. She couldn't see anything in the darkness, so she closed the heavy drapes and went back to the sofa.

"We do have something in common," Beatrice said. "We both want to see the end of the Nether. The difference is that I know how to bring that about. I just need your help to do it."

"Wait, what?" Cathy held up her hands. "Do you mean destroy it? But what about the people who live there?"

"They would be forced to live in the real world, just like everyone else."

Cathy reeled. The end of the Nether? Really? Without that place, not even the Patroons could keep every member of the Great Families fully closeted away. With multiple influences instead of just one monochrome Nether Society, the change she craved would be inevitable. Perhaps more; perhaps Society would simply disappear, with everyone scattered amongst millions of other, normal people, like salt grains spilt on sand. It would be so much easier for those who wanted no part of it to just slip away, find their own path. Maybe even freedom. "How would you do this?"

"I have some knowledge and skills of my own." Cathy had the feeling it was an understatement. "But I need Lord Iron's assistance and he is unconvinced by my plan. This is where I need your help."

"You want me to persuade him?"

"I do. He will listen to you in a way he won't listen to me."

"I don't know…" Something about this made Cathy uncomfortable.

"Surely you want to see the end of the Nether? There would

be no need to hide here anymore. The prison they want to put you back into wouldn't exist."

There was a tug in her heart. Life in Mundanus without the dread of being pulled back to the Nether…Cathy could barely imagine it. "But it's not enough, not for me. The Fae won't leave me alone just because the Nether isn't there anymore." She doubted Lord Iris would abandon his plan for a child just because she'd changed address. And Lord Poppy would still seek her out, just to torment her, regardless of the existence of the Nether.

"Ah, I see." Beatrice nodded. "Then I propose this: you help me to succeed in my plan to destroy the Nether, and I will teach you all you need to protect yourself from the Fae."

Cathy raised an eyebrow. "Look, I'm sorry, I barely know you. And I've been screwed over so many times lately, I just can't believe that you're just going to make everything I've wanted to happen come true, just like that!"

"It was my twin brother who betrayed me," Beatrice said after a pause. "We have both known what it is to be moulded by men, grown into shape by the confines of a prison of their making. We have both known what it is to fear being our true selves, to push ourselves into their spaces. Spaces which are not theirs to keep. That they stole. That they cling to now, like fat dogs who fear hunger. We have both been punished for wanting more, for being more, for needing more than they deign to give us."

Cathy couldn't breathe, as if her chest was filled with something else. Her skin tingled and her pulse raced and she suspected magic was being worked, but it was unlike anything she'd felt before. There was something compelling in the rhythm of Beatrice's words.

"You carry within you the purest force of destruction," Beatrice continued. "When the time is right, together we will destroy the prison they wove with lies and false promises of protection. We will unleash such a freedom upon the people you care for that there will be no man, no rule, no fear that can bind them."

New tears started to roll down Cathy's cheeks, but not of shame or fear, not even of guilt. Of hope. Then the doubt seeped back in. Magic usually meant manipulation. "But how can I trust you?"

"We will make an oath than binds us both. And when it is done, I will teach you the way to work that magic too."

Cathy closed her eyes, forced her senses inwards as best she could, needing a moment to check that she wasn't about to do something stupid. "Wait…you killed your twin brother?"

"Yes." Another pause. "When we are bound by the same oath I have with Lord Iron, I will tell you why it was necessary."

"Will it bind my will to yours?"

"No. It will mean that each of us will know if we are about to betray the other. And if we do, we have the right to destroy each other. If you have no intention of harming me, then it shouldn't be a concern."

Cathy frowned and opened her eyes, looking at Beatrice as boldly as she could. "I have no intention of that *now*. What if that changes?"

Beatrice laughed more heartily than Cathy thought she'd be capable of. "Life is risk. And to pass on my knowledge to you is one I am willing to take. I have worked so hard for so long to make this happen. I want to find a way to work with Lord Iron, rather than resorting to working against him. You will make that possible."

Cathy was about to reply when the sound of the front door opening and then closing again soon after interrupted her. She paused, listening for the sound of Sam calling her name, as he'd taken to doing every time he got back from the forge or whatever else he got up to, but there was only silence. Maybe he thought she might be in bed.

She balanced the risk of tangling herself up with this strange and obviously powerful woman against the risk of being trapped in Sam's house for the rest of her life. Freedom was all she'd ever wanted, and if it meant throwing her lot in with Beatrice—the only option she could think of—then she had to take it. Having a direction again, just a thing to do, was better than stewing in her own misery.

"Agreed," she said. "But you might want to know that Lord Poppy thinks my true potential is to destroy everything. Not just the Nether."

Beatrice's smile was devilish. "It is written across your soul for me to read like poetry. It's the reason we are having this conversation. The only people who need fear it are those who wronged you."

"Okay. I'll take the oath."

Beatrice came to sit on the sofa. "We rest a hand over the other's heart," she said, and Cathy rested her hand over Beatrice's heart at the same time as hers was covered. "When I speak a secret to you, you will know it for what it is and its worth. When you speak it to another against my wishes, you will know if you are about to betray me, and in betraying me, yourself. The same for any secret you share with me. Now, Catherine, you say the same to me, and mean it."

Cathy said the words back with Beatrice's guidance. She didn't feel anything happen. When it was done and Beatrice returned to her chair, Cathy tried to remember the times she'd interacted with Ekstrand and his magic. "What kind of magic was that? It didn't seem like sorcery, but it was too structured to be Fae magic."

"It is a hybrid of the two. We will go through it in detail tomorrow. Now, tell me how to persuade Lord Iron to assist me."

Cathy shrugged. "He's not a machine. I can't tell you the right buttons to press." At her blank expression, Cathy realised that maybe Beatrice didn't have a frame of reference for that analogy. "What does Sam object to? He hates the Nether. I don't understand why he's not helping you already."

"I believe his main concern is the fact that the Fae will be free once more."

Cathy twitched. "What?"

"The Nether can only exist in the place between the Split Worlds; the only way to destroy it is to undo the work of the Sorcerers and restore reality to the way it should be. No Exilium, no Mundanus. Just one restored world in which humanity and the Fae co-exist."

For a moment, all Cathy could do was blink at her. "*That's* the plan? No wonder Sam won't go along with it! It's fucking bonkers!"

Beatrice looked away, mouthing Cathy's last words to herself, as if she didn't understand them. "I am still unaccustomed to discourse. It seems I need to persuade you that my plan is correct, yes?"

Cathy twisted the corner of the cushion in her fist, trying to keep control of her anger. "I'd rather you just lay it all out for me, rather than persuade me. You deliberately left out information so I would be more likely to bring Sam onside."

"Ah. I understand. Will it help if I tell you that I have already killed one thousand three hundred and fifty-two people in the pursuit of my goal? My brother was only the first."

"Holy shit! No, that doesn't help at all!"

"Why not? I thought you were concerned about my deliberate obfuscation of the truth. I am being truthful and accurate."

Beatrice seemed calm while Cathy pressed her hands against her face in shock. "Shit."

"Would it help if I explained that I only did this because if I hadn't taken such action, and if I don't continue to pursue my goal, millions of people will die?"

"I don't know if it will help, but I need to know why."

"The Elemental Court is destroying the balance of life on Earth. Despite all of the evidence proving this to be true in the language of science, nothing is being done, because the Elemental Court are driving it. They are being driven mad by their own nature, as they are left unchecked by the Fae. Splitting the worlds and forcing the two courts to exist in separate realities is making both of them more extreme and more dangerous. The Sorcerers would not accept this. I tried to persuade them when they thought I was one of them. I showed them the proof. They refused to accept it, because they had become too accustomed to their power and could not accept that their greed could lead to their destruction."

"Wait, are you seriously telling me that everything that is wrong with...industrialisation and modern technology is because the Fae are in Exilium?"

Beatrice considered this. "It is a woefully inadequate summary, but the essence of the causality is correct."

It took a moment for Cathy to parse Beatrice's strange phrasing. "I know there are all sorts of terrible things being done by the Elemental Court, so I don't disagree that there's a problem with them. But solving that by bringing the Fae into Mundanus is like… like solving an itch you can't reach by jumping into a river full of piranha fish."

After the same careful consideration, Beatrice said, "I disagree. If I interpret your analogy correctly, you assume that restoring reality to what it was before the worlds were sundered would be worse than it is now. That the Fae would cause lethal damage to humanity."

"Not necessarily always lethal," Cathy said. "They specialise in worse than death. I mean, why the hell do you think I'm so keen to trash the Nether? One of the reasons is to stop them having access to the people there! If you'd told me you wanted to dump Exilium into Mundanus wholesale when we first talked about it, I'd never have promised to persuade Sam." How could she have been so stupid? She'd been so desperate to have hope she'd walked into this without asking the right questions. Maybe all the lessons she'd learned in the Nether had leaked out of her with all those bloody tears.

"Please understand that I am seeking to restore something that was broken, rather than forcing one thing into another. You speak of Mundanus as if it is something to be protected. It is not. It is the impoverished remains of a brutal magical ritual that never should have been done. Both Exilium *and* Mundanus are false constructs."

Cathy buried her face in the cushion, trying to keep track of her thoughts as her anger and self-loathing buffeted them. "Look, the worlds were split to protect people, so how can you—"

"Ah!" Beatrice cheered as if she'd had some sort of lightbulb moment. "This is the root of the problem. Of course, I should have realised that you would be just as corrupted by their lies as everyone else is. You believe the Fae were 'put into Exilium' to protect people from them. This is not the truth. This is what the Sorcerers wanted everyone to believe. Like all victors, they ensured their version of history was believed above anyone else's. Even those of the Fae-touched."

"If that's the case, why didn't the Fae tell us the truth?"

"They are bound by the Treaty." Beatrice sat very still, her back ramrod straight, but she seemed to be relaxed. Like they were talking about an interpretation of a painting, rather than the nature of reality. "As much as I despise the Sorcerers, I cannot help but admire their command of language. The word 'treaty' implies an agreement, yes? Something that both parties have committed to after reaching an accord?" She waited for Cathy to give a nod, like a tutor waiting for a student to confirm they are still following along. "But that's a lie. The Sorcerers split the worlds to protect themselves from the magic they were incapable of controlling. To form a new reality in which their magic was dominant. Logic. Rules. The patriarchal control of information. None of it had anything to do with protecting people." Beatrice smiled. "The idea is strangely amusing when considered from your point of view. If they truly cared about people, they wouldn't have created Arbiters. They wouldn't have ignored the Nether. They would have closed the loophole that permitted its existence. It was in their power to do so. It was in the Sorcerers' power to stop the Fae from doing anything. The crowns made sure of that."

Cathy hugged the cushion tightly, feeling like too much of what she knew was being challenged at once. "Look…I'm struggling to see this any other way. The Fae are…they are the cruellest, shittiest creatures who have done the cruellest, shittiest things to people, myself included. Needing to protect people from them makes a lot of sense."

Beatrice sighed. "The Fae have treated the people in the Nether—and those they steal from Mundanus—this way because they too are unbalanced. If I locked you in a prison, starved you, and assigned jailers from your own family, would that not change your behaviour towards the tiny amount of food you could find? Would you sit nicely, use cutlery? Or would you snatch that food, make sure no one else could steal it, and then devour what you could?"

"Wait, are you saying we're like food?"

"No, but human emotions and memories nourish the Fae. Of course they are cruel to you. It creates so many more emotions than contentment does."

"And that's still going to be true if you undo the magic. Right? I mean, they're going to gorge themselves."

"You forget the balance. There might be a period of readjustment, but ultimately, all would return to the state it should be. A world in which both the Fae and the Elementals co-exist with humanity. Both of the courts in balance again, neither able to become more powerful than the other. Magic would become part of everyday life again. Humanity's soul would be soothed by its return. The Elementals' need to steal and destroy would be tempered by the Fae's roots in the chaos of nature. The Fae's hunger for the emotional fruits of humanity will be sated by their immersion in human society and its constant change. They will be just as cruel and just as kind as any other creature with a mind and desires."

Cathy shook her head. "It just sounds too good to be true."

"Regardless of your ability to believe me about the result, you cannot deny the need for radical change. Without it, the Elemental Court's actions will be so environmentally destructive that millions of people will die. This has nothing to do with magic. It has everything to do with them extracting their elements from the ground unchecked and perpetuating a system that puts profit above humanity's survival. The only solution is to undo the work of the Sorcerers and restore the balance the Fae will provide. Permanently. The worlds must be unsplit to bring this about. If you cannot see this, then you are of no use to me and our agreement is void."

The possibility that the magic tuition she'd been offered, promising true freedom, could be taken away so easily made Cathy's stomach cramp with panic. "Wait!" She hugged the cushion tighter, trying hard to untangle her selfish needs from the revelations she'd just been buried in and the legitimate doubts they'd caused. "Wait. I just…I need some time."

"People are dying. Now. In mines. In cities with tainted air. In droughts and in floods. I have taken too long already. Bring Lord Iron around to my solution and fewer people will die needlessly."

"But the Fae…" Cathy simply couldn't see them as victims. "I just can't agree with unleashing them upon the world!"

Beatrice stood. "Then there's nothing left to discuss. And nothing I am prepared to teach you."

"Wait!" Cathy dumped the cushion, holding her hands up to placate her. "You haven't lived with the Fae controlling your life. It's irresponsible to just rush into this without thinking about the immediate impact."

Beatrice folded her arms, but appeared to be listening.

Cathy paused for breath, trying to figure out whether she even believed it all. She had vague memories of old stories about the Fae protecting people and natural places, mythical tales passed down the Great Families, but she'd always hated them. What if they had some basis in truth? There was no doubt that the Elemental Court was awful, and Sam's hope of changing them was diminishing daily. But this seemed like such an insane plan she couldn't even hold it fully in her head.

Then she remembered the ride in the carriage with Tom on the way to see Natasha at the Tower, the way he'd made it clear that nothing could change and that she had to just accept it. He was right. There was no way to change the Nether. But just because she refused to simply abandon the people in the Nether, did that mean it was right for her to help this woman destroy it? And more than that—to change the world forever?

It was too big to agree to after one conversation, a weird and difficult one at that. Cathy needed time. Information. A plan. And she needed to keep Beatrice on her side. No one else in the worlds was prepared to teach her sorcery. No one else in the worlds could give her the freedom she'd been promised.

"I propose this," Cathy said, the plan forming just ahead of her words, like train tracks being laid ahead of a moving train. "We go ahead with your plan and unsplit the worlds. But we only do it after certain things are put in place. Like protections and setting up information ready to disseminate once it's all been done. Because the people who have always lived in Mundanus need to be educated on how to protect themselves from the Fae. They really do. Otherwise the Fae will just fuck everything up in a matter of days."

"That seems reasonable."

"And you'll still teach me?"

"Yes. If you still commit to persuading Lord Iron to assist me."

Cathy nodded. "I will definitely be having a very long conversation with him about this." Whether they'd agree it was the right course of action was another matter. "Look, he's not here at the moment, and I've sat around crying for long enough. Are you willing to start teaching me now?"

Beatrice nodded. "I have no other commitments this evening."

Cathy grinned with relief. "All right. I want you to teach me how to protect myself from the Irises."

• • •

After what seemed like an age, Will saw a movement at the side of the road. He got out of the car as Carter scrambled up out of the ditch. Will could hear the other three men close behind, but they were invisible in the darkness.

"Where is she?"

"Your Grace…"

"Where is my wife?" Will shouted with frustration.

"We…we tried, your Grace, but there must be some other magic in force at the house. As soon as we touched the windows or the doors we just…we just couldn't go in. The others just walked away. I managed to get the front door open, but then I couldn't stop myself walking away before I'd even gone inside."

"The front door? For the love of… Did the need for caution or discretion not occur to you?"

Carter, clearly affronted, was trying hard not to show it. "It was *not* my intention, your Grace. I tried to go to the other doors, but—I have no idea how that happened, truth be told. I'm so sorry, your

Grace. There's something else at work there. We couldn't even get into the house, let alone near to the Duchess."

"Damn it!" Will banged the roof of the car with his fist. "Did you even see her?"

"Yes, your Grace, through the living room window. The Duchess looked distressed. She was talking to a woman with long blonde hair. Not someone I recognise. And the Duchess looked thinner, and pale, your Grace. I'm not sure that Lord Iron is looking after her very well."

Will turned away and rested his arms on the car, feeling suddenly exhausted. "I don't understand. It sounds like Fae magic, but that doesn't make any sense."

"Indeed, your Grace. We did all we could. I'm so sorry."

Will scowled at the distant lights of the mansion. A place that broke magic yet was protected by it. It seemed that only an Arbiter would be able to enter such a place. Fortunately, he knew a corrupted one.

Will pulled out his mobile phone, walked a few paces away from Carter, and dialled the number for Faulkner. It rang twice and then a flat, emotionless voice said, "Hello, Mr Iris."

"Faulkner, I need you to do something for me. Lord Iron has kidnapped my wife and is holding her at his estate and it seems to be protected by magic."

"The last I heard, Lord Iron's estate is in Cheshire."

"Yes, that's right."

"I work for the Camden Chapter, Mr Iris. Cheshire is in another Kingdom. I can't help you."

Will was gripping the phone so tightly he heard the plastic casing creak. "I will handle all of the arrangements. No one else needs to know. I'll pay you, if—"

"Mr Iris," Faulkner cut in, "I have been instructed to turn a blind eye to any of your activities in the Kingdom of Essex. Nothing more."

"Then give me the number of the Chapter here."

"They will not be interested, Mr Iris. Your wife is not an

innocent, and I suspect the local Chapter will be keen to maintain good relations with Lord Iron. And if you are desperate enough to contact me, you might be tempted to involve the mundane police force. Don't. If you do, the local Chapter will get involved and you will be facing accusations of a breach regardless of whether you use magic or not."

His chest feeling tighter by the moment, Will glanced back at Carter, who was waiting by the car as the rest of the men arrived. "Is there nothing you will do to help me?"

"No. Good evening, Mr Iris."

The call ended, along with Will's hope. What the hell was he supposed to do now?

4

Lucy never thought she'd be able to muster any great sympathy for Nathaniel Reticulata-Iris, but this evening it was easy. His first grand public event since becoming Chancellor of Oxenford was not going well. Despite the impressive interior of the Radcliffe Camera dazzling visitors from the rest of Albion, it was clear to those who had any social understanding that something was very wrong.

Even though there was dancing and music and the champagne was flowing, key people were missing. At first Lucy had thought they might be tucked away on one of the upper galleries that looked down into the central circular space. There were many clusters of people watching the dancing, obscured by the huge stone pillars, and it would be easy to miss someone's presence. But as she and Tom moved through the ballroom and then the galleries, nodding and smiling at those he felt should be greeted warmly, she'd heard several remarks that supported her suspicion. None of Nathaniel's family had come. The Duke and Duchess of Londinium—the Chancellor's own brother and sister-in-law—were conspicuously absent. Several guests had even asked Tom where they were, placing him in the awkward position of having to give a satisfactory answer that was bland enough to cover all possible explanations yet leave the enquirer feeling they knew more than before they'd asked. Lucy noted that he'd gone from saying that he was sure the Duke and Duchess would arrive presently to saying that he understood the Duke had been unavoidably detained but should arrive soon. That was what he'd told Nathaniel, who'd demanded an answer through the gritted teeth of a public smile. Unlike all of the other casual enquirers, Nathaniel had left the exchange looking angrier than he had before.

None of the Aquae Sulis Irises had arrived either. Neither Nathaniel's own parents nor his unmarried, highly eligible sister had deigned to arrive and it was starting to look like the family was snubbing their eldest. Lucy couldn't believe that; it was clear that the entire family and their patron supported Nathaniel's controversial rise to power, but that actually made her more worried. What could possibly have happened to keep so many of them away? It felt as if something was building, like the way it used to feel back home before a storm broke, as if the oppressive sense of worry might soon reach the point when it tipped into a social tempest. It didn't help that the person whom she'd expected to arrive in Londinium earlier that day had also failed to appear.

"Where in the worlds are the Duke and my sister?" Tom remarked. "They're never this late."

"I guess they had better things to do," Lucy ventured.

Tom leaned down to whisper in her ear. The brief thrill of the movement's intimacy rapidly faded when he said, "'I guess' sounds dreadfully colonial, dear." Reddening, Lucy looked away, searching the crowds for any sign of Cathy. She could do with an ally. Someone who found this event as tedious as she did.

"Excuse me, Mrs Rhoeas-Papaver?" She turned at the sound of the voice to see one of the servants holding a silver tray with a folded piece of paper resting on it. "A message for you."

"Thank you." She took the note from the tray.

"Is it from Cat?" Tom asked. "What's the excuse this time?"

Lucy recognised the handwriting immediately. "It's from Edwin! He's right outside!" When Tom frowned in confusion, Lucy sighed. "My cousin, Tom, from California."

"Oh, yes, he was coming to visit. Why is he here and not Londinium?"

Lucy snapped her fan shut in frustration. She'd been through all of it with Tom earlier that week. "Because I secured him an invitation. As we discussed." He nodded in that vague way when he wanted her to think he was listening, but she knew he was probably thinking about the way the building was constructed or which historical events happened within the anchor property or which king killed which queen here or something. "He's waiting outside; I'm going to bring him in." When Tom didn't move off with her, she paused. "Aren't you coming with me?"

Something had caught his eye. Elizabeth was on her way over and she didn't look happy. "I'm going to diffuse whatever this is first," he said. "She looks angry. It's probably about Harold's hat. Or it's Cat. Probably Cat."

Lucy bit back a comment about Elizabeth's husband and left the siblings to it. How Cathy could be related to Elizabeth never failed to astound her. The fact that Elizabeth was related to him was something Tom often seemed bemused by himself.

Poor Tom. Lucy reminded herself of the pressure he was under as she descended the stairs to the ground floor. Will had barely been at the Tower all week, leaving Tom to handle the fallout from Bertrand Viola's scandalous fall from grace. Secretly, Lucy was glad that horrible man had been expelled from Society, even though it was such a headache for Tom. Bertrand had been the wealthiest public supporter of Will's Dukedom. Now everyone was trying to secure an opinion from Harold, who was now the head of the Viola family in Londinium (a fact that pleased Elizabeth no end) but no one had succeeded in getting anything useful from him. Lucy suspected the man was quite mad, and probably needed professional help, but all the times she'd tried to raise the issue with Tom he'd shut her down. Really, these Brits were just too private for their own good.

She managed to slip past most of the guests without drawing their attention—sometimes it was useful being very petite—and headed out of the main doors. Carriages were still arriving, bringing guests who were stretching the boundaries of what was considered fashionably late. As she looked for her cousin, Lucy couldn't help but admire the beauty of Oxenford's reflected buildings surrounding the small road around the camera. The lawn had been reflected too, no doubt to make some sort of statement about wealth, and its dull green made her miss the sunshine.

"Lucy!" Edwin stepped out from behind a carriage sporting a huge grin, waving to her.

Her heart leapt at the sight of him and she ran over to let him gather her in his arms and spin her around. "Jeez, am I glad to see you," she said as he set her down and held her at arm's length.

"Well, don't you look the fancy lady?" he said, and she laughed. The sound of his American accent was the sound of home and she felt a horrendous pang of homesickness that brought tears to her eyes. She hugged him again, fiercely, until it passed.

"You look well," she said.

His eyebrows shot up. "What kinda accent is that?"

She shrugged. "Survival British," she replied, and enjoyed his chuckle. "What happened to you? You were supposed to be in Londinium this morning."

"Yeah, I thought taking the plane over would be faster. Bad weather in Philly, so I missed my connection. Ended up having to stay over and fly today. I couldn't get a message to you, sorry about that." He looked at the Radcliffe Camera. "So that's where the ball is?" He gave a low whistle. "Mom would go nuts for this place."

"Whatever you do, don't say a word about how old it is. It's like the most colonial thing you can say."

"Oh, I can think of plenty more things to say that are more colonial than that!" Edwin said, with that grin she'd missed so much. The one that promised the most delicious mischief. "How about 'Wow, do you seriously consider your wife to be your property?'"

"Shush!" Lucy said, looking around them to see if anyone had heard.

"No, no, I got it: 'The United States has been doin' just fine without the Brits for quite a while now.' Or I could just say 'Ya know, Patroons are really kinda passé now, doncha think?' Aw, Luce, don't tell me you lost your sense of humour!"

Lucy took his hands and squeezed them tight. "It's been a long time since I really laughed."

Edwin kissed the knuckles on her right hand, then on her left. "I know it's been tough for you, kiddo. I could tell from your letters. From what you *didn't* say."

She looked into his big brown eyes, saw the love in them. How soothing to be looked at by someone who genuinely loved her. "I couldn't be sure who else would read them."

He nodded, understanding. "I'm here now, cuz." He frowned at a couple climbing out of a nearby carriage who stared at him as they straightened their clothes. "I get the feeling they don't get many black men coming to these balls of theirs."

"Seriously, it's worse than we thought here," Lucy whispered. "A lot worse."

Concerned, he looked back down at her. "I'm not gonna like it here, am I?"

She shook her head. "I almost told you not to come, but…"

"Hey," he said softly. "It's okay. When you left, I told you that if you ever needed me, I'd be there. You need me. I'm here."

Lucy's eyes welled up before she could stop them. "It's so hard."

"I know."

"It's just awful here."

"I know."

"And I'm getting nowhere. All the things Mom and Dad suggested, and your mom and dad, I tried them all. None of it worked."

"Have you had a chance to get to the Patroon?"

She shook her head. "No. He married us and then I saw him at a ball once, but there were dozens of people there. It was impossible to get him alone."

"Okay, well, then we go back to the drawing board. Maybe we forget about the Patroon. Go straight for our patron. That was always Plan B, right?"

Lucy bit her lip. "It was Plan A at one point, remember?"

Edwin nodded. "Yeah," he said with a sigh. "But we all thought that getting you into Albion, right into the lion's den, was just too good a chance to pass up. Were we wrong?"

Lucy shrugged. "I don't know."

"Shit, we were wrong." Edwin grimaced. "I *never* wanted them to send you here."

"It's okay." Lucy did her best to smile. "I'm fine. Especially now you're with me."

"So the new plan, once we're done, is to kill your husband and you come back to California, right?"

Sometimes it was hard to tell when Edwin was kidding. "No," Lucy said firmly, just in case he was serious. "None of this is his fault. Tom is…I think he could be better than he is. He just needs a bit of time."

"Why do I have the feeling we're not going to get along?"

Lucy was about to reassure him when she saw George Reticulata-Iris climb out of a recently arrived carriage to turn around and help his wife and daughter out after him. All three of them looked incredibly grim-faced, and a feeling of dread settled in Lucy's stomach.

"Who are they?" Edwin asked.

"The parents of the Chancellor of Oxenford," Lucy replied as George Iris noticed her. He said something to his wife and then headed over. "Good evening, Mr Reticulata-Iris," she said with a smile.

"Good evening," he said, the frown not lifting from his face.

"May I present my cousin, Edwin Californica-Papaver? Edwin, this is George Reticulata-Iris, of Aquae Sulis."

George looked momentarily confused and then shook Edwin's hand. "A pleasure." He looked back to Lucy. "May I have a word in private? I have some grave news."

Edwin clasped his hands behind his back to stroll around the lawn as George gently steered her away. "I'm afraid there's no easy way to put this. Charles Papaver was found dead earlier this evening, in his home. He…" George swallowed, ashen-faced. "He took his own life."

Lucy clamped a hand over her mouth. She'd seen her father-in-law less than a fortnight ago, at Elizabeth's wedding, and all had seemed well. "Oh my God!"

George rested a hand on her shoulder. "I'm so sorry. If there's anything we can do…"

"How is Isabella? Is someone with her?" Had she found her husband dead? Lucy couldn't imagine how awful that would be.

The look on George's face flickered between discomfort and embarrassment. "You didn't know. Oh dear. Lucy, Isabella left Charles a few days ago. She hasn't been seen since. That's why he…"

All Lucy could do was stand there for a few moments. She hadn't been close to Charles, far from it; he wasn't the sort of man one could even be close to. And knowing about how he beat Cathy— well, she'd never really wanted to get to know him. But the thought of his being so distressed that he'd resorted to suicide shook her to the core. She'd never known anyone who had died in the Nether. "Who…found him?"

"One of the servants. It was shortly before we were due to go over for sherry before coming here. We assisted the staff and the Censor has been informed."

Lucy didn't want to ask the question that came to mind, but once it had, she had to know. "How did he…"

George swallowed. "He shot himself with a service revolver. The one he kept from the First World War, I believe."

She started shivering. How was Tom going to—"Oh, Tom!" she said. "He's at the ball! He doesn't know!"

"Would you like me to inform him?"

"No, I will. I'll…I'll go and fetch him now. And Elizabeth is there, too. She'll need to be told. I'll find her as well."

"William can break it to Catherine," George said.

"But they aren't here yet," Lucy said, to George's evident surprise. "Thank you for telling me, Mr Iris. If you'll excuse me, I need to find my husband."

• • •

39

Sam yawned as the car pulled up outside one of the hotels he owned in Chester. He hadn't been sleeping well, and the meeting he was about to have was only one of the reasons why. He still wasn't used to the different distribution of worries in his role as Lord Iron. So many things that would have stressed him out before were nothing now. So many things he used to be utterly ignorant of were now keeping him awake at night.

Faced with the pressure to do something as ridiculous as unleashing the Fae upon a world with the internet and reality television, he had to prove to Beatrice that it was possible to temper the behaviour of the Elemental Court. The fact that he himself wasn't like them didn't seem to be enough to satisfy her. He had to admit that if he was the only one, things weren't going to change fast enough for either of them to be satisfied. But writing off the entirety of the Elemental Court without even trying seemed like madness.

He had given up on Copper; when a guy sends assassins to kill you in your own bed, there's no coming back from that. Earlier that day he'd visited Susan, his former employee, and made it clear to her that he knew she'd helped Copper. He didn't feel good about threatening a woman—even if it was only with legal action—but he had to make it clear he knew what she'd done. He'd told her in no uncertain terms that his people were keeping a very close eye on her. She knew, more than many, just how good they were.

Now he was gearing up to meet Mazzi and he was nervous. If he could change the behaviour of just one other member of the Elemental Court, there was hope.

There was a dusting of snow on the pavement and on the shoulders of the doorman waiting to let him into the hotel. Des was waiting in the lobby. "Your guest is five minutes away, sir. If you'll follow me." It was the usual polished-marble-and-swanky-lighting affair that he'd come to expect from the hotels he'd inherited from his predecessor: as posh as it was energy inefficient. It was on a long list of properties that were going to be overhauled in the next three months. For now, he just had to grin and bear it, consoling himself with the memory that his new staff benefits packages and wage scales had been implemented there. The staff certainly looked happier.

The small conference room was on the ground floor, with the files in the security boxes he'd locked himself and put into Des's car. The projector screen was already pulled down and ready to use, and coffee and his favourite chocolates were there too. He popped one into his mouth and moved the remainder so the space wasn't obvious, with a grin at Des, who'd seen what he'd done.

Des left him to his nerves and mental rehearsal. Sam sat and then stood up again, too wired to stay still. He went to the window and looked into the tiny courtyard with its ventilation ducts and bird droppings slowly being hidden by the snow. He wondered if Cathy was enjoying the weather. She was never far from his thoughts. He didn't want her to leave, but he couldn't say that. He didn't want to be the kind of arsehole that had plagued her life before.

A knock on the door made him jump. Des opened it and said, "Lady Nickel is here."

Sam nodded, left the window to stand near the table, and realised he hadn't unlocked the boxes. *Shit!* With trembling hands he managed to get two of them open before Mazzi arrived at the doorway.

"Hi, Sam," she said with a business-like smile.

"Come in. Coffee?"

"Please." She wore a green trouser suit, her long fingernails painted to match. She set her briefcase on the table, glanced at the boxes and the projector screen, and then accepted the cup from him. "So, you wanted to see me. Is this about Copper?"

"Sort of," Sam said, picking up the projector's remote control. He knew Des was next door with the laptop, ready. "You don't agree with what I've done."

She leaned back in the chair, folding her arms. "I thought we'd had a moment of understanding, down in those caves. You seemed to get it. When I saw what you did to Copper after that, it felt like a punch in the guts."

"Why?"

"Because I've been trying to bring you into the fold, Sam. And you threw it back in my face. Copper might not be the nicest man on Earth, but he's one of the Court, and we've got to stick together."

"Why?"

"Because…" She scowled. "Stop acting like a goddamn child! You know why. We have a lot of power and we influence a lot of people's lives. If we start attacking each other, nothing good will come of it."

He wanted to make a snide comment about the fact that Copper had already attacked him, but he didn't want to lose focus on the real reason for the meeting. "Did you see the stuff I released about his mines?"

She sipped her coffee, remaining silent. Sam pressed the button on the remote. On the screen appeared an image of a river with dead fish floating on the surface and clumped at the shore. He changed the image to a close-up of a cluster of dead fish showing the smears of chemicals in the water. Then a third image of a man with brown skin, wearing ragged overalls and no shoes, dragging a net through the water as part of a woefully underfunded local clean-up. Then another shot of a different river, running orange through a forest. Then another of cars on fire partially crashed into a wire security fence.

Mazzi sighed. "If you're trying to turn me against Copper you've got to try harder than this."

"You don't recognise these pictures?"

She shook her head.

"They were sent to you in a report a couple of years ago by a Mr Neugent of Pin PR. There were about fifty of them, along with details on how the local youths were throwing firebombs into your nickel mine in Brazil when a spill killed over a thousand fish in the local river. The report covered the strategies that were going to be employed to reduce the harmful impact on your company's image." He clicked the button again, showing a page of the report with a portion highlighted.

We've ensured that the environmentalist groups that usually report on this area have been suitably distracted. One group has obtained the attached images but we have persuaded them that it would be in their best interests to only release them to a particular news contact under our control. They believe it will be run as an exposé in the local area. It will in fact be buried and featured as a minor column article in the lowest-circulation newspaper. The information about the spill has reached international news aggregators but we have taken steps to delay its reporting in the western press to ensure that the local unrest will have been brought under control and downplayed by local law enforcement by the time anyone significant arrives.

Sam glanced at Mazzi's face, her eyes bright in the glow from the projector screen. No change in expression. He clicked the button again. It showed a man's leg, mangled beyond recognition, only identifiable as his limb by virtue of the fact that it was attached to him. Then another of a pair of hands, covered in burns, followed swiftly by another man's leg, this time with a deep gouge in the thigh.

"These pictures never made it to the press, of course. Nor to any of the local agencies that are supposed to monitor industrial accidents. Or any of the international watchdogs that your operations are obliged to submit data to. These came from the doctor working at that same mine. He was found dead a couple of months later. Hanged himself. Apparently. I guess the details didn't even make it out of the local police report. If it was ever written. I'm not sure if that information reached you, in fairness. Maybe you just skimmed that bit of the report. You get so many, after all."

Mazzi looked at him. "What do you hope to achieve here? Are you showing me these to warn me that I'm next after Copper?"

Sam chucked the remote onto the table, turning to face her fully. "Jesus fucking wept, Mazzi. I'm showing you these to see if you give a shit."

"It's very sad, of course," she said, with a voice that suggested it was about as sad as a fly being smashed against a windscreen. "But if you're hoping for tears or promises of—"

"I'm hoping for a shred of fucking humanity!" Sam shouted. She bristled and he held his hands up. "I'm sorry. I'm looking for a sign of...of anything that might suggest you could care about another human being."

"Do you want me to cry? To make promises that I'll change things? Are you that naive about the way the world works?"

Sam rubbed the back of his neck, feeling constricted by his suit jacket. "I want to understand why you can just let this stuff happen and not lose sleep over it. Nothing about the way you and your company have handled any of the disasters you're responsible for suggests that. All I've seen is the usual scapegoat sacking, the same old CEOs making some bullshit statement before they got another cushy job. I mean, Jesus, it's the most depressing shit I have ever read and I don't have to live through it like those people have. I'm lucky to be depressed by it! I could be one of those poor bastards being destroyed by it!"

"No, you couldn't," Mazzi said, taking another sip of the coffee. "Those people only take those jobs because they haven't bettered themselves. They could strive for more but they don't. Why should everyone else feel bad about the fact that they've let themselves slip to the bottom of the pile?"

Sam felt any reasonable responses fly from his mind. How could he deal with a complete absence of compassion? He rested his face in his hands, elbows propped up on the table, trying to sift out a useful thing to say from his internal raging.

"I wonder how you would have done in that man's village," he finally said. "Where the only jobs are the ones offered by your mine, because all of the other things they used to do to survive were trashed by your company. The land was sold from under them. The farms they used to live off were taken from them by a corrupt official, paid off by your people. There are no alternatives, short of packing up and leaving. To go where? The Rio slums? Would you want to take your kids there?"

"That mine you are so upset about paid for the roads, the school, the clinic, the—"

"Yeah, to service your workforce that you don't pay enough. The clinic that can only be used by employees or their families, and they have their pay docked for the privilege. The school that doesn't make any effort to match its curriculum to the national standard, that has all the kids in one big room with a couple of underpaid, under-resourced teachers. Yeah, your company is doing so much good for that community."

Mazzi stifled a yawn. "The world isn't fair, Sam. If we let bleeding hearts like yours—or, what are they calling them online now? Social justice warriors! That's it. If brave warriors like you ran everything to be fair, the global economy would collapse. Society would collapse."

"That's the same old bullshit the career politicians churn out to keep things the way they are because it suits them. I know you personally fund people in parliament, under the table. Jesus, it's like all the shittiest conspiracy theories were just scraping the surface!"

Mazzi plucked a chocolate from the plate and held it, pinched between thumb and forefinger. "It's late, Sam, and the weather is closing in. What do you want?"

He wanted so many things, but it was clear she was incapable of giving any of them. "I wanted you to…I dunno, react like a human being. To care!"

She put the chocolate in her mouth, watched him as she let it melt within. She was looking at him like he was a child. A stupid idealist with no sense of anything beyond his own emotions. It made him want to fling the remote through the window, to smash the cups against the wall and rip the projector screen down from the ceiling. How could he make her see what she was doing in the way he did? How could she not? It was like she was some sort of psychopath, able to look at these pictures of human suffering—that her company was responsible for—and simply feel nothing.

And then a sinking dread poured into him. What if Beatrice was right?

"Is there anything else?" she asked, finishing her coffee.

He shook his head, defeated, unable to see any way of moving forwards.

"You'll be getting a letter in a day or so, from Copper's lawyers. Don't ignore it." She stood and looked at him, sadly. "I had such hopes, Sam, that we could be friends. Like Amir was."

"I had high hopes too," he said, also standing. That she could show an ounce of humanity, for one thing.

"I tried to help you. And because Amir was such a good friend, I'll give you this warning. Copper is not going to just let you carry on with your campaign against him, and the rest of the Elemental Court see you as a threat. The lawyers are a polite warning shot across the bow, Sam. If you don't re-evaluate, they will destroy you."

"You know nothing about the murder attempt, then?"

A twitch of an eyebrow told him she didn't. "I've seen what he does to people who don't just go away," she said after a pause. "Murder would have been kinder. I'll see myself out."

He watched her go and flopped back into the chair. "Shit," he muttered, looking at the boxes of evidence. He hadn't even started on those. Not that it would have made any difference.

With a sigh, Sam started to think that Beatrice might be the only person who could change things. But how could unleashing the Fae upon the world make anything better? How could he trust her with something so risky, so huge?

After locking the final box he noticed the remaining chocolates. He left them on the plate for the cleaner to enjoy. He'd lost his appetite.

5

When Will's carriage drew up outside the Radcliffe Camera, he didn't wait for the footman; instead, he jumped down from the carriage as soon as it came to a stop, pausing only to grab his top hat and pat it into place. He walked briskly to the steps going up to the entrance, only to be intercepted by one of the Chancellor's footmen. "Good evening, your Grace. This way, please. The Chancellor has asked that you be brought to him as soon as you arrive."

Will was almost of a mind to go straight into the ball, rather than be dressed down by his brother in private first. But he didn't want to give Nathaniel's staff something to gossip about, so he nodded and followed the footman round the circular building to another door, behind which were steps down. It felt like he was some sort of smuggler sneaking to meet a contact, rather than an honoured guest. Was this some sort of trap?

"The Chancellor is waiting for you below, your Grace."

Will set off down the steps. When he heard the low rumble of his father's voice, he relaxed slightly and knocked on the door.

"Come in," Nathaniel called, and feeling most relieved, Will entered.

A large study with huge bookcases and intricately carved wood panels covering the walls lay on the other side of the door. It had the feel of an academic's retreat, rather than anywhere Nathaniel would have created for himself.

Nathaniel was seated behind his desk, their father seated opposite. "Where the hell have you been?" Nathaniel barked as Will shut the door.

"Good evening, Father," Will said, removing his hat. "Dear

brother. My deepest apologies. Circumstances entirely beyond my control delayed me. Though it seems, from the sound of it, that the ball is a great success." He rested his hat on a nearby shelf and sat down. "Now, why are we gathered?"

Nathaniel opened his mouth and then paused, looking at their father. Will had a sudden sense of there being something dreadfully important going on and felt his inner defences rise. Did they know that Cathy had run away?

"Charles Papaver is dead, Will," George said.

"Good God! How?"

"Suicide."

"I beg your pardon?"

"He shot himself," George said. "This evening."

Will tried to swallow, but his mouth was too dry. Cathy didn't know. Would she be upset, after all the beatings that man had given her? Then his stomach tightened. "Is this because of Isabella?"

George nodded. "Couldn't take the shame of it. Poor chap."

So Cathy's mother had actually gone through with it and abandoned her husband. Will remembered Cathy telling him about it, that last perfect morning when he gave her the choker. And how he'd betrayed her confidence by telling the Patroon later that same day.

"I only told him the truth," George added.

"What exactly did you say to him?" Will asked.

"I pointed out that a man who could not control his wife's behaviour would not be supported in his position in the Council of Aquae Sulis. The residents wouldn't respect him once the scandal broke and he would be an embarrassment to us all. I merely suggested that it was better to resign his post before that happened, and advised him that as his property portfolio could only be held by a member of the Council, it would be of more benefit to him to sign the properties over to me so that I could support him financially. Just until he found his feet, you understand. I made it clear that it would be a discreet arrangement between friends."

Guilt rumbled at the back of Will's mind. His father was

painting this as a noble act, when they both knew that he'd had the opportunity to plan and execute this move thanks to Cathy's information. Will struggled to wrestle the guilt into something less pernicious. He couldn't have known how weak Charles was! Besides, what Father said was true; the man was socially doomed. The residents of Aquae Sulis were obsessed with anchor properties and their reflections. A man with a failed marriage controlling who could live where, and the rent charged for the privilege, simply would not have stood.

But Will couldn't quell the feeling that he'd contributed to the man's death. Unwilling to dwell upon his place in it all, he looked at his father. "So where does this leave Aquae Sulis? I take it he committed suicide to deny you the properties, if he had no intention of accepting your help?"

His father's smile actually reached his eyes. "On the contrary. He signed it all over to me. We have the city. I've already apprised the Censor and Master of Ceremonies of the situation. Claudia and Richard understand their position perfectly."

"Which is?"

"They can continue in their roles as social figureheads, but they are aware of the need to consult me on their plans and in particular, any guest lists."

Nathaniel chuckled. "I wish I could have seen their faces."

George smirked. "They were a picture. And they know there's nothing they can do. I own the vast majority of the properties in Aquae Sulis now, including the most prestigious guest apartments they depend upon to impress the right people. All they have now is their home and the one the Rosas tried to take from Richard. I made it clear that, should the city make too much of a fuss, I would be prepared to install a new person on the Council to take Charles's place. Someone of my choice, of course."

"I think you've been far too generous, Father," Nathaniel said. "With the majority share you could have booted them out, surely?"

George twisted one of his cufflinks. "I could have, but it would not have been the decent thing to do. There was a time, before you were all born, when things were very precarious for us in Aquae Sulis. The Sorcerer of Wessex took a great dislike to Lord Iris for some reason and we were almost thrown out. The Master of Ceremonies intervened on our behalf. I said I would never forget the kindness. I consider the debt paid now."

Will wondered if the Lavandulas would see it the same way. "Charles signed every single property to you?" Will asked. "Even those in Great Pulteney Street?"

His father nodded.

"He didn't leave one to his children?"

"He wasn't in his right mind, Will," he said with a dismissive smile. "So, while it's all very sad for the Papavers, it's time to look forwards. Lord Iris wishes us to take all of the major cities of Albion. Between the three of us, we hold all of the South. Only Jorvic remains. It still hasn't recovered from the fall of the Rosas and is ripe for the plucking."

"This is appalling timing," Nathaniel muttered. "I have to break the news upstairs and end the ball. We can't...it wouldn't be right."

"I agree. Everyone will understand," Will said. "And they need to know why the family was late."

"Why *some* of them were," Nathaniel said pointedly as he stood up. "I won't be long. Now, if you'll excuse me..."

Will went after him. "I should be seen with you when you make the announcement."

Nathaniel closed the door to the study and paused next to Will at the bottom of the steps. "Why were you late? I needed you here hours ago. It looked terrible."

It was tempting to confide in Nathaniel; they were closer after his brother's confession about losing Margritte from his custody, and Will felt the need of a confidant keenly. But to confess it was his fault Cathy had fled was too much. "Cathy has been kidnapped," he whispered.

"Good God, man, no wonder you look so wretched. By whom? Do you know?"

"Lord Iron, with the assistance of a rogue Arbiter." Now he was telling the lie again it almost felt true. "I can't get her back; there's bizarre magic involved and Lord Iris is…impatient. Nathaniel, I don't know what to do."

Nathaniel squeezed his shoulder. "Don't tell anyone else, not even Father."

"I have no intention of doing that," Will said. "You're the only one I can trust. It's all going wrong."

Nathaniel's grip was strong, reassuring. "Let's get rid of the guests, hear what Father has to say, and then when he's gone, we'll talk."

• • •

Tom hadn't believed the news when he first heard it. A mistake, surely? People didn't die in the Nether. The only death he could remember in his lifetime was that of Freddy Viola, and that was in a mundane brothel, not the Nether. His father was nothing like that man.

He'd thought Lucy had pulled him outside to meet her cousin. When she'd said his father was dead, he'd just blinked at her, certain he'd misheard. When she said it the second time, there was a momentary confusion—how could she believe something so absurd? Then somehow his knees had buckled and Lucy's arms were around him and it felt like the worlds had stopped. It was as if the buildings of Oxenford that surrounded them faded into the mists. When he recovered enough to tell Elizabeth, it sounded unreal again. She'd fainted and had to be sent home with her husband. From the way Harold bumbled around her as she was carried to the carriage by a footman, Tom wasn't sure he'd be much use. It wasn't his place to suggest such a thing, though.

Now he was in a carriage riding through the streets of Aquae Sulis at an unsociable hour, with a bag packed in haste and his wife and her cousin left behind in Londinium. "I'm coming with you," she'd said as he waited for his valet to pack a small case for him.

"No."

"But you need support. You're still in shock."

"It isn't something a lady should be exposed to." *It isn't something anyone should be exposed to*, he'd thought, but didn't voice.

"Look, this isn't the time for the whole stiff upper lip thing."

"For the last time, Lucy, no!"

He'd regretted shouting, but she'd left the room before he'd gathered himself together enough to apologise. She didn't understand that he couldn't bear the thought of having anyone with him. He needed to be alone when he learned the facts. He needed to make sense of it all without worrying about maintaining his composure around her. He was afraid of how he would react, given his momentary weakness outside the Radcliffe Camera. He didn't want her to see him break.

The carriage crossed Pulteney bridge, passing the ice cream shop his father had taken him to when he was ten years old as a reward for reciting Owen's "Dulce Et Decorum Est" from memory. Tom looked away, fearful of somehow seeing himself as a child standing outside of it, his father with one hand on his shoulder, straight-backed as though he were about to march off on parade any moment. It was the first time he'd ever been into the Nether reflection of Bath and while the strawberry ice cream had been the best he'd ever tasted, the silver sky had terrified him.

Thanks to the hour, Great Pulteney Street was empty of people and carriages, much to Tom's relief. Perhaps the news hadn't yet spread. The carriage drew to a stop in the familiar place and Tom closed his eyes and clasped his hands together, as he used to before poetry recitals. The carriage rocked gently as the footman climbed down from the back and then the clunk of the door being opened and the step being unfolded told him he had to move.

He had to be strong.

Tom climbed out of the carriage and stared at his parents' house. A movement in his peripheral vision made him snap his head to the left and notice another carriage parked just ahead of his own with Iris livery painted on the door. George Reticulata-Iris was standing next to it, waiting for him, it seemed.

"Thomas," he said, holding out his hand as he approached. "May I offer my deepest condolences?"

Shaking his hand, Tom merely nodded, put off balance by his presence.

"I knew you would come and I wanted to reassure you that if there is anything you need, anything I can do, please don't hesitate to ask. Your father was a dear friend of mine and…" He paused, swallowed. "And we are all so dreadfully shocked."

"Yes," was all Tom could manage. His throat was tightening and he was afraid he'd say something regrettable, so he clenched his teeth instead.

"Please do tell me if I am taking liberties," George continued. "But as this is such a rare…tragedy, I thought it likely that the next steps would be unknown to you. As soon as you are ready, everything can be set into motion. Rest assured that I can assist with all of the arrangements for the funeral. It will take place in Mundanus, of course."

"Of course," Tom muttered. He hadn't even considered it. This was too soon!

"It isn't the time for that, though, my apologies," George said, making Tom worry that he'd been inadequate in hiding his opinion. "We're only a short carriage ride away if you need us, dear boy. I shall give you some privacy. And don't worry about the house, take as long as you need."

George climbed into his carriage and it was well on its way before Tom realised it was a strange thing to say. Why should he worry about the house? Perhaps it was regarding the wake. Would there be a wake? He'd only ever read about funerals in Mundanus. What did they do in the Nether? Whatever the Violas did for Freddy, it was a private affair.

The front door was opened before he even reached it. The butler looked dreadful and his eyes filled with tears when he saw Tom. "Sir," was all he managed to say, and Tom's throat went tight again.

"Good evening, Wilson," Tom forced himself to say as he entered the house. "Is anyone else here?"

"I hope you don't mind, sir," Wilson replied in a tremulous voice as he shut the door, "But I sent the maids and the cook to your house round the corner. They were so distressed. They heard the...we all heard the shot, you see, and one of the maids saw..." he trailed off. "I'm so terribly sorry, sir. I should have..."

Tom put a hand on his shoulder and was horrified to see a tear slip down Wilson's cheek. "Go and make some tea, Wilson," he said in the hope that an ordinary task would help focus the poor man.

Wilson nodded and looked askance at Charles's study. "He..."

"I understand," Tom said. "Go and make the tea. I need a little time alone."

"Of course, sir," Wilson mumbled, and hurried off.

The house was so silent it chilled him to his bones. The grandfather clock had been stopped. The door to the study was shut, as it usually was. Tom knew he had to look, but couldn't make his legs move. Standing there, looking at the study door, he could imagine his father sitting at his desk on the other side, writing a letter or frowning at one he'd received. Perhaps if he just stayed still and didn't open it, that would be the reality. It was the only one Tom could imagine.

With an inordinate expenditure of willpower, Tom took a step towards the door and felt like he was ten again, palms sweating and heart thumping as he tried to keep lines of poetry, dates of battles, and names of military leaders in his mind. He found himself about to knock, his knuckles less than an inch from the wood, before remembering there was no need. And yet, he couldn't help himself, couldn't bring himself to disobey his father's wishes even now. So he knocked three times and waited for the voice that never came.

His hand drifted down to brush the door handle with his fingertips, resting there as he waited for that call, as his mind tried to imagine his father in the drawing room instead. Then he gripped the handle, unable to bear a moment more of this twilight state, and opened it.

It took mere moments to see what lay within, before he turned away, squeezing his eyes shut as the assault of images flicked through his mind. The desk as it always was, the swagger stick in its rest as it should be. The walls filled with bookcases and so many books they'd read together. The display cabinet, pristine, the military regalia inside. His father in his chair. Slumped to the left. Eyes open and glass-like. His skin so waxy and pale against his dark moustache. His uniform, rarely worn, buttons highly polished.

The blood.

There was a high-pitched whistling sound and sparkling prickles of light edged his vision. Tom lurched to lean against the wall of bookshelves to the left of the door. His legs gave way beneath him as his lips tingled and his vision tunnelled to a single coin of light. He sucked in a breath and gripped one of the shelves until the fainting spell passed.

A memory surfaced, like flotsam following the sinking of a ship, of the day he'd successfully recited his father's favourite poem by Wilfred Owen. How the stern expression throughout his recital had been broken by one of his father's rare smiles, followed by the opening of his arms and the swift, congratulatory embrace and a firm pat on the back for his efforts. He could still remember the smell of his father's cologne and hair oil as he was picked up and sat on his knee.

"And what did the poem say to you, Thomas?" he'd said.

"That war is bad. Is it bad, Papa? It doesn't seem bad in the stories."

"An unjust war is bad, son. How do you think Wilfred Owen felt when he wrote that poem?"

"Sad."

"And angry too, perhaps? He wanted everyone to know the cost of war. The cost of duty. He was angry at everyone merrily sending their sons off to war without knowing what horrors it held."

"Did you see a man die in the war, Papa?"

His father had looked away then, haunted. "Many of them, son. Many friends amongst them. But they did their duty. Duty above all else, Thomas, that's what matters. They did their duty and they died well."

Now, his forehead resting against the hard wooden shelf, Tom wanted to scream at his father's body, *Is this dying well? What about your duty to us?* But he kept his mouth tightly shut and forced himself to stay still as the rage tore through his heart and left a howling, terrifying grief in its wake.

He managed to get back onto his feet but not to look at his father again. The sound of rattling crockery at the doorway made him notice that Wilson had returned. "The tea will be in the drawing room, sir," Wilson said, just as unable to look at the far side of the study.

Keeping his eyes away from the body and the worst of the blood, Tom scanned the floor near the desk and saw his father's service revolver lying where it had fallen from his hand. He needed to pick it up and take out the bullets, but he simply couldn't bring himself to do it. Shivering, he staggered from the room and closed the door behind him, half falling against it to rest there for a moment and gather the strength to join Wilson.

"Pour a cup for yourself, Wilson," he said when he finally made it to the drawing room. "I…have some questions."

Wilson looked as though he'd been expecting as much. "Yes, sir."

Tom sat heavily in an armchair and clasped his hands together in an effort to hide how much they were trembling. "When did it happen?"

"Just before nine this evening, sir," Wilson said as he poured the tea. "The Irises were due to call at nine for sherry before they travelled to Oxenford. No one was sure whether Mr Rhoeas-Papaver would be joining them, given the…" He blushed. "The…difficult circumstances regarding Mrs Rhoeas-Papaver, but at half past eight Mr Papaver came out of his study and asked the valet to dress him in his uniform. We assumed he intended to go to the ball in his regalia, as he's been known to do so in the past. If you'll forgive my personal speculation, sir, I wondered whether it was to help fortify him to go into public since Mrs Papaver left."

"So Mother really has gone?"

"Yes, sir. A few days ago."

The thought of his mother abandoning his father sat nonsensically in his mind as Wilson continued.

"Only Mr Reticulata-Iris knew. He visited the same day she left and I think Mr Papaver told him in his distress. Mr Iris has been very supportive over the past week. Of course, we've all been hoping she'll return, after whatever it was blew over. But…" Wilson noticed he was still holding the teapot long after he'd finished pouring. He set it down and picked up the milk jug. "Where was I? I'm so sorry… Yes, it was just before nine and I was checking that the footman had sent for the carriage to be prepared in case Mr Papaver needed it. I was in the back parlour, the scullery maid was clearing the fireplace in the dining room, and Cook was having her break in the kitchen. The valet was tidying the dressing room. We all heard it. Just one shot. Out of nowhere."

"Was his valet the last person he spoke to?"

"Yes, sir. He's with Cook at the other house now. He said that Mr Papaver seemed…fine, as he normally was. Quiet. He's been very quiet all week but that was understandable. What with…" He looked down at the milk jug still in his hand, unused. "I got to the study first. I saw…the…I…I saw how bad it was and there was a knock at the door and I…" He carried on staring at the milk jug. "It was the Reticulata-Irises, all dressed in their finery and I was so confused and shaken I…Mr Iris saw something was wrong and pushed past me and so did his wife and…" Wilson jolted, as if noticing the jug for the first time. He poured some milk into both cups and set it down. "I shouldn't have let them in. I'm rather ashamed to say I shouted at them, for seeing it, and forced them into here. By then the rest of the staff had come from their various places and I had to settle them and…" He passed a cup to Tom. "It was awful. Cook was very helpful and gathered them up and took them out of the house." His intense stare was broken with a jolt and he reached into his inside pocket. "Oh my goodness, I am so sorry, sir. I'm…I'm not quite myself. I forgot to say…" He pulled out a letter and Tom recognised the paper and envelope immediately. Without having to see the handwriting, he knew his father had written it. "This was on his desk. I haven't told anyone else about it. It's too private."

Tom took it. *Thomas* was written in the familiar hand on the front of the envelope. There was a red wax seal on the back and the poppy motif was misaligned. What he thought was a speck of wax was actually blood, and he put it beside him on the arm of the chair until he felt stronger. "Thank you," he forced himself to say. "And please, do sit down, Wilson. You must be exhausted."

Looking distinctly uncomfortable, Wilson sat in one of the other chairs and they drank their tea in silence. Tom felt as if the tea were the only real thing he could comprehend and drank it in three uncouth gulps, each one pushing down a surge of emotion. He had to be still, to stay calm and be strong for Wilson. It wouldn't do to fall apart in front of the staff.

Wilson stood and placed his cup and saucer on the tray with care. "Sir…I don't quite know how to say this, but the…the body. Should I contact the Agency for guidance?"

It seemed as though the floor lurched beneath his chair, and Tom had to put the cup down on the saucer for fear of spilling the tea dregs. He had no idea what to do. It felt like he needed to look for a responsible adult and for a ridiculous moment he thought to ask his father what would be best. Tom clamped his hand over his mouth, but the sob escaped nonetheless. Appalled, he gripped the arm of the chair with his other hand, trying to steady himself and rein it all in. The envelope crinkled beneath his palm and then any hope of maintaining his composure was abandoned as he leant forwards and wept uncontrollably.

By the time he came back to himself, Wilson was gone. Tom was left with the dregs of his tea and the letter. It lay on the floor, crumpled, and he snatched it up, horrified by his own carelessness. He flipped it over to look at his name and back to the seal, trying to find some mote of strength within himself to open it. Eventually, the fear of what was inside was outweighed by the simple need to just get it over with. Better to know than to dread.

There was a single sheet of paper inside. He opened it to see his father's familiar handwriting in its usual black ink.

Thomas,

There is nothing I can say that will make this any less cowardly, but I want you to understand why. That's the least I owe you.

I simply cannot carry on in this life as the failure I am. Your mother has made it clear that she will never return and I have found myself considering why she left, now the rage has passed. Now that the three of you have lives of your own, the prospect of eternity with me alone was too much for her to bear. I find myself agreeing with her.

I haven't been a good husband. I was a passable father to you and to Elizabeth, I hope, but I failed to curb Catherine's wilful nature and upon reflection I wonder if I am more to blame for her behaviour than I have cared to admit. Please tell her I am sorry for all that I did to her. I do not deserve her forgiveness but perhaps the thought that I regret my actions will offer her succour.

Thomas, my boy, you are everything I could have hoped for in a son. I am so very proud of you and you do not deserve to be embarrassed by the sight of my fall from grace. George R—I— has made it clear that it is inevitable, but I will not permit him to take your birthright. All of my properties are yours. The deeds are in the leather wallet accompanying this letter. Simply sign your name on the transfer document for each one, beneath where I have written it, and say that you did so yesterday or whenever your schedule could have made it possible. It is imperative that the Irises do not take A— S— and that you resign your position as Marquis and protect our tenants now that I am unable to do so. I should have brought you here to do this in person, but in truth, I cannot bear the thought of you seeing me this way. How can I look you in the eye now? How can you see me as anything but the man who could not even keep his own wife happy?

Forgive me, Thomas. Be a better man than I.

Father

Tom carefully placed the letter back in its envelope and tucked it into his inner jacket pocket to sit safely over his heart. He rested his head in his hands, trying to understand the letter. How could he think about properties and resigning as Marquis now? Did his father think his love for him was so shallow that he'd be able to care about anything, having seen his dead body? What state could he have been in to think such a thing?

And then he was weeping again, not caring about whether he was being strong or not. Why didn't his father send for him when he was struggling so? How could he have only found out about Mother now, days after she'd left? Was it all because of his father's pride?

As he sobbed, he was only dimly aware of a knock on the door, unable to care about who it could be and confident that Wilson would turn them away. He soaked his only handkerchief and there was no sign yet of the tears stopping. Tom couldn't remember the last time he had cried. He must have been very young. For as long as he could remember he'd always stopped himself, knowing that Father wouldn't have been impressed by such weakness.

There was a hand on his shoulder, the familiar scent of warm spices, and he looked up to see Lucy there, tears in her eyes. "Oh, Tom," she whispered, stroking away a tear with her thumb as she knelt in front of him. "You don't have to go through this alone." And then he was clinging to her, his face buried in her shoulder as he cried. Her hand stroked his back in slow circles until there was nothing left but a hollow ache inside.

"I know you didn't want me to come with you," she said after handing him a fresh handkerchief from her reticule, "but I couldn't bear the thought of you—"

"No, I'm glad you came," he whispered. Her eyes widened as something like hope filled them. Had he starved her so? He cupped her face in his hands and kissed her tenderly. "Thank you for thinking of me."

"Is there anything I can do?"

"You're already doing it." He wiped his cheeks and sighed

heavily. "I don't know what to do with myself. And I need to deal with…"

She watched his eyes flick to the hallway. "You don't need to deal with anything right now. I'll speak to Wilson and we'll figure out what we need to do, and we won't do anything until we've talked it through, okay?" There was another knock on the door. "Did Wilson call for some help already?" she asked.

"Not that I know of."

They both watched the butler pass the open doorway and listened when he opened the front door.

"Is my nephew here?"

It was his uncle Lavandula, the Master of Ceremonies. With a start, Tom realised he probably should have informed his aunt and uncle about what had happened.

"I'm afraid Mr Rhoeas-Papaver is not receiving guests, your Grace," Wilson said.

"I'm family, and I need to see him. Thomas?"

"Come in," Tom called. "There's no point arguing with him," he whispered to Lucy.

"Thomas, my poor, darling boy!" his uncle said, dabbing at his eyes with a powder-blue silk handkerchief that matched his frock coat and breeches. "Lucy, a pleasure to see you, dear, despite the appalling circumstances."

Tom helped Lucy up and went to shake his uncle's hand. "You know, then?"

"Of course I do! That toad came and delivered the news himself. Pure greed dressed in false sympathy."

Exchanging a confused glance with Lucy, Tom held up a hand. "I don't understand what you mean."

His uncle hid his mouth behind his handkerchief. "Forgive me, sweet nephew, I am behaving as poorly as the one who sent me into this rage. Allow me to express my condolences properly. I knew your father for hundreds of years and frankly, I'm still in shock." He glanced around the room and then shut the door behind him. "The toad I referred to was George Iris. I came to tell you that your aunt and I won't stand for it, Thomas, and we are fully prepared to do whatever it takes to put him back in his place."

Sensing his confusion without even looking at him, Lucy spoke when Tom couldn't find the words. "I beg your pardon, Mr Lavandula, but we have no idea what you're talking about."

Tom watched his uncle's eyes widen. "Well, much as I hate to be the one to lay more awful news upon you, dear ones, I feel you should know. George Iris has claimed all of your father's properties, Thomas, even the very house we stand in now."

"But my father left them to me," Tom said, thinking of the note in his pocket. "The deeds are in his office."

"They're not, dear boy. The Irises have them, and George's signature was upon the transfer documents. I saw them with my very own eyes, along with the seals of authenticity. The Irises have all but taken Aquae Sulis, Thomas, and we must get it back!"

Now the comment George Iris had made about taking all the time he needed made sense. Tom closed his eyes, exhausted. Not this, not now, not on top of everything else. There was nothing left inside him and not even the anger at the Irises exploiting his family's tragedy was enough to stir more than a flicker within him.

He felt Lucy's hand slip into his and squeeze it gently. Such a small gesture, but at that moment it felt like the most important in the worlds. "Mr Lavandula," she said, "I understand that terrible things are happening in this city, and I understand your justifiable anger, but my husband has had the most appalling shock and he needs time to catch his breath."

"Yes, but—" Uncle Lavandula began, but Lucy cut him off.

"It will all still be there tomorrow," she said firmly. "And the day after that. The Irises have made their move and there's nothing to be done about that in this moment. There are more important and pressing matters that Tom and I have to deal with right now. Okay?"

There was a pause and Tom opened his eyes, wondering if his uncle was going to make some sort of comment about the use of that colonial vernacular term. Surprisingly, he found himself ready to tear into him if he did. "Dear girl, you are indeed correct. I have behaved abominably. Forgive me, Thomas, darling. I have quite lost my head."

Tom could only nod, and after another squeeze of the hand Lucy broke away to go over to Uncle Lavandula, smiling warmly at him as she touched his upper arm. "We understand. It's a terrible time. May I see you to the door? I have some questions I'd like to ask you, regarding certain practicalities."

"Of course, dear, of course. Thomas, we are just across the way, as ever."

They left the room and Tom let himself drop back into the armchair, listening to the conversation fading as the other two went into the hallway. In the moments Lucy was gone, the horror of his father's study returned, and he covered his crumpling face lest she see it when she returned.

Then she was back, sitting on the arm of the chair, stroking his hair, soothing. "I'm going to contact the right people to move your father out of the house, Tom, is that okay? I mean, is that all right?"

He dragged his hands down his face and looked at her. Her brown eyes were large and sad, her petite features so delicate. It felt like he was really seeing her for the first time. "I don't think I can..."

"You don't need to. I'm here. We're gonna get through this, Tom. Okay? I promise."

Tom sighed and then nodded. "All right," he said quietly. "Okay."

6

Max pulled down a side street and parked next to a huge red brick building. He'd set off from Bath before dawn but several hours later there wasn't much change in the light. The rain hammered on the car so loud that it was hard to hear when the idling engine was turned off.

His coat was resting on the back seat. The gargoyle was crammed into the car's boot and had finally stopped grumbling about that fact. Thanks to the weather, and the fact that it was Sunday in an industrial part of Manchester, the streets were deserted. Max was counting on there being very few innocents about.

Max found the new app that Kay had set up on his phone, along with the gadget Rupert had given him the night before. He managed to look at the map that the app was now displaying, work out that the small red arrow flashing on it was where he was, and how the shading of the area around him changed to indicate proximity to the target before a thud from the back of the car made him look in the rearview mirror.

"We're on a public street," he said to the boot. "You can't come out here."

There was another thud and the central armrest for the back seat flopped down, opening a small gap through to the boot's interior. "I hate it in here. Are we getting out or what?"

"That's what I'm trying to work out. I don't think so. As far as I can tell, the target isn't in Manchester at all." He tried pinching the screen and moving his fingers outwards to try and zoom out, but it didn't work the way it did for Kay. She'd made it look very easy in the office the night before. He tried again, and the third time all he achieved was moving the map to Scarborough and then closing the app by accident.

"Listen," said the gargoyle, whose fidgeting was making the car rock a little too much for Max's liking. "Do you really think that Rupert is going to start sorting things out after this woman has been dealt with?"

"That's what he said."

"'Cos I was talking to Kay and we're not so sure. Rupert doesn't seem fussed about finding a better way to do things."

Max undid his seat belt and twisted round to see the gargoyle's snout just visible through the gap in the seat back. "You don't think that these phone 'apps' are better? The information management seems much faster to me."

"No, we don't mean that. We mean Arbiters. Kay and me were talking about it, and she's really pissed off about the way we've been treated."

"Why?"

"Because it was wrong!" the gargoyle growled. "We were torn in two and conditioned to think and believe things and we had no say in it. We can't let it happen to anyone else."

Max faced front again, trying to examine whether he agreed with that appraisal. He could consider the factual aspect of what had happened to him. He could remember the pain of it, but only in an intellectual manner, without any emotional discomfort at all. At the very most, he felt a reluctance to see another child go through what he had, but that was only part of his remit. That was one of the reasons why his work was so important; to prevent any breaches and thereby make it less likely someone would see too much and need to be removed from mundane society. He simply could not share any sense of injustice, however, nor feel anything else at all about his becoming an Arbiter. It simply…was. And it was a necessity. "I don't agree that the technique is wrong. The dislocation of the soul is the only robust protection against Fae magic."

"Yeah but there's iron and copper and—"

"That was tried a long time ago. There's always a weakness.

Armour has gaps, for one thing, and the Fae and their puppets soon learned how to exploit them. Dislocation is the only way."

The gargoyle muttered something Max couldn't hear, though he had the distinct sense it was derogatory. "Kay's going to make sure that Rupert looks for an alternative. And if there's anyone who could do that, it's her."

"She's a young woman with no esoteric skill. He is a Sorcerer with hundreds of years of experience. I doubt she will be able to sway his working practice enough to satisfy either of you." As the gargoyle chewed that over, Max made a second attempt to use the app and failed. A text arrived from Kay: *The target is not in Manchester. Drive ten miles south-west and then stop again.*

"And when are we going to go and free those people in the Agency headquarters basement, eh? I know we were distracted, nailing that Iris bastard, but come on. I've been really patient and those people are suffering."

"I'll speak to Rupert about it once we—"

"He doesn't give two shitty pebbles about anyone except himself. If we don't push this—if we don't just go and bloody get it done—it won't happen. Let's go find Cathy. I reckon we could come up with a plan and—"

"No. This isn't the time." Max was certain that letting the gargoyle spend any more time in the company of strong-minded young women was not going to be productive. Another text arrived: *Rupert says you need to get moving. You must get as close to the target as you can.*

"Eh?" the gargoyle said from the back. "What exactly does he want us to do?"

Please clarify instructions, Max texted back.

After a pause, a reply came through. *Rupert says you need to get as close as possible. He needs an exact reading on her location.*

"I don't like this," the gargoyle said. "We've seen what that woman can do. She'll mash us up and serve us with peas."

Another text arrived. Kay typed them much faster than he could. *I don't agree with Rupert. Trying to get a better idea of what you're supposed to do, but he's watching your location, so go to the estate and I'll see what I can find out while you're en route. Either way, you need to come back to Bath soon. We just got word via the Agency that the head of the Poppy family in Aquae Sulis has died in unusual circumstances.*

"Cathy's dad?" the gargoyle asked. "I wonder how she's taken that."

Yet another text from Kay arrived. *And talk to the gargoyle. It's important.* Max deleted it, like all the others he'd received, as basic security good practice. "Kay says we need to go ten miles south-west. Why does she think I need to talk to you about something important?"

"We're not very far from where our sister's children live. Our niece and nephew. And their children, and *their* children and the ones that have just had their fourth birthday party. Twins. Our great-great-great-nephews."

"I didn't realise Jane had so many descendants."

"Kay looked into it. They're having a family get-together tomorrow. Kay found it on the Google booking faces thing. Our niece, Joy, is having her eighty-fifth birthday party in Chester. It's not that far from here, actually."

Max tried to work out why that should be of interest, and failed. "We should go to the next location to get a new reading."

"Yeah, but we have to go to the party tomorrow, right?"

"Why? I can't speak to them. I can't risk them recognising any family resemblance and creating a breach. There's no point."

"Yeah...what point could there be? Oh, wait a minute! Because they are our only family in the world! That couldn't be a better point if you sharpened it with a bloody big knife!"

"You pay too much attention to Kay," Max said, starting the engine. "You are far too easily swayed by her. Dislocation doesn't just protect us from the Fae."

"Dislocation isn't the only thing that makes you an arsehole."

Max gave one last look at the road map on the passenger seat next to him. He checked his mirrors, flicked the indicator, and pulled out, ignoring the gargoyle's insults as they drove away.

• • •

Cathy looked at the formula and went over each part in turn, referencing her notes and double-checking the symbols she was still unfamiliar with. After this cup of tea she'd take her work to her new tutor. She'd stayed up all night, devouring the lesson notes and exercises that Beatrice had given her the night before. She'd planned to stay up to speak to Sam when he got back, but she'd been in the library at the back of the house, engrossed in her work, and he'd got back so late he must have assumed she was in bed.

There was no better reason for insomnia than the glimpse of a way to protect herself. Beatrice had written out the formula she'd need to ward herself from the Irises, but if life in the Nether had taught Cathy anything, it was to never accept magical assistance based on trust. She'd insisted on learning everything that underpinned it before actually using it, to be sure it really said what she wanted it to.

After the last slurp of tea, Cathy gathered her work and went up to Beatrice's room to find her door slightly ajar. Cathy could see her working at the desk within, so she knocked on the door softly. "Beatrice?"

Her tutor turned to face her. "Have you finished the exercises already?"

"Yes. I worked through the night. Would you mind checking them?"

Beatrice stood up. "Let's work in the library."

The return to the library was welcome, as was the scent of the books. It was Cathy's favourite room, even though it sent a pang through her for her old library, abandoned with the rest of that life. She'd thought it was such a romantic gesture, so thoughtful. She'd read far too much into it at the time. Just another example of Will's manipulation.

"This is excellent work," Beatrice finally said after reading it all through. "You have a natural aptitude for sorcery. And your practical experience with Fae magic will serve you well."

"It's like algebra," Cathy said, "and conjugating verbs. It's all…

tidy in my head. Using the Fae magic with it is like a part of the formula bracketed off, isn't it? Like a shorthand for stuff that would be too broad to express with sorcerous terms."

Beatrice stared at her long enough to make Cathy uncomfortable. "That is correct."

"Where did you learn all the Fae magic? I'm married into the Irises and I wasn't taught pure Iris magic. I had to buy it. Or have it inflicted upon me," she added bitterly.

"I made deals," Beatrice said, casually, as if she were talking about buying potatoes. "In return for knowledge of Iris magic, I instructed the Arbiters in London to ignore the activities of the Irises. Lord Iris felt that was of great worth."

Cathy gawped at her, remembering the day she and Max had worked the Charm on the statue of Nelson in Trafalgar Square. "You were behind all that? How did you corrupt the Arbiters?"

"I didn't. They think I am my late brother."

Cathy couldn't help but admire her, despite the fact that murder underpinned the admiration. "This hybrid magic of yours is insanely powerful. I think I understand this protection formula now. That clause must refer to Lord Poppy. And you've used the Fae magic here so you don't have to write a clause for every single member of the Iris family and Lord Iris and all the different interpretations of that concept, right?"

Beatrice nodded. "That's a very simplified way to describe it, but the essence is correct. This one is an additional clause to cover third parties employed by your husband and his patron. And you have discovered the fundamental weakness of sorcerous magic. It is too rigid. That's why I had to develop the hybrid approach to achieve my goals."

Cathy thought about all the artefacts and potions and Charms she'd ever directly experienced. Shadow Charms and that damn choker and the Charm to make her able to paint that picture to satisfy Poppy...all of them had a specific purpose. But then again, when she tried to think of a way to express their effects in sorcerous magic, she simply couldn't do it. How could one define the concept of "stay hidden" in a precise formula without having to define where, when, and from whom? How could she express something as broad and subjective as improved artistic ability?

Then she considered the sorcerous artefacts she'd seen. She could understand how the function of the messaging tube that Ekstrand gave her was very narrow; it could only send that particular message capsule to one specific location. While it didn't matter *where* it was screwed into the ground, it still had to be. It had to be activated in a very specific way. What else had she seen? She'd certainly heard the knocks made by Arbiters on the doors of Nether properties. Probably made with some sort of device held by the Arbiter and literally struck against the door. She could imagine the shape of the formulae involved: define the door, determine whether there is a Nether property anchored to it, send the sound to all doors mapped to the one being struck. Something like that, anyway. The pin Max had put into the keyhole of her drawing room when they needed to speak in private—simple! It would just define the sound within the space enclosed by the door and walls and stop it from penetrating them.

Her heart began to race as she started to understand the fundamental differences between the two types of magic. She had to persevere, to seize as much knowledge for herself as she could, so she could put the days of fearful ignorance behind her.

But then Cathy remembered the Truth Mask that Max had threatened her with that one time things had turned sour between them.

"How would an Arbiter's Truth Mask work?" she asked. "How would a Sorcerer define a concept as loose and subjective as someone telling the truth or not?"

Beatrice's eyes took on a wicked glint. "There is no sorcery used in a Truth Mask."

"What?"

"It's not needed. A Truth Mask employs simple torture and fear to achieve the result. All Arbiters are trained in torture techniques and all have a special set of tools designed to maximise pain in the

Fae. After all, there is no better torturer than a man literally incapable of feeling guilt or any sort of empathy with their victim."

The thought of it made Cathy feel sick. "Is that why you killed all the others? Because they did more harm than good?"

Beatrice's face took on a contemplative expression. "That is an interesting question. I certainly believe that of the Sorcerers. But I destroyed the Chapters because I had to remove the tools of their power and oppression, rather than because of a judgement about the people themselves."

"But...but don't you feel bad about what you've done? All those people—lots of them victims of the Sorcerers themselves—are dead because of you."

"It was not a decision I made lightly. But I have reconciled myself with my actions. To create change, to disrupt a system of control, one must carry out radical acts. One must be prepared to destroy so that something new can be created. Those in control will never give up the power afforded to them voluntarily. It must be taken. If that requires the deaths of a few to give freedom to the many—and *survival* of the many—then so be it. This is not a gentle act."

Memories of Miss Rainer's lessons resurfaced. Debates about violence, about what was acceptable behaviour in the struggle for equality, and when the line could and should be crossed. There was nothing gentle about the more radical acts committed in the name of the women's suffrage movement. Cathy had loved those lessons the most.

Cathy stared out at the snow-covered garden. "Be militant each in your own way," Emmeline Pankhurst had said. Destroying the Nether was the most radical act she could consider. But it was more than taking away property; she would be destroying a way of life. Did she have the right to do that? Did anyone? She wasn't sure, but she was certain that the Patroons had no right to keep their control over it. She didn't want to hurt anyone, though. Aside from reflections of properties, the only things she was willing to destroy without guilt were those fragile male egos and their toxic masculinity. How

71

far would she go to destroy the Nether? Beatrice had told her it was possible to warn the Fae-touched beforehand, but given her track record, was she trustworthy? Having killed all those people, would Beatrice care if a few more died?

"Besides," Beatrice said. "I find it more productive to focus on what is still to be done, than what is in the past."

"Do you plan to kill any more people?"

"No. All of the Sorcerers and the Arbiters—save a small number I keep in London in case of emergency—are dead."

Cathy thought of Max and the gargoyle and kept silent. She was certain Max had told her that Ekstrand had been replaced. Perhaps Beatrice had killed him since they'd had that conversation. She didn't want to raise any of it, not wanting to put Max at risk.

She was learning from someone she was afraid of. Cathy pushed the fear down, knowing there was no other way to gain this knowledge. "This clause here, can you explain that? I wasn't too sure about it."

"This one defines you. It is possible to define yourself in sorcerous terms, but it's very difficult. Even though it can be shorthanded once defined, it's slow and unwieldy."

"Okay then. So if I wanted to leave the estate, would I just write this on myself?"

Beatrice nodded.

"Anywhere?"

"There are subtleties in Fae magic. Where would you write it?"

"Over my heart," Cathy said. "Because of what it means to me, rather than physical proximity to the organ."

"Yes. That is correct."

"Okay. So I'd write this on, then add the Fae bits with spoken Charms?"

Beatrice nodded. "Fae magic is more powerful when spoken from memory. And jewellery that holds the magic can always be lost or broken or stolen. This way binds it directly to your soul."

"That oath last night was more Fae-based than sorcery, wasn't it? Hang on, didn't you say that Sam was bound by the same one?"

When Beatrice nodded, Cathy said, "But how? Fae magic doesn't work on him, so neither will hybrid magic."

Beatrice's smile was frightening. "It seemed Fae, but it employed purely sorcerous magic, executed with words alone. The sounds themselves acted as sigils. It's very advanced. You need to concentrate on the written form."

"But…to make that oath work, you'd have to define betrayal in all of its forms, before you even get to the words!"

"I did define it. Completely." Beatrice replied. "It took me over ten years. The books I wrote the definition in could easily fill this room. The shorthand notation expressing it would fill one of those big ones over there." She pointed at one of the huge leather-bound tomes. "Condensing that into a sigil that I could visualise perfectly enough whilst verbally working the magic of the oath took over a year to develop." She tilted her head at Cathy's shocked expression. "I knew that once I had killed all the Sorcerers, I would need to work closely with Lord Iron. Sorcerous magic is only as powerful as the preparation put into it." She reached for her pen. "I prepared extensively. Now, you understand the oath that binds us, you understand that if I were to put anything into this formula that we have not discussed would be considered a betrayal, and you would know. This ward will do exactly as I have described and even if your husband, or Lord Poppy, or Lord Iris himself were to find you, they would be powerless to do anything to you that is against your will."

Cathy nodded. "Okay then. And once you've taught me the Fae Charms to go into those clauses, just writing it on whilst I cast those makes it work?"

Beatrice held up a finger. "All sorcerous magic requires intent behind it. If Mrs M wrote this onto herself, it would have no effect, even if she knew the Fae components. These symbols are the language of human will. Without that will behind it, it is just writing. When you study sorcery, you must also be a student of concentration, of the focusing of intent. They are just as important."

"I'll make sure I understand it all completely, then after I write it on myself, I'll get it tattooed."

Beatrice looked appalled. "That would be very unwise. I would never advocate any sort of permanent warding on the body."

"Okay. But what if this smudges? Or I get wet and my clothes rub it off?"

"I will show you how to make a robust form of ink for warding. But it will only last as long as it should."

"What's that supposed to mean?"

"Don't you see? The Charm to express you in this formula would be worked on a particular day, and who knows how you will change over the next week, the next month, the next year? The only way for this ward to be truly permanent would be for you to refresh it, often. We never stay the same, physically, spiritually, and emotionally. Trying to hold yourself to who you are now for the sake of maintaining this protection would be unwise."

"But the Fae magic is only notated. If I refresh the Charm myself, why not make the rest of the formula permanent?"

"Are you so certain that you will always need to be protected against Iris magic? What if you needed to use it one day? What if you found yourself in a situation where you required Lord Iris's assistance? What if you were to reconcile with your husband and his family?"

Cathy snorted. "That's never going to happen."

"Iris magic is very useful. Warded against it, you cannot wield it or any artefacts with that magic bound into them."

Thoughts of that choker returned and Cathy grinned. "Good."

Beatrice shook her head. "You are very young."

"Fuck the Irises," Cathy said as she saw Sam heading across the garden towards the forge. "Can you set me more exercises? I want to learn everything."

"I do not have time to teach you all of my sorcerous knowledge. I will show you as much of the basics as I can."

"Thanks." Cathy stood, stretched, and felt the pull of her bed. But she needed to talk to Sam before she could rest.

7

Cathy could hear the heavy clang of Sam at work in the forge way before she got there. She was wearing one of his coats and an old pair of Mrs M's wellies but she'd left the umbrella back in the house. She wanted to feel the snow on her hair and skin.

"Hi," she said at the doorway to the forge. Sam paused his arm halfway up to the next strike and turned to face her. He was wearing just a T-shirt and jeans beneath his blacksmith's apron, thanks to the heat of the furnace behind him. Sweat had made the grime of his work collect in rivulets describing the curves of his muscles. Cathy studied them as he laid down the hammer and thrust the piece of iron he was working into the plunge bucket.

"Bloody hell, Cathy, there are umbrellas up at the house, you know!" He hurried over to pull her towards the fire. "You're shivering!"

"I know, it's wonderful. I've never been in proper snow before. It doesn't tend to settle in Bath. There was nothing but rain when I was a student. And in the Nether, there's obviously no weather at all." She shuddered and tried to push that dreary silver sky from her mind. "What are you making?"

Sam wiped his face on the cloth he kept by the sink in the corner, then washed the back of his neck as she squeezed out a trickle of water from her ponytail. "Haven't decided yet. I was practicing a technique."

"How about a spear for Lord Iris's heart?"

"Does he even have one?"

"Probably not." She warmed her hands with the heat from the furnace and then hung her coat from one of the huge hooks on the wall as she tried to work out what to say to Sam. "So…I spent some time with Beatrice yesterday."

Sam came over to stand next to her, holding his own hands out to the flames level with hers, flexing his fingers as he often did after working the metal. She could see calluses, and dirt under his nails. They couldn't be more different to Will's soft, manicured hands. "Did you two get along?"

"I'm not sure Beatrice could 'get along' with anyone. We had some interesting conversations. We need to talk about her plan."

Sam swiped back a lock of damp hair from his forehead. "She told you about it?" When she nodded, he asked, "After you swore that oath?"

"Yeah. It was…weird."

Sam started to form a word, then paused, started to move his lips again, and then sighed. "Tea. Tea first." He went over to the shelf next to the sink and filled the small kettle. He took off the apron and hung it up before rinsing out a mug and plucking another from a higher shelf. Cathy couldn't help admiring the broadness of his shoulders, the way his torso slimmed to his waist. She looked away, back to the furnace, silently chiding herself as the kettle boiled. He poured the water over teabags he'd dropped into the mugs and turned to face her. "Jammie Dodger?"

She laughed. "What?"

"Jammie Dodger," he repeated, smiling. "You know, the biscuit?" He grabbed a tin from the top of the nearby fridge and pulled off the lid, holding out the contents to her. There were pale biscuits made of two layers with jam sandwiched between them, glimpsed through a heart-shaped hole at the top. She took one, inspecting it.

"Shit, you've never had a Jammie Dodger?"

She shook her head. "Bourbons, custard creams, and…um… jaffa cakes. Not these."

"Please tell me you've had chocolate digestives?"

"No. Should I have? I didn't get round to trying those."

He slapped a hand over his heart and acted like he'd been

wounded. "Oh, Cathy, it's just too sad. I'll ask Mrs M to get some. And Rich Tea, too. For dunking. Obviously."

"Obviously." Cathy smiled. She nibbled on the biscuit experimentally as he swirled the teabags around and finished making the tea. By the time the cup was being handed to her she was brushing the crumbs off her fingers. Wordlessly, Sam came back with the tin and she took another. He shook the tin and when she looked up at him he waggled his eyebrows with a grin and looked back down. She took another and he seemed satisfied.

"When I was a kid, I used to eat the top layer first, then the jam, then the bottom layer," he said, coming back to her side with tea mug in one hand, biscuit in the other.

They munched the biscuits in companionable silence, the crackling of the flames filling the air for them. Cathy considered how safe and relaxed she felt with Sam. Far more relaxed than she'd ever felt with Will. Here, with Sam, there were no expectations pressing upon her. No pressure to please him. She took a slurp of tea and it was noisier than she intended. Trying not to laugh, she saw Sam's smile from the corner of her eye and then he slurped so loudly it sounded like bathwater going down the plughole. He smacked his lips and said, "Ahhhhh, there's lovely," and then grinned at her. She grinned back.

"So, Beatrice is teaching me a ward," Cathy said, wanting to say something positive before they tackled the really tricky stuff. "I've still got a couple of bits to learn, and I need to practise it, but it means I'll finally be safe."

Sam's face fell. "You'll always be safe with me."

"But I can't stay here forever."

Sam looked down at his shoes. "You could if you wanted to."

"That's..." Cathy suddenly felt she had to choose her words very carefully, as if she'd stumbled into some sort of emotional minefield and could blow everything up with a careless step. "That's really kind of you, Sam, but staying here because it isn't safe to leave isn't...a choice. I'm not saying I don't like being here—I do—it's that...I'd rather stay here because I don't want to be anywhere else, rather than because I *can't* be anywhere else."

He nodded. "Yeah. You're right."

Cathy wanted to say something about the way she feared he was unwittingly using her to fill the gap left by his wife, but she couldn't think of a way to raise it without sounding horrible. "Look, things are already changing. Beatrice is teaching me some things that I thought would be much harder but they're not. Soon I won't have to depend on you to keep me safe from Will and that is officially a Really Good Thing, okay? Because I don't want any of that crap to mess our friendship up. Yeah?"

"Yeah."

His smile was still a little sad, but she was satisfied that he knew where they both stood. "Okay, so you should know that she's teaching me about her hybrid magic in return for me trying to bring you onside. But I'm not here to do that. I want to talk it all through with you. Not persuade you."

He nodded. "Maybe I misunderstood," Sam said, in a tone that suggested that wasn't true at all. "But the way she talked about it, she believes the Sorcerers split the world into Mundanus and Exilium and that made the Fae go insane, and is making the Elemental Court into total arseholes. Present company excluded."

"I thought the Fae were arseholes before they were even put into Exilium," Cathy added. "In fact, I thought that was the whole reason why! I can't speak for the Elemental Court. I don't really know anything about them, apart from the bits you've told me."

"Oh, they are definitely arseholes," Sam said. "More tea? This is a two-mug discussion at least."

She nodded and watched him refill the kettle. "Beatrice talks about undoing the Sorcerers' work like it's the only option. Are we sure that it is?"

"As far as I can tell, it is," Sam said as he rinsed their mugs. "I haven't handled the Elemental Court very well, I admit that, but even if I had, it wouldn't change the fact that they're heartless bastards. And they're insanely shortsighted. They just can't see how bad an impact they have on the world. No, that's not right—they know it intellectually but they just don't care. I don't know how to make them care. It's like some bit of them is just missing."

"Can't we persuade Beatrice to…adjust the members of the Elemental Court? Shit, that sounds so fucking dodgy, I can't believe I'm even saying it!"

"Don't feel bad; I already asked her that, before you arrived," Sam replied. "I asked her if she could just give them a conscience or something. She said Fae magic doesn't work well enough on the Elemental Court. She said she tried it, before I was born, but it always failed."

Cathy wondered if some part of their soul had been cleaved away, something similar to what had been done to Max. Sam's soul seemed intact, though. And if Beatrice had already rejected that option, it was academic anyway. "And the members of the Elemental Court are definitely the root of all the planet's environmental problems?"

"Oh yeah," Sam said grimly, dropping new teabags into the mugs and pouring in the boiled water. "I've got all the evidence. I just can't find a way to use it well enough."

"Is this because of being in the Elemental Court, or just a cultural thing, though?" Cathy asked. "If there's anything I learned from the Nether it's that once people take control they don't give it up, and they don't let anyone close unless they're cut from the same cloth. But then, I suppose you disprove that."

Sam shrugged. "Sort of. Amir—my predecessor—woke up, somehow. He deliberately chose someone who wouldn't be like him. But that was because he was killing people he knew, by accident, and his potential heirs were doing that too. He was doing all sorts of terrible stuff around the world and just didn't give a fuck about it. I don't know if the Court is the way it is because it's a self-selecting group of arseholes, or if the splitting of the worlds is making them mad, like Beatrice thinks. All I know is that short of removing them all from power—which would be bloody hard even if I was the sort of person that was happy to go around murdering people for the greater good—I can't see how anything is going to change. None of them are going to pick someone like me to take over from them." He made the tea and handed her mug over. "But the thought of the Fae coming into Mundanus…shit. It makes me feel sick, you know?"

"Me too, but we have to do something," she said, more to rally herself than to express her frustration.

"Yeah, but…the Fae? Seriously? I cannot think of any situation in which they would make things better."

"Beatrice thinks that they will get better if things are put back to what they were before the world was split. But it's a leap of faith, isn't it? That's what this comes down to. Do we believe that Beatrice is telling the truth?"

"Is there any way to find out?"

Cathy shrugged. "I don't know if the Sorcerers were into writing stuff like that down. And anyway, we can't trust anyone when it comes to this. The Sorcerers were complete fucks. We both know that. And I would be the most unsurprised person in the worlds if I found out that Beatrice was right and they were split to give a few blokes a lot of power. I mean, we see it in the Nether, we see it in Mundanus. It's not outlandish to believe they did it just for their own gains."

"But look at the Fae," Sam said. "We both know they are just as bad. We've both seen what they do to people. I feel like we're stuck in a river with bloody crocodiles on one side and hungry lions on the other and Beatrice is saying the best way for us to survive is draining the river." Cathy squinted at him. He squinted back. "Okay," he finally said, "that wasn't the best way to describe it, but you know what I mean!"

"Yeah…" Cathy dumped her mug in the sink. She was so tired. Tired from lack of sleep and from being emotionally wrung out several times over. So much guilt and fear.

And anger. It was still there, beneath it all, that rage driving her on, because the Nether was still there, still holding so many prisoner to its ideals. The Agency and the horrors the gargoyle had told her about were still there and hundreds of servants in houses across Albion were still effectively slaves. How many wives had been beaten last night? How many men had forced themselves on women they considered their property whilst she'd been here, hiding away, blubbing on the sofa? "But it's not like we're just some bloody rabbits stuck in the river hoping we won't get eaten and that's the way we're thinking. Lord Poppy was really scary and horrible to you before you were Lord Iron, but what about when you went there and kicked his ass? I'm assuming that actually happened, right? You didn't just make that up?"

"That really happened," he said.

"And I'm not the same person who got screwed over by Poppy either. I'm learning sorcery. And I know that it isn't like that for everyone else and that they'll be at just as much risk as we were, but the point is that we're sitting here, worrying about what to do and whether to believe Beatrice like…like we're stupid children hoping that we're listening to the right grownup to tell us what to do. You are Lord Iron and you break their magic. And once I've learned more, I'll be able to protect places and people too. We can't do anything to stop the Elemental Court as things stand now. But we can do a lot to protect people from the Fae." She paused. Was she really arguing to rejoin the worlds?

Sam placed his mug in the sink next to hers. "Okay. So what you're saying is that things are fucked now. They could get more fucked, but we could maybe make sure they are less fucked than otherwise."

She nodded. "But I'm biased, Sam. I want to see the end of the Nether. I want to take that power bubble from the Patroons and I want the people there to be free to choose how they live. And we already agree that the Elemental Court has to change too. Else we're all screwed. And Beatrice might be telling the truth and it might all rebalance and get better. Of course, she could be in cahoots with all of the Fae and tricking us into freeing them so they can torment the entirety of humanity. Shit, that actually sounds quite plausible."

"Jesus," Sam whispered. "I hate this. I might be Lord Iron but I don't know anything about this sort of stuff. Not really."

"But we know she needs you to do this," Cathy said. "And it's got to be for an esoteric reason. Something you have to do, actively, otherwise she'd have used sorcerous magic to get what she wanted instead of having to take the time to persuade you."

"She wants to know where the forges are," Sam said. "There are seven of them apparently, and they connect to Exilium in a really freaky way. There are these…cables, big enough to walk on, that go from the forges to Exilium. I walked on one from my forge to Exilium that time I kicked Poppy's arse. Maybe she wants to break them?"

"I reckon that if a map of their locations was all Beatrice needed from you, she'd know that by now," Cathy said. "She's ruthless. She'd torture you, mundane medieval style, to get it out of you."

Sam nodded with a grim frown. "I know I can do…weird shit. But I can't see how any of it can be any use. And anyway, it doesn't solve our problem."

Unable to stay still, Cathy started to pace. "Okay. Let's take a step back. There's really only one choice, as I see it, anyway. We do nothing, after putting Beatrice in a box or something so she doesn't kill us. And that'd be hard, thanks to that bloody oath we swore. Or we unsplit the worlds. That's it. Do nothing or do something, and that something can only be what she suggests, because you can't change the Elemental Court and I can't change the Nether."

"If we do nothing," Sam said, "then environmentally, we're fucked."

"And the Nether keeps on going forever," Cathy said. "Nothing changes. The slavery goes on, the rape, the kidnapping of innocents…" She stopped pacing and they looked at each other. "Shit," they said, simultaneously.

"Well, that's that, then," Sam said. "We have to do it."

"But we do it our way," Cathy said. "We prepare. We determine when we're ready. We set stuff up ready to help people."

"Agreed," Sam said. "I've got some ideas."

"Good." Cathy stretched. "I'm going to have a nap and then

I'm getting back to work. Want to have lunch together?" She could tell he'd been hoping as much.

"Yeah. We'll work it out, Cathy. I think that, together, we could do some pretty amazing stuff."

For a moment, she almost believed him. But she'd learned the hard way that it wasn't worth putting her trust in any man. "I'll see you later."

8

There was a pile of correspondence on Will's desk, but after reading through the first letter he'd realised he was in no state to handle any of it. He went to the sofa, thinking he would sit nearer the fire and try to rest. There was nothing else to be done that evening. Not that he could face, anyway. He let his head fall back, thinking there was no way sleep could take him, when a knock at the door jolted him awake. Snapping his head round to look at the clock, he realised he'd only been asleep for twenty minutes. He jumped to his feet. "Come in."

Morgan entered. "A messenger is here for you, your Grace."

"An Arbiter?"

"No, a delivery boy, one who worked for the Emporium some time ago. He says his delivery is for your eyes only."

Had Lord Iron learned of the attempt to get Cathy back? Or was Lord Iris behind this? "Show him in."

Morgan bowed, withdrew, and soon returned with a young man, still in his teens. He was carrying a plain wooden box and was dressed in a smart black suit with a red waistcoat and red cravat. Will saw a pin at the boy's throat glittering. A tiny poppy made of gemstones. The breath caught in his chest. Had Lord Poppy discovered that Cathy was gone?

"Begging your pardon, sir," the young man said. "I was told I must put this box in your hands and no one else's."

"Show me your marque, boy."

"I don't deliver for the Emporium anymore, sir," he said sadly. "This is the only marque I can show you." He lifted his left trouser leg, revealing a glittering band around his ankle.

Will nodded. "I see."

The boy dropped the trouser leg back into place and held the box out towards Will. "Please take it, sir, else I'll get into terrible trouble." Will took the box and the boy sagged with relief. "Thank you, sir." He gave a small bow and left.

The last thing Will wanted to do was open a box sent by Lord Poppy. There was no possibility of anything good being within. His imagination put all manner of awful things on the other side of the wooden lid and settled upon a knife engraved with *cut out thine own heart*, as was reputedly delivered to another who had wronged the Fae.

As tempting as it was to just leave it on the table—or better still, at the bottom of a well in Mundanus—Will knew that Poppy would be waiting for the box to be opened and would know the moment it had been. Better to get it over with than face the contents along with his wrath at having been kept waiting.

Will returned to the sofa, balanced the box on his knees, and opened it. It was lined with black velvet and the object inside was wrapped in poppy-red silk. Partially unwrapping it revealed a handle made of wood. Resting within the lid of the box was a note that he plucked out and read. *Warm the glass with a fearful sigh.*

It wasn't difficult to muster such an emotion as Will lifted out the ornate scrying glass. He thought of Lord Iris's dwindling patience, and of what Poppy was about to unleash upon him, and breathed gently on the mirror. As soon as the breath misted on the glass it began to ripple, just as if he'd instructed it to show someone like any other scrying glass.

He was being shown Exilium. It was too colourful, too beautiful to be anywhere else. He could see trees and a scattering of the red flowers before Poppy's face came into view, as if he were darting in front of a film camera to get in shot. His grin was the epitome of delighted mischief, but there was something horribly cold about it too.

"Ahhh, William, the caretaker of my favourite's heart. I trust you are well?"

"Yes, Lord Poppy, thank you," Will said, hoping that the booming of his own heartbeat was audible only to him.

"And my favourite? How fares she in this difficult time?"

Difficult time? It took a beat for Will to remember that her father was dead and Poppy thought she knew. Was this a trap to reveal she was missing? Of course; Tom would have been expecting her to join them in Aquae Sulis...

"Catherine has chosen to keep her feelings private, Lord Poppy. Grief is such a personal thing."

Lord Poppy's eyes widened as if he were about to fly into an appalling rage, but then just as swiftly he flicked a lock of his long black hair from his face and smiled broadly. "Indeed. Grief can do terrible things, can it not? But I wonder if you have ever experienced it, William. Your life has been blessed. Everything you could possibly want, simply handed to you on the proverbial platter. Wealth. Power. Love. A wife more interesting and exciting than the rest of the women of Albion put together. Has she surprised you lately, William?"

"Yes, Lord Poppy," he replied with bitter truthfulness. "Very much so."

Lord Poppy's eyes narrowed. "You don't deserve her," he hissed into the glass. He drew back, staring at him with those horrifying black-on-black eyes. "I hope you are making her happy, William. I would be most displeased if you were not."

"It is all I think about, Lord Poppy," he said. What did the hateful creature want? Had he tried to find Cathy and failed?

"In times of grief," Lord Poppy said, starting to stride through the trees, "I find that causing untold misery to the enemies of those one loves does ease the pain somewhat. Don't you agree?"

Will felt an awful prickling cold run down his back. Poppy had evidently discovered that his family had lost their share of Aquae Sulis. But why take it out on him? Had he found out that he'd tipped his father off about Cathy's mother? "I imagine it is most satisfying, Lord Poppy." There was no choice but to play along.

The view through the scrying glass seemed to follow him,

and Will wondered if the magic was connecting what one of Lord Poppy's faeries saw with that being shown on the glass. It certainly bobbed about in a way reminiscent of the way those creatures flew. The sound of birdsong and a breeze through the trees was incongruous with the feeling of dread. Poppy was leading him somewhere. Will dared not look away, just in case Poppy looked back over his shoulder and somehow knew. There might be a corresponding glass floating in Exilium, for all he knew, showing the Fae what he was doing.

Then Will caught a glimpse of colourful gowns through the gaps between branches. Was he being led towards a party? His theory about a corresponding glass in Exilium faded when he saw several Fae come into view as the trees around Poppy opened into a clearing.

The first that Will recognised was Lord Iris, by virtue of his long white hair. Then Will noticed how he and the other Fae present all smiled and greeted Poppy without even glancing at whatever was sending him the sound and images.

At the far left of the view through the glass, he saw a tree stump that had been fashioned into some sort of display stand. On it stood something that appeared to be carved of wood. Then he noticed another plinth with what looked like a piece of jewellery upon it.

An art exhibition? Will had no idea the Fae had them.

Poppy drifted past some of the displays and whatever was following him turned to take in the exhibits that he passed, as if distracted by them.

"It's the best piece my slave has ever created," Will heard a female voice, light and soft, saying as Poppy passed by one of the sculptures. "He said he can't possibly do any more, that he's too sad, and then he carves this."

"Sadness is one of the best sources of inspiration," came a male voice from out of sight. "But it's hard to strike a balance in their fragile hearts. I told mine that his children had died since I took him from Mundanus, in the hope he'd write something truly moving, but all he does is lie there all day now. I think I broke him. I need another."

"But he was so talented." The source of the female voice came into view as Poppy approached. It belonged to a Fae in a lilac gown embroidered with a familiar motif. Lady Wisteria. Will had never seen her before. Unsurprisingly, her beauty was terrifying. "Why not bring him a new child and make him think it is his? He'll adore you and be so delighted he won't be able to stop composing music."

"And if he grows dull again I can use the child against him," her companion said. Lord Buttercup, Will deduced from the tiny bloom tucked behind his ear, bright against his blond hair. He kissed her hand. "Darling Wisteria. A marvellous idea."

"Take care to give your little Patroon clear instructions," Poppy said. "Your pets are the most incompetent in Albion."

Lord Buttercup scowled at Poppy. "I'm surprised to see you here. You've never been able to extract anything artistic from yours."

Pets? Will clenched his teeth. He knew they had little regard for them, but hearing the Fae talk so casually about stealing children made him feel sick. Then what Buttercup said actually sank in. Was that the purpose of this? Had Poppy created an exhibit to torment him?

Poppy's voice refocused him. "I simply waited until I had a piece that I knew would win."

Lady Wisteria's eyebrows arched. "The Princess has very particular taste, Poppy."

"I am well aware of it. Look as doubtful as you wish, Buttercup. You'll be the first I'll look to for congratulations."

Poppy moved on until a painting of the Royal Crescent in Aquae Sulis came into view. Will's sense of impending doom heightened. Why was there a painting of his family home in Exilium? He couldn't remember any of his family being artists and couldn't imagine why anyone else would want to paint the home of another family. Was this in fact Iris's exhibit, painted by someone held in Exilium, like the composer they'd been talking about?

Lord Iris wasn't looking at the picture. Instead, he was standing next to one of the sculptures and Will wasn't sure if he'd even seen it. Surely he would take an interest in a painting of the home of one of his most powerful family lines?

"Is that your offering today, Iris?" Poppy asked him.

"No. I haven't commissioned anything of late," he replied. "Nothing...artistic, anyway."

Poppy laughed, but Iris didn't seem to think he'd made a joke. "Very witty," Poppy said. "Have you seen mine?"

"No," Iris replied. He seemed bored, but Will wondered if he was in fact distracted. "I thought you found the Princess's whims too difficult to satisfy."

"We shall find out," Poppy said, gesturing to a place out of sight. "Here she is."

Whatever he was watching through turned and Will drew in a sharp breath at the sight of the Princess entering the clearing. She was accompanied by an entourage of beautiful slaves, each one wearing a glittering band around one ankle, and flitting clusters of faeries. As far as he knew, no one other than the Patroons of the Great Families had ever seen any of the Fae royalty.

He didn't think it possible for the other Fae to be diminished by another, but the Princess made them look commonplace somehow. Even though her eyes were still inhuman in their appearance, a solid green with no pupil or iris, somehow they weren't frightening. She wore a crowning circlet of oak leaves and a gown which seemed to be made of the same. Will couldn't pull his gaze away from her and felt awed to the point that it felt wrong to be sitting on a sofa, even just looking at her through a scrying glass. He knew that if he were there, he'd be on his knees.

He forced himself to look away and saw that the rest of the Fae, even his own patron, were universally cowed by her presence.

"Only five pieces today?" Her voice made Will shudder. "Well, let's see if there is anything worthy of further attention." She walked past the sculpture and jewellery with barely a glance. Her hair, a deep chestnut brown, rippled down her back in luxuriant waves. Following behind her, Poppy looked back at Will through the mirror with obvious excitement and Will heard a tiny giggle. So he was watching through his faerie's eyes somehow. At least with her back to him, the impact of the Princess's Charm was less intense.

She paused briefly by one of the paintings which elicited a tilt of her head and then a disappointed sigh before she moved on. It was clear that Poppy's offering was going to be the last.

"It used to be so different," the Princess said as the Fae court gazed at her. "There used to be so many for us to inspire and nurture. Now we squeeze meagre offerings from stolen souls and pretend they are impressive. This"—she waved a hand at a painting of the sea that Will could only see a part of—"this is beautiful but so dull. I'm bored."

Worry flickered across the faces of everyone there, everyone except Poppy and Iris.

"The Elemental Court have taken an interest in artists," Lady Wisteria said. "It's so hard for our pets to bring them in now."

"They've always been interested in them," the Princess said. "Really, Wisteria, you need to find better excuses than that." She waved a dismissive hand at the seascape. "This doesn't make me feel anything. And I don't see any of you weeping or reacting to it in any way. Have you all forgotten what art is?"

None of them spoke. Will watched Iris more carefully. He didn't seem as besotted with her as the others, but every time her gaze swept across him he took care to appear to be enraptured by her—at least as much as Iris could ever appear to be so.

"Poppy, you seem excited," the Princess said.

"I have something to offer," he replied, leading her towards the painting.

"The Royal Crescent?" The Princess sounded unimpressed. "I have seen so many like this."

"Ah…that's the beauty of this piece," Poppy said, beckoning to her and Iris, who stood close by, now interested himself. "Look closer, if you will, your Royal Highness."

"There are people in the windows," she said. "The Irises, I

presume. Strange one of yours would paint them. Yes, there's the Patroon. What do you think of it, Iris?"

Iris took another step closer. He was frowning, his blue eyes moving from one window of the painted building to the next until he straightened and clasped his hands behind his back. He turned to Poppy with a piercing glare that made the faerie Will was watching through pull back. "Who painted this?"

"I'm sworn to secrecy," Poppy said, placing his hand on his chest. "It's part of the art, you see. This painting is called *The Secret*."

Iris looked back at the picture and then at Poppy, his glare sending a sharp spike of terror through Will—even though it wasn't aimed at him—before turning and leaving without even a bow to the Princess.

But what had made his patron so angry?

The rest of the Fae remained silent until Iris left, and then a burst of speculation and blossoming gossip erupted between them. The faerie drew closer to Poppy's shoulder as he and the Princess turned their backs to the others and inspected the painting together.

"I have never seen Iris look so...emotional," the Princess whispered to Poppy.

"Neither have I, your Royal Highness. I cannot think of a better indication of good art. If it can stir such a reaction in the coldest of hearts, it's..."

He left the sentence incomplete and the Princess took up the thread. "Surely the best piece here. Is there really a secret in the picture?"

"Yes, but one even I am unaware of," Poppy replied, unable to stop himself from rubbing his hands together like a gleeful child. "And the not knowing is an exquisite torture."

"Oh, it is," the Princess said, breathlessly. "I think Iris knows the secret, though. Bravo, Lord Poppy. Yours is the best art I have enjoyed in a long, long time."

As they spoke, Will studied the painting, focusing on the windows as his patron had. He recognised his mother, father...there was Imogen, Nathaniel... His breath caught in his throat. The face of a small girl peered out from one of the windows. Sophia. She was the secret in the painting! That's why Iris was angry—he knew his family had hidden a child from him!

Horrified, Will threw down the scrying glass and it shattered on the table as he jumped to his feet. Lord Iris would come for Sophia. He had to hide her.

9

By early afternoon, Max had pulled over, taken a reading, and received his instructions from Kay three times. They were close now, within five miles. The gargoyle had not said a word for hours. Max focused on the road as they crossed the county border and went into Cheshire. The heavy rain that was currently drenching Manchester was turning into snow the further west they drove.

"What do you think Rupert's going to do to with that Sorceress?" asked the gargoyle through the gap in the back seat.

"Imprison her or kill her," Max replied as they paused at traffic lights. There were so many cars on the road now. "Maybe both. It depends whether he wants to know why she killed them all."

"It's hard to tell with him," the gargoyle said. "I don't suppose it really bothers you, but I'm not sure I want to…you know…actually kill her."

"You won't have to," Max said, pulling away again at the green light. "It would be me."

The frustrated sigh that percolated in the gargoyle's throat sounded like the motorcycle that had been idling next to them at the lights. "Yeah, but muggins here will have to mop up all the emotional fallout. But you go ahead, who cares, right?"

Max didn't have anything to say to that. It seemed there was very little of benefit to say when the gargoyle got sulky. Another couple of miles and then he would pull over again.

"I suppose something has to be done to stop her," the gargoyle said, a mile later. "I mean, you can't just go around killing people. But it bothers me that we don't know why she did it. I mean, it's a pretty select group of people she's been targeting. Why Sorcerers and Chapters?"

"The Chapters support the Sorcerers and their control over the Heptarchy. Perhaps she is in league with the Fae-touched to give them more freedom to abuse the lack of supervision. Or even the Fae themselves. She had to learn that magic somewhere."

"She must have cut a deal," the gargoyle said. "How else could she have both types of magic under her control? And anyway, aren't they supposed to be the opposite of each other? How does that even work?"

Max thought about when they found her in the tower close to the former Sorcerer of Essex's home. How easy it seemed to be for her to work the magic that killed all of the Oxford Chapter. He'd never seen Ekstrand at work. Perhaps it was easy for all of them. "She didn't kill the Camden Chapter, though. I wonder if she has a use for them."

"Maybe they just aren't a threat, seeing as they're in her pocket. We saw that, didn't we?"

It was an interesting question. Had they actually seen that? They had found the Tower she lived in by going through the corrupt Chapter Master's office, but he didn't actually mention her explicitly. In fact, when he thought back to it, the Chapter Master was still under the impression that he was working for Dante. He didn't know about the Sorceress at all. He thought that the orders to turn a blind eye to the activities of the Fae-touched came from Dante. "That Chapter doesn't know about her," Max said to the gargoyle. "If anything, the corrupt Chapter in London is actually in the pocket of the Irises." There was a moment of something he would describe as satisfaction, as two pieces fell into place. "That's the deal I think she struck," he said to the gargoyle. "I think Iris gave her knowledge of his particular...flavour of magic, and in return, the Irises in Londinium had free rein. Remember how they ignored Cathy's breach at Nelson's Column? I think that's why."

"What about the Arbiters that tried to kill us? That dodgy Chapter Master said they weren't his."

"Maybe the Sorceress has another Chapter elsewhere that she's been using the same way. We've never had a chance to investigate the state of the other parts of the Heptarchy. She could simply have sent them. Or he could have lied."

He saw a lay-by up ahead and pulled over. Following the same procedure as he had at the previous stops, he waited for Kay's text. This time, his phone rang instead.

"Max? I think we might have a problem."

"I'm listening."

"So…I might be wrong but it looks like the target could be on Lord Iron's estate. I double-checked the file and it's the address we have listed for him. Rupert isn't here, so I don't know whether it's okay to just go there. Do you know?"

"We're on good terms with all of the Elemental Court, as far as I'm aware," Max said. "I'm going to head to his address and try to verify the target's presence there."

"Um, okay, but be careful. She sounds really dangerous."

"Yes, I know," Max said. "I'll update you later."

"Kay cares about us," the gargoyle said once the call was ended. "Surely even you can tell that."

Max gave that comment the amount of attention it deserved and pulled back onto the road after consulting the map and the address that Kay had texted. They were less than a mile away, so he put the time to good use and ordered his thoughts before arrival.

There were three possibilities. The first was that Lord Iron had no idea the Sorceress was hiding at his estate. While his mundane wealth was significant, the mundane security it would pay for might be circumvented by her peculiar skill set. Saying that, Max wasn't sure if her strange hybrid magic might be rendered useless there, as Fae magic was reputed to be.

The second possibility was that Lord Iron knew she was there, perhaps even hosting her as a guest, without knowing who she really was and what she'd done. This seemed more likely than the third possibility: that Lord Iron knew she was a murderer, and simply didn't care. From his own interactions with the man, Max had the impression he was not the sort of person who would condone such behaviour.

Whichever of those possibilities was the actual truth, Max had to identify whether the target was there, and in the interest of good relations being maintained between the last Sorcerer of Albion and the Elemental Court, surely he was obliged to warn Lord Iron about her nature?

"Cathy is probably there," the gargoyle said. "I mean, where else could she go and be safe from those Fae bastards? We should see if she's all right."

"She either will be or she won't. Our knowing it won't make any difference," Max replied. He ignored the gargoyle's groan.

Soon enough they reached the short road that led to the edge of Lord Iron's estate. Max headed for the gatehouse, parking the car in the space next to it so he could leave the gargoyle well out of sight.

A guard opened the door of the small stone building when Max got out of the car, staying inside the threshold to avoid the snow. "Good afternoon," the man said with a polite nod. "Can I help you?"

"I'd like to see Mr Ferran," Max said. "My name is Max. We're acquainted, but he isn't expecting me."

"I'll make a quick call and see if he is available. Would you like to wait inside? It's warmer in here."

"Thank you."

Max was guided towards a small sitting room at the back of the gatehouse with a window overlooking the parked car. He checked to see that the gargoyle wasn't moving around and then, when the guard went to make the phone call, he pulled the gadget out of his pocket. Instead of showing mostly red lights, the majority were now green. A text came through from Kay. *Target is less than a mile to the east of your location. That puts her in Lord Iron's house. Go carefully. He might be on her side.* Max deleted the text and dropped the phone back into his pocket.

The guard returned, the polite smile still in place. "Mr Ferran is on his way."

"I can't go to the house?"

"Mr Ferran said that he will come to you here. Please, make yourself comfortable; he'll be a few minutes."

So Lord Iron didn't want him to go to the house. He was inclined to agree with Kay's appraisal. But he still felt that he was obligated to warn him. It was unlikely that the Sorceress would be open about her crimes, after all.

He watched the snow fall. Why would the Sorceress come here, of all places? Did she need Lord Iron for something? To commission a piece, perhaps, as the Sorcerers sometimes did? Or to bring him onside? Both of those explanations suggested that killing the Sorcerers on the Isle of Man was not the completion of her plan.

The sound of a car drew his attention back outside again. A large 4×4 was parking next to Max's old estate. Mr Ferran got out, followed by Cathy. Max knew the gargoyle wanted to see her, but he conveyed his warning to stay hidden as best he could. He didn't want the guards to see it.

After a brief conversation, during which Mr Ferran seemed to be checking something with Cathy, both of them hurried from the car to the gatehouse. Cathy was dressed in a coat far too big for her and Mr Ferran looked very smart indeed. He kept looking at Cathy, concerned, which puzzled Max momentarily, but then he realised they were outside of the formal estate boundary and probably wary of any Iris Seeker Charms. Cathy appeared to reassure him and then they both came into the waiting room.

"Hi, Max," she said brightly. "How are you?"

"I am well, thank you."

"Look, I wasn't in the best state of mind when I last saw you. I know you came to see Sam, but I wanted to say thanks for helping me. Has Bertrand been punished for what he did?"

"Yes, he was expelled from Society. His family have been given permission to remain in the Nether, but have been excluded socially."

Cathy nodded. "Good. Exactly what we hoped for. Thanks. Has…has Will hassled you?"

"No."

"Do you want to speak in private?"

Max shook his head, thinking that having two of them to watch might reveal more. "No. If you are resident here, it's a matter that concerns you, too."

"I don't mind," Sam said. "Let's all sit down. Is it the Irises? We've been expecting them to make a move."

Max moved his chair to sit opposite them, and to be able to see out of the window to keep an eye on his car. "That's not the reason I came. Is there another woman staying in your house, Lord Iron?"

The way they both looked at each other said a great deal about how both were reluctant to talk about it. "That's a personal question, Max," Sam said. "Since when would you be interested in any of my houseguests?"

"Since one of them is a murderer."

"It isn't as simple as that," Sam said.

"So you don't deny that she's at your house, nor that she is a murderer?"

"I'm saying that this is complicated," Sam replied. "Look, I'm not happy about what she's done, in principle. I don't condone murder, but the Sorcerers weren't innocents, let's face it."

"Look at how Ekstrand refused to help me," Cathy said. "And all the other people in the Nether who suffer every day because they have no one outside of that world to help them. And what was done to you! Did you want to have your soul dislocated?"

"What I may or may not have wanted is irrelevant," Max said, aware that his car had started to rock on its suspension as the gargoyle started moving about.

"I went to Ekstrand and asked him for help to protect my wife," Sam said, "and he didn't give a shit. I tried to save those people from Exilium and neither of you lifted a finger to help them. Now, I know you are bound by rules, but Ekstrand could have helped and he didn't."

"Are you arguing that because he didn't help people who fell outside of the remit of the Split Worlds Treaty, he deserved to be murdered?" Max asked.

Sam rubbed his chin, agitated. "No. No, I'm not saying that. I'm just saying that she has her reasons. And seeing as the people she killed had been screwing people over for centuries, I'm not going to lose any sleep over it."

"Ekstrand didn't care about anyone except himself, Max, you know that," Cathy said. "He saw all those people in the basement at the Agency, didn't he? The ones the gargoyle told me about."

There was a thud from outside and Max had a flash of the gargoyle knocking the entirety of the back seat upright into the main space of the car.

"Didn't he?" Cathy pressed. "And he didn't give a shit about them."

"You are both arguing to defend a murderer," Max said. "Based on your judgement that the Sorcerers deserved it. What about the others? She has also killed the Arbiters of their Chapters and all of the researchers who worked to support them. Over fifty people in my Chapter alone. My colleagues. She murdered them all. There were dozens of Chapters, all over the country. I believe she did the same to them."

Both Sam and Cathy looked distinctly uncomfortable. Behind them, Max saw the car's rear passenger door open and the gargoyle slink out, keeping as low as a panther on the prowl, staying below the eye line of the 4×4 driver. At least it was being discreet in its disobedience. Wanting to avoid the gatehouse guard seeing it, Max opened the window, allowing the gargoyle inside.

"Cathy," it said, and went over to her. She rested her hand on the top of its head. "Are you okay?"

She shrugged. "Things are complicated," she said.

"I take it you won't object if we seek to remove her from your property?" Max asked.

"Hang on a minute!" Sam said. "Look, this is all...there are things going on here that are…important. I'm not going to just hand her over to you. Not until I understand it all."

"What is there to understand?" Max said, thinking that Sam was so flustered he could reveal what he knew about the Sorceress and her motivation. "She's a murderer."

"But there's a reason why she killed them," Sam said. "She's not just some psycho who did it for kicks."

"And what would that reason be, Mr Ferran?"

Sam closed his mouth, exchanging another look with Cathy. She held his gaze for a moment, looking very troubled. After taking a deep breath, she turned to the gargoyle. "Do you think that what the Sorcerers did to you was right?"

The gargoyle's heavy stone brow furrowed. "No."

"It was necessary," Max said, but the gargoyle growled.

"We were thirteen years old!" it said. "We shouldn't have even been taken in the first place."

"How else is the Treaty to be policed?"

"Kay will find a better way. Better than bloody Rupert ever will. He's just as bad as Ekstrand."

"Is Rupert the one you mentioned to me before?" Cathy asked. "Ekstrand's replacement? He's still alive?"

"Yeah," the gargoyle said. "He tricked her into thinking she'd killed him."

"Get in the car," Max said, pointing to the gargoyle. If Rupert knew what had just been said, they'd be slaughtered.

"Shit," Cathy muttered. "She thinks they are all dead."

"We should probably tell her," Sam said.

Cathy looked at Max and the gargoyle. "No. We can't. If she finds out about him, Max and the gargoyle will be in danger. Best she doesn't know about any of them."

Sam leaned back, looking very stressed. "Cathy…I don't think we can hide it from her. She'd want to know."

Cathy rested her hand on the gargoyle's head, looking into its stone eyes, deep in thought. "We shouldn't be divided over this," she finally said. "Max, Gargoyle, you shouldn't work for Rupert.

He's not trustworthy. And Sam, we need to look out for Max here. These are my friends. They've helped me and they didn't barter for it, either. Beatrice is using us, as much as I am using her to learn what I need to. We need to talk this through together, without her or Rupert being involved. I trust everyone in this room. I don't trust the Sorcerers. Any of them."

Sam rubbed the stubble on his chin, keeping silent.

"Look," Cathy said, keeping her hand resting on the gargoyle. "Max, regardless of what that woman has done, we have to face up to the fact that the Treaty is failing a lot of people. People like me, and you, and Sam's wife. People who should have been protected and weren't." She looked at the gargoyle. "This Rupert, is he really just as bad as Ekstrand?"

"Don't answer that," Max said.

"He's just as selfish," the gargoyle said.

She nodded. "Does he know about the people in that basement?" When it nodded, she looked at Max. "Don't you think that we have to at least look at—"

Max didn't want to be derailed from his assignment. "You are harbouring a murderer, Mr Ferran. I am asking you, with all respect, to consider your position on this very carefully."

"It's not that simple," Cathy said. "Beatrice has a plan that—"

"Cathy!" Sam sounded almost panicked. "We can't say anything to them about it. Remember?"

"Can't we at least talk about working together to help those people held by the Agency?" Cathy said. "Max, come on, this is important! I can't do it by myself! I need your help."

"Mr Ferran," Max prompted.

"As long as Beatrice is my guest, she's under my protection, whether you think she deserves that or not. I don't give my permission for you or your spare Sorcerer to come onto my estate. Not until all this is sorted out."

"Then I think it's best for us to leave," Max said.

The gargoyle's growl deepened. "So you're just going to walk away when we need to work together?" it said. "Cathy's right, we're the only ones who can do anything about the Agency. If we ignore this now, we're no better than the bloody Sorcerers!"

Max opened the door and stared at the gargoyle. "We're done here. It's not our place to get involved in things like this any more than we already have."

Cathy jumped to her feet. "Not your place? What kind of bullshit is that? You can't keep avoiding this. What they did to you was barbaric. You need to face up to it and you need to work with me. Otherwise all of these other people will keep making decisions for us, whether it's the Fae or the Sorcerers or whoever else holds the bloody leash! Beatrice is planning to—"

"No, Cathy!" Sam said, louder. "The oath! She'll know!"

A loud beep made Cathy jump, and Max knew another text had arrived. Normally he would have ignored it, but with clarification from Rupert needed now more than ever, he opened the message.

About to call. Pick up but DO NOT SPEAK OR SAY ANYTHING. Just listen.

"Something's wrong," the gargoyle said. It looked at Cathy. "We should all hear this." It moved away from her to rest its haunches against Max. "There's something bigger than us happening here. Cathy's right. We look after each other. We all need to be informed."

It was definitely an unusual message. He held up the phone screen for Cathy and Sam to read. "That's from Kay, who works for Rupert," he said.

They both nodded. "You can put it on speakerphone," Sam said, and when Max looked at him blankly, he took the phone when it rang and pressed something.

"Okay," they heard Kay say. "So I get that accuracy is a good thing in sorcery. I get that. But I can work out exactly where she is from the data we have now. She hasn't moved for the past ten minutes. Look, you can see that here. And we know she is in the house. Is it a three-dimensional issue or something?"

There was the slap of Rupert's lips as he chewed on something. "What do you mean by that?"

"I mean, do you need to know if she's on the ground floor or the first floor or something like that?"

"Your brain is brilliant," Rupert said. "Have one of these jelly snakes. They help me think. If you had one, you might think up something really spectacular."

"I don't want one," Kay replied. "I want you to explain this to me. You want me to learn. This is important. Why do you need Max to get closer?"

"Are you worried about him?"

A long pause. "It's like trying to do a crossword with only half the clues. How can I use this data efficiently without knowing what the plan is?"

There was nothing except the sound of Rupert working on a jelly snake for a few seconds. "All right. Fair enough. Your instinct is sound. Why else would I want my man up close?"

"But that's what I can't work out," Kay replied. "I thought this woman was too dangerous to risk that. What can Max do to her? He doesn't have a weapon to subdue her, capture her, or…kill her. If that's what the plan is?"

"Sure you don't want one of these snakes? There's a red one, they're the best. You can have it."

Another pause. "The only things he has are the tools. None of them have anything that could be used against her as far as I can tell. Then there's the tracker, but that—"

Max reached into his pocket and pulled the tracker out so Cathy and Sam could see it. It was longer and heavier than the Sniffer Rupert had made him, and he had assumed that it was because it was a more complex device. Was that assumption drawn from his experience of mundane objects? He considered the phone he held and how much it could do. The tracker wasn't that much smaller. They were hardly comparable, but something about the fact that Rupert hadn't made the tracker smaller was…unsatisfactory on some level.

"Unless the tracker itself has more than one purpose," Kay said. Rupert must have reacted in some way, as Kay said, "Oh my

God, I'm right! Okay, okay, so the tracker does something else and you need Max to get it as close to the target as possible. So that means it must have some sort of effect. Something that can only happen when close enough to her. Maybe it needs her presence to trigger it…no, that doesn't seem right. Maybe because whatever the effect is, it's only short range…"

"Warmer," Rupert said.

"Maybe only within a small radius…"

"Warmer."

"Shit, like some sort of bomb?"

"Close enough. Not a bomb, those are messy, but same effect. See, I reckon she is warded to fuck against anyone or anything designed to attack her, right? Which means Max is the ideal choice. So I designed this thing that destroys all flesh within a two-metre radius using this badass formula that only completes when—what? Why are you looking at me like that?"

"Destroys all flesh?" Kay's voice was louder, higher-pitched. "What do you mean 'destroys all flesh'? Even Max's?"

"Well, yeah, duh. I needed to be sure."

"But Max is a person, Rupert! And so is she, for that matter! You can't just go around melting people!"

"Eh? What did you think I planned to do with her? She tried to kill me! She killed all of the other Sorcerers!"

"And so that makes it okay for you to melt her and your own staff?"

"It's an acceptable loss."

"No, it fucking isn't! Max? Max, did you hear that? Don't go to the target! It will kill you!"

There was the sound of a paper bag being crumpled. "What the fuck?" Rupert shouted and then there was a muffled scuffling noise and then a thud. Max heard Kay cry out, as if in pain, but she sounded farther away. Had the phone been knocked from her hand? "I fucking trusted you!" Rupert shouted, but again, it sounded further away, as if the phone were on the other side of the office.

Cathy's eyes filled with tears and she covered her mouth and they listened to the sound of someone choking, and then another thud.

"He killed her!" the gargoyle shrieked, and pounded the floor.

Max turned away, cupped his hand over the phone more to try and block out the sound of the gargoyle's distress. He couldn't hear Kay, only approaching footsteps. "Fuck!" Rupert's shout was much closer, and then the call ended.

The gargoyle snatched the tracker from Max's hand and threw it out the window. "Fuck Rupert," it said to Max. Max was still processing what he'd heard during the call. The gargoyle grabbed his arm and there was a staggering rush of rage and betrayal and grief. "Fuck Rupert," the gargoyle repeated, its grip tight as Max reeled. "We are so done with being screwed over by Sorcerers. Right? We're on our own."

But how? Max thought, struggling to think clearly as he was bombarded by the gargoyle's anger, and somewhere deeper, that he didn't understand, a building…panic? Was that the right label for it? He did his best to suppress it, to focus on more pressing concerns: How could they sever themselves from the last Sorcerer of Albion? Where would they go? How could they police the puppets without Rupert's assistance? What was he for, if not to do that?

"We can't trust Sorcerers," the gargoyle said. "We can trust Cathy."

"You can't go back there, Max," Cathy said. "Rupert knows you heard that. He won't trust you now. Sam, Max and the gargoyle need to stay here, with us."

"But that Sorceress is there!" the gargoyle said.

"We'll have to tell her that you two are different," Cathy said. "You don't have anywhere else to go. And we need to stick together. Sam?"

"She's waiting for me to tell her…that thing I told you about in the forge," he finally said to her. "I'm going to give it to her now. I think once she has it, she'll leave, and Max and the gargoyle can stay with us then. Wait here until I give the all clear." He went to the door, coaxing Cathy along with him. "Don't say anything more," he said to her quietly, as they embraced. "And if there's even a hint of any magic, come through the gates, right away."

"Don't worry. We'd know if the ward wasn't working by now." She watched him go. "I'm so sorry about your friend," she said to Max and the gargoyle once Sam had left. "That Rupert sounds awful."

"The woman that Lord Iron is protecting killed dozens more of my colleagues," Max said, disliking the way that the gargoyle's proximity was making his throat clog with unshed tears.

Cathy groaned and dropped back into her chair. "This is all a such a huge fucking mess."

"What's going on with that Sorceress, Cathy?" the gargoyle asked. "Why are you both defending her?"

"She's taught me how to protect myself from the Irises with her kind of magic, and it seems to be working," Cathy said. "And… and she explained why she killed all those people. It's all part of a plan." She nibbled her thumbnail, staring at the floor for a few moments before swearing beneath her breath and looking back up at them. "She wants to unsplit the worlds."

"Eh?" the gargoyle sounded just as confused as Max felt.

"I know it sounds insane. And I don't condone what she's done so far, but I think she's right about the Sorcerers not being the saviours they've painted themselves to be. Sam and I decided to support her because the Elemental Court need to be counterbalanced by the Fae. That Court has lost its way and Sam has done everything he can to change them, but they're hellbent on trashing everything. Have you met any other people in the Court?"

"No," Max said as the gargoyle moved away from him, letting him think clearly again as it curled up next to Cathy. "I was told we should be careful as Arbiters to maintain a respectful distance, lest we be compromised." He rubbed his leg, thinking of the titanium within that the gargoyle had been so worried about. "It seems it's not as much of an issue as the one who trained me believed."

"Beatrice said the Sorcerers split the worlds because they couldn't control the Fae, rather than because they wanted to protect people from them. We both know the Sorcerers don't—didn't—give a shit about looking after people."

"And you believe that undoing the work of the Sorcerers will be best for everyone?" Max said. "Even though you have experienced the interference of the Fae firsthand?"

He watched her nibble her nail again. "We're damned if we do and we're damned if we don't. We think that the planet is screwed if we don't do this. And we're putting together a plan for educating people about the Fae, ready for when the worlds are put back together again. I think if people know how to protect themselves, that will be much better. At the moment, it's all on your shoulders to protect them."

Max could see some sense in that; in the early days of being an Arbiter he had wondered whether it would better to give people as much information as possible to help reduce risk, rather than preserve their total innocence. He'd never been given a satisfactory answer for why that wasn't the done thing, and the decision had been made so many hundreds of years before his birth, it was generally agreed that there was no way to change things.

"I'd really like you to help us, Max," Cathy said. "You have so much experience. You'd be invaluable."

"I've been trained to keep the Fae out of Mundanus. If there were no distinction between the worlds, that would change things a great deal."

"Yeah, it would. No more Arbiters will be made, for a start," Cathy said. "And I think it'll be pretty chaotic. Your being immune to Fae magic will be critical."

"You're speaking like this is definitely going to happen."

She nodded. "I think it is, if Rupert doesn't screw things up for Beatrice first." She looked down at the gargoyle, who had covered its muzzle with its paws, thoroughly miserable. "Are you going to be okay?" she asked it.

It shrugged. "How are you coping so well?"

"I didn't know Kay."

"No, I mean, how are you coping so well after your father died?"

What little colour was left in Cathy's face drained away. "What?"

The gargoyle groaned. "You didn't know. Shit. Sorry. Kay told us, just before we arrived. She wouldn't get that wrong."

"Tom," Cathy whispered, standing up. "Stay here. I...I have to write a letter. I have to make sure my brother is all right."

The gargoyle looked at him after the door closed behind her. "We staying? We going along with this?"

"We're staying," Max said. "I don't trust that Sorceress. We need to see if she is telling the truth. And if she is, we'll do more good with Cathy and Lord Iron than with Rupert."

The gargoyle nodded, settling down again. "Good. I was worried you were going to be an arsehole again, and I don't have it in me to fight you right now."

10

Will paused at the green baize door that led to the nursery wing. He didn't want Sophia to think anything was wrong, so he made sure his brow wasn't wrinkled and a smile was on his lips when he went through.

With every step from his study to that door he'd imagined Lord Iris summoning the Patroon and demanding to know who the child was. It was easy to imagine the conversations that would ripple outward from that encounter and it would be only a matter of minutes before his father would be summoned.

He could predict his father's denial of any knowledge when faced with the head of the family; there was no way he would want any of his superiors to think he could not only sire an illegal child but also hide it for years. The only thing Will found difficult to foresee was what his father would do after his conversation with the Patroon. Would he want to hide Sophia somewhere else? It wasn't what Will feared the most. He'd heard a number of rumours of how ruthless his father could be. How far would he go to preserve his own honour and status? Surely not harming his own child?

But the fear wouldn't leave him and Will found his thoughts bouncing between the threat of Sophia being delivered to Iris and his father killing her or taking her into Mundanus and abandoning her there like an unwanted child in a fairy tale. Every time he told himself his father would never do anything like that to his own child, the next thought was that his father had never even seemed fond of the poor girl. Not even Mother wanted her back home. The temporary arrangement of having Sophia live with him had stretched into normality. Even after the attack that had scarred her, they hadn't pressed for her to go back to Aquae Sulis. Perhaps they were satisfied that she was happier there, but Will suspected they'd been glad the problem of hiding her away was no longer their concern.

"Sophia!" he called, and was answered by the sound of running feet. The smile he'd fixed in place became genuine when she peered round the schoolroom door and beamed at him.

"Will-yum!" She wriggled her fingers, covered with paste and snippets of newspaper, at him in delight as she ran to him for the usual hug. "We're doing papaver-mashey! I'm making Saturn and Uncle Vincent is making Mars. We're doing the whole solar syphon, and then we're going to hang them from the ceiling. Then I'm going to make a rocket for my dollies so they can fly to them and do sciencing. Where's Cathy? Why hasn't she come to see me?"

As she babbled, Will scooped her up into his arms and carried her to the schoolroom. "Cathy had to go and visit a friend who is unwell."

Uncle Vincent was standing when they reached the schoolroom, wiping his hands on a damp cloth, pieces of the shredded newspaper clinging to his trousers. The table was covered in a riot of paste and balloons partially covered with papier-mâché. His face was grim, his mouth set in a hard line that told Will he was ready for trouble. Will set Sophia down. "Now, I need to talk to Uncle Vincent so you carry on whilst I talk about boring things with him next door, there's a good girl."

Vincent followed him out and they stepped into the room next door. "I'm not going to Jorvic," Vincent said. "I don't care a jot for what George thinks is best, he can send some other poor bastard to do his dirty work. If he—"

"Forget Jorvic," Will snapped. "Lord Iris knows there's a child he wasn't informed of. No doubt the Patroon knows by now and I'd be surprised if Father wasn't being given a grilling as we speak."

"Hell's teeth." Vincent went to the window and looked out onto St James's Park. London rumbled on around them, oblivious. "Iris can't summon her; he doesn't know who she is, so that's something. How did he find out?"

"Something Poppy cooked up, but I've no idea how. It was a painting, but the only Papaver who knows about Sophia is Cathy and she can't paint her own fingernails."

"Could she have told anyone else? Poppy even?"

"No," Will was certain. "You know how fond of Sophia she is. Cathy would never do anything to endanger her. I made sure she knew how important it was to keep her true identity secret."

"I'd like to wring the neck of the one who did it."

"After I've run him through," Will said. "But we need to get Sophia to safety first. I have to keep her out of Londinium; no doubt Father will come for her."

Vincent turned, arms crossed in front of him, shoulders hunched. "You're afraid he'll hand her over?"

Will moved closer and lowered his voice. "I'm afraid he'll do worse. Do you think he'd…" He couldn't bring himself to say it.

Vincent chewed his thumbnail, his eyes shadowed by his brow. "If it came to his position or her…I don't trust my brother to do the decent thing. We have to keep her away from him."

Will hoped to keep one step ahead of his father, but as soon as Iris knew who she was, no Charm in the worlds would protect her from being summoned by their patron. For all he knew, Iris might just be able to summon her, without even knowing her name. "Do you think he'd tell Lord Iris who she is?"

Vincent shook his head. "No. I think he'll cover it all up. The only question is how thoroughly he'll do that. We'll keep her in Mundanus whilst—"

"Not in London, though," Will cut in. "The Arbiters here are corrupt. The Patroon may well know that and use them against us. I wouldn't be surprised if he used them to raid our houses. No one can deny an Arbiter entry, after all."

"The staff here are loyal, at least," Vincent said. "I'll take her to—"

Will held up his hand. "Don't tell me. They could get the

location from me." He stopped as the idea of Vincent whisking Sophia away to a location outside of his knowledge sunk in. His chest tightened at just the thought of it. No, there had to be a better solution. He would be better at hiding her than his uncle would, with everything at his disposal.

Lord Iron could protect her. The idea slipped into his mind like a foul snake.

No. He couldn't bear the thought of taking Sophia to that house. But Cathy was there, and Sophia adored her, and—as Cathy was exploiting so effectively—it was the only place she could be protected from Lord Iris. Perhaps it was the best… No. He couldn't give that odious man such ammunition against him.

Tate. Yes, Tate made all the artefacts and potions supplying the Emporium of Things in Between and Besides. Surely she would know a way to make the Shadow Charm more potent. Permanent, even. "I have an idea, but I can't tell you." As Vincent's frown deepened, Will added, "You'll be implicated far too much should all this come out."

Vincent snorted. "It's all over for me, Will m'boy. And anyway, you've got far more to lose than I do. We don't have time to argue. I'll take her—"

"No," Will said, and put a hand on Vincent's shoulder to take the sting out of his tone, even though he outranked his uncle. "No, I—"

They both jumped when a squeal came from next door. Will burst out of the empty bedroom and reached the doorway to the schoolroom in time to see his father pick up Sophia. He hadn't heard him arrive! Where did he come through? "Father," he said, taking a step into the room. "We need to talk."

His father shook his head. "Too late for that, son. This has gone on long enough. Say goodbye to William, Sophia."

Sophia's bottom lip stuck out at the best angle to express displeasure. "No, Papa, I want to stay here."

"Please," Will stepped forwards. "Father, please just put her down and we'll go and talk about this."

"He knows, son."

"I can hide her!" Will moved forwards again. "I can help!"

Sophia, seeing Will's barely controlled panic, started wriggling. "I want to stay with Will-yum."

"Now stop that," Father said, adjusting his grip on her. "We're going to go somewhere very exciting. You'll love it there. It's the prettiest place you can imagine."

"You're taking her to Iris?" Will yelled, not even believing it himself. How could his father even consider it?

His father's glare made him nauseous. "Don't make a fuss, William," he said, then looked at Sophia. "Time to go."

11

Tom looked at the brochure with its pictures of gravestones beneath a blue sky and trees laden with blossoms. Promises of peace and respectful treatment with a note on the back about different payment plans available. He threw it onto the fire. Why the Agency had sent it to him, he had no idea. It wasn't as if there was a choice about where to bury Father. All the Papavers who had ever died were buried there. None of them close relatives. The thought of burying his father still had the edge of absurdity to it. His grandparents and great-grandparents were going to be at the funeral. Cousins he'd never met. Aunts and uncles he'd only heard stories about, brought back from places all over the world where they'd been sent to best serve their patron.

Would Lord Poppy be at the funeral? No, of course not, it would be in Mundanus. But at the reception afterwards, perhaps. He'd been expecting a summons, or at the very least a demand to know the circumstances, but Tom had only had one message from him, delivered by one of his tiny faeries, the day before. "My Lord says that he is aware of the events in Aquae Sulis and to tell you that the Irises will soon know a pain to rival your own," the tiny creature had said with delight. All he could do was nod and sigh with relief when it disappeared in a shower of poppy petals.

The one person he'd been waiting to hear from—no, to arrive in person—had remained infuriatingly silent. He knew Cat and Father's relationship had been difficult and he could understand how the news of his death would be a shock, but to not even send word? Such cowardly behaviour. Even selfish, spoiled Elizabeth had come to see him every day. She didn't say much, just asked him how he was and if the arrangements for the funeral were progressing, whilst perched on the edge of the armchair cushion. She seemed utterly lost, poor thing.

"Are we orphans now?" she'd asked him the night before.

"Mother isn't dead, darling. So, no."

"She might as well be," Elizabeth had said bitterly. "She and Cathy are the most hateful, selfish witches I've ever known. I'm so glad I have you, Thomas."

She'd clung to him at the door, as if she hadn't wanted to leave. When she finally went, Lucy had taken his hand, led him back to the living room, and draped a blanket around his shoulders. She'd listened when he talked through his thoughts about the funeral, made good suggestions, held his hand. When he'd moaned about Cat, she'd frowned a little, but said nothing. Now, two days after father had died, his patience was running out. Even if Cat couldn't face coming to the family home—which was understandable, considering how she'd been treated there—surely she could take two minutes to dash off a note?

Lucy came in with the post, having realised how distressed it was making him the day before. There was a large stack of letters, tied with string, that she put on the coffee table. "These are all condolences, all very kind, nothing unusual."

"Anything from Cat?"

She shook her head.

"William?"

"No. Nothing. Tom, I'm getting worried. What if something has happened to her? I know Cathy gets caught up in her own business, but she loves you. No matter what her relationship was with your father, she would want to know if you are okay."

Tom grabbed the poker and stoked the fire. "We didn't part on the best of terms, the last time I saw her," he said. "I closed down her printing operation and exiled our former governess who'd been helping her distribute those damn pamphlets." He saw Lucy wince. "I had to do it! I couldn't let the Patroons trace the distribution of seditious material to the Duchess of Londinium! Cat didn't see it that way. Obviously." He jabbed at a partially burned log, watching chips of glowing wood spark up. "It seemed so important at the time. Now it just seems ridiculous."

Lucy came over and rested her hand on his arm. "I think this sort of news would make Cathy feel the same way. That's why I'm worried. I don't think she's petty enough to let something like that come between you at a time like this."

Tom nodded, tucking a wayward strand of her hair behind her ear affectionately, and stroked her cheek. He wanted to say how much it meant to him to have someone to talk to, someone to carry the load with him. He wanted to tell her that he was glad she was there, that she was making this all bearable. But somehow he couldn't quite grasp the right words to express it all. So he looked back at the fire and put his arm around her, pulling her close, hoping she could tell.

"I was thinking that I should go back to Londinium for a few hours this afternoon," Lucy said, wrapping her arm around his waist. "I need to make sure Edwin is okay."

Tom had forgotten about her cousin and felt wretched for doing so. "Of course," he said. "I was planning to go through Father's study. I think Edwin will be better company."

"Are you sure? It's very soon, darling."

He didn't want to do it, but he had to be certain those deeds hadn't been misplaced. The Irises could have forged them, after all, and his uncle wasn't going to wait for long to resolve the problem. Besides, it was Father's last wish to take care of the family's responsibilities. What kind of son would he be if he hid away whilst the Irises capitalised on his grief? "I need to face up to it at some point. It's been...cleaned in there."

Would he ever stop seeing his father slumped at that desk? He felt Lucy's embrace tighten and placed the poker back in its rest so he could wrap his other arm around her too.

The rattling of a Letterboxer made them jump and separate. Lucy went over to collect the envelope as he readied himself for whatever could be within.

"It's addressed to me," Lucy said, sitting down.

"I'll ring for tea," Tom said, pulling the cord next to the fire.

He watched Lucy open it and turn straight over to the end to see whose signature lay there. "It's from Cathy!" she said, frowning. "But it isn't the usual paper, and it looks like it's been written with a strange pen."

"What does she say?"

Lucy read, her eyes growing large with shock. By the end of the first page her jaw had dropped open. She flipped over and read swiftly as Tom's sense of dread built. What had Cat done now? He was certain it was something terrible.

"Oh, Cathy," Lucy said, then covered her mouth. She looked horrified.

"What is it? Is she unwell? Does it say why she hasn't come?"

Lucy held up her hand and Tom swallowed down his irritation at the gesture. When she reached the end of the letter, she rested it on her knee, staring into space for a moment. "Tom…Cathy has left Will."

He swore under his breath. "She's run away? Again? I cannot believe this!"

"Tom—"

"How can she think that is the best course of action? Can she not see how the Irises will—"

"Tom!" Lucy's raised voice cut through his rant. "Darling, I don't know how to say this. She…had good reason. Will did something terrible. Truly terrible, and she fled. She's staying with someone she won't name, being protected from Iris magic."

He could see she was shaken. "What did William do to her? Did he hurt her?"

Lucy nodded. "He didn't hit her. It was worse. He…made her…" She looked away and then after a slight nod to herself, looked back at him. "I think you need to know this, Tom, but it's horrible."

The sensation of rising anxiety filled him, just waiting for something to land on, like a flock of birds sent into the air by a farmer's gun. "Tell me."

"He gave her a Charm to make her unable to resist his advances and he raped her. Repeatedly. Whilst the Charm tricked her into thinking she was falling in love with him. Then when she wanted to delay having a child, he put a choker on her that contained a jewel to make her more…" her lips curled in disgust at the very thought of it, "…compliant. Like a slave, without her knowing it."

Tom pressed his fist against his mouth, trying to separate out all of his tangled emotions.

"Tom?" Lucy sounded worried. "We're not going to have a problem here, are we?"

"Why did he do that?"

"Which part?"

He was referring to all of it, but that wouldn't help with the detangling. "The first Charm."

"Because he thought his right to have sex with her was more important than the fact that she didn't want to sleep with him. She didn't want to marry him, remember? And she barely knew him."

"But…they were married."

He looked at Lucy and saw a glare so potent, so fierce, she looked like another person. "Are you seriously going to tell me she had no right to refuse? Because if you are, I don't think I can handle that."

Pressing his fist back against his lips, he wrestled with the conundrum. He'd always been taught that once you were married, you enjoyed conjugal rights. It was expected. Cathy would have known that. Lucy hadn't resisted. They had both been nervous and there was a certain amount of embarrassed fumbling on his part, but there was never any question of whether Lucy was willing or not. In fact, she'd kissed him first. He remembered it clearly. He'd been worried about how to start and had been so shocked when she'd tugged on his cravat and pulled him down to kiss her, as if she'd waited long enough.

Had Lucy been reluctant, would he have forced her? A shiver went through him. He tried to imagine what was going through Will's mind to cast magic upon his wife and take her against her will. Even with a Charm that removed the need for violence, having that intimacy and knowing it wasn't real? His fist clenched tighter. It was disgusting.

"I could never do that to you," he said, and Lucy's glare melted. "I could never force you, even if it seemed you wanted to, not if I knew it was because of a Charm." He couldn't quite believe he was talking about such things with her. But nothing about the past two days had been normal. She leaned forwards and kissed his cheek. "Lucy, this is a terribly forward question and...I find this very difficult but...you didn't mind...having to...with me...that night? And since?"

He hoped for an immediate denial, an instant soothing of his fears, but she said nothing for what seemed like an eternity. "I was relieved that you were so handsome," she said. "And I would have preferred to know you better first. To have had the chance to fall in love before we consummated our marriage. But...but I'd prepared myself for it."

"You make it sound like an exam!"

She laughed. "No, nothing like that! I meant emotionally. I mean, surely you must have, too?"

He knew he was blushing and he hated it. "I might have considered it when the engagement was announced, I suppose."

Lucy laughed again, but it didn't seem unkind. "Oh, Tom. You are so British it hurts."

Not understanding what she meant, he just smiled. But then he remembered when he found Cat after all those years of searching, how he'd literally carried her out of her flat over his shoulder. While he hadn't felt good when he did it, now was the first time he'd feared it had been the wrong thing to do. He'd dragged his own sister back to a world where she could be married against her wishes, to a man who had done that to her.

Then he thought of his mother and how he hadn't once considered why she'd left. He'd just been furious at her for leaving Father and abandoning everything. But had she been married to him against her will? Had she been forced to endure years and years with a man she hated? With a man who might have— He stood up and went back to the fire, taking the poker from its rest and stabbing at the embers, trying to push such awful thoughts away.

"She says she's never coming back," Lucy said. "And that she's just been told about your father, but she can't believe it's true; that's why she wrote this and sent it to me. She didn't want to upset you if it proved to be a mistake. She's worried about you, Tom. So, you see, she isn't as bad as you think."

"No wonder Will has been so absent of late," Tom said. "He must be distraught."

"He must be feeling guilty as hell," Lucy said, without sympathy. "He can't hide this forever. This will be the end of him."

Tom turned and looked at her, their eyes meeting in a moment of mutual understanding.

"We could make that happen," Lucy said.

Tom shook his head. "No! That just wouldn't be cricket."

"What the hell are you talking about?"

"It wouldn't be the decent thing to do."

"Tom, are you hearing yourself right now? This is the man that raped your sister and collared her like a slave! His dad stole your inheritance! Taking down William Iris is the only decent thing to do!"

It was too much, all at once. Everything he'd had an unshakeable faith in was crumbling around him. There was no desire to fight, nor to hurt another, despite the fact that at his core he agreed with her, and wanted to see Will destroyed for what he'd done. But what sort of a man would that make him, to give in to such base urges? His head hurt too much to think. "I have the most appalling headache," he said, putting the poker back. "Tell Wilson to turn away any visitors. I need to lie down."

• • •

Fearing that if he just snatched at Sophia, there would be violence, Will followed his father out of the schoolroom in the hope he could persuade him to leave her there. Sophia's bottom lip wobbled as she stretched over their father's shoulder towards him. "Father, does anyone know about the specifics here? Do you really need to fall on your sword?"

His father threw a puzzled glance over his shoulder. "Hardly falling on my sword. This is the best we can do in a difficult situation. I know this isn't what you want, but I have to do what is best for our family."

"But taking her to Iris isn't the best for Sophia!"

"Where's Iris?" Sophia sniffled. "I don't want to go there! I want to stay with Will-yum!"

"You're just upsetting her," George said as he reached the green baize door. "I think it's best you stay here. Once I've straightened everything out I'll come back to you."

George opened the door. Will looked behind him to see Vincent standing white-lipped down the corridor. Frustrated with his uncle's weakness, Will beckoned him to follow with a scowl. Did his uncle not see that he needed him? That Sophia did too?

"How is taking Sophia to Iris straightening this out? Won't he be furious with you? With all of us?"

"Better to face that head on. Did I not teach you anything?"

"How has hiding her for five years been facing this head on?" Will couldn't help his voice rising at the flagrant hypocrisy. "And you always taught me to do everything I could to keep our patron happy. How is admitting this going to do that?" Sophia started to cry and Will felt terrible for upsetting her. "It's all right, darling. Father and I just disagree, that's all."

"I want to stay here!" she wailed, throwing her head back and arching her body, pushing against their father's shoulders so suddenly that he almost dropped her as they crossed the landing.

George stopped and gave her a shake. "Stop it!" he said so sternly that she just stared with huge, horrified eyes. Will doubted she'd ever been told off by him before.

Will looked back, seeing that Vincent followed them like a shadow. "Uncle Vincent, tell him there's another way!" Will said with desperation as George started to head downstairs. He remembered the doorway between his study and his parents' house. No doubt George saw the covered mirror in there on his way through before. Vincent opened his mouth, then closed it again. He looked like he could pass out any moment.

Getting over the shock of being chastened, Sophia sucked in a breath and started to sob, tears running down her cheeks as George reached the bottom step. Will raced down the stairs after them, reaching out to brush Sophia's hand before George twisted her away.

"Iris will punish you, and Mother," Will said as they went down the hallway. "Can't you stop and think about Mother? How angry Iris will be with her? With both of you?"

"It will be nothing compared to his rage if we continue this charade," George said, opening the door to the study. "It's only a matter of time before he finds her, son, and you need to accept that and take it like a man. Like a duke."

Will faltered at the doorway, feeling like he'd been gut punched, before rushing into the study to step in front of his father before he could get to the mirror. "Forgive me, Father, but I thought that being a man was all about protecting and fighting for those we love. As I fought for you when that Arbiter falsely arrested you. If I hadn't gone to the Patroon, you'd be in Mundanus now, rotting away!"

His father's eyes fixed him with an angry glare but then softened. He put his hand on Will's shoulder. "Your loyalty is admirable. But in this case, Will, it is misplaced. Let it go."

Will trembled, his fists clenched. Vincent appeared at the doorway behind George. *Do something, damn you!* Will thought at Vincent, but his uncle just leaned against the door frame, as if Sophia had already been taken from them.

"Let it go, Will," his father repeated, squeezing his shoulder.

Will looked his father in the eye as Sophia sobbed. "No." He readied his fist to punch him. There was the briefest look of disappointment on his father's face and then he spoke something so quietly, so quickly, Will didn't realise what his father had done until it was too late.

George stepped around him as Will struggled to move, frozen in place by the Doll Charm, so all he could do was stare straight ahead at his uncle. Vincent looked away, covering his face with his hands until he staggered out into the hallway, unable to watch any more.

No matter how hard he strained against it, Will couldn't even move his eyes, couldn't blink, couldn't breathe. As the panic built within him, all he could do was listen to Sophia screaming his name until even that was abruptly cut off and Will was left alone, trapped in his own skin.

12

Just when Will was certain he was about to suffocate to death, he lurched forwards and then stumbled into the sofa, released at last from the Doll Charm. His ears rang as he sucked in lungfuls of air, coughing and gasping himself back to normality. His eyes watered and he couldn't stop blinking, now that he was able to do so, nor was he able to stop shaking. Gripping the back of the sofa, he took a minute to steady himself before being certain he could walk.

Wiping his eyes, he looked at the mirror and saw only the reflection of his study. He pounded his fist into the sofa cushion and went to the door. Uncle Vincent was sitting on the floor just outside, his back against the wall, weeping into his hands. Morgan lurked down the hallway, clearly at a loss about what to do. Will waved him away angrily. "Get up!" he shouted. "We haven't got time to sit around crying!"

"He always was a heartless bastard," Vincent sniffed. "I can't believe—"

"Get up!" Will repeated in disgust.

His uncle just looked up at him with reddened eyes. "What for? She's gone. It's all over now. I'll be next. Oh, my life!" He covered his face again, shaking with each sob.

"What do you mean 'what for'? We need to get her back!"

"Don't be a fool, boy!" Vincent said into his hands.

"Coward!" Will went back into the study. He'd lost Cathy. He wasn't going to lose Sophia too.

He rifled through the desk drawers until he found an envelope he'd acquired shortly after he'd become Duke. Something he never thought he'd need. "What's that?" Vincent asked from the doorway. "Is it opium?" he added hopefully.

Will gawped at him. "What in the worlds…? No!" He tapped the corner on his palm to ensure the contents were settled, then tore it open. "It's a Charm. To open a Way to Exilium."

"Have you taken leave of your senses, boy? No one goes into Exilium without a summons! It's madness. You'll be lost for sure!"

"I am not going to sit here and weep whilst my father makes a terrible mistake. I have to bring Sophia back. Did you see him step through?" Vincent nodded, unable to meet his eyes. "And did you see our patron on the other side?" Vincent shook his head. "Then Father may not have reached him yet."

"Listen to yourself! Surely you cannot believe that," Vincent said as Will went to the mirror. "I know you love her, but Will, m'boy, you're the one making a terrible mistake."

Will made no effort to hide how low his opinion of his uncle had fallen. With a last, withering glance, he poured the sparkling powder from the envelope into his cupped hand, drew in a breath and then blew it towards the mirror before pressing his palm to the glass. He felt it ripple beneath his skin and before his doubts got the better of him, he walked forwards.

Will had never been to Exilium without having been summoned, and he was shocked by the open countryside that surrounded him. He couldn't see any wooded glades, even in the distance, and when he turned, there was no Way back to his study. Only then did he appreciate how little he had thought this through.

There were rules about Exilium, everyone knew that, all to do with what one should or should not do in order to avoid slavery or death. Every single one of them flew from his mind. The only thing that remained in the blossoming panic was the need to find Sophia. He listened for her, hoping that her cries would lead him to her, but all he could hear was the breeze caressing the meadow grass around him.

He had to stay focused. Yes, that was one of the rules; he had to stay focused on why he was there. He turned around, scouring the horizon, looking for any sign of Sophia. When he turned a third time, he noticed that the ground nearby was sloping upwards into a small hill that wasn't there before. With no better direction to head in, he started to walk up it.

After taking a breath to call for Sophia, Will decided against it. What if Lord Poppy heard him and pounced on the opportunity to torment him more? Instead, he thought of Sophia's little hand in his, the way she hugged him, her ringlets and the way she said his name. He needed to see her, needed to hold her and tell her everything would be all right. He needed it so badly it felt like a rope had been tied around his heart and was pulling it out of his chest.

At the crest of the hill he saw a copse of trees not far away— impossibly close, given what he'd seen when he first arrived. But this was Exilium; he had to expect such things here. He headed towards it, keeping thoughts of Sophia foremost in his mind, having to push away momentary flashes of anger towards his father. He'd deal with that later. All that mattered now was finding his sister.

As he approached, Will saw familiar blue and purple flowers bobbing in the breeze. Irises. And it felt like every single one was watching him. *Nonsense*, he thought to himself, *they're merely facing the sun*. He ignored them as best he could and stepped in the shadow of the leafy trees.

It felt different here. When he turned around to glance behind him, all he could see was forest, stretching so far back he couldn't see the edge of it. He shivered. *Just think of Sophia*, he told himself, *not the bloody trees*.

He walked, passing irises that always seemed to be tilted towards him, a sense of unease growing all the while. He hadn't been summoned, and worse than that, he was uninvited. This was his patron's domain; he'd been here before, but had always been brought straight into the heart of it. Now it felt like he was a trespasser, creeping into a private estate to steal valuables.

A movement up ahead made him stop. He could hear someone's voice. A woman's.

His mother!

Will hurried forwards, eager to find her, yet terrified of being caught. She sounded upset. He was too late. Why else would his mother be there but to answer for her crime? Was that what it was? To have a child and love her?

Close enough to hear her words, Will slowed to a stop as the light of the clearing ahead illuminated his parents kneeling before Lord Iris. Will scoured the trees for Sophia but couldn't see or hear her anywhere. Had Lord Iris whisked her away to some hidden place so he could focus on his parents? "Don't get attached to her, Will," he could remember Imogen telling him, shortly after his return from his Grand Tour. "She shouldn't be here." He shivered. Was she even still alive?

He moved forwards slowly, carefully, until he was right at the edge of the clearing, mere yards from his parents. He could see both of them clearly whilst he was obscured by the dense foliage, having positioned himself to the rear of Iris's organic throne in the hope that his patron wouldn't see him.

"I know it was wrong." His mother's voice wavered with fear. "I should have come to you as soon as I knew, Lord Iris, and I beg your forgiveness."

"What for, *exactly*?" Lord Iris said.

She looked up, frowning in confusion, her cheeks wet with tears. "For having a fourth child, my Lord. Against your wishes."

"And what else have you done that requires my forgiveness?"

Will saw his mother visibly flinch and then look at his father, terrified. She started to speak but broke down before the words left her mouth.

"Anna-Marie!" his father said harshly. "Comport yourself!"

"Speak!" Lord Iris commanded.

"Sophia…" she began, tremulously, "Sophia…is not your daughter, George."

Will watched his father's face, saw the utter confusion there, which was mirrored within himself. "But the Charm," George said quietly. "How could you betray your vow? Only an Iris man can touch you."

"Sophia's father *is* an Iris man," Anna-Marie said, fearfully. "He's your brother."

"What?" George shouted, and then remembering where he was, looked at his patron with a mixture of shame and barely contained anger.

As he too reeled from the shock, Will expected to see either rage or complete disinterest on his patron's face. But the hungry anticipation Will saw there instead was so much more frightening. "You were married and yet you dared sleep with another man?" Lord Iris said, his voice gentle, his tone…fascinated, almost. It was hard to place. "You knew how highly I value loyalty and respect and yet you cuckolded your husband and bore another man's child?"

"We love each other!" Will's mother wept. "Vincent loves me and…and…" She looked at her husband. "And you never have. It's like being married to a statue! No, a golem, made of judgement and constant disappointment. I was never good enough, never anything enough for you! But Vincent…he is actually capable of loving someone in a way you simply aren't."

Will realised he'd clamped his hand over his mouth. He couldn't believe what he was hearing, but at the same time, it all made sense. The way Vincent had come to the hospital so soon after the attack. How he'd never left Sophia's side. How he'd practically abandoned life in Society to be with her, day in, day out, and why he'd been so upset at the prospect of being sent to Jorvic. Now the terror that his uncle had shown when his father took her made sense; now Will understood that it hadn't been just about Sophia's fate, but also his own.

George stared at his wife, his expression mutating from one of shock, through varying shades of disgust and shame to settle upon pure, unbridled fury. "My own brother?" he hissed. "That *failure*?" His eyes widened. "Is Sophia the only bastard you've given birth to?"

"George!"

Lord Iris held up his hand. "Enough. The first three are yours," he said to George, and Will breathed again.

"My Lord, I had no idea about any of this!" Will's father lowered his head as if waiting for it to be chopped off.

"That is of no interest to me," Lord Iris said, still focused on Anna-Marie. He leaned forwards, his white hair slipping from his shoulders, until he was close enough to kiss her. "I want you to think of the moment you first wanted to betray your husband." Somehow, as if carried by the breeze, Will could hear his whisper clearly. From the horrified look on his father's face it was evident he could too. "Hold it in your mind. Yes, good. And now I want you to remember when you first acted upon it, knowing your vow, knowing you were breaking rules set by Society and your patron."

His mother was so pale Will feared she was about to collapse. It was as if Iris was a mesmerist and she could not look away.

"I want you to remember," Lord Iris whispered, lifting her chin with his fingertips, "the moment you felt your private needs were more important than your obedience."

Will heard his mother gasp and saw the tendons in her neck stand out as she strained against something. A choking cry slipped from her and then, faster than he could see, Lord Iris's hand was around her throat. For an awful moment Will thought he was going to strangle her, but there was no change in his mother's behaviour and Will realised Iris was holding her still.

"Yes," Iris's whisper held such anticipation, such desperation, as the Fae stared deeply into her eyes.

Then something seemed to be oozing from her tear ducts, something thick and greenish yellow, that made Will's gorge rise. Her breath sounded ragged, strained, and Will wanted to turn away but simply couldn't.

A sigh from Lord Iris was enough to pull his attention and Will saw the delight on the Fae's face. Lord Iris opened his mouth and as Will stared, utterly horrified, a long thin tongue emerged to lick the ooze from his mother's face. Sweat burst across Will's forehead and a dreadful lurch in his stomach made him spin round and hunch over in the grass, panting for breath as he struggled to stop himself from being sick. By the time he'd got his gut under control and turned around to face the clearing again, Lord Iris was withdrawing, that inhuman tongue hidden from sight. He let go of Anna-Marie's throat and she collapsed.

Was she dead? Will tried his best to see, and was rewarded with the sight of her back rising and falling with each breath. Her eyes were shut, her face clean and a sickly grey white.

"She won't break a vow ever again," Lord Iris said, settling back into place on the throne, looking genuinely happy in a way Will had never seen before. "She is incapable of it."

George was just as pale and as horrified as Will felt. "I…"

"When you take her home, she will sleep and then be well. And obedient," Iris added, with a cruel smile.

Will's father looked from his wife to his patron, speechless. He closed his eyes, swallowed, opened them again as he rallied himself. "And my punishment, my Lord?"

"Have you done something I am unaware of?"

The same confusion struck Will as his father. "Regarding hiding my—the child, my Lord."

Lord Iris waved a hand, disinterested. "It is forgotten."

"And…and my brother's betrayal?"

"I will see to him. You must focus on Aquae Sulis now. I am pleased with your progress, but now it's time for the rest of Albion to know who controls the city. You must impose harsh rules upon the residents. Restrict their freedoms. Make them struggle to keep your favour."

"But…Lord Iris, Aquae Sulis is stable and prosperous. The jewel of Albion. If I…" His voice withered away beneath Lord Iris's glare. "Of course, my Lord. Whatever you wish. I was considering sending Vincent to Jorvic, but now…"

"Focus on Aquae Sulis and its misery. And I need more mortals from Mundanus. No musicians, unless they have the qualities I desire. Talent alone is not enough."

"How many, my Lord?"

"As many as you can pluck without drawing undue attention to yourself." Lord Iris clicked his finger and a faerie darted from the branches of a nearby tree. "Return them to Aquae Sulis." The faerie zipped off to the centre of the clearing and then its flight described a large circle with a sparkling trail. Will saw his father's study on the other side.

George stood, bowed deeply to Lord Iris and then picked up Anna-Marie, who was still in a dead faint. Will watched them leave and the Way close behind them. Only then did he think about his own predicament.

"William," Lord Iris said, and with a jolt, Will understood that his patron had known he was there the whole time. Of course he did. How could that not be true?

Will stood, brushed off his trousers, and walked into the clearing, trying his best to look unafraid. "My Lord," he said, and bowed.

"You did not announce your presence."

"You were indisposed," Will replied, and was rewarded with a twitch of Lord Iris's mouth. He tried not to think of the tongue. He failed.

"Why have you come?"

"I'm looking for my sister. Sophia. My father brought her into Exilium." He stood as tall as he could. "I've come to take her home."

The fact that Iris looked amused rather than offended was little comfort. The Fae shook his head. "But she's mine now."

Will looked out of the clearing, into the trees, desperate for a glimpse of her. "But, my Lord, she's only a child and she wants to be with me."

"How do you know that? How do you know if she even remembers you now?"

It felt like a spike was being driven through his chest. "I remember her, my Lord, and my love for her will have to be enough."

"Where is your wife?"

Will looked down. "I am still working on the solution to that problem, my Lord."

"I've been waiting, William, for so long. For this marriage. Then news of a child. Now it seems to me that you have neither."

"But Iron took her, my Lord! Any other man and it would have been nothing to bring her back. Please understand how difficult this is!"

Lord Iris held up a hand. "I do, William. That's why your skin remains on the outside of your body." He leaned back. "You have not given me what I want. I see no reason to give you what you desire."

"But Sophia is just an innocent child, my Lord! Why should she suffer when none of this is her fault?"

Iris frowned. "Suffer?" He indicated the woods. "Does this appear to be a place of suffering?"

Will clenched his teeth. He wasn't thinking before he spoke. "I simply refer to her separation from me, my Lord."

"I *could* make her suffer," Iris said, as if Will had inspired him. "Perhaps that would be better motivation for you."

Will held up his hands. "No! No, my Lord, I could not be motivated more, please believe me!"

With a tilt of his head, Lord Iris scrutinised him. "I could make the child forget you, but I wonder if making her long for you would be more entertaining. What would you be willing to do, to prevent her suffering, William? What lengths would you go to?"

I'd kill you, was the first thought that came to him, and then he remembered his mother, the way Iris had spoken to her...*the moment you felt your private needs were more important than your obedience.*

He had to be smarter than this. He'd put his own head into this bear trap and Iris wanted him to trigger it. He wanted his disobedience. With a sudden horror, Will realised that was what the Fae had physically extracted from his mother.

He always known that obedience was one of the qualities his patron favoured most highly, but he'd always believed it was because Iris was obsessed with perfection. But having watched the way Iris had deliberately drawn out his mother's disobedience and made it manifest physically, Will had less faith in his own appraisal. And now Iris was forcing his father to be so strict it would encourage rebellion in Aquae Sulis. With a shudder, Will realised that was probably a better explanation for the exacting standards Iris placed upon his family: not to pursue perfection but to put them all under so much pressure that one day they would disobey him. And he'd insisted upon his marriage to Cathy, despite her many flaws. Now Will had a feeling it was because she embodied this quality that Iris craved. No one in the Nether was more disobedient than Cathy.

With a racing heart, Will felt that he'd brushed against part of something much bigger than he, something he and Cathy were at the centre of—had always been at the centre of—unknowingly and innocently.

He didn't fully understand it yet. All Will knew was that he wasn't going to give this creature what he wanted now. He was just as powerless to help Sophia as he ever was, and dancing to this tune was not going to get her back. He had to find another way to save her.

Letting his shoulders fall and the tension go from his back, Will bowed. "Forgive me, my Lord, I forgot myself. I should not have allowed myself to be distracted by such matters. With your permission, I shall return to the Nether and concentrate upon the most important task of seeing my wife returned to me, safe and sound."

After a fleeting expression of disappointment, Iris nodded and directed the faerie with a pointed finger. Will bowed again and stepped through the Way that had been opened to the mirror in his own study. Once the glass had returned to normal, he replaced the covering silk with trembling hands and then poured himself a brandy. Knocking it back, he rested against the sofa once more and let the glass slip from his fingers as the full horror of his situation crowded in upon him.

13

Standing outside the house she'd grown up in, Cathy felt sick. There was the window in the nursery wing that she'd spent so many years staring out of, watching the real world whenever she could get away with it. How many times had she been shooed away by her nanny whenever she was caught gawping at the cars, wishing she could sit in one, then later, wishing she could drive one. Wishing she could escape.

She wore a hoodie and one of Mrs M's coats and it felt like a disguise, even in Mundanus. But she still couldn't bring herself to walk up to the house and use the Charm of Openings right there, on the open street. She walked back down to the bridge, then back up Great Pulteney Street, avoiding looking at the Holburne Museum as much as possible as she tried to muster some courage. Then she walked round the back, to the high wooden gate that separated the garden from the street. Away from the traffic and people, the back lane still had traces of snow in the corners, and Cathy found herself staring at cat pawprints in a tiny drift.

"Come on," she muttered to herself. "Just get it over with." She whispered the Charm of Openings at the gate and stepped into the Nether on the other side. Just the sight of the silver sky was enough to make her pause, heart thrumming, tempted to turn and run. Surely the Irises would know she was back? Surely Will or Lord Iris would be mobilising now?

She rested her hand over her heart, recalling as much of the formula as she could. She was warded.

Cathy let the gate close behind her and looked at the Nether reflection of the house. All of the curtains were drawn and there was a black ribbon tied over the door knocker. A wreath of yew leaves hung from it, with another black ribbon decorating it. Cathy finally believed her father really was dead.

All she could do was stand there, staring at the wreath. He wasn't in that house anymore. He wasn't at his desk, nor standing in front of it, swagger stick in hand, waiting. He would never look at her with that mixture of rage and disappointment.

He would never hurt her again.

Then she was crying and she didn't know if it was relief or guilt or sadness. It just was.

She was only vaguely aware of the sound of the door opening and then her brother's arms were around her, holding her tight. For once, his height and broad shoulders felt like a shield between her and everything else and she wrapped her arms around his waist and cried into his chest. When the worst of it was done, Cathy pulled back enough to look up at him, seeing his cheeks were wet with tears too. It was such a shock, to see a man of the Nether weep, that she returned to the embrace. She held him tight, becoming aware of the slight shaking of his body as he wept silently.

"I'm here," she said. "I'm so sorry, Tom. I'm so sorry."

"I am too," he said, kissing the top of her head. "For everything." He let her go, swiped his hand across his cheeks, and tried to smile at her. "Come inside. Let's have a cup of tea together. Lucy is in Londinium but I'm expecting her back soon."

"Elizabeth isn't here, is she?"

"No. She was earlier. She's actually been quite sweet."

He took her hand and she let him lead her in, closing the door behind them once they were in the back hall. She took off her coat and pulled down the hood, expecting him to comment on her mundane clothes, but he didn't seem to care. She followed him through to the living room, taking care to avoid looking at the study door. At the doorway her breath caught at the sight of the familiar space with black crepe veils draped over the portraits and sprite globes. It took her a moment to place what was missing: the ticking of the clock. She supposed that they had all been stopped for mourning.

Wilson appeared briefly at the door, gave her a sad smile, confirmed the need for tea, and left again. The room was stuffy with warmth from the fire and there were letters scattered over the coffee table, most of them bearing the Agency marque at the top.

"Funeral arrangements," Tom said, gathering them up into a neat pile.

She was shivering, despite the warmth. It all felt like a terrible unreality. How could she be back in this house again? How could her parents not be here? How could Father be dead? None of it made any sense.

"Sit down," Tom said, pulling a blanket from a nearby chair. "Oh, Cat, sit down. You've gone so white."

She sat and he put the blanket around her shoulders and rubbed her back. "I don't think I really believed it," she said. "Not until I saw the door."

"It's still sinking in," Tom replied. "I'm so glad you're here. Lucy told me everything. Cat, I never should have brought you back. If I'd known what was going to happen, I never would have."

Was this her brother? She stared at him, seeing the dark circles under his eyes, the drawn cheeks. There was something different about him. "You mean when you found me in Manchester?"

He nodded. "I've been thinking. About Father. About what he was like. And why he was like that. I've found myself regretting things I've never really even thought about before. I was so angry with you. I thought you were selfish and…and I blamed you for everything I lost out on when I was looking for you. But then, I thought about Mother, and the way Father treated you and…oh, Cat." His voice cracked and he covered his face in his hands, sinking onto the sofa beside her. "I don't want to be like him."

Tom's shoulders shook as he wept again. She wrapped her arms around one of his and rested her head on his shoulder and it was like they were children again, together against everyone else. It felt like the time of their lives when they both thought Elizabeth was ridiculous and stupid and they were both so scared of their father and Tom came to her room after a beating and sat with her, guilt-ridden, upset. But now it was he who wept, instead of her.

"You're nothing like him," she whispered. "You're gentle and thoughtful and—"

"Gentle? I threw you over my shoulder and carried you out of that flat. And I threatened you. I didn't listen to you. *You* didn't deprive me of a Grand Tour. I allowed that to happen because I was too weak to stand up to Father. Too weak to fight for what *I* wanted. Like you did. It just…it feels like nothing is actually what I thought it was, Cat. And I feel so bad for thinking this way about Father. I loved him, I really did. But I was scared of him too and…and I'm starting to realise that he might not have been the person I made him into, in my mind."

"Father was angry, all the time," Cathy said, thinking of that ride in the carriage to the Oak on her wedding day. "He was twisted up inside because of it, I think."

"But this is my point," Tom said, resting his hand over one of hers. "*I* was angry all the time, too. Angry with you. Furious with Mother for leaving. I've even been angry with Lucy. Lucy, of all people! There is not a gentler soul in the worlds and yet I've found myself shouting at her about the most ridiculous things."

"This is what happens," Cathy said, softly. "It gets passed on. Father to son, over and over again, all of these things that no one ever questions. All these ways women are treated. How men are treated, too. Oh, Tom, I hate to see you so upset but I'm so glad you're crying and that sounds horrible but…the men here are like stone. Not allowed to be anything but strong, you know?" When he nodded, she tightened her embrace around his arm. "But right now, I think you're being stronger than you ever have before. It's so brave to admit these things. Father never could, and I think that's why he was the way he was. He kept it all locked up inside and just lashed out. When he beat me, it wasn't really about what I'd done. I don't think so, anyway. I look back and I think about how I was just this kid, you know, just messing up stupid stuff and he treated me like

I'd done something a million times worse. So that was all about him. Not me."

"I should have stopped him," Tom said.

"You were a kid too. You shouldn't have had to do that. It was his fault." She pulled the blanket tight around her, covering his arm too. "It took a long time to figure this stuff out. Time in Mundanus. Reading stuff there, learning from people who talk about things in a way that never happens in the Nether. You never had that opportunity."

"I spent a lot of time in Mundanus, Cat."

"Yeah, but not sorting yourself out and learning stuff. You were still under his thumb and stressed out of your mind. How could you have had the space and the time to do that?"

They both fell silent as tea and an assortment of sandwiches and cakes were brought in. Cathy had no idea what time it was, but she hadn't had anything since breakfast and it was a welcome sight.

"Thank you, Wilson," Tom said, and extricated himself from Cathy's arms to see to the tea. As he fussed with the teapot, Cathy wondered how to ask the one question on her mind that she didn't feel able to speak. She wanted to know what had happened, but decided to let Tom tell her in his own time. He'd never spoken this way with her before, not even when they were children, and she dared to hope that this wasn't just a state of mind brought on by grief. Could Tom really have changed?

"Miss Rainer and Margritte are both well," he said out of the blue. "I asked Lucy to write to them and make sure they were finding their feet." Cathy forced a smile, remembering how he had exiled Natasha. "I'm not proud of what I did," Tom said as he handed her a cup of tea. "As I said to Lucy, it seemed very important at the time. Now…I regret hurting you. And Miss Rainer. I just couldn't see any other way to handle it."

"Is that what you think of what Will did?"

The look of horror on Tom's face made her feel terrible for doubting him. "No, Cat! Do you think of us the same way? Am I really as terrible as him?"

"Sorry. Look, I want to talk to you about all this stuff, but…I've never been very good at being delicate about things, have I?" His lopsided smile reassured her. "I think the two of you have a lot in common, but hear me out. All the stuff you did before, that you just said you regret—that was all to keep men happy. Father. Or the Patroon. Or just Society in general—keeping it as it always has been. You put the needs of those men above mine and Miss Rainer's and all of the other women—and some men, too—who want it to change. That's exactly what Will did. He just went further. He put everyone else's needs and demands above mine and when I refused to comply, he forced me, rather than listening and trying to find another solution with me."

Tom stared at his teacup. "You're never going back to him, are you?"

"No."

He nodded and looked her in the eye. "I support you. I understand."

The tears came back, rolling fat and hot down her cheeks out of nowhere. She'd never realised how much that mattered, how much she'd needed to hear that from him, until this moment. He reached across and touched her shoulder. "I'm okay," she said. "Really. I'm okay. Thank you. It means a lot."

"Does it mean you have to stay with your friend?" Tom twitched. "My God, Cat, the Irises could find you here! Did anyone else see you?"

"No one else knows I'm here and I've got protection from them, don't worry. I'm working on a long-term solution." She meant the sorcery, but then she wondered whether she should tell him about the bigger plan to just destroy the Nether. No. This wasn't the time. "Has Will been hassling you to find me?"

"No, he hasn't told a soul. He's been saying you're unwell, which is a flimsy excuse at the best of times. Lucy said a few people in Londinium are gossiping about you being pregnant and it going badly."

Cathy rolled her eyes. "It's going to come out sooner or later."

"Would you be very upset if it did?"

"Of course not."

"Even if it meant he'd lose everything?"

Cathy finished her tea, feeling better for it. "You mean the Dukedom?" When Tom nodded, she found herself actually thinking about it. She hated Will, but actively wishing harm upon him? But then, it was only his social status. "He dug his own hole. He can dig his way out of it." She noticed how uncomfortable Tom looked. "What is it?"

"Cat...I think you should know what's happened. With Father. And the Irises."

"What have the Irises got to do with any of it?"

"From what I can tell, they found out that Mother left Father somehow. Even though he didn't see anyone after she left and as far as I know, he didn't tell anyone. I think what must have happened was that the Irises had a dinner or something arranged, and pushed him to confide when he sent an excuse. Either way, George Iris acted very quickly to exploit the situation."

Had Will told his father about her mother leaving Father before she had? Cathy was back in her dressing room for a moment, Will's hands all over her, trying to tempt her out of her underwear as she dressed for the wedding, just before he put the choker on her. She remembered confiding in him, so thoughtlessly, not even considering the possibility that Will would use that information against her family. They'd been allies for so long and she was distracted and stupid and...

And now her father was dead. She felt the tears run over her hand as she covered her mouth, trying desperately to ride out the urge to throw up again.

"Is this too hard, Cat? Would you rather not know?"

She shook her head. "Go on," she said through her fingers. She had to know.

"George Iris was pressurising Father into signing over his properties before he was publicly disgraced and lost his seat on the

Council. You know no one here would ever let a man whose wife had left him keep his status."

She hadn't considered it, not for one moment. Cathy had only thought of her mother and the freedom she'd gain. "What happened? Did he refuse?"

Tom was struggling too. He pretended to choose a cake from the stand, but she could see his hand shaking. "He…" Tom's hand dropped as he stopped trying to hide his distress. "He shot himself, Cat. In the head. With his service revolver. He did it in his study just before the Irises were due to call."

Hand still firmly over her own mouth, Cathy squeezed her eyes shut as another wave of nausea passed through her. "Does Mother know?"

"I don't think so. I have no means of getting in touch with her. Not even a Letterboxer works. The letters come straight back. Even when you left, they went somewhere."

"Oh God, Tom, it's so awful. I had no idea he'd…I thought it was a heart attack or something." She couldn't bring herself to tell him her part in it. She couldn't bear the thought of Tom blaming her as well as the Irises.

"There's more. George Iris stole our inheritance. He said Father signed all the properties to him. I know he didn't. Father left me a letter. I don't know whether you want to see it. It isn't easy to read."

How was she supposed to deal with this? She didn't know whether to cry, to rail against the Irises, to mourn her broken father, or to hate him for all he had done. No. She couldn't find it in herself to do that. But she didn't love him, either. Was that okay? The thought of reading his last words made her feel ill, but the thought of never knowing, of leaving this house and never truly knowing what he'd left behind seemed just as awful.

"I'd like to read it," she finally said. "Otherwise I'll always wonder what it said."

Tom pulled the envelope from his inside breast pocket and handed it to her. It was crumpled and warm. It took a while to open it, Tom busying himself with the teapot in an adorable effort to stop her feeling pressured. She read it in silence, the tears returning. Afterwards, she folded it, put it back into the envelope, and handed it back. "You've been carrying this all alone?"

"Lucy has been a rock, but no one else has seen this letter, Cat. Not even Elizabeth."

"I do forgive him," she said. "But I can't say I loved him."

Tom nodded, tucking the letter away again.

"When will the funeral be?"

"I was hoping tomorrow. It depends on you."

It was one thing to speak to her brother in private, another thing entirely to face the rest of her family. And while she was confident the ward could protect her from Lord Poppy, if he saw her, there was nothing to stop him from ordering one of the family to hold her for Iris. Knowing Poppy, it would be Tom. She couldn't bear the thought of putting him through anything more than he'd have to face already. "I can't risk it, Tom. It wouldn't be safe, for me or for you, if Poppy decided to get involved."

He tried to hide his disappointment. "I understand. Lucy will be there." He frowned. "And the Irises, no doubt. It will be so hard seeing George Iris. I think the pressure from him pushed Father over the edge. And now he's declared himself as Duke, apparently. He's behaving despicably."

"Well, he's an Iris," Cathy said. "It's what they're good at. Sorry. That sounded flippant. What do you want to do?"

"I'm not going to let them get away with it," Tom said. "And I'm not going to protect Will either. But I wanted to speak to you first before I work out what to do. I need to know if you want to come back. Not to the Irises. To the Papavers."

"No. I'm not coming back to the Nether at all." Again she felt the tug to tell him it might all change soon anyway, and just as quickly, she suppressed it.

"I won't pull any punches when it comes to Will, then. Figuratively speaking, of course."

"Don't. He deserves all the figurative punches you can throw at him." *And worse*, she thought. She'd been stupid to tell him of her mother's plans, but it was the height of betrayal for him to use that knowledge. "Actually, Tom, I'm not just happy for you to take him down. I want to be part of it. If the Irises stole the deeds they must have forged the signatures. I have a friend who will be able to help me prove that. If you can guarantee an evening when the Irises won't be at home, I can make that happen."

His concerned frown was both adorable and frustrating. "But Cat, you shouldn't get involved in this. The Irises will—"

"Don't worry about me." She found a discarded envelope on the coffee table and grabbed a nearby pencil. "This is my phone number. Don't give it to another soul. Get George Iris out of the house for an evening and I'll get your proof. Then you can take them down. Deal?"

He nodded. "Deal."

Cathy kissed Tom's cheek. "Thank you for asking me first. And for what it's worth, you were already a better man than Father. I think you might be one of the best."

They embraced. "I'll do everything I can to help you," he whispered. "Let me get this nonsense with George Iris resolved, then we'll see about getting your marriage annulled. There must be a way."

"Don't worry about me," Cathy said, holding him tight. "I'm sorry I can't be at the funeral. I love you."

His embrace tightened. "I love you too, Cat. We'll get through this. I'll be in touch soon."

14

After an appalling night's sleep, washing his face had done little to make Will feel better. He patted his face dry, tried to stretch out the pain across his shoulders, and let the towel fall to the dressing room floor.

The day stretched ahead of him, filled with worry and empty of hope. Now there were only servants in the house, and the thought of the vacant nursery wing made his eyes sting. Uncle Vincent had been summoned soon after Will had been returned home, and he had not come back. The anger was the most difficult to manage. After everything he'd done for his father, Sophia was gone, his uncle was no doubt facing Lord Iris's wrath, and his mother…well, he had no idea what state she was in now. All because his father had refused to find another solution.

What could he do now? Out of all the people in his life, the two he'd been most desperate to keep safe were beyond his reach.

He was out of ideas. Cathy ignored his attempts to communicate and he'd exhausted every mundane and magical means of reaching her, short of hiring an aeroplane and having a message scrawled in the sky above that bastard's house.

It was just a matter of time before Lord Iris's patience ran out. If only he could understand what lay beneath his patron's demands. All night he'd lain awake, staring at the ceiling, trying to work it out. If Iris really had pulled out the disobedience, somehow made manifest, from his mother, why not do the same to Cathy? He'd said that Mother would be incapable of breaking a vow again. Did he want Cathy to be even more rebellious before taking it from her? Or was he unable to do that, with her being born a Poppy? Was that why Iris was obsessed with getting a child from them? It would have Iris blood, but even if Iris was willing to wait until their child grew, there was no guarantee it would be anything other than a diligent Iris, too terrified of their patron to dare emulate their disobedient mother. Something about it didn't add up.

Will was certain it all had something to do with someone Lord Iris had lost. He remembered the intensity with which his patron had urged him to find Cathy. What had he said? Something about not finding her leaving him ghostlike…Who could it have been?

He had half a mind to contact Dame Iris. Eleanor was well disposed towards him, and knew Lord Iron and Cathy. Perhaps she could act as an intermediary. And she would know more about their patron's past. He needed to know more.

A quick wash wouldn't do. He summoned his valet and once he was shaved and dressed properly, he felt marginally better.

He went to the study to pen a note to the Dame when a tapping sound made him pause. Will looked at the window, saw no one was there, then listened again. It sounded like it was coming from the cheval mirror, hidden beneath the silk.

Resting the pen on his desk, Will closed his eyes, fearing the worst. Then he remembered that Lord Iris would not send a faerie to knock politely. He would summon him, violently. Composing himself with a few flexes of his fingers, Will went over to the mirror and pulled the silk away.

Exilium was on the other side of the glass, a tiny faerie pressing its nose against it. Its tunic was made of acorn leaves, and Will's heart flipped unpleasantly in his chest. Which patron's faerie would wear—"William Reticulata-Iris!" the faerie cheered. "You're the one? How interesting! You are such a lucky mortal! The Princess has decided to bless you with a visit. I see you are adequately attired. Good!"

Without even giving Will the chance to respond, the faerie flew off, away from the glass. It was then that Will noticed the castle in the distance, a huge, white-stoned palace with turrets that looked straight out of one of Sophia's fairytale picture books.

The Princess? His mouth went dry at the thought of meeting the Fae whose majesty had been so devastating, even when only witnessed secondhand. Whatever she wanted with him, he knew he would be struck dumb by the magic she wielded unless he took precautions. Noting that the faerie was now out of sight, he dashed to his desk and rummaged through the drawers. In the bottom one he found a ring that gave clarity of thought, something Tate had made for him to wear when dealing with difficult meetings. He had just enough to time to put it on and dart back in front of the mirror before the Princess came into view.

It looked like she was walking at normal speed when she got closer, yet somehow she had covered the distance between the palace and the glass in moments. Her green eyes glittered and her lips were deep pink, forming a smile that Will found himself reflecting before he realised it.

Will dropped to one knee, forcing himself to look down and gather himself back together again before her majesty unravelled him completely. Rather than making it easier to think in her presence, it seemed that the ring merely made him all the more aware of how her beauty struck him dumb. He'd never experienced anything like it. No Charm, no magic he'd ever fallen victim to before was even close to the impact hers was having on him.

Looking away helped. He readied himself for whatever she had to say; then a touch of the top of his head startled him so much he almost lost his balance. He looked up to see that she had reached through the glass as if it were a film of water to touch his hair and was now stepping into his study.

Her gown, cut in a medieval style, was a shimmering dark green, her cloak made of thousands of oak leaves, matching the ones that formed her royal circlet. When her touch left his head he felt a shiver and feared she had placed a Charm on him, but he didn't feel any different. Not that that was any sort of guarantee. In fact, he felt better able to focus his thoughts. Perhaps the ring was starting to work.

"Rise, mortal," she commanded, and he did so, turning to see her moving towards the fireplace as if drawn by the flames. The rest of his study seemed to fade in her presence, as if she were the only real thing present, the difference in the vibrancy of colour as striking as that of a fresh bud resting against old newspaper. He found himself worrying about whether she liked what she saw, whether she judged him dull and disinteresting from the way her eyes skimmed over his possessions for only the briefest moments.

For the first time, Will had no idea how to treat his guest. Should he offer her a drink? Surely not? How could the Princess of the Fae be satisfied by anything in the tantalus? The thought of ringing for tea was absurd, but equally the thought of not offering any refreshment at all was appalling.

"May I offer you any refreshments, your Royal Highness?"

She waved away the offer with a flick of the wrist and he breathed again. He watched the cloak, the leaves seeming to cling to each other rather than being sewn to any fabric, as she went to stand near the hearth. The fire seemed to fascinate her more than anything else in the room, including him.

"You were in Exilium recently," she said. Her voice was so soft, he found himself moving closer. "You were distressed."

When she turned to look at him he focused his gaze on the rug between them, deferent, and not a little defensive too. He feared that if he let her look deeply into his eyes, she would tease out his soul. Looking away helped him to think. "I am flattered that someone such as I could be noticed by you, your Royal Highness."

"Why were you upset?"

"It is a trivial matter that could not possibly be of any interest to someone of your majesty," he said, hating the fawning tone of his voice.

"You were looking for someone. You left Exilium before I could help you."

He had the distinct impression that her idea of helping him would not match his own. "I thank you most humbly for your concern, your Royal Highness. However, I discovered the whereabouts of the one I sought."

"Yet you did not return more happy than when you arrived."

"I am the Duke of Londinium, your Royal Highness. There are many burdens upon my shoulders." *Your visit is one of them*, he thought to himself. *What does she want with me?*

"The Duke of Londinium, yes, but I care little for that. I care more about the fact that when I cast a Charm to find the person who knows a particular secret I seek, it led me to you. It led to Iris too, of course, but he is so very dull, and besides, I would much rather you tell me than him. You have such a pretty face."

Will recalled the art exhibition. Was that the reason for the visit? He kept his mouth shut and his eyes fixed on the rug, hoping he was wrong.

"Lord Poppy entered a most interesting painting into an exhibition recently. Of the Royal Crescent in Aquae Sulis." She gasped. "Oh! You know of it! I can smell the fear radiating from you!" She stepped away from the fire, coming closer, the scent of summer flowers coming with her. "It was called *The Secret*. Did you paint it?"

"No, your Royal Highness, I did not. And I have no idea who did."

"But you have seen it. Look at me!"

Steeling himself, Will looked up and saw the excited flush across her cheeks. "I am aware of the painting, your Royal Highness," he said, hearing the quiver in his voice.

"Tell me what the secret is, the one hidden in the painting. I must know!"

His mouth opened and for an awful moment he almost told her, without even thinking about it. Then he remembered Sophia, how she was already at the mercy of Lord Iris. What if the Princess took an interest in her too? It was clear that the Fae were powerless to refuse her. If she took Sophia from Iris, there would be no hope of getting his sister back ever again. He'd never be able to embrace her and tell her that it was all over and there was no need to be afraid.

It was as if he'd been drunk and was suddenly, horribly sober. He still had to protect Sophia from this monster before him. "I am so sorry, your Royal Highness, but as a loyal Iris, I cannot tell you without the permission of my patron."

He felt her anger, as if the fire across the room had become an inferno, a heat across his face that made him shut his eyes and lean back. "You cannot refuse me!" she cried. "I am the Princess! No one may refuse me anything!"

Will thought of Sophia, thought of her saying his name in that way of hers, of the tiny kisses she scattered across his cheek. He forced himself to open his eyes and to wear his most charming smile. "But, your Royal Highness, if I were to simply tell you the secret because you demand it, would I not steal the thrill of anticipation from you?"

The glare that had made her face so terrifying melted away and she smiled again as if she'd never been angry in the entirety of her existence. "Oh, you are a Duke indeed. Such courage! You deny me what I want and dare to smile as you do it? What a creature you are!"

"If I may be so bold, your Royal Highness, I prefer to think that instead of denying you something, I am instead giving you a gift. It must be so dull, having everyone give you exactly what you want the instant you desire it."

"Oh, it is, it is! But now I want both! Such sweet anticipation and yet the need to know is torture."

Will took another step back, masking his need for distance with a desire to sit down. He gestured towards the sofa but she shook her head, so he remained on his feet too, the arm and corner of the sofa now placed between them. "Then, may I humbly suggest a game?"

She clapped her hands, reminding him sharply of Sophia in her delight. "I adore games!"

"It seems to me that we both want to know a secret about my patron, though not the same one. I propose that we each take turns, trying to guess the secret we desire to know. We both must tell the truth, but only answer the question asked with yes or no. The person who guesses the secret first wins. The other must accept that they will not learn the other." It was a game he'd played for hours and hours with Oliver Peonia on their Grand Tour. Will had the dreadful suspicion that the Princess would be better at it than his old friend.

"Such delicious fun! Yes, we must both play and we must both accept the result. And when you lose, William Iris, I will take you as a slave. For I believe you would entertain me well in Exilium."

Will's heart felt as if it had burst into his throat. "But, I have a duty to Londinium and my patron, your Royal Highness."

"Neither is as important as my happiness. I will go first because I am the Princess and that is the way it is always done. Is the secret related to the Royal Crescent?"

"No." At her frown, he added, "Your Royal Highness." It did little to change her expression. "My turn. Has my patron lost someone he loved?"

The frown was swept away by a look of sheer delight. "Oh! *That* secret!" She laughed. "I know all about *that* one! It's one of my favourites. Yes. He has. Now…my question…is the secret related to a specific member of your family?"

"Yes," he replied, thinking more about his next question. Lord Iris clearly loved the one he'd lost. And he would never let anyone he loved far from his sight, not given how possessive the Fae were about their favourites. "Was Lord Iris's love taken from him, against his will?"

The Princess giggled. "Yes. How he wept! I've never seen such misery, it was wonderful! My brother—" She covered her mouth with her fingers. "Oh, I almost forgot myself. That's the thing about secrets, especially the best ones. They have a life of their own. They fight for their freedom."

So the Prince was involved? Yes, that would make sense. Will couldn't imagine any of the Fae lords and ladies being able to trick Iris into giving someone up; he was too calculating for that. Could he leap to the conclusion that the Prince stole Lord Iris's love, though?

"Is the secret I seek connected to your *immediate* family, William?"

His brief thrill at learning more than she had faded as he realised how close she was. "Yes," he said. He had to gamble. A correct guess this soon wouldn't give him enough information, but leaving it another round or two could be the end of him, and Sophia's chances. He needed to learn enough to decide whether he could use the information to bargain with Iris for Sophia's freedom. From the look on the Princess's face when she spoke of this love of Lord Iris's, Will suspected that she was actually desperate to tell him. The Fae were not like people, guarding a secret to protect the ones they loved, after all. Then he realised there was one thing he needed to know above all else. "Is the person whom Lord Iris loves, the one who was stolen from him, still alive?"

The Princess bounced up and down, barely able to contain herself. "She is! All this time she's been out of his reach in the one place he couldn't find her! Oh, it is so exquisite a punishment! So beautifully cruel and perfect to hide her with his mortal enemy!"

She covered her mouth again and he could see how she struggled not to tell him. He couldn't push her too far, though. But then he realised he'd never defined the secret he needed to know! He laughed and bowed to her. "I win! That was what I needed to know! Lord Iris's love is still alive. Thank you, your Royal Highness, for such an exciting game!"

The look on her face was like a storm about to break, filling Will with a fear for his life. "But I always win!" she yelled. "I am the Princess and I win all the games!"

She was like a spoiled brat, but with the power to kill him or worse. He dropped to one knee again, lowering his head. "But your Royal Highness, was the game not enjoyable? Did you not relish the opportunity to let that secret free after all this time?"

"But what about the one *I* need to know?" She moved towards him and he prepared himself for a blow, but she stopped and lifted his chin instead, reminding him of Iris. "Tell me the secret!"

"I cannot," Will said, forcing himself to stop quivering. He thought of Sophia again, armouring himself. "You would have to pull it from me, and that would break the rules of our game. You said we must both accept the result."

She screeched with frustration, her fingernail digging into the skin below his chin so sharply he was sure he was bleeding. "Then I will have a forfeit from you."

Pointing out that he had won, and therefore owed nothing to her whatsoever, would not go well for him, he suspected. Will caught himself before he protested, knowing her wrath had to run its course.

As quickly as it had descended, the stormcloud frown lifted and her lips curved enough to make Will genuinely frightened. "I know what it will be! As you are so fond of games, let this be your forfeit. The next time you enter Exilium, you will come straight to the palace. You must try to find me there, without my brother seeing you. And when you find me, you must kiss me. If you can do that without falling in love with me, you may leave again." Her look of complete satisfaction told him it was an impossible task. Would his resolve be enough to resist her there?

"Your desire for my affection fills my heart with gratitude," he said, and she laughed.

"That silver tongue can't mask your true feelings." She leaned closer until she was all he could see. "You are wise to fear me, little man," she whispered. "Enjoy your minor victory. Once you love me, I will torment you until you beg me to let you speak that secret. You'll regret guarding it so closely."

She went back through the mirror and in moments he saw himself reflected in it once more, pale-faced, the white collar of his shirt stained red with his own blood from the wound beneath his chin. He let himself lean against the back of the sofa, exhausted, scrabbling to feel anything other than despair.

No. All was not lost. He knew his patron's love was a woman who was still alive and hidden from Iris with his mortal enemy. All he had to do was work out who that was, find her, and then bargain for Sophia's return. How could something so difficult be summarised so simply? As for Cathy... He sighed. One crisis at a time.

15

Edwin prodded the crumpet. "What's this thing called again?"

"A crumpet. It's nice. Try it."

He took a bite and Lucy laughed at his confused expression as he chewed. "What the hell is that made of? I mean, that texture... it's bizarre."

"I don't know. Probably some sort of butter and flour combination. Practically everything has butter in it and then you have to spread more on, it's like a rule or something. The butter here is dark yellow and tastes so good on toast."

"Aww, man, you've really gone native. We gotta get you home and back on pancakes and coffee, stat!"

Lucy laughed and kissed him on the cheek. It was the first time she'd relaxed since that awful night they got the news and she felt guilty for leaving Tom. She couldn't expect Edwin to tiptoe around a grief-filled house, though, and Tom was barely keeping himself together, let alone able to entertain a guest. "I'm so sorry I haven't been around as much as I would normally be," she said.

"It's not your fault. How's he holdin' up?"

Lucy rested her elbows on the table, her cup of tea held in both hands, making the most of being able to relax. "He's taken it hard. And there's other stuff going on too. This is gonna sound terrible, but I think it might actually do him some good. Charles Papaver was a scary guy. He used to beat Tom's sister and I'm like ninety per cent certain he is the reason why Tom tries so damn hard all the time. A chance to live out of his shadow is a good thing. I could never tell him that, of course."

Edwin nodded. "Must be tough, losing a parent. I've always

wondered what it would be like to live in Mundanus and watch your parents grow old and die." He shook his head. "I guess that only sucks if you like your parents."

Lucy nodded. "I guess they all gave you a pep talk before you came over, right? Something about making sure I'm on track, that I haven't forgotten why I'm here, blah, blah, blah?"

"My parents wanted to know if you need anything to help get things moving." He shrugged. "Not that any of us could think of anything. We don't know enough about the Patroon to figure out some leverage."

Lucy poured more tea. "If you're not gonna finish that crumpet, I will."

"Knock yourself out," he said, pushing his plate over. "I'll stick to the bread and butter."

"I think the Patroon is a bust," Lucy said. "We were all hoping that something of Mundanus would have seeped through to them here, but they'll never let the Colonies go. Not willingly, anyway."

"Yeah, but, we never really believed they would, right?"

Lucy shrugged. "Some things have started to change. Thing is, the one who was spearheading it all has left the Nether, just when things were starting to get interesting." She told Edwin about the educational pamphlets, about the young ladies who'd come to the last ball of the Aquae Sulis season dressed as men and about how Cathy had spoken out in the Londinium Court. "I even heard a couple of rumours at that ball that there are feminist groups springing up all over Albion."

"You gonna get involved?"

"I thought about it, but I need to keep my eyes on the prize, right? I don't think I've got a chance of achieving anything with the Patroon; I'm just a colonial married into Albion. He probably thinks I'm grateful to be brought into the fold."

Edwin rolled his eyes. "Jeez. Okay, so it's Poppy himself. We could just…call for him."

Lucy gawped at him. "Are you kidding? No, we need to impress him first, then ask for independence. And it's gonna be tough. I have the beginning of a plan…"

"Which is?"

"Destroy the Irises."

Edwin sat up straight, pretended to hold a teacup with his pinky finger stuck out. "Destroy the Irises, no big deal," he said in a mock British accent. "Cuz, you need to back up a bit."

"The Irises have taken Aquae Sulis, stealing all the properties my father-in-law left to Tom. George Iris sent a letter to Tom yesterday that I intercepted and it gave me an idea." A knock on the door made her pause. "Come in."

Grayson entered with a silver tray. "Two visitors have arrived, ma'am." Lucy took the calling cards from the tray, both with the top left corner folded over. It took her a moment to recall that it meant they were here in person.

The Lady Censor,
Claudia Angustifolia-Lavandula
Aquae Sulis

The Master of Ceremonies,
Richard Angustifolia-Lavandula
Aquae Sulis

Lucy took a deep breath, recalling her mother's words when she'd kissed her goodbye at the port. "They're gonna think that they're better than you. They're gonna act like that's true and they're gonna try and make you feel small so they feel bigger. Now you remember this, honey: you are smart, and brave, and you have made a sacrifice that few people would. I am proud of you. Now go get 'em. You show them what us 'colonials' are made of."

"Want me to go do the tourist thing for a while?" Edwin offered.

"No, I'd like you to stay so I can introduce you."

Edwin peered over at the calling cards and scratched his chin. "I don't think that's a good idea."

"Don't you want to get a sense of what we're up against?"

He nodded. "I do...I just..." He shrugged. "You've got a plan and you know how to talk politics with these people. They're too high up for me to screw things up for you." He held up a hand when she took a breath to protest. "I've got some stuff I wanna do anyway. It's cool."

She frowned. It wasn't like Edwin to avoid people. "Only if you're sure."

He kissed her cheek. "I'm sure."

Lucy dabbed at her mouth with the napkin. "We'll meet them in the drawing room, Grayson." Lucy stood, smoothing down the skirt of her day dress, and waited for Grayson to leave before hugging Edwin. "Wish me luck."

"You can buy eggs for that, you know." He grinned. "Good luck, cuz."

The Censor was wearing a powder-blue silk travelling gown with panniers that made her shape utterly bizarre to Lucy. It was trimmed in a darker blue satin which also covered the buttons and formed the ruffled trim on the gown. Her hat was a large brimmed affair with three dramatic ostrich feathers. How she'd managed to fit it into the carriage along with her brother, Lucy had no idea. The Master of Ceremonies wore pale pink silk breeches and a long powder-blue jacket with remarkably big cuffs, cut to reveal an exquisitely embroidered waistcoat decorated with stylised lavender and pink humming birds. Both wore white powdered wigs and makeup. Lucy felt distinctly underdressed.

She curtsied deeply to them both, earning a broad smile from him and a satisfied nod from her. "It's such a pleasure to see you both," Lucy said.

"Dear Lucy," Richard said, scooping her hand up to kiss it lightly. "Tell me, how is my nephew?"

"I think he's past the initial shock," Lucy said, "but he's still very shaken." She gestured to the two large sofas positioned opposite the one she planned to sit in. The Censor would need one to herself in that outfit.

"It's utterly dreadful," Claudia said, manoeuvring around the sofa with a grace Lucy was certain she wouldn't have with such undergarments. "I have no doubt that my disgusting sister was responsible for Charles's distress." Richard frowned at that, but didn't challenge her.

Lucy wondered how to navigate that landmine as she sat down. "Have you heard from Isabella?"

Both of them shook their heads. "We don't even know if she's aware of what's happened," Richard said. "Though I suspect that it wouldn't make any difference. She knows she can never show her face in Society again."

"I can only hope that her patron devises a suitable punishment for her," Claudia said, pulling off her gloves with dainty precision. "No wonder Catherine turned out the way she did. Isabella tried to blame it on the governess, but now the truth is out. I haven't seen Catherine in Aquae Sulis. Did she simply neglect to pay her respects to us?"

Lucy didn't want to get sidetracked, especially when she hadn't quite decided what to do with the knowledge she had. "Catherine hasn't visited Aquae Sulis, as far as I know, Lady Censor. She wrote a beautiful letter to Thomas, though."

The Censor pursed her lips as Richard said, "I heard tell that she has been absent from the Court."

"As have I, sir," Lucy said. "I cannot confirm or deny her presence, I'm afraid. I've been devoting all my time to Thomas."

"And rightly so," the Censor said. "Perhaps William has finally come to his senses and realised that she is a liability in public."

Lucy could have kissed Grayson for choosing that moment to appear with the refreshments. There was the distraction of serving tea, and delighted comments from Richard about the macaroons— just enough for her to gather her thoughts and courage for what she was about to do.

The Censor was looking at her expectantly over the rim of her teacup. Richard seemed more interested in the macaroon held delicately between his fingers. It was time.

"Thank you for taking the trouble to come and see me in Londinium, I do appreciate it," she said. With these two, it was always important to pay them in gratitude first, at a level vastly outweighing the effort they'd actually made. "I need to speak with you about a delicate matter and I felt it was very important that I discussed it with you before Thomas becomes aware of it. He has so much to deal with at the moment, and I fear this would be too much." It was a lie, but she felt it was worth it. She knew they'd pay more attention now she'd said that.

Richard was sufficiently intrigued to only take one bite of the macaroon before pausing to hear the rest. Claudia leaned forward the slightest amount, indicating that she was interested but not yet convinced this was worth her trouble.

"I've been dealing with the correspondence relating to the bereavement. Thomas has so much to arrange, he asked me to do so. A letter arrived yesterday that I haven't shown him. I was so shocked by it. I thought it would be wiser to show you first and ask for your advice." Lucy hoped she sounded sincere. She'd known exactly what to do when she saw it, but the Lavandulas were the sort of people who needed to have their egos fed—and besides, there was no better way to get them in the right frame of mind for her to steer them. What did the Brits call it? "Buttering up"; that was it. Like a crumpet! The phrase suddenly made sense.

Richard placed the remaining macaroon on his plate and set it down, wiping his fingers on his napkin. "Why do I have the feeling this letter was sent by George Iris?"

Lucy nodded. "I'm afraid so." She glanced at the Censor, whose lips were pressed into a thin line. "It isn't just the fact that he has increased the rent on our house and that of Thomas's parents that's offensive, not even considering the insensitivity of the timing. It's how he signed it."

Richard frowned. "What do you mean?"

Lucy folded her hands on her lap. "He signed it, 'George Reticulata-Iris, Duke of Aquae Sulis.'"

"Duke!" the Censor shrieked. "Duke? There has never been a Duke of Aquae Sulis in the history of the city!"

Richard's mouth had fallen open. "Do you have the letter?" he asked after a few moments.

"The Irises have gone too far!" the Censor said as Lucy went to her desk and unlocked the drawer. "What a cowardly, underhanded way to state his intentions."

"I believe signing a letter with a title is further down the road than merely stating his intentions, dear sister," Richard said. "It's clear he already considers himself to be so."

"How many other letters has he signed so?" Claudia scowled into her tea. "This is simply unacceptable."

"This is a coup," Richard said quietly. "A coup d'état *au lettre*."

Lucy handed the letter to him, which he read silently and then passed to his sister, who snatched it from his hand and read in moments. "I will destroy him," she whispered beneath her breath. "I will expel him from the city immediately, and—"

"Claudia," Richard reached across and touched her arm. "Darling, it's too late for that. Don't you see? He must have sent a similar letter to all of his tenants. Not one of them has brought it to our attention. They see which way the wind blows. First Londinium, then Oxenford and now Aquae Sulis. They probably think Jorvic will have an Iris Duke before the month is out. None of them have told us because they already consider our authority to have been removed."

"But he told us we would remain Censor and Master!" Claudia said. "You were there, Richard!"

"He obviously changed his mind," Richard said.

Claudia threw the letter at him with a frustrated cry. "How can you be so calm? This is an outrage! I have a mind to go to Lady Lavender and petition for—"

"No," Richard said as Lucy returned to her seat. "Not yet."

Lucy marvelled at how still he was. For a man who fussed and cooed and giggled at parties, a preternatural calm seemed to fill him now his power was threatened. She watched his eyes as he stared at the teacup, so intensely focused on his thoughts that it was as if he were alone in the room.

In contrast, the Censor fidgeted and unfurled her fan that had been dangling from a bracelet. She waved it with such ferocity that the curls of her wig twitched and the feathers of her hat looked like they were clinging on in a gale. "I simply cannot believe this is happening. And to think I was upset that Cecilia Peonia danced with a servant at the ball!" She looked at Lucy. "Did you see that?"

Lucy shook her head. "I did not, Lady Censor. Was it one of the forfeits?"

The Censor wrinkled her nose. "It was not. The Peonias are well aware of my displeasure. Perhaps I should have another wartime bomb discovered in the grounds of the Royal Crescent..."

"Claudia," Richard said sternly. "This is not the time. We need a better solution than causing them a petty inconvenience."

As Claudia stared at her brother in shock, Lucy poured more tea. "If I may be so bold," she began, having observed the effect the phrase had had in several delicate conversations, "I have given this considerable thought since receiving the letter and I would like to make a humble suggestion."

The look on Claudia's face expressed so much in silence. It was clear the Censor didn't believe a colonial like her would have anything intelligent to contribute on the matter. Richard, however, was looking at her with interest.

"George Iris has stolen my husband's inheritance, of that I have no doubt whatsoever. Thomas is so certain his father left the properties to him that I suspect there may have been a letter saying as much, but he hasn't told me about it. It's probably too painful. Now George Iris has stolen the city from you. He is a thief and a bully and must be stopped. But"—she paused to pour some milk into her cup, wishing it was a strong black coffee—"it must be done in such a way that not even his patron will be able to defend him."

She stirred the tea, taking a moment to enjoy how Claudia's disdainful expression had been replaced by one of interest.

"There are two objectives," Lucy continued. "One is to prove, irrefutably, that George Iris has no rightful claim to my husband's inheritance and the second is to restore your power in Aquae Sulis. I believe that one leads to the other."

"As I said to your husband, dear girl, I saw the deeds. Charles transferred the ownership the day he died."

"Has a signature never been forged in Albion?" Lucy asked.

"There are protections in place to ensure it cannot be done to the Aquae Sulis property deeds," Richard replied.

"Protections can be broken," Lucy said.

"If George Iris has the gall to declare himself Duke illegally, he certainly has the gall to ask his patron to give him the power necessary to break those protections," Claudia said to Richard. "I know you think they are indestructible, but if Lord Iris wanted it to be done, he could do it. Everyone knows that he was behind William taking the throne. He would have lost that duel without his patron's support." Claudia looked at Lucy. "I can see you have an idea. What is it?"

"We all want to see George Iris go down, and to be honest, I'd like to kick him into next week, but we have to be smart about this." She noted the way that Richard's mouth twitched as he tried not to smile. "He's declared himself Duke. He's expecting you both to kick up a fuss. He's expecting us to refuse to pay that rent. I suggest we do the opposite."

"By which you mean welcoming his pathetic coup with open arms?" Claudia said.

"By which I mean you throw him a ball."

"Ha!" The Censor stood up. "This is just the sort of nonsense one from the Colonies would believe to be a—"

"Claudia!" Richard said her name so sharply she jolted with surprise. "I know you are upset, but there is no excuse for such appalling manners." He looked at Lucy. "My most sincere apologies. Please, do carry on." Claudia stood there for a moment, as if she couldn't quite believe what had just happened, and then sat down again.

"I know it sounds absurd," Lucy said after giving Claudia a

brief smile to let her know that all was well. She was used to such treatment, after all. It would take far more than that to upset her. "But my thinking is this: he clearly has the support of Lord Iris, as without it, declaring himself Duke would be a dumb—I mean, stupid—thing to do. And while George Iris lacks many things, intelligence isn't one of them."

"Go on," Richard said.

"So imagine this: you say to him that he's entirely right; the Council of Aquae Sulis simply doesn't work without a third party who holds power, and in light of the fact that Charles signed the properties to him, it makes sense that he be declared Duke. So much sense, you'd be delighted to hold a ball in his honour, to demonstrate your support."

Claudia looked like a woman who'd taken a sip of a drink expecting it to be tea only to find it was coffee. "He would never believe us! And besides, the season is over. We cannot hold another ball for at least six months. It simply isn't the done thing!"

"Forgive me, Lady Censor, but declaring oneself Duke by signing demands for unreasonable rent increases is hardly the done thing either. We find ourselves in dire circumstances and the need to survive surely outweighs any traditions regarding when one can hold a ball?"

"Quite so," Richard said, giving Claudia a look that spoke of her need to agree in no uncertain terms. "Besides, Aquae Sulis has never had a Duke before. It will hardly be the most scandalous breach of tradition, will it, now?"

"Well, when you put it that way," Claudia said. "Though I still don't see any need to give this toad any public credibility."

"Ah, well, I haven't got to the heart of the plan yet," Lucy said, putting her empty teacup and saucer back on the table. "You see, if we can convince the Irises that they have seized the city, then they will think we have accepted George's story about the deeds. The family will go to the ball en masse, as they always do, meaning we will know when they are definitely out of the house. Giving someone the perfect opportunity to get the deeds and have them tested for forgery. The local Arbiter will be all too happy to do that. I heard through the grapevine that George Iris was arrested by him not that long ago. I'm sure they'll be very interested in anything involving Mr Iris."

"Are you seriously telling us that the purpose of the ball is to distract the Irises whilst we break into their house like common criminals?"

"She is and it is brilliant," Richard said with a broad grin. "Darling, it's the last thing they'd expect!"

"Yes, and when we have the proof," Lucy said, "the entire family and the residents of Aquae Sulis will be conveniently gathered in one location. We'll be able to publicly shame George Iris, leaving him no opportunity to cover up his crime." She didn't mention the fact that William would be there too, and that she had every intention of publicly shaming him as well. She needed to keep the Lavandulas focused on their enemy. "Imagine the satisfaction of destroying him so publicly, while making it very clear that you were both still in control the whole time."

Claudia's face was transformed by the most delighted smile whilst Richard laughed. "My dear girl, I have underestimated you," she said. "George Iris will be incapable of predicting such a turn of events. Yes, we'll make this happen, will we not, Richard?"

"Indeed we will, dear sister. And Lucy, dear, do feel free to call me Uncle. We are related by marriage, after all."

Lucy smiled. "Why, thank you, Uncle." She looked at Claudia, who held up her hand.

"I will not accept anyone calling me Aunt," she declared, standing up. "No matter how much they have impressed me," she added. "Now, of course, we won't mention anything about a ball until the funeral is over. Do you have a date in mind?"

"It hasn't been confirmed yet, but as soon as it is, I will make sure you know."

Richard stood and kissed her hand once more. "We shall turn our minds to the more…subtle aspects of this plan, whilst we wait, so we can move quickly. Who knows what else George Iris will do with his power? We need to hold the ball as quickly as possible."

Lucy escorted them out to the front door. "I look forward to finalising the arrangements with you," she said to them both, and after accepting a kiss on the cheek from the Censor, she waved them off as the carriage pulled away.

She maintained the smile until the door was shut, and then leaned against it with a heavy sigh. The first part of the plan was in place. She just hoped that she could pull off the rest of it. As satisfying as destroying the Irises would be, considering all they'd done to hurt Tom and Cathy, it wasn't the ultimate goal. And she knew that impressing Lord Poppy would be much harder than winning over the Censor of Aquae Sulis.

"Interesting times ahead," she whispered, and then went off in search of her cousin.

16

With Cathy away in Bath, Sam felt able to leave the house and go to the office without guilt. Beatrice had left with the locations of the seven forges without mentioning a word about Cathy. Perhaps protecting Max didn't constitute betrayal. Either way, he was relieved Beatrice had gone, even though she'd promised to return for him "when the time was right."

He'd only been there a minute when there was a knock on the door and Des came in. "What's happened?" Sam asked. "You've got that look on your face."

"What look?"

"The 'something really big and bad has happened but I'm going to look calm and professional' look."

Des put a large sheaf of papers and several full document wallets onto Sam's desk, obviously trying not to confirm or deny the appraisal. He opened the topmost wallet and took a moment to check the first page. "We had a letter from Lord Copper's lawyers," he said, and handed the wallet over.

"Wait, all of this is one letter?" When Des nodded, Sam handed it back. "Sum it up for me."

Des flipped through the sheaf of loose papers and pulled out a smaller clump of pages stapled together. "This is the summary from our lawyer. It's ten pages long."

"Okay. Summarise that one."

"Basically, we're screwed if we try to do anything else along the lines of what you've done so far. And Martin Barclay is already screwed. He's being prosecuted for libel. The lawyer that's been set on him is a real Rottweiler, apparently. He's asked for some help from you. Your lawyer thinks that's unwise. It's all a bit complicated. The long and the short of it is this: we need to back down. We need to make the right noises to Copper and we need to distance ourselves from Barclay and his environmental group. And we can't do anything like the same leak for anyone else in the Elemental Court. They've made it clear that this will be a group prosecution if it comes to it."

"Okay," Sam said.

"So we're backing down?"

"No. I meant, 'okay' as in I understand what they're doing. Fuck them. Fuck their bully boy tactics."

Des took a deep breath before replying. "Mr Ferran, I'm not a lawyer, so maybe I haven't summarised well enough here, but Francesca, the lawyer who wrote this summary for you, said that this isn't a shot across the bow. This is the real deal. We're one step away from a brutal prosecution. We can't afford to fight this."

There was a time when any sort of threat of legal action—even just a fine for a parking ticket—would have sent Sam to the pub to drown his worries. Now? He knew he had to stand firm. "They can go fuck themselves. Make sure Martin has all the help he needs. The very best lawyer, with as much experience as possible. Make it clear to that lawyer that I am one hundred per cent behind Martin."

"But, sir…" Des was actually starting to look flustered. "Have you read the report that your CFO sent you? We're going to make a loss this year for the first time. Ever. All of this environmental work you're doing, all the changes, they're laudable and I really admire you for doing all the things you are, but…it's expensive. It might even be worth staggering things a bit."

Sam shook his head. "No. It's all long overdue. We stick to the planned changes. And there's another project I'll need money for soon. Can you get someone to sell that island Amir owned? I own that now, right? How much would that get?"

"I think it cost your predecessor somewhere in the region of thirty million dollars, but the resort wasn't built then."

"Right. Okay. What other stuff can I sell? Property-wise, I mean, stuff that's just for my private use."

"I haven't looked at the portfolio recently. There are several properties, all worth several million each. And a few other assets that could be liquidated."

"Can you put a list together for me? With estimates of how much I can get for each one?"

"Sir, you're not going to force them to take you to court, are you?"

"Eh?" He couldn't fathom why Des would think that. "Oh, this is to raise funds for another project. Not to pay a bunch of bloody lawyers! And I want you to get a report together on steel manufacturing in the UK."

"It's been in decline for decades, sir. Amir couldn't see the point of shoring it up here when he could make more profit elsewhere."

Sam nodded. "Yeah, but Amir was an arsehole. I want you to give me a report of what it is now, what it used to be, and what the capacity for UK production could be if there was sufficient investment. I'm not bothered about profits. Just tell me how much it would cost to get it working to full capacity again."

Des fidgeted, picked up a couple of the wallets, and tidied them before setting them back down again. "Sir, I know I'm just your PA, but I really think you need to speak to your CFO about all this first. The global demand for steel is falling, now China is slowing down. The numbers just aren't adding up and you could go bankrupt if you're not careful and—"

"Des," Sam held up his hand. "It's going to be okay." He knew that once the worlds were restored, the demand for iron would go through the roof. He needed to get the industry in the best shape he could before then, and bringing as much of that production home felt good. "There's more to all this than just making money. And anyway, I'm just talking about selling stuff I don't even use. I don't need it. I'm not interested in swanking about, playing at being rich. Not when there's more important stuff to be done. Leave the reports with me, I'll read it all."

Des lingered, as if he had more on his mind. He made it to the door before saying, "Mr Ferran, I'm really proud to work for someone like you. Someone who genuinely cares. But I can't help feeling that you're not taking Copper and the others seriously enough."

"It's all going to be okay, Des. Really. Go find that stuff out for me. Okay?"

A text from Cathy came through as Des left and Sam opened it.

Sam, I want to go and shut down the Agency. Do you have a couple of buses and drivers that could help Max and me?

He grinned at the message and typed a reply back.

I'm on it.

17

Max could hear the bus driver's snore from where he stood, at least five metres away from the vehicle, even with the wind whipping around him. The driver of the second bus looked asleep too, headphones in his ears, utterly disinterested in why they'd been sent to a remote rural location near Stirling at zero notice. The men had been told they were going to rescue some people being illegally trafficked. It was the same cover story used for those rescued from the asylum, so they accepted it without question.

It was almost midnight. The gargoyle was still curled up in the van Sam's PA had hired for them and Max had got out to walk around in an effort to keep his leg from getting too stiff. Cathy was due any minute. He'd brought all of the tools at his disposal with him, including a crate full of hastily made sandwiches and drinks that Mrs M had insisted they take as soon as she heard there might be people brought back with them.

Cathy had insisted on introducing them before she'd left for Bath, even the gargoyle, despite his reservations. Mrs M hadn't reacted like most people would at the sight of an animated gargoyle. She'd just asked if it was housetrained and when she was certain it wouldn't "pee on the carpets," she'd been very welcoming to them both. After the van was loaded up, Mrs M had pressed a small box into his hand, given the gargoyle a flask to carry, and pecked Max on the cheek. "Something to keep you goin', pet," she'd said. "I'll make sure all the guest bedrooms are made up and that the hotel is ready for people. What must they think, eh? All these strange people turning up, paid for by Mr Ferran. They must think he's involved in something right dodgy." The box had contained a cheese sandwich and two pork pies. Now only crumbs remained. The tea had kept him warm enough, but now the cold was starting to bite.

There was a low rumble in the distance and the gargoyle's head popped up inside the van, its ears swivelling to follow the noise. A car. Max checked that everything he might need was in place as the car Cathy had borrowed from Sam came up the hill and parked.

"Hi," she said. "Everything's ready, then?"

Max nodded. "We need to make a plan."

She came and sat in the van with him, reaching back to scratch the gargoyle behind the ears. "I've had a hell of a day. Max, do you have anything that would be able to detect whether something has been forged?"

"I can detect if Fae magic has been used to commit a forgery," Max replied. "But not if it was carried out by a person with the correct mundane skills."

"I reckon magic would have been used," she said. "I know you're not part of a Bath Chapter any more, but would you still be willing to help me and my brother?"

"Arbiters aren't permitted to help puppets unless it involves an innocent."

"Oh, come on, Max. You've left all that behind now. If George Iris gets away with this, I reckon a lot of innocents in Bath are going to be at risk."

"George Iris?" the gargoyle snarled. "What's that pond scum done now?"

"Stole my brother's inheritance and used it to declare himself Duke of Aquae Sulis."

"That bloody—"

"We will help you," Max said, knowing the gargoyle would only get louder unless he agreed. He was prepared to take the risk in returning to Aquae Sulis. He doubted Rupert would be anywhere near Bath, or its reflection, after what he'd done to Kay.

"I'll help nail George Iris to a wall. Any time," the gargoyle added.

Cathy grinned. "Good. When we're done here, we'll make plans." She peered out into the darkness. "So where is this place, anyway?"

"The Agency's building only exists in the Nether," Max said. "The foundations are present in Mundanus, about a yard beneath the grass over there. That's all. I don't know how the magic is worked to create the building without a mundane anchor, but I am sure it has something to do with the people I saw in the basement."

"There were models of the building and they were staring at them in a really creepy way," the gargoyle said. "It was horrible."

"Sounds bizarre," Cathy said. "I don't see how that could be done with just sorcerous magic. But then, I'm not an expert. Yet."

"How much did that Sorceress teach you?" the gargoyle asked.

"Not nearly enough," Cathy said. "I can protect myself and I know some basics." The gargoyle's throat rumbled. "What is it?" Cathy asked.

"The Sorceress is teaching you her special hybrid magic?" When she nodded, the gargoyle said, "Don't you think it's a bit strange that a woman who went to all that trouble to kill all the other Sorcerers seems perfectly happy to make a new one?"

Max could see the thought hadn't even occurred to Cathy. "Can we deal with one really frightening thing at a time, please?"

"After this is done," Max said, "we need to think carefully about your involvement with the Sorceress. We don't know what her agenda is."

"Rescue first," Cathy said, pulling on the door handle. "Difficult conversation second. But I'll tell you this now: you're not going to stop me from educating myself. If we want to make sure that Beatrice isn't pulling the wool over our eyes, we need to understand what she's doing and the only way to know that is for me to learn more sorcery. Now, what's in the rest of the building?"

"A very large room which serves as an office with multiple desks is on the ground floor," Max said. "Lots of filing cabinets in there, which we should keep. That's why we brought this van. Even though I'm not part of a Chapter any more, that may change, and information on the puppets is critical."

"There are files on everyone in the Nether?"

"Yup, far as we could tell," said the gargoyle. "It's where we got that file on Miss Rainer for you."

"The rest of the building is accommodation for the group of people who run the place, headed by a man called Derne, and the entirety of the top floor is divided into male and female living quarters. There may be babies there, too. There's no way to know how many staff are being trained there without going inside the building."

"Trained?" the gargoyle growled. "Brainwashed, more like."

Cathy's expression was equally grim. "Are there guards?"

"I saw four on the top floor," Max said, recalling his earlier reconnaissance trips carried out for Ekstrand. "One on the stairs down to the basement and several in the room with the prisoners there."

"Okay." Cathy chewed on her thumbnail. "So let's make sure we're clear on our objectives. I want to get the prisoners out of the basement and get them whatever care they need to recover. I want to get the people being trained to be Agency staff out of there and given the freedom to do whatever they like. I think keeping that information in the files safe and in our possession is a good idea and it'll help us to get in touch with people after the worlds are unsplit. I'm not sure what I want to happen to the people running the place, and the guards. We can't exactly take them to the police."

"We can decide what to do with them after the prisoners are freed," Max said. "At the very least they need to be restrained so they don't interfere."

"Right, okay. Is there anything else you two want to achieve?"

"I want to bang some heads together," said the gargoyle.

"I don't think that's a good idea," Cathy said, making the gargoyle's muzzle wrinkle with disappointment.

"All right, then. I'll be good, as long as we make sure they can't start this racket up again. We get everyone out, and the files, like you said. Then we trash the place."

"Nuke the site from orbit?" Cathy grinned.

"I think that is a step too far," Max said.

"It's from a film!" she groaned. "I agree that we take the place down."

"I suspect that we when remove the prisoners from the basement, the magic creating the Nether property will fail," Max said. "That being the case, we deal with the rest of the building first, the basement last. If the Nether property disappears, we might end up with all of the furniture and possessions—and people, if they're not removed first—crashing down onto the foundations."

They sat in silence for a few moments. "I know a Charm to make people sleep," Cathy said. "I learned it when I was a kid, but I haven't used it on anyone before. I remember it, though, it's very easy. We could sneak in and every time we find an owner or a guard, I make them sleep."

"Too risky," Max said. "If there's more than one they could raise the alarm."

"We could ask the Sorceress to come and help," the gargoyle said. "Not keen on the idea, mind you, but she knows how to make everyone in a building drop dead. I reckon making everyone in a building fall asleep would be dead easy for her."

"Is that how she killed the people in the Chapters?" Cathy asked.

The gargoyle nodded. "Turned all the hearts to stone. She wrote on the building and they all dropped dead."

Max watched several expressions cross Cathy's face. He picked out horror at first, then after a couple that he wasn't certain of, she looked excited. "I think I could do that! I mean with sleeping, not turning hearts to stone. I know the Charm needed already, I know how to define a space—and of course, marking a building would make it easy—and I know how to link the two. Theoretically." She stared up, biting her lower lip as she thought. "Yeah. I think I could. I could make sure the basement is left out and put everyone else to sleep."

"Then I could go in, restrain the owners and guards, then you lift the magic, yes?" Max asked. "If there's a Fae Charm involved, I would be immune."

Cathy nodded. "Yes, that works. Do you have any chalk?" Max found some in a pocket and gave it to her.

It took her an hour to chalk the formula onto the Nether building once they'd gone through. As she worked, the gargoyle kept watch on one side of the building, Max on the other, both taking care to stay close to the walls and avoid being spotted from the windows. Max was counting on the fact that now it was moving into the small hours of the morning, most of the people inside would be in bed already. Eventually she came over, twisting the chalk nervously in her hands. "I think it's ready. I've checked it. Three times. I think it's right."

Max nodded. "Do it."

She went to the nearest set of markings, readied herself, and then stopped, turning to look at him. "I can't do it when you're watching me."

"Why?"

"You're making me nervous."

Max walked round the corner to wait. He had enough time to check that the cable ties were easy to find in his pocket. He then pulled out his Opener and waited.

Cathy poked her head round the corner. "Done."

Max nodded, pushed the pin of the door handle into the mortar between the stones, and watched the outline of the door appear. "Wait here until I come and get you," he said to Cathy, and went inside.

Like the first time he had entered the building weeks before, it was quiet and empty of people downstairs. He peeped into the large room with the desks and files and saw that nothing had changed. He went up the stairs, listening carefully. The sound of snoring made him pause for a moment. Carrying on, he reached the top, went down the hallway, and saw a man, dressed in a suit like the security guards had been before, lying in the middle of the corridor fast asleep where he had fallen. Cathy's hybrid magic seemed to have worked.

Reassured, Max pulled a couple of cable ties from his pocket and bound the man's hands behind his back. He used three to bind his feet together, then joined them to the one around his wrists. The man would be uncomfortable when he woke, but unable to even shuffle off for help. Good. The plan could work.

He moved swiftly through the first-floor rooms, finding the members of the management team asleep in their rooms. He restrained them all in the same way as he had the guard. Derne was the only one not asleep in his bed, instead slumped over a desk in his room, ink staining the page that his fountain pen had been left resting against when he fell asleep. Max bound him to his chair, trying his best to ignore the man's stinking breath as he snored loudly.

There were four guards sleeping in the hallways of the second floor, all dealt with in exactly the same way. Once he was certain all of them had been restrained, Max went through every room, counting the number of people asleep in the male and female dormitories. Ten men and fourteen women in total, one of whom was heavily pregnant. He found dormitories for children, too, three girls and five boys, along with a nursery containing six cots, filled with babies sleeping peacefully, along with a nanny asleep in a bed next door. She wasn't dressed as a guard and he considered whether she should be treated the same way. He decided against it, seeing as all the men and the management team had been taken care of. If he recalled the number of people in the basement correctly, it was likely that the two buses would easily be enough.

Satisfied that everyone in the main part of the house was accounted for, Max went back outside. "Twenty-four adults, one nanny but I'm not sure if she is a mother or staff or part of the management team, eight children, six babies. They can all fit in one bus if there are no more than twenty prisoners in the basement. We use the other bus for guards and the staff."

"But where do we take them?"

"Back to Cheshire for now," Max said.

"We can't do that! It's kidnapping," Cathy said. "Look, I hate those people, but we can't have them prosecuted in Mundanus. There are no Chapters left to deal with them. I say we drive them to a mundane service station or something and let them fend for themselves."

"Agreed," said the gargoyle. "I might give that Derne bloke a black eye first, though."

"No," Max and Cathy said simultaneously.

"So shall I break the formula now?" Cathy asked. "They're likely to stay asleep, especially if they're already in bed, given the time."

Max nodded. "You should probably wake the staff they are training and the nanny. Explain what's happening, give them a chance to pack and get them onto the black bus. We'll get the guards and the management team out and into the red bus, then we'll load the files into the van before we deal with the basement."

"If there's any noise upstairs, won't it alert the guards below?"

The gargoyle grinned. "I'll be very happy to make sure no one comes upstairs to make trouble."

"We keep everything as quiet as possible," Max said. "And we block off the door from the basement to the main part of the house to give us time if we need it. You," he said to the gargoyle, "will be more use getting files into the van. We'll park it round the side next to the windows and out of sight of the bus drivers. I need you to carry the guards and management team down to the hall first. I'll escort them to the buses after I've explained the situation to them." With a grumble too low-pitched for anyone to make out, the gargoyle agreed.

"How are we going to explain all this to the bus drivers?" Cathy said.

"They're Mr Ferran's people," Max said. "They've been given the human trafficking story. It worked well for the ones rescued from the asylum."

They got to work. Cathy ran upstairs to start mobilising the people on the top floor while Max and the gargoyle started shifting the others downstairs. Each of them protested when they woke, but soon realised there was nothing to be done but accept what was happening. Some of them just needed an extra threatening growl from the gargoyle to make them settle down.

The woman that Max had always suspected was high up in the Agency's hierarchy, Matilda, was already awake when they got to her room, sitting on the edge of her bed, hands and ankles still tied. "These are very uncomfortable," she said. "I'm not going to fight you." She eyed the gargoyle. "That thing is clearly much stronger than I."

Max cut the cable tie connecting the ones around her ankles. "You can walk, then."

"Did the Duke tire of this portion of his empire or is this yet another change in ownership?"

"Duke? What Duke?" the gargoyle asked. "We're from Ekstrand, the one who took over."

Matilda smirked to herself. "I told Derne that Ekstrand had no idea. The Duke of Londinium has been in control of this establishment for some weeks now. Were you unaware?"

"It doesn't matter anymore. This place is being shut down."

He ignored her protestations as he escorted her to the bus. The driver was now wide awake and took responsibility for her at the door. "They're trying to bribe me with all sorts of things," he said. "Don't worry, though. I know what these dodgy bastards are like."

Only Derne was left to remove. Max could see the other bus was filling up too, all of the passengers staring up at the moon and stars in varying degrees of shock. A baby was crying and a couple of people were moving around inside the bus, reunited with each other, from what he could tell.

The gargoyle was waiting for him at the top of the stairs. "Cathy is upset."

"She'll recover."

"It's horrible. All of this is horrible. It's all right for you. You don't have to—"

"We haven't got time for this," Max said. "Let's get Derne onto the bus, then move the files."

It was silent in Derne's bedroom when they opened the door and at first Max assumed the lack of snoring meant that he had woken up, before he saw the empty chair.

"Oh shit," the gargoyle said as they approached. "He got away."
It went out to fetch Cathy as Max picked up the cut cable ties.

Cathy arrived with the gargoyle. Her eyes looked reddened.
"What's happened?"

"Derne is gone."

"Oh shit," she said, coming closer.

"That's what I said," the gargoyle replied.

"Oh my God, look at this!" she cried, pointing at the book
resting on the desk. "This is a sorcerous formula! Derne was
a Sorcerer?"

"No, he wasn't one of them," Max said. "Not of the Heptarchy,
that is."

"Maybe he was an apprentice," the gargoyle suggested. "One
that got away and set up shop here."

She started to rifle through a trunk at the foot of the bed and
then pulled out a couple of huge books. After flipping through the
pages, she grinned. "Books! This one's basic-level stuff, by the look
of it; I recognise some of the exercises from what Beatrice gave
me." She picked up another. "Whoa, that one is more advanced.
That explains the weird way this building was made. He probably
set it up."

"Maybe he left the Sorcerer he was apprenticed to because he
didn't like the way he was doing things," Max suggested.

"It certainly wasn't over ethical concerns," Cathy said. "It's sick.
All of it. He probably just realised he would make more money and
have more power if he broke away and set all this up. They're all
monsters. All the Sorcerers. They dislocated your soul! Rupert killed
your friend. Beatrice has killed over a thousand people. I mean…
what the fuck? I don't want to spend another moment with her.
But I need her to teach me. These books are only going to get me
so far."

"There has to be another way," the gargoyle said. "You seem
pretty good at it. What if we got some more books so you could
teach yourself? Ekstrand's place is still full of them."

"I'm not sure this is a good idea," Max said.

"Why?" the gargoyle said.

"We've seen the damage this knowledge can do."

"We've seen what it can do when arseholes have it," the gargoyle countered. "Cathy is different. She's one of us."

"Us?"

"One of the people that's been screwed over by them. Remember what happened to Kay. Remember what nearly happened to us! And what actually did happen to us! Cathy could put things right."

"How?"

"I don't know, but at least she'd bloody try. Wouldn't you?"

Cathy blinked at the gargoyle's expectant face. "I wouldn't kill anyone with it, I can promise that," she said. "And I wouldn't make any more Arbiters. And if you wanted me to undo what happened to you, I'd try to find a way."

"Now isn't the time for such decisions," Max said. "We haven't completed all of our objectives. The people are still in the basement."

Cathy stripped a pillowcase from the bed to carry the books in and slung it over her shoulder. "Come on, then. Let's get this finished."

When she left, the gargoyle looked at Max. "She's already started to learn, you can't stop that now. We should help her. Better to have a friend who's a competent Sorcerer rather than an incompetent one, right?"

"I'll think about it," Max replied.

"Don't you trust her?"

Max considered the question. "I don't trust sorcery," he replied. "Whether Cathy can be trusted with it remains to be seen."

18

Cathy couldn't shake the nebulous feeling that something bad was going to happen. Since the night at the Agency she'd been studying hard for a few days, then catching up on sleep, so she had barely seen Sam, who was busy preparing for being in demand when the worlds were unsplit. She was glad to have the time to herself, while Max and the gargoyle sorted out the files taken from the Agency. She'd helped them debrief the victims and make sure they had all they needed in the safehouses Sam had provided before closeting herself away. It was frustrating not having Beatrice around to tutor her, but it was also a relief.

Then one morning she realised her father's funeral had taken place the day before and she hadn't even thought about it. One moment she was looking out at the snow, thinking about the formula she was developing, then the next she was sobbing into her coffee. Once it had passed, the sense of dread lifted. Right up until she received a call from Tom telling her a ball had been arranged in Aquae Sulis to keep the Irises busy and out of the house at the appointed time. She and her brother finalised the plan, agreeing that Lucy had handled the Lavandulas perfectly.

It was time to return to the Nether and strike a blow against the Irises.

The time away had not made Aquae Sulis more palatable. Cathy scowled at its silver sky. She knew that with everyone at the ball there was no real risk of being spotted, but she was still tense. It was worth the risk, though. There was no way she was going to sit back and let the Irises get away with their crime. And if Will went down in the process, all the better.

She'd come into the Nether at King's Circus, as close to the Royal Crescent as she dared to come through. Dressed in the most innocuous clothes with her black cape, she had to simply hope that no one would notice her.

"Cathy, dear, wait for me!"

Uncle Lavandula stepped out from behind the trunk of one the huge sycamore trees reflected into the Nether, dressed in black satin and white hose. The elaborately embroidered black waistcoat and frock coat glittered with tiny gems.

"Uncle Lavandula, you're supposed to be at the ball! You'll be missed!"

"Nonsense, dear girl, Claudia is taking care of everything. I'll only be gone for ten minutes at the most." He came over and kissed her hand. "I'm coming to enjoy some delightful criminal activity with you."

"You can't," Cathy said. "It's too much of a risk."

"But I had this outfit made specially. Watch and learn, dear girl. One must always be suitably attired for every occasion. Just because one is about to break into another's house, it does not mean fashion should be overlooked."

There was no point arguing with him, so Cathy headed out of the Circus towards the Royal Crescent. "This is the plan," Cathy said. "I have a sorcerous door handle that we'll use to go through the wall, so we aren't seen by any servants. I've got a Charm to deal with the safe, I get the deeds, I get out. I can't see the point of putting us both at risk. What if he has wards in use? Traps?"

His uncle laughed. "My dear girl, George Iris is dreadfully dull and one of the most unimaginative men in Albion. It simply won't have occurred to him that anyone in the worlds would ever dream enter his study without his permission, so he won't have taken precautions. Be thankful it wasn't a Digitalis who stole your brother's inheritance. That would be another kettle of fish altogether."

Cathy decided it would be best to stay silent for the rest of the walk. When the Royal Crescent came into view her step faltered. This was madness.

But then she remembered the suicide note. If she walked away from this now, her father's last wish to protect his family would not be honoured, Tom would not have his inheritance, and he would have to bow to that disgusting man and accept this injustice. No. She had to help Tom to take the Irises down, publicly, before the worlds were rejoined and they lost the opportunity.

Uncle Lavandula was strolling as if they were promenading, and any moment Cathy expected someone to emerge from one of the many doors in the crescent. No doubt her uncle would simply bow and wish whoever it was good day. She wasn't confident she'd be able to handle it with as much grace.

Cathy sneaked up to the correct space on the wall of the sweeping crescent of houses and pushed the pin in. She twisted it and then stood back as the outline of a doorway burned its way into the stone. When the new door appeared she stepped inside with her uncle and pulled out the handle. The fake entrance disappeared as if it had never existed.

The study was so neat it felt as if it wasn't actually used day to day. There were the usual bookshelves, large desk, chair, but not a single thing out of place. "Very tidy people, the Irises," Uncle Lavandula commented. "Keep your gloves on, dear girl."

"Fingerprints…yes, of course," Cathy had been so focused on the magical aspects she'd forgotten about leaving mundane clues behind.

"More to maintain the thrill of thievery," her uncle said. "I'll look through the desk, you look for a safe."

"The deeds won't be in there," Cathy said, heading over to the nearest painting of bleak moorland.

"I agree. I just want to see what he keeps in here."

Trying her best to ignore her uncle's dreadful nosiness, Cathy tried to move the painting aside, but it was so large the frame had been screwed to the wall in several places. Not willing to waste any more time, Cathy pulled out the pouch containing the Charm Tom had given her. "Look away, Uncle," she whispered. "I'm going to use a Charm." She jiggled the pouch from its strings and her uncle nodded.

Once he was looking away—magical dust in the eye was dreadfully painful—Cathy emptied the contents onto the palm of her hand. "I seek the deeds of the Aquae Sulis properties," she whispered into it, and then blew it as hard as she could, sending a sparkling plume of dust into the air.

It swirled randomly for a moment and then swiftly coalesced, reminding Cathy of a murmuration of starlings she'd seen in Mundanus. It rose up, twisted back on itself, and then shot towards a section of wooden panelling on the wall opposite the window, sticking to the wood and making it sparkle. The sparkling faded when she touched the panel.

There was no obvious opening, so she ran her fingers around the edge, hoping for a groove or button. Perhaps it would only open for someone of Iris blood. Maybe her protection against the Irises would prove to be a disadvantage here.

"Press the top right corner," Uncle Lavandula said as he thumbed through a stack of papers he had pulled from a drawer. "Then the bottom right, then top left, bottom left."

Cathy followed the instructions and with a click the panel slid across, revealing a simple safe with a keyhole, rather than a numbered dial.

"How the hell did you know that?"

Her uncle chuckled. "I didn't just get this outfit made to prepare for this," he said with an appalling smugness. "I had a...special conversation with Imogen. Before her father declared himself Duke, fortunately, otherwise she never would have told me."

"Imogen knows we are doing this?"

"Of course not, silly girl. She thought I was planning to do something completely different. There aren't merely property deeds in there, as you'll see." He tossed a tiny key over.

There was more to her uncle than she'd appreciated. How could she have done this without his help? She was so woefully underprepared.

Inside the safe was a familiar wallet, and with a pang in her chest Cathy saw that it still bore the simple red poppy on the clasp that held it shut. It rested on top of another containing the Iris properties and beneath that was a separate piece of paper. She took it out, along with the top wallet, leaving the Iris property folder inside.

There was a list of ten names, most crossed out, all men's names with surnames abbreviated. She saw her uncle's name right at the top, and *Oliver M-P* at the bottom, but didn't recognise any others. "Your name is on this list, uncle, with others that are crossed out. Shit, this isn't a list of people to kill, is it?"

Uncle Lavandula stifled a laugh and took it from her hand. "No, dear girl, this is the fabled list of suitors that has kept Imogen awake at night. And I am still at the top."

Cathy wrinkled her nose. "She's far too young for you, even by Nether Society standards."

Her uncle glared at her. "How rude! Besides, the Master of Ceremonies is never too old to constitute an excellent match. I suppose George was too busy imposing his wishes on his newly acquired empire to take the time to cross me off. Well, it's irrelevant now. Pop it back inside, Cathy dear, so George can find it tomorrow and fully appreciate just how difficult it will be to marry off his daughter when his reputation is worth less than that of a Buttercup."

Cathy did so and closed the safe before sliding the panel back into place. After checking that the deeds were in fact in the wallet as expected, she went back to the wall. "I have them; we should go." Her uncle was reading something so absorbing he didn't hear her. "Uncle! We need to go and meet Max."

He tutted at the page, shaking his head in theatrical disapproval. "Well, well, well. I knew George Iris was a dutiful son, but I had no idea he'd stolen so many from Mundanus. It seems Lord Iris has a great appetite for rebellious mundanes. How interesting."

Cathy frowned, mentally filing away the information to discuss with Max. Then, thinking there was no point in worrying about her father-in-law discovering the robbery, she took the list from her uncle and stuffed it into the waistband of her trousers. Catching a glimpse of the mundane clothing previously hidden by the large cloak, her uncle raised an eyebrow. "Catherine, dear, I assumed that all was not well in your marriage, considering your eagerness to expose your father-in-law's crime, but…trousers? Are you quite well?"

She put the pin of the Opener into the wall. "Everything is just fine," she said. "Max is waiting down the road for us; I want to get these documents to him right away. Once he's confirmed the forgeries, you need to get the evidence to Tom as soon as you can. Come on! Let's go!"

19

Will stifled a yawn, uninterested in the ball. Hiding his anger at his father over Sophia was exhausting, especially now he was Duke of Aquae Sulis, and he was thoroughly bored of deflecting enquiries about Cathy. Even the former Master of Ceremonies had been unable to fake his interest in the event; Will had spotted him slinking back into the room after presumably finding a distraction. He was just about to make his own excuses and leave when there was a gasp from the far side of the ballroom, near where the former Censor stood. The guests swiftly parted to reveal Lady Lavender stepping from Exilium, through a gilded mirror. She wore a ball gown made of a lilac fabric so fine it looked like layered mist. Her hair, a rich dark blonde, tumbled in tight curls swept away from her face and down her back, reaching the floor. She smiled at Claudia Lavandula, then Richard, both of whom were bowing more deeply than Will had ever seen. He too bowed, as any sensible man would in the presence of the Fae. The smile their patron gave them made him worry. Surely she would be angered by the fact that they'd lost control of Aquae Sulis?

"We are honoured by your presence," said the Duke of Aquae Sulis. Lady Lavender barely acknowledged him. When her gaze fell upon Will he bowed his head again, not prepared to stare it out with one of the Fae.

When he straightened, he saw Lord Iris and Lord Poppy step through the glass just before the mirror rippled and was restored to showing a reflection again. Lord Iris was as cold as usual, while Lord Poppy looked utterly delighted by the shocked expressions around him.

"My Lord," Tom said, stepping forwards from the crowd. "I have an announcement to make, with your permission?"

Will frowned at the way Tom ignored the Duke. "Oh, please, entertain us!" Lord Poppy said with a wave of his black cane. Seeing the look in Tom's eyes, Will knew he was about to be betrayed.

"I am not an orator, nor a showman, so I will get straight to the point," Tom said. "I have indisputable proof that my inheritance has been stolen by George Reticulata-Iris, who, having exploited the untimely death of my father, has seized power in Aquae Sulis by means of forgery and deception."

As an excited murmur rippled across the crowd, Will looked at his father, who was glaring at Tom, ready to defend himself. When he opened his mouth to do so, Lord Poppy held up his hand, crossing the room in a few graceful steps to stand between him and Tom. "No, little Iris, I want to hear more about this from my favourite's brother."

"I have obtained the deeds to the properties owned by my family and an Arbiter of the Bath Chapter verified that powerful Iris magic was used to forge the name written on the transfer document for each one. This has been verified by Lady Lavender. My name was replaced with that of George Iris, who claimed that my father signed over his properties to him before his death, giving the Irises the majority in Aquae Sulis. He used this imbalance to force out a power structure that has kept this city civilised and stable for centuries, claiming that my father's last act was to support his coup." Tom's face crumpled for a second, then he regained control of himself. "My father's last wish was that I protect the tenants that my family have managed with the same care and fairness that we always have, and, specifically, protect them from the likes of you!" He jabbed a finger at Will's father. "You have stolen my inheritance, twisted my father's last wishes, and lied to everyone in this city for your own personal gain. You do not deserve the title of gentleman, let alone Duke of Aquae Sulis."

When Poppy twisted round to look at the accused, his face was a picture of theatrical shock, his blood-red lips forming a large O shape and his black eyes wide. "You took from my family?" he asked in a harsh whisper. "You stole what was rightfully ours? You stole from the Lavandulas?" He held out a hand towards Lady Lavender, who swept across the ballroom to come to his side as Lord Iris looked on, excluded. "Oh, George. This simply won't do. Will it, my dear?"

Lady Lavender's pure violet eyes darkened to a deep purple. "It. Will. Not."

Will's father looked to their patron for support, only to see Iris turn away, seemingly disinterested. His mother hung her head, looking as though she wished she could disappear. Imogen, who had been enjoying her new status as daughter of a Duke mere moments before, stared in horror.

It felt as if he'd somehow tumbled into a nightmare. He'd had several since destroying the Rosas, where it was his own family being condemned instead of theirs. Now it was playing out around him, Will could only appreciate how inaccurate those nightmares had been. This was far more terrifying than anything he'd ever woken up from.

"Do you deny it, sir?" Tom asked, his voice hard.

"I do not," was George's reply, and Will couldn't bear to look at him as the room reacted with shock. "I sought only to further the interests of my patron and for this I have no regrets."

"Well, your patron doesn't seem very interested in you anymore, *Mr* Iris," Poppy said. "I, however, am extraordinarily interested in your punishment. What shall it be?" he said, looking to Lady Lavender. "Perhaps we should curse him to smell like rotting flesh, or simply—"

"I will decide," Lady Lavender said. "My family has suffered far worse than yours."

Lord Poppy laughed. "I think not. But out of love for you, Lady Lavender, I will accept that we need to discuss the punishment at length." Poppy smiled at Will's father. "You may remain intact for now. But we will be seeing each other again, little Iris. And it will not be a day you will enjoy."

"Claudia, Richard." Lady Lavender beckoned to them and both went to attend her with another bow and curtsy. "Even when the Irises appeared to have taken the city, you never failed in your vigilance. This pleases me. You remain, and have always been, Censor and Master of Ceremonies of Aquae Sulis. And may another Iris never seek to take that from you ever again."

Will focused on the back of Lord Iris's head, silently begging for an intervention. How could he abandon them now, when all they'd done was what he'd asked?

"We are, as ever, your humble servants, Lady Lavender," the Censor said. "Let it be known that the Irises are exiled from Aquae Sulis. All of their properties are now forfeit and compensation to the Papavers will be discussed forthwith. The Irises will never own property here again, nor will they be permitted to attend salons, balls, or any private social event within the boundaries of this city. All of the properties once owned by Charles Rhoeas-Papaver are now the property of Thomas Rhoeas-Papaver, by right of inheritance. And let no man declare it otherwise." She turned to look at Will's father. "You failed, George. Now take your foul family and get out of my city."

Imogen glared at Tom with the purest hate before bursting into tears. She and their mother were guided out of the room by the former duke. Surely, Will thought, the Collectors would be here any moment? Or were they to be spared, seeing as his father hadn't physically hurt anybody? Terrified, Will felt like his feet were rooted to the floor. He didn't know where to look or how to contain the tumult of shame and embarrassment. Feeling someone's eyes upon him, he glanced up to see that Tom's stare was now focused on him.

"With your permission, my lords and ladies, I have a question to ask of a certain Iris before he leaves." After their nods, he asked, "William, where is my sister?"

Lord Poppy's dark eyes fell upon Will. "Yes! Where is my favourite?"

For the first time, no clever rebuff, no witty evasion presented itself. There was nothing but fear. Tom was looking at him with the purest of hate, and Will realised he knew that Cathy had left him.

"Well?" Poppy prompted. "Where is she?"

A strange relief flowed through Will as the constant fear that his shame would be uncovered evaporated. It was no longer needed, after all; that which he had dreaded for so long was happening. Will rallied, pride surging once more. He wasn't willing to go down without speaking a few home truths first. "Cathy has proven that Papaver women are flighty creatures with no sense of loyalty. Just like her mother, she has run away, abandoning her duties to the residents of Londinium and to me." He tried his best to ignore the murmurs fluttering around the room, trapped behind fans, keeping his attention firmly on Tom. "I should have known she'd do this. After all, it's not the first time Cathy's run away, is it? Didn't you spend years hunting her down, Thomas?"

"Don't try to distract us from the fact that you have failed as a husband," Tom said. "I'm sure the residents of Londinium would agree with me when I say a man who cannot maintain his marriage cannot be expected to maintain his rule over a city."

"You attack me for the same failings as your own father?" Will gave a bitter laugh. "It seems that Papaver men have problems with loyalty, too."

"I merely hold you to the same standards as I held my father," Tom said evenly. "He suffered for his failure. I see no reason why it should be any different for you."

"You promised to keep her safe. You said you loved her," Poppy said. "And yet you couldn't keep her happy. Unless there is another reason behind this? Iris?"

Will felt the attention of his patron upon him. "I was told a *different* story," Lord Iris said, glaring. "I have been patient. No more. You are no longer an Iris."

It felt like the air had been sucked out of his lungs, and Will staggered back a step, struggling to breathe. One by one, every person in the room turned their backs on him, all save Nathaniel, who looked like he'd gone into shock. Their eyes met and Nathaniel looked at the doors, pointedly, before walking out of them himself. His brother was telling him to leave. There was no coming back from this.

Lord Poppy narrowed his eyes at him, as if promising something awful, and then even he turned his back, his shoulders shaking with laughter. Only Tom looked at him now. There was no smug self-satisfaction, no sense of gloating, in Tom's expression. He simply appeared to be burning the moment in his memory. He gave the slightest nod, as if all was as it should be, and turned his back too.

Will knew how the Rosas had felt, and it was so much worse than he'd imagined. He felt a sting of tears and then clamped down on his emotions, pushing them down as best he could. There was nothing to be said. Nothing to be done. Will forced his legs to move, one step, then the next, towards the door. He'd allow himself to think later. He'd allow himself to feel later. He left the ballroom, then the Guildhall. Down the steps he went, seeing no one else until he heard Nathaniel call his name.

His family were clustered together down the road. Imogen was hysterical, sobbing in their carriage as their mother tried to console her. His father looked ill, leaning against the carriage as if he were about to keel over. Nathaniel's hand was on his shoulder. He waved Will over.

"You're all coming back to Oxenford with me," he said.

"You're the only Iris duke left," Will said.

"For now." Nathaniel's confidence seemed as strong as ever. "Tom Papaver will regret his actions. And I don't care what was said in there, Will. You're my brother. You'll always be an Iris. Our patron had to say something in there, in front of everyone. I'm sure he'll summon you once it's all over and—"

"Don't bother," Will said. "It's over."

"Will!"

Father straightened up. "This is a blow, Will, but we will rally."

He wasn't convincing. Did he say it for himself or his sons? Will had no idea. "Go back to Oxenford, if that's what you wish," he said. "I won't join you."

"But Will!" Nathaniel gripped his shoulders. "Come on now. You're just shocked, that's all. We'll go back to my castle, have a drink, and plan our revenge. You can't let the likes of bloody Tom Papaver be your downfall!"

"If anyone finds out you're harbouring me, I could be yours," Will said. He pulled himself free, took Nathaniel's hand, and shook it with both of his. "Take care of them."

"But where will you go, Will?"

Will walked away.

"Will! Where will you go?"

His brother's calls went unanswered until they faded behind him. Will knew exactly where he was going. And for the first time in his life, he didn't have to worry about what his family would think of it.

20

Lucy had been gripping Edwin's hand so tightly as Tom saw justice done that her fingers had gone numb. When she turned her back on Will, along with the rest of the room, she couldn't keep the grin from her face. *This was for you, Cathy*, Lucy thought. If only she'd been there, in the ballroom with them, to see it. They'd all agreed it was too much of a risk for her to witness the result.

"You're shaking," Edwin whispered. "Wanna sit down?"

She released his hand and tried to flex some feeling back into her fingers. "I'll be okay."

"Now, let us dance!" called the Censor after the doors closed behind Will, and the musicians struck up the opening chords of a country dance as people found their partners. Lucy was relieved that she could just stay with Edwin as her nerves settled. Being officially in mourning had its advantages.

She turned to look for Tom, wanting to have just a moment with him, but he was in close conference with the Censor and it looked very serious. Lord Poppy stood nearby, watching Tom too. Lord Iris stepped back into Exilium as if nothing of import had happened but moments before. She had expected him to defend his own; that was why she and the Censor had agreed it was important to make sure that Lady Lavender was involved. It seemed they had overprepared.

A glance at the mirror at the far end of the ballroom showed that the way to Exilium had closed. Did Lord Poppy intend to stay? Tom was oblivious of their patron's interest in him. It was only then, with a sharp shiver that ran through her whole body, that Lucy realised this was her chance.

"C'mon, cuz, I think we both need a drink." Edwin extended his arm to her.

"Lord Poppy is right there!" she whispered. "Should I...?"

"Drink first," Edwin said. "I have something I need to talk to you about, now the drama's over."

Simply walking over to the punch table was a horrible experience when her patron was in the same room. It reminded her of a time back home when she was a child and a snake was in her bedroom. Everything else faded, her attention solely on the thing that could kill her. She'd been so paralysed with fear that she couldn't call out for her nanny. It was only when the woman walked in and the snake had rattled its tail that she had started screaming.

Now, as she moved around the women lining up opposite their partners, Lucy felt the same urge to stare at the worst threat in the room, keeping it firmly in her sights so she could dart away if it chose to strike. But the Fae were harder to deal with than rattlesnakes and staring would only increase the threat. So she forced herself to keep her eyes focused on Edwin, who gave her an encouraging wink for her trouble.

Thankfully the dance had cleared the small crowd around the punch. "So what have you been up to for the last few days?" Lucy asked as Edwin filled her a glass. "You weren't there every time I popped back to make sure you were okay."

"I've been spending time with Princess Rani."

"I heard she'd left Albion."

His smile suggested there was far more to the story than she was aware of. "That's what she wanted everyone to think. She had a few...delicate matters to attend to first, and I managed to catch up with her just before she left. I cut a deal. You are looking at the man who has single-handedly negotiated a preferential trade agreement with the newly independent Rajkot Court, cutting Albion out altogether. It's fair, it's going to make us more money, and it's going to safeguard Rajkot's income. Those guys have got some difficult times ahead."

"I can't believe we haven't heard any gossip about their declaration."

Edwin shrugged. "She wasn't impressed with Cathy. She said that the Duchess was more beautiful than she expected, but far less quick-witted than she'd been led to believe."

That sounded like the opposite of her sister-in-law. Lucy wondered why Cathy hadn't said anything to her about it. Maybe it was so close to when she left Will, she'd forgotten. "Have the Patroons given a formal response?"

"Not yet. She's leaving today, before they decide to use her as ammunition against her parents. I like her. A lot. I was thinking about maybe going out there for a visit. To…make sure all the contracts are sorted out. Ya know."

She nodded. She knew, all right. "Just don't let Oliver Peonia know your intentions. He was making eyes at her at the masked ball."

"I ain't worried about that guy. Look, this trade deal…do you think that would impress *him*?" Edwin asked with the slightest tilt of his head towards Poppy.

"It impresses me, but I don't think the Fae care about things like international trade agreements," Lucy replied. "I have to try something, though, Edwin; this might be my only chance."

Lucy watched her patron laughing at one of the Buttercups. She hadn't given up her home, her freedom, just to stand here quivering. Tom was still in deep conversation with the Censor, now joined by his uncle. Now was as good a time as ever.

Right after a glass of punch. Her mouth was horribly dry and she needed a moment to collect herself.

She knew that politics would bore Lord Poppy unless it involved dramatic showdowns like the one that had just happened, and only when it directly involved his family. She knew Edwin would say the wrong thing and get turned into a frog. She was likely to do the same herself. What could she say that would even get his attention?

"Ahhh! Thomas's teeny tiny wife! There you are!"

She almost dropped the punch glass, sending half of the contents sloshing back into the bowl. She dumped it on the table, hastily wiped her wet fingertips on the tablecloth, and turned to face her patron. He stood about a metre away, cane held out at an elegant angle. She took in the white breeches and open-necked shirt worn without cravat, the blood-red frock coat and his long black hair, disturbed by how beautiful he was, before she dropped into a curtsy.

"I can't imagine why," he began, moving towards her, "but I had the most profound impression you wished to speak to me."

Lucy straightened, reminding herself not to simper or fawn or giggle or do any of the things that the majority of the women here would. Cathy was his favourite, so she was the better role model. With a nod, she said, "I do indeed, Lord Poppy." When he glanced away, already losing interest, she added, "I have a secret I thought you would like to know." He looked back, head tilted like a bird who'd spotted a worm. "Perhaps we could sit at the table over there, away from the crowds?"

He inclined his head and waved a hand for her to lead the way. As Lucy crossed the room, Lord Poppy looked in the other direction and Edwin held up his fingers, crossed.

Poppy raced ahead of her at the last moment, pulling one of the chairs away from the table and gesturing for her to sit in it with exaggerated movements, as if he were performing a mime study of an eager gentleman. When she sat, he teased out a lock of her hair from its arrangement and let it play through his fingers. "Your hair is the colour of sunlight on water," he sighed. "Perhaps I could keep it."

Breathe, breathe! "Don't you want to hear my secret?"

"Oh yes!" With a twirl of his cane, he sat in the seat next to hers. "I'm listening."

"My family didn't marry me to Thomas for the reason his family thought at the time," she said, and was gratified to see him lean closer. "It was because I had a secret mission to achieve. One that involves you, my Lord."

"I thought you were married into the Rhoeas line because they needed the money. That's what the Patroon told me. Are you saying he's a liar?"

"He is merely misinformed, my Lord." Lucy tried to swallow, but her mouth was so dry her tongue stuck to the roof of her mouth. "I came here to persuade you to support a declaration of independence that my family, and others in America, would like to make, should you support us."

Poppy wrinkled his nose. "Independence?"

"From the Patroons of Albion." Poppy looked away, evidently seeking something more interesting. "The drama this evening only happened because of my actions, Lord Poppy. I alerted the Censor and Master of Ceremonies to the coup and I formulated the plan to obtain the proof of the theft of my husband's inheritance, and for the Irises to be shamed here." Poppy looked back at her, mildly interested once more. "I demonstrated initiative and cunning in regaining what was rightfully ours and I also orchestrated the defeat of the Irises." She paused for breath, remembering what her mother told her at her coming of age. *Honey, if you don't ask, you don't get.* "I would like to think my actions demonstrate how much my people could achieve if we were freed from the yoke of Albion rule. If you were to declare us free, then…"

Lord Poppy sighed. "If I didn't support this, what would you do?"

I'd fucking do it anyway, was her first thought, but it wasn't one to be voiced to her patron. But she couldn't lie. He would know. "I would find that very difficult, my Lord. I feel most passionately about this."

He seemed interested again. "How passionately?"

This was it, the thing she feared the most. The moment of self-sacrifice she had always known would come. "I would be willing to…to go to extraordinary lengths to earn your support for our freedom, my Lord."

"Would you be willing to have your soul forged into a little diamond pin I could wear on my cravat?"

Lucy clenched her teeth, fighting down the little squeak that threatened to emerge from her throat. Then she thought of Cathy, of that moment she must have had with Poppy that made her his favourite. Surely Cathy wouldn't have given in to his outlandish demands. She didn't seem the type. Not the woman who asked to go to university for her coming of age. Lucy fixed her most charming smile in place and leaned forwards slightly. "I think that would be a dreadful waste of my soul, my Lord."

He laughed, eliciting a moment of pure triumph within her. "Perhaps it would," he said. "You have fifteen minutes to impress me. If you succeed, I will tell the Patroon to release his control of your family's affairs. If you *delight* me, I will persuade the Court to say the same to their Patroons. Of course, if you fail, I will put your soul to better use. Now fly, little golden bird. Time is against you!"

She stood, curtsied, and then hurried over to Edwin. "I've got fifteen minutes to impress him."

"Holy shit." Edwin looked around the ballroom, as if inspiration could leap out from anywhere. "Incoming," he whispered.

"Lucy," Tom said behind her. She turned to see him standing there with flushed cheeks, looking a strange mixture of shocked and excited. "I may have accidentally become the Duke of Londinium."

"Huh?"

"The Censor said that Aquae Sulis will back me, and my uncle said that after seeing what I just did, the Londinium residents here tonight will be grateful to me, and…are you all right?"

It was the worst timing, but she managed an encouraging smile. "I'm fine. Darling. Do you want to be Duke?"

"I don't know. It all seems rather sudden. What do you think about it? Would you like to be Duchess?"

I'd like to still be alive in twenty minutes, she thought. "I think that making a decision this important after everything that's happened this evening isn't a good idea. How about we get through the rest of this ball, go home, and talk it over after a good night's sleep?"

Tom smiled. "You're right. Of course." He took her hand, kissed it. "That level-headedness would make you an excellent Duchess." *You don't know the half of it,* she thought.

"Thomas?" The Master of Ceremonies rested a hand on his shoulder. "Come and speak to Mr Digitalis. He's very interested in becoming Marquis of Londinium once more. You'll be needing one of those, after all."

"But Uncle, I'm in mourning, I can't—"

Lavandula patted his shoulder. "Come on, dear boy, your father wouldn't mind. And while your filial loyalty is admirable, there's nothing noble about a power vacuum."

"Forgive me, dear," Tom said, kissing her hand once more before allowing his uncle to steer him across the room.

Lucy's gaze followed him until Lord Poppy stepped into her line of sight, looking pointedly at a pocket watch before giving her a wicked grin. She smiled and spun around to face Edwin. "Okay, we need to brainstorm."

They stood there in silence as the next dance began. "I'm guessin' that me doing that dance that got me thrown out of the New Orleans ball three years ago wouldn't cut it," Edwin said.

"Cathy ran away, then when she was found, Poppy decided she was his favourite," Lucy said. "She's like the opposite of what Society wants women to be like. And Poppy is contrary and mercurial. Maybe if we bucked a trend somehow...did something that Society would disapprove of."

"Cuz, I got a million ways I could upset people here. Just watch me."

She put a hand on his arm. "No, it has to be more than showing them up. It has to be something...something shocking but clever too."

That moment, her eyes fell upon a corner of a grey pamphlet, hidden underneath Cecilia Peonia's gloves and reticule. It was one of Cathy's, the very same as the one Tom had thrown onto the fire when he'd found it in their house!

"I've got an idea. Let's read something out that will really upset some people."

"Let me do it," Edwin said. "I know you want this, but if you do it, Tom will never forgive you."

"This is more important than Tom! We've been fighting for this for so long!"

"Cuz, I know we always said you'd come home when you did this, but I've seen the way you look at him. What if you want to stay?"

Lucy bit her lip.

"And I am definitely going home after this, so if I rock the boat, it's no big deal. It keeps your options open."

He was right; she did care about Tom and how he would be affected. While she was pretty certain he wouldn't burn the pamphlet if he found it now, he would lose the chance to be Duke if she did as she planned. "All right. Meet me out in the corridor in five minutes."

Cecilia Peonia was so busy dividing her time between giving the Censor the evil eye and watching a particularly handsome servant that she didn't notice Lucy sliding the pamphlet from its hiding place to be folded and held beneath her fan. Once it was hers, Lucy went down to the lobby to speak to the messenger boy from the Emporium of Things in Between and Besides, ordering the glamour she needed, promising him a healthy tip if he could bring it back to her within five minutes. With only seven minutes left to go before tiepin time, the boy returned, flushed and out of breath, to give her a small wooden box.

She raced back up the stairs, collected Edwin, went with him to the narrow staircase leading up to the minstrel's gallery, and cast the glamour on him.

"What the f—" he started, but she shoved the pamphlet into his hands.

"Go up to the gallery. This dance is about to finish. When the music stops, step out in front of the musicians and read this as loud as you can."

He flipped through the pages. "Holy sh—"

"Go!"

She dashed over to the ballroom doors, paused, composed herself, and then entered. Lord Poppy was standing at the back of the room, twisting his cane as he watched the dancers, only to stop and smile as she approached. "I am, as yet, unimpressed," he sighed.

"Lord Poppy, at the end of this dance, I have arranged something that will make at least one lady faint, at least one gentleman choke on his punch, and several women will hide their faces behind their fans. It will be the talk of Aquae Sulis—no, of Albion—for weeks to come." She glanced up at the gallery. "And, I hope it will entertain as well as impress you, my Lord."

The last chords played out and the dancers bowed and curtsied as Lucy held her breath. Then Edwin stepped out in front of the musicians, appearing to be dressed in a flowing red ball gown, complete with puffed sleeves and gold trim.

"Ladies of Nether Society!" Edwin called out in his deep voice. "There is more to life than what we are told to believe. There is more to life than looking beautiful and dancing nicely. There is more to life than being someone to marry off for the profit of one's family."

As he read the first lines of the pamphlet, both Lucy and Lord Poppy looked at the Censor, whose mouth had fallen open as she stared up at the gallery, her hands in the air as if she were being held at gunpoint.

"There is more to life than bearing children for a man you did not choose to marry. There is more to life than being someone's property and devoting yourself to supporting your husband's ambition."

One of the Wisteria women fainted and one of the Buttercups swayed unsteadily too, but Lucy didn't believe the woman was doing anything else than trying to mask her delight, having seen the grin that had been on her face just beforehand. Cecilia Peonia and a couple of her friends clustered together, giggling behind their fans as someone else dropped their glass. As if jolted out of her shock, the Censor lurched forwards, striding towards to the door. Lord Poppy caught up with her in a few steps and put a hand on her shoulder. "No, Lady Censor," he said. "I would very much like to listen to what he has to say."

"You are being kept in ignorance by the men who control Society and the women who support them," Edwin read. "We are taught how to dance, how to play instruments, how to speak dead languages, how to run a household and how to keep oiling the cruel wheels of this Society in which we are trapped for the benefit of men. We are not taught about how our own bodies function, nor that we can control when we conceive a child, nor the changes that have taken place for women in Mundanus.

"You have the right to know more.

"You have the right to *be* more."

Edwin flipped the page, his eyes widened at the diagram of female reproductive organs, and then he flipped past that to start reading from the next. "Life is very different in Mundanus—but the gentlemen of Nether Society don't want us to know how different it is! In Mundanus, women have more choices about how to live their life than you might imagine.

"Women are no longer the property of their husbands, have the right to inherit property, other assets and money, rather than it being passed straight to the husband. Women have the right to own property and to an education equal to that given to men."

Lucy watched the women of the room starting to really listen, instead of focusing on how they should be seen to react, as more rights were read.

"Women have the right to enjoy sexual intercourse for the sake of pleasure, without fearing pregnancy."

Another Wisteria fainted at the sound of the words "sexual intercourse" while Oliver Peonia's cheeks looked hot enough to fry eggs upon them. All the while, the Censor stood, Lord Poppy's hand on her shoulder, forced to listen to the sentiments she so clearly disagreed with.

"As a lady of Nether Society YOU HAVE NONE OF THESE RIGHTS!" Edwin boomed across the ballroom. "Furthermore, in Mundanus, men are not permitted to beat their wives, nor have sexual intercourse without the consent of their wives. They are not permitted to imprison their wives, nor restrict her freedom of movement in any way. If a woman wishes to divorce, she can." Edwin lowered the pamphlet, looking down on the shocked guests. "Why do *you* not have the same rights, ladies of Albion?"

In the silence, Lucy looked over at Tom, who looked shocked, but not angry. As if he could feel her gaze, his eyes dropped to her, the slightest questioning frown on his face. He didn't seem like a man incensed by what was happening. To think, only weeks before, he'd burnt a copy of those words in their house. Perhaps he really had changed.

Edwin gave an elaborate bow, and seeing his performance was over, everyone looked expectantly at the Censor. Lord Poppy was whispering something in her ear, then came back towards Lucy, grinning merrily. The Censor gave a false laugh. "Oh! Our colonial cousins are so witty! How amusing!" She clapped her hands at the musicians. "Play something for us to dance to!" she snapped at them as Edwin left the gallery.

Lord Poppy scooped up Lucy's hand and kissed it. "I enjoyed that. It reminded me of my favourite. And it made the Censor tremble. The head of the Californicas will answer to me directly. The Patroon is very boring, after all. And I will speak to the rest of the Court. Perhaps the Colonies are more interesting than we've been led to believe…" When Lady Lavender approached, Poppy released Lucy's hand to skip over to her. "Lady Lavender! I've decided that Colonies are so very unfashionable. Independence is where the excitement lies. After all, my favourite has shed her awful husband and struck out without him. Why can't our pets do the same further afield?"

Lucy left Poppy to his conversation, choosing instead to rescue Edwin from the Censor. "I'll take him home straight away, Lady Censor," she said, stifling a laugh as Edwin stood there at the bottom of the stairs in the absurd gown. "Too much punch, perhaps."

The Censor gave them both a hard stare and then went back into the ballroom. Lucy threw her arms around Edwin. "We did it! It worked! We're free of the Patroon and I'm not a tiepin!"

Edwin picked her up and spun her around. "Awesome! Mission accomplished, cuz! Now all you need to do is decide whether you want to come home."

"Lucy?" Tom was at the doorway to the ballroom.

Edwin put her down and straightened his dress. "I'll get back to you on that," Lucy whispered to him. "Are you angry, Tom?"

He shook his head. "No, but the Censor is. Time to go, I think. That's quite enough drama for one evening." He looked at Edwin. "The red suits you, sir," he said, po-faced, and Edwin's laugh echoed up the gallery's stairwell.

"And progressive thinking suits you, sir," Edwin said. "Let's go find something decent to drink."

21

Once the initial shock had passed, Will felt a clarity he hadn't experienced for a very long time. Not since his Grand Tour, in fact, when decisions were narrowed down to where he and Oli were going to eat that evening or which town they would visit next. Now the constant, nebulous stress of being Duke had gone, and with it the ache in his back and the tension in his stomach that he hadn't realised had become permanent. Now that everything had been taken from him, his options were so narrow, so limited, he felt almost euphoric.

Leaving his family behind in the Nether, he'd stepped through to mundane Bath to find it was a bitterly cold January evening. The pavements glistened with newly fallen rain and he realised he'd left his cape and top hat at the Guildhall cloakroom. He'd look a fool in them here, though—the white tie and tail coat were bad enough.

"Gettin' married, mate?" some lout yelled on the way into a pub. Will ignored him, but it brought home the precarious state of affairs. If he didn't act swiftly his newfound freedom could rapidly become starvation.

Using an emergency Charm he'd kept on his person since the day Rupert caught him and put him in that box, he used a nearby doorway to disguise a Way that opened directly to his study in Londinium. He needed money, Charms, as much as he could grab before the news from Aquae Sulis filtered to his household. It was a wonder the Collectors hadn't been called on his family, and the thought made him pause. His father's crime was not dissimilar to that of the Rosas—it could be considered worse, in fact. So why the leniency? Did the Arbiter not feel the local Sorcerer should be involved, whoever that was now?

But it wasn't the time to speculate about such things. He grabbed a large briefcase from the cupboard in the corner, pulled out the extraneous dividers inside, and emptied the contents of his desk drawers into it. He opened the safe and removed all of the cash, gold, and the details of the various mundane bank accounts in which he had mercifully squirrelled away money earned from his diverse business interests. All of those were established on his Grand Tour and he was thankful he'd had the wherewithal to think of such things while Oli chastised him for being dull.

He wouldn't need his white tie anymore, so, keeping the case with him should he need to flee, he left the study and ran up the stairs, hoping the staff wouldn't realise he'd come home. He didn't count on his valet being in his dressing room, packing away newly starched shirts.

"Oh! Forgive me, your Grace, I thought you'd still be at the ball."

"Change of plan," Will said. "Bring me two suitcases, would you? Where are my mundane clothes from the honeymoon?"

"Packed away in the chest in the corner, sir. I hadn't anticipated your needing them."

Will freed himself of his bowtie. "I do now. Pull out a pair of jeans and a shirt and jumper for me, will you, then get the cases."

His valet went over to the chest. "Are you planning a trip to Mundanus, sir?" At Will's nod, he said, "May I suggest packing the stout walking boots, the wellingtons and the cashmere coat, sir? It's rather cold there at the moment."

"Yes, pack them all, please."

While his man was busy, Will changed as quickly as he could, keeping an eye on the briefcase all the while. He needed to eat, and while things still seemed normal, he'd chance his arm at one last meal in this house before…

It suddenly hit him, like a knee to his stomach, and he sat down heavily. This house, the library he had made to make Cathy smile, was no longer his. There would be no more visits to the Tower, no sense of pride as he entered, everyone bowing before him. It was all over. The nursery wing would never be filled with Sophia's laughter again and would never shelter his own children. Everything he'd strived for, everything he'd done despicable things to gain and to keep, was for nought.

A knock on the door distracted him from the lump in his throat. "Yes?" he said without thinking, and then wondered if he should just open a Way and bolt right now.

Morgan entered. "Your Grace, I'm sorry to disturb you, but I understand you are taking a trip into Mundanus?" When Will confirmed it, Morgan paused as if searching for the correct words. "Your Grace, I wouldn't normally concern you with domestic matters, but the steward and I are at a loss. It's regarding the Agency. They haven't responded to several requests we've made over the past few days. I made discreet enquiries at other households with whom I am acquainted and it's the same for them. I don't suppose anyone has contacted you, or…"

"No, they haven't," Will said. Had the Agency been taken from him too? No, surely not; no one knew he controlled it. There was a time when he would have followed it up instantly, but now he couldn't care less about what was going on. None of it mattered any more. He had the briefest thought about whether he could withdraw to the Agency and try and exploit the information there to somehow claw back his status—but without the support of his patron, it was futile. He wasn't even an Iris anymore.

All that mattered was getting Sophia back and the only way he could do that now would be to find Lord Iris's lost love in the hope he would return Sophia as a reward. Will rested his elbows on his knees, considering what the Princess had told him. She was still alive, but she must have been taken a long time ago, because according to his father, Lord Iris had been as cold and difficult to please for as long as he and *his* father could remember. That meant she had to be hidden in the Nether. The princess had said this mystery woman was with one of Lord Iris's mortal enemies. The Nether aspect ruled out Lord Iron, and if it had been one of the Fae, he was certain that someone as calculating and ruthless as Iris would have found her by now.

That left the Sorcerers, enemies of the Fae and resident in the Nether too. Or perhaps an Arbiter. No, the Prince of the Fae wouldn't hide someone with a mere Arbiter. A Sorcerer, then. But which one?

"Your Grace?"

Will jolted, having forgotten Morgan was still there. Shouldn't he tell him what had happened? After all, they were all unemployed, strictly speaking. He couldn't bring himself to say the words, though, stoppered up as they were behind a thick plug of shame. "I'll send a letter on my return. It's not urgent, is it?"

"Not yet, your Grace. How long will you be away?"

"A few weeks, most likely," Will lied.

"And…forgive me, your Grace, I know it's a sensitive matter, but will the Duchess be returning in the foreseeable future?"

Will sighed. "I think not, Morgan. Tell the staff they can take a short holiday, if they wish. Yourself included."

"Thank you, sir. I hope you have an enjoyable trip. Will you require the carriage?"

After a shake of the head, Will was left alone once more. Why would a Sorcerer keep someone beloved by the Fae? Stupid question. The Sorcerer in question must hate Lord Iris, and would have leapt at the chance to torment a Fae. But which one was it?

Then Will remembered the comment his father had made about the time when the Sorcerer of Wessex had had a falling out with Lord Iris and how the family's position in the city had become precarious as a result. The Lavandulas had protected them. Could that have been part of an ongoing feud between that Sorcerer and his patron? His heart sank. *Former* patron.

He'd return to Bath; an Arbiter was definitely in the city, as Tom had mentioned one being involved in the earlier catastrophe. The Lavandulas had banned Irises from Aquae Sulis, not the mundane reflection—and besides, he was no longer of the family. He could go where he liked. Finding the Arbiter would lead him to the

Sorcerer, and with any luck, to the woman hidden from Lord Iris all these years.

By the time Will got back to Bath and checked into the Gainsborough Hotel, he had a plan. What better way to find an Arbiter than to lay a trap in Mundanus? Once he had broken a luck egg over his head, showered, and ensured that his most valuable belongings were in the safe, he went out to reacquaint himself with the mundane city. He hadn't realised how much he missed the feel of fresh air and the bustle of city life.

He made his way down the street between Jacob's Coffee House and the Pump Rooms, heading for a crowd gathered to watch a fire-eater. Strange to think the ball was still happening in the reflection of the Guildhall a mere street away. He put that from his mind as he unstoppered the bottle he'd brought with him and surreptitiously shook the contents onto people he passed a few drops at a time. Then he dropped the bottle into a nearby bin, including the handkerchief he'd wrapped around it to protect his glove, then stepped into the nearby coffee house.

"We're closing in half an hour," said the young man behind the counter. "But you're still welcome to order."

Will sat by the window of the first-floor room with a hot chocolate, watching the crowd below as the magic took effect. It was a mixture of two separate Charms that as far as he knew wouldn't last more than an hour and would be relatively harmless. The first was a very mild curse to have a bout of hiccups. He'd procured it from Tate, having discovered from an Agency file that one of the Buttercups had a horror of them and he wanted something at hand just in case he became a problem at Court. The other he'd bought for Sophia but hadn't had a chance to give her. Now its effect unfolded below.

Dozens of sparkling butterflies, nothing but glamoured puffs of breath, were popping out of people's mouths with each hiccup. He chuckled at the sight of children trying to catch them, just as he'd hoped Sophia would. There was a mixture of confusion, awe, and delight amongst the rest of the mundanes, with some looking quite frightened.

Will shifted his attention to the edge of the crowd as others arrived, drawn by the commotion. Most of the new arrivals watched as if they were observing a piece of street theatre, a few even applauding and fishing coins from purses, looking for somewhere to drop them. One enterprising fellow took off his hat and began collecting the money, passing it off as his work. Will couldn't help but admire his quick thinking.

Then he saw a man approaching who, even from the warmth and safety of the coffee shop, made a shiver travel down Will's back. He was wearing a hat and coat like everyone else, but the way he was observing the crowd, with a deadpan expression on his ugly face, made him leap out to Will.

The Arbiter was holding a mobile phone and moving around the edge of the crowd, heading straight for the bin in which Will had disposed of the bottle. Will watched him pause beside it, then switch the phone for a torch, which he shone inside. He pulled out the bottle and handkerchief and moved a little way away. Will couldn't see what the Arbiter pulled out of his pocket, but he held it against the bottle for a few moments and then seemed to read something off it.

Will watched the Arbiter patrol around the crowd, no doubt looking for the perpetrator. He didn't intervene. Did he know how harmless it was? Did he just care about finding the one responsible? Either way, the man did nothing to engage with the people affected.

Now was his chance. The plan was simple: follow the Arbiter until he went back to his headquarters and, hopefully, where the Sorcerer lived. He had a memory of being told the Sorcerer had changed, but it was of no matter. He could only hope Iris's lost love would still be there, if he'd guessed the right jailer. Better to act, rather than worry, even when it was the flimsiest of plans.

"We're closing now, sorry," said the man from downstairs. Will put his coat back on, turned the collar up, and stepped outside.

It was easy to move closer to the Arbiter unnoticed. All Will had to do was pretend to be watching the spectacle. The Arbiter loitered for another half an hour or so, then left just as a TV news camera crew were arriving. Will took just as much care not to be noticed by them either.

Following the Arbiter without being seen was fairly easy; the man didn't seem to be concerned about anyone tailing him. Will was still cautious, and feared that to a casual onlooker it would be obvious. There was no way for him to hide it, so he just kept vigilant for any sign the Arbiter was about to turn around.

Will was most concerned that he'd get in a car and drive off, but he kept limping along with his walking stick, right across the centre until he reached a hotel. It was one Will had almost gone to stay in himself.

Why a mundane hotel? Perhaps this was the anchor property for the Sorcerer's house, or the place the Arbiters lived. Then another possibility popped into his mind. Could Cathy be staying there? It could be the same Arbiter with whom she'd left Lancaster House. He'd assumed she was still with Lord Iron, but if she'd learned of her father's death, she could have come to Bath to help Tom with the funeral arrangements, and to grieve with him. That he could have stumbled across a hotel in which she was staying was a long shot, but she wouldn't have felt safe in any property reflected into the Nether or associated with her birth family. Where else could she stay in Bath?

He had to see if it was her. He followed the Arbiter in, watched him enter an empty lift, and waited to see which floor it stopped at from the numbers lit above the doors. When he saw it was only the next floor up, Will raced up the stairs two at a time. Panting, he emerged cautiously from the stairwell to catch sight of the Arbiter knocking on the door of a room down the hallway. When he saw the Arbiter enter he crept to the same door, still catching his breath, and pressed his ear to it.

He could hear the murmur of voices, one male, one female, and his heart splashed against his chest. Was that Cathy? It was hard

EMMA NEWMAN

to tell when it was so faint. It certainly wasn't a Way to a Nether property, though.

Now it was a choice between speaking to the woman in that room—surely it was Cathy; who else would an Arbiter be visiting in a hotel room in Bath?—or following him once he left. Of course, the room could contain a Way through to the Sorcerer's house, but it seemed unlikely.

He decided to wait until the Arbiter left and then confront the occupant. If she wasn't Cathy, he might still learn something he could use against the Arbiter, some leverage that could make the Arbiter tell him if the Sorcerer had someone hidden away from Iris.

Back in the stairwell, Will tried to work out what he'd say if it was Cathy. Now Lord Iris was no longer interested in him, and by extension, a child of their making, the pressure was off. He could let her go.

The thought sat uncomfortably within him. At first he thought it was simply a matter of being dissatisfied with things left unsaid. Apologies unmade. Then he wondered if it was his pride; he hated the thought of her out there, thinking him a monster without hearing his side of it all. He wanted to tell her how much he regretted his actions—not just what he'd done to her, but to all the people he'd hurt—and how he intended to get Sophia back and lead a quiet life away from such foul social engines that made men monstrous. He wanted her to know he had woken up to what he'd done. He could only hope it wasn't too late and that she'd forgive him.

Then he remembered that kiss in his study, when she'd been filled with that fire of hers and he had wanted her so badly. He pushed away the memory of what came after—the former Dame Iris's horrific death—choosing instead to remember the feel of Cathy pressed against him. The need to possess her resurfaced, to somehow capture that fire, but not with magic and tricks. With love.

The lift bell rang and when he peeped back into the hallway he saw the Arbiter stepping into the lift, alone, only now carrying a suitcase. He waited until it had closed again and was well on its way before stepping back into the corridor and moving to the room the Arbiter had visited. In front of the door, he hesitated, trying to work out how to open the conversation. He knocked with the same pattern that the Arbiter had, confident that once he saw her, he'd know what to say.

The door opened right away, a blonde woman he'd never seen before, saying, "Did you forget something, M—" She frowned at him. There was something familiar about the set of her lips, the shape of her cheekbones, even though Will was certain they'd never met. "Oh. I thought you were someone else," she said with an uncertain smile. "I think you have the wrong room."

Will ran a hand through his hair, crushed by the fact that she wasn't Cathy—and that he'd just lost the Arbiter. His judgement was clearly impaired when it came to his wife. "I was hoping to find someone else here," he said. "This may sound dreadfully…forward, but are you sharing this room with another lady? With brown hair?"

She was staring at his hand, then his hair, her eyes darkening as they dilated. "No. Who are you? You…you seem familiar."

"My name is William," he said. "May I come in? Or, if you'd be more comfortable, perhaps we could continue this conversation downstairs in the lobby."

She stepped back, waving him in, still staring as she closed the door. She rested her hand on her stomach, as if trying to steady her nerves. "I'm not in the habit of letting strangers into my room, William, but I am almost certain I know you. Or…perhaps a relative of yours."

Will appreciated how striking she was, tall, elegant, and poised, even in her confusion. He looked at her hand, at the ever so slightly crooked index finger, and with a start, he realised Imogen had exactly the same-shaped hands. "My God, I believe you're right." The sense of familiarity wasn't born from having met her before; it was the simple instinct that they were of the same family. The features that marked his family as different from the Rosas and the Papavers were there in her face too. He dared not say it, but he would have wagered a small fortune that she was either an ancestor of his or the product of a secret branch of the family. The former was far more likely, but why hadn't he met her before? He reached for her hand, which she gave him. He held it gently, laying her fingers over his palm. "My sister has exactly the same-shaped fingers as yours. As does my grandmother." A strange mixture of relief and uncertainty played across her face. "Who are you, dear lady?"

"I only know my name," she said with a sigh. "Petra. Does that mean anything to you?"

Will shook his head. "I'm afraid not. Only your name? Have you lost your memory?"

"I've lost everything. But this is a strange conversation to have with someone I've only just met. And yet…there is something about you…" She closed the distance between them and for a moment Will thought she intended to kiss his forehead. Instead, she merely sniffed his hair. "You smell of…magic!"

He released her hand. This was no mere mundane; she recognised the scent of the luck egg! Could this be the woman Lord Iris had lost? The slightly crooked finger—something his sister and grandmother took great pains to keep secret—and the way her features reminded him of them made him suspect she was a relative at least. Perhaps, when the Sorcerer who kept her died, she'd escaped with the Arbiter's help, and then he'd unwittingly led him to his prize. "This is going to sound like a rather strange question, but have you recently been a prisoner of a Sorcerer?"

Her eyes, round with surprise, filled with tears. "Yes! Well…it didn't feel like I was a prisoner. I worked for him. I was his librarian. But there was a spell on me, and it was broken after he died. And now I have no idea where I came from nor how I came to be in his service. It's…absolutely awful. But how did you know? Do you know who I am?"

"I have a suspicion," Will said. "I've been looking for you, in the hope that returning you to the one who loves you would…make things better. For all of us. I thought it likely that the woman I sought was kept with a Sorcerer, and probably the one who lived in Bath. I simply didn't expect to come across you this way. I thought you'd still be in the Nether."

"I was, for years and years...centuries. But while the spell was intact, I didn't question it. I...just wanted to please the Sorcerer, and take care of him." She pulled her hand back, wrapping her arms about herself as if suddenly cold. "I have no idea how Ekstrand could bear someone clouded with Fae magic to be in his employ, but that's the truth. He was too skilled to be ignorant. Either he knew and was glad to benefit from my addled state, or he knew and didn't care. Either way...I'm lost. I've been trying so hard to find something of what I was before, but it's like I'm...empty. Just a shell." She paused. "Wait. Returning me to someone who loves me? That's what you said, isn't it? Who do you think I am?"

His heart was racing to keep up with his thoughts. It was hard to think it all through rationally, he was so excited, but it all seemed to fit. He tried to regain some clarity of thought. It was a dangerous conclusion to leap to; if he presented her to Iris and she wasn't the one he loved, he could take out his wrath on her. On them both.

"I think you could be Lord Iris's love. I think you might have been taken from him, by the Prince of the Fae, and hidden somewhere my patron couldn't find you."

He'd hoped for some flash of recognition, but there was none. "Can you take me to him?"

Will wanted to, but he had to be certain it was her. "I need to be sure I'm right. Could I take a lock of your hair? If it is you, he'll know, just from that."

She went to a chest of drawers and for the first time, Will took in the nice, but fundamentally impersonal, hotel room. *How awful to lose oneself*, he thought. He would much rather be disowned and left intact than be put into this twilight state she suffered. What could possibly have made the Prince do something so terrible?

Newly armed with scissors, she cut a lock of her hair, wrapped it in a tissue, and handed it to him. "I'm so grateful. Who were you hoping to find here? Perhaps I can help you in return."

"My wife. No one you would know. I'll be back as soon as I can with the answers we need, but it may be a few hours, perhaps even a day."

She opened the door for him. "I look forward to seeing you again, William. And thank you. You're very kind."

•••

"Lord Iron. It's time."

Sam looked up from the arrowhead, resting his hammer on the anvil as he wiped the sweat from his forehead. Beatrice was standing at the doorway to his forge, dressed only in her white dress, her silk slippers sodden and covered in mud. "Forget your wellies?"

She looked down at her feet as if they belonged to someone else, disinterested. "You need to go to the forge near Bath. Tell none of your people. Take nothing modern with you. No phone, no wristwatch. Wear no metal. Once you are there, I will give you your instructions."

He didn't like the way she treated him as if he were an employee. "I was waiting for Cathy to get back. Can't I—"

"No. You must leave now. And tell no one where you are going. It reduces risk of interference. Anything else would be a betrayal of my trust." The slightest crease appeared in her brow as she studied his inaction. "Please?"

With a sigh, he put the hammer into its usual place where it hung on the wall and began to take his apron off. "So what do I do when I get there? Just wait?"

When he turned to see why she hadn't answered, Beatrice had already gone. Sam went to the door and looked out over the darkening meadow but she was nowhere to be seen. "Bloody Sorcerers," he muttered, and set off for the house.

22

Back in his hotel room, Will made sure the door was locked before he went into the bathroom and cast the Charm on the mirror to open a Way to Exilium. He had to climb onto the sink and then stoop to step through, which was horribly undignified.

When he straightened up on the other side of the mirror, the green fields and blue sky that he'd seen through the glass were no longer ahead. Instead, the white stone of the royal palace stretched up before him, blocking everything else out of his sight. He staggered back a couple of paces, momentarily confused, before remembering the Princess and her insistence that he pay a forfeit after he had won their game.

He swore at his own forgetfulness. He'd been so thrilled to finally have something to take to Lord Iris to bargain for Sophia's return that he'd forgotten everything else. What did she say he had to do? Sneak into the palace and reach her without being seen by the Prince. That was it. And perhaps something awful involving a kiss.

The oak doors that he stood in front of now were framed by beautifully carved stone. It had the same splendour as the building he and Cathy had been married in, simply scaled up. It was so big he couldn't see all of it from where he stood. Unprepared, he had no idea how he'd find the Princess in there with no Charms or artefacts that could help.

The only thing he could be certain of was that standing there, despairing, was the most direct route to failure. There were no guards outside, nor patrolling the palace perimeter as far as he could see, so he pushed experimentally on one of the doors. To his surprise, it opened.

The cool interior felt like one of the many impressive cathedrals he'd visited on his Grand Tour. The high vaulted ceiling was painted with a blue background and gold stars, not unlike several of the medieval buildings he'd seen in Mundanus, but this one was lit by what looked like hundreds of sprites flitting about. In the Nether they were always trapped in globes of glass and fixed to walls or lamps. It was strange to see them flying free. Worried that one would spot him and cause a spectacle, Will darted behind one of the many stone columns that stretched up from the entrance hall floor. It was carved stone, like everything else he could see, a stylised design of oak leaves and branches weaving in and out of one another, each of the leaves a vibrant green. Unlike many of the comparable mundane buildings he'd seen, it was riotously colourful everywhere he looked.

Quiet, and seemingly empty of people or Fae, it was eerie, rather than a bustling centre of rulership he'd assumed it would be. The Fae palace felt more like a tomb.

There had to be dozens of rooms and he daren't ask any of the sprites for help in case they alerted the Prince to his presence. The ridiculous forfeit was getting in the way of what he needed to do, so he picked a nearby archway that was straight ahead and went through it, finding himself in a long corridor with an arched doorway leading off it on both sides, taking him right into the heart of the palace.

Pressing his ear against the door on the right, he heard the faint sound of a harp being played and risked opening the door just far enough for him to peep inside. The room had a high ceiling and windows opposite that looked out on the countryside. The back wall that he was closest to was covered by a huge tapestry showing a party with hundreds of revellers. He was just about to risk peeping round the door to see the rest of the room when a movement made him freeze.

The figures in the tapestry were moving to new positions, as if the party were being played out in the threads. Breathing out in relief, he looked round the door to see a very long room that seemed to stretch the length of the corridor with a small dais at the far end.

A woman was seated there, playing the harp, dressed in a gown that looked like it was made of oak leaves. One of her legs was visible where the dress had slipped and he saw a sparkling band around her ankle.

There was no one else in the room. Who was she playing for? It was a beautiful melody, but sad, especially coupled with her solitude. He knew better than to approach a slave, having heard tales of how they were bound to answer their masters with only the truth. Fearing she would be compelled to tell the Prince of his presence, Will withdrew without speaking to her and closed the door. He tried not to think about who she used to be and how long she'd been in this place.

He crossed the corridor and listened at the opposite door. It was silent, and a brief peep inside revealed an empty room which was the mirror of the one he'd just seen. Its tapestry showed a night sky with the tiny stitched stars twinkling and steadily moving across the fabric sky.

There was one more door right at the far end of the corridor, very elaborately decorated with oak leaves and branches like the column he'd hidden behind in the entrance hall. He approached it slowly, uncertain, wondering if the throne room was on the other side. Just over halfway down the corridor he decided to turn back, thinking it far more likely that the Princess would be elsewhere, but when he paused he heard the sound of weeping.

It was definitely coming from the far end of the corridor. He moved closer, trying to work out if the sniffling could belong to the Princess, when the doors flew open. He barely had time to register a rush of something behind him and then the dozens of sprites he'd seen before were pushing and pulling him towards the newly visible throne room ahead. They were surprisingly strong for such tiny things.

He was deposited just inside the doors, which swung shut behind him. The throne room was dazzling in its beauty, every inch of its cavernous vaulted ceilings decorated with gilded stars and over a dozen of the oak leaf pillars supporting it. The walls featured exquisitely carved friezes of cavorting revellers that reminded Will of classical nymphs he'd seen in museums, only unlike these, they'd been static.

There were two thrones on a dais before him and seated upon them were the King and Queen of the Fae wearing robes of shimmering dark green embellished with golden oak leaves. The crowns upon their heads were a striking combination of golden circlets and green oak leaves that sparkled with the reflected sprite light. Shafts of sunlight illuminated the thrones too, pouring through the huge windows high on the walls showing the blue sky outside.

Will tugged his clothes back into place, regretting having changed out of his white tie, and then bowed deeply. He could barely look at the monarchs, such was the power of their presence.

"What's this?" the Queen asked. "A new slave?"

"No, I think not," the King said with a miserable sigh. "Would it make you happy, dear, if I were to make him one?"

"We have so many," she said with a sniff. "None of them have made it better."

"Stand straight, mortal," the King said. "Tell me how you would make the Queen happy."

They hadn't even asked who he was or why he was there. Will straightened himself. "I would offer no entertainment as a slave, your majesty. I cannot sing, dance, or perform an instrument to the level you'd require."

"Surely you can suffer?"

Will did his best to look straight at the Queen, but it was like trying to stare into a gale force wind; all he wanted to do was keep his head down. "I have the feeling many slaves have suffered for your entertainment, your majesty, and yet you remain sad. Were I to retain my freedom, I am certain I could end your sadness more effectively."

"I doubt that," the Queen said, sighing heavily once more.

"Who are you, entering the palace without announcement?"

Will lowered his head beneath the King's scrutiny. "A mortal man named William."

"How did you come to be here?"

"A Charm that opened a Way, and then the effect of a forfeit demanded by the Princess, your majesty."

"You're no mundane, then." When Will agreed, the King asked, "And who claims you? I see no family written on your soul."

Will remembered how he'd felt in the Guildhall. Had Lord Iris's statement actually done something tangible to him? "I have no family, no patron, and no allegiance to any others, your majesty." He raised his chin. "I have no Patroon and no master. I am my own man."

The King and Queen exchanged a look of excitement, a sudden shift from the misery moments before. "You may approach the royal thrones," the King said, and Will moved closer. "How would you bring an end to our sadness?"

"I would begin by asking if there is a specific cause."

"There is," the Queen answered. "Our nobility."

Confused, Will stepped forwards again. "The fact that you are the King and Queen is making you miserable?"

"This is beyond misery, mortal!" the King boomed, and Will staggered back, dropping to one knee as soon as he found his balance again. "This is the leeching of any mote of happiness from our existence. This is the horror of isolation, of being hated and feared for eternity!"

"Forgive me, your majesty; as a mere mortal, I cannot possibly comprehend the depths of your suffering," Will said, hoping he sounded sincere enough. What had he stumbled into? Was the damn luck egg still working? It didn't feel like a stroke of luck to fall under their scrutiny. Like so many of his interactions with the Fae, it was apparent that he was little more than a moment of interest in a dull day.

But then he thought of the look they'd exchanged when he'd said he was his own man. Why be excited by that? He risked a glance at the King, who was having a whispered conversation with his Queen. Both of them seemed excited again. Damn these Fae and their mercurial nature.

"What would be your next question?" the Queen asked. Will felt like he was skirting around the edge of a bottomless pit. Not a game with dubious rules, like he'd played with the Princess, this felt more like a bizarre audition for royal problem solver.

"Well, it seems to me that the fact that you are King and Queen is making your lives insufferable," he said, watching them both nod. "And I can only assume that you cannot pass the weight of your office to the Prince or Princess, otherwise you would have already." Both looked eager. But neither had confirmed it. "Am I correct?"

"What would be your next question?" the Queen prompted, a hint of frustration in her voice. Perhaps they couldn't confirm it. Like a curse.

"I would ask if you had both been cursed, your majesty."

They both shifted forwards on the thrones, like children waiting to hear whether they'd won a prize. Again, neither said anything to confirm or deny. He was right—they were cursed, and like all curses, there were strict rules to prevent it being lifted.

"So…my instincts are telling me that you were both cursed to be King and Queen and your royal existence is unbearable but you're unable to bestow it on…anyone else?"

The Queen gripped the King's hand.

"So, unable to pass your crown to another one of the Fae, perhaps you could pass it to a mortal?" The King's frown was thunderous and Will looked down again. "Of course not. No…if this royalty is a curse, you cannot give it up at all. But…" He stood up again, moving forwards. "Perhaps it could be taken."

There was no mistaking the hope in the King's eyes, the desperation in those of the Queen. All thoughts of a quiet life were discarded as Will imagined all he could do if he were King of the Fae. Was there anything to stop him? Any formal requirement that they had to be ruled by their own kind? Perhaps that was the reason for their excitement when he'd told them he was his own man and no mere mundane. The odds of someone who fit those criteria ending up in the royal throne room were so small, he was willing to bet the curse had no protection against him if he decided to take the crown himself.

As King, he could order Iris to give Sophia back and restore her without the need for a fearful negotiation. He could command him to explain all he wanted to know, and force the Prince to reveal what he did to Petra and why. It would all be so easy!

He'd always wanted to get to the top of the ladder, and in his ignorant youth, he'd thought that was simply a matter of clawing his way to being Patroon. But now he knew that not even being the head of the Irises would be enough. He would still be Lord Iris's pawn. What freedom would that be? There was only one freedom he wanted now, that given by control over the ones that had ruled his life and destroyed so many others.

He would be king.

Closing the distance between him and the thrones, Will focused on the King's crown, feeling himself having to battle to reach it— not only against his own doubts but also a physical sensation of something pushing against him. He thought of Sophia, of Petra, of being able to tell Cathy it was truly over and they were both free of Lord Iris's schemes. He made it to the dais and reached up.

The King's hands were now gripping the arms of the throne. "Stop. I cannot allow you to take this crown without telling you why you cannot possibly want it," he said with effort, as though fighting the words. Part of the curse, no doubt. "If you take this crown, you will command the Fae Court, but they will despise you. You will never be loved by them; you will never be seen as anything other than their jailer. You will be bound to obey the Sorcerers of Albion in all things and to ensure that any breach of the Split Worlds Treaty by your subjects will be punished harshly, no matter your feelings."

Will had no care for how the Fae felt about him if he commanded them. He had spent all his life being frightened of them. Hating them, more recently. He would never want to be loved by them— that always led to misery. "I can live with that," he said.

"And!" The King raised a hand to stop Will moving any closer. "Once you take this crown and place it upon your head, you will never be able to leave Exilium. You may enter any domain here, you make take whatever you wish from any of your subjects, but you will never be able to enter the Nether, nor Mundanus, as long as you are King."

That did make him pause. But what was there for him in the Nether? His family could come and visit—even shelter here under his protection if they needed it—and as for Mundanus...there were a million things he would miss but he could live without them if it meant Sophia was safe and he answered to no one. And if Cathy were here...

"If I were to become King, would I be able to choose my Queen?"

"Whoever wears the Queen's crown is the Queen," the King said.

Will withdrew, grateful he hadn't acted too swiftly. Considering the misery of the Queen, and the fact that there did seem to be some form of love between them, surely the King would have released her if he could? Of course, there was no accounting for the cruelty of the Fae, but it wasn't an unreasonable assumption that once you wore a crown, you wouldn't be able to take another crown from someone else. It fit with the rest of the curse.

"Your majesty, would you be able to summon the Princess here? I need to see this forfeit done, then start unpicking this curse in the correct order."

The Queen clapped her hands with delight. "The Princess has made so many mortals suffer, but for the first time, her cruelty has led to something truly exciting!" she said. "To think, if she hadn't bound you to this forfeit, you never would have been able to enter the palace!"

"Were it anyone else, I would consider this part of a clever design," said the King, and snapped his fingers.

Moments later the Princess entered the throne room and curtsied to the thrones before noticing Will. "You! This is cheating!"

"Silence!" shouted the King and the Princess obeyed. "You will not harm this mortal, nor will you try to influence his soul in any way. You will stand still and wait until I tell you that you may move again."

The Princess pouted. "But that's no fun at all, your majesty." But then she caught a glimpse of the Queen's glare and became meek. "As you wish."

Will approached her, feeling like a man sent into a sleeping bear's cave. The Princess watched him and even though she wasn't actively trying to influence him, her presence and beauty were still able to shake him to the core. When he reached her, he armoured himself with thoughts of Sophia as he cupped her face in his hands. He closed his eyes and kissed her lips, feeling a terrific thrill throughout his entire body. It reminded him of when he kissed Amelia and that helped harden his heart against her. When it was done, he reached up and put his hands on the circlet.

She gasped and grabbed his arms. "Be still!" the King's voice boomed, and she stopped pulling at Will, her face becoming ugly with rage.

Will lifted the circlet of oak leaves from her hair, which was much heavier than it looked, and she screamed with fury, the oak leaves on her gown crumbling into golden dust, leaving a simple silk dress that was a pale purple colour. The impact of her beauty diminished; she was merely one of the Fae again.

"Why?" she screamed at the King. "I was such a good Princess!"

"And now you are Lady Dahlia once more," said the King. "Return to your domain and breathe life back into it. Find your pets and take comfort in them. Your time as royalty has come to an end."

She headed towards the doors, bound to obey, but with a supreme effort, she paused long enough to give Will a withering glare. "I will not rest until you have been sent mad with torment."

He watched her leave, still holding the circlet. There was something uncomfortable about holding it, as if it were incomplete. He went back to the thrones and laid it down behind the dais.

"Why you made Lady Dahlia the Princess I will never understand," he overheard the Queen mutter to the King.

"And now the Prince," the King said, neglecting to answer her.

Will moved round to stand before the King. He wondered if this was the time to ask the Prince about Petra, but he didn't want the other Fae to hear his answer. No, better to ask once he was King.

The Prince was summoned and ordered to be still by the King, just as the Princess had, but the Prince was so tall he was also asked to kneel on one knee. It felt utterly bizarre to approach him, and again Will felt he had to draw deep on his own determination just to get close. Without Sophia as his motivation, and the lifetime of frustration that had built within him, he wasn't sure he'd be capable of taking the circlet. The Prince remained silent throughout, seeing that complaining would be futile, but he didn't make it easy for Will. He stared at him as he approached, and just as Will started to reach for the circlet, the Prince said, "You were once an Iris."

"I was. Does that bother you?"

"The family is inconsequential. Lord Iris is another matter."

Will recalled what the Princess had said about Iris's lost love. "Why did you punish him?" Will whispered.

"He watched me give up the one I loved yet kept his own. He believed his love more important than mine. I was lenient."

Chilled by the hatred in the Prince's voice, Will lifted the circlet. The oak leaves forming the Prince's cloak turned to dust, leaving him dressed in a simple burgundy tunic and hose.

"You are Lord Chrysanthemum once more," said the King.

"You didn't pay attention when I was a Prince," the Fae Lord said to the King, standing once more. "And now that which I foresaw has come to pass. I knew Iris would orchestrate your destruction."

"Go, for the sake of all that is joyful!" said the Queen. "You were such a sour Prince. Be gone!"

Will placed the Prince's circlet next to the other and went to stand before the King and Queen. He watched the King take the Queen's hand and kiss it. "Have I not been kind to you, my Queen?"

She smiled, took his other hand, and kissed it. "You have. I will not forget it."

"I command you to be still and to not harm this mortal," the King said.

Will approached, a little tired now, this being the third time he had to push against the urge to withdraw and kneel at a polite distance. As he reached up to the Queen's crown, he felt tears pricking his eyes, a sudden appreciation of how he was about to destroy something perfect and beautiful. But he remembered Sophia and told himself that, unlike his love for her, these emotions weren't real. He needed to do this, no matter how awful it felt.

As soon as the circlet was lifted from her head, the emotional onslaught ended abruptly. He stepped back, his legs unsteady, as she leaped up from the throne, brushing away the dust left by the disintegrating oak leaves. Her gown was now a delicate lilac colour, her hair lightening to a white blonde with streaks of purple. She skipped away from the throne, pirouetting like a ballet dancer, laughing all the while.

"Lady Orchid," the King said softly. "It has been too long."

She stopped and rushed back to him, kneeling at his feet to kiss his hands. "Your majesty. I am yours, as ever." He stroked her hair, letting the purple streaks run through his fingers. Will had never before seen such tenderness in the Fae. He looked away, feeling he was encroaching upon something private.

Will waited until Lady Orchid left the dais before focusing on the King. But to his surprise, she stopped next to him. "The curse will force him to repel you," she whispered. "Forgive him, please. I will do all I can to help, but I cannot Charm you or lend magical aid. Otherwise your soul would be tainted, and you wouldn't be able to take the crown."

"What would you advise I do?"

"Don't look into his eyes. Don't pay attention to anything you may feel. Focus on the need to succeed. He helped you take the rest of the crowns. This time will be different. But he will do all he can to fight the curse, too. I hope that is enough."

Closing his eyes, Will nodded and felt her hand leave his arm. He shut out the room and the King as best he could and thought of Sophia, filling himself with the need to protect her. When he opened his eyes again, he forced himself to look at the crown, but just that alone took so much effort.

He moved forwards.

"Stop," the King said, and Will found himself unable to move, as if the command had simply bypassed his conscious thoughts and spoken straight to his body. Mercifully, unlike a Doll Charm, he could still blink and breathe. Asserting his control over his limbs by thinking of each in turn and flexing his toes and fingers, Will leaned forward as if into a headwind and managed another step. He could hear the King muttering to himself, locked in his own struggle, and pressed on.

"I command you to leave!" the King shouted, but Will clenched his fists. *I'm no Fae*, he thought. *And no Fae rules me.*

The next two steps were easier, and he planted one foot on the dais with a sense of triumph. Just as he started to reach up to the circlet, he felt a hand around his throat. There was a moment when his breath was choked off, then the grip relaxed and he could just about draw a breath before it tightened again.

"Quick!" the King hissed, and Will was acutely aware of the Fae's own battle. No doubt there were a thousand ways the King could repel or kill him, and he wasn't sure how much longer the King would be able to fight the compulsion to use them.

He clawed at the King's hand instinctively but after the initial moment of panic, his focus returned. The only way to save himself was to take the crown. He tried to think of Sophia, but the love he felt for her seemed so far away, such a sweet, warm memory, he almost wanted to give in, then and there, just to be left alone to wallow in it.

Delving deeper, he remembered his anger at his father for giving her up, which swiftly transmuted into rage at his patron for encouraging such cruelty. If he died now, he'd never get his revenge. Will didn't want the freedom of insignificance and anonymity. He didn't want the freedom of death, even though his burning lungs demanded it. All he wanted was the purest freedom of being so powerful that no man, no Fae, could ever again tell him what to do.

He gripped the crown as pinpricks scattered across his vision. With the last of the air in his lungs, Will lifted it from the King's head before falling backwards, the metal oak leaves digging into his palms as he gasped for breath. Then he was in someone's arms, and as his vision cleared he saw Lady Orchid's radiant smile as she held him. After a single kiss on his forehead she helped him to stand. The palace seemed to shudder around them, as if the lack of a king had made it shiver.

Will put the crown on his own head and felt a surge of raw power flood his body. He had only the vaguest awareness of another Fae stepping down from the dais as he struggled to contain it, feeling like the sheer potential of everything he could do with just a whim was going to subsume him.

Then just as swiftly, it passed and he remained. Will sat on the throne with a triumphant surge of satisfaction. Now he ruled over his tormentors, nothing and no one could stop him. The days of struggling to survive, of fearing his patron, of desperately trying to please his Patroon…they were over. He laughed, just briefly, barely aware of the joyful celebration between the former King and Queen.

The sheer relief alone was enough to make him feel almost drunkenly euphoric and with the knowledge that he could command any creature in Exilium to do his bidding, it was a heady combination. Beneath it all, however, was the sense that his domain was incomplete. He thought of the other crowns, left unworn, imperfect. He needed to make it all right again. He needed his wife by his side once more. He needed his Queen. He knew exactly how to bring her back to him, but first, he had to see Sophia safe once more.

23

"He went out, love," Mrs M said to Cathy when she and Max got back to Sam's estate. "Drove himself. Didn't say where he were goin'."

Cathy hung up her coat as Max did the same. "Oh well. Seems as good a time as any to carry on with the prep. Could you help me, Max?"

She took him through to the games room. Boxes were stacked everywhere they could fit, even on top of the billiard table, with little walkways between them.

"What's all this stuff?" asked the gargoyle.

"I started planning it after Sam and I agreed to go with Beatrice's plan. The bigger boxes are for the staff who work in the Nether, the medium-sized ones are for the women in the Great Families, and the smallest are for the men. They contain a sort of emergency pack for life in Mundanus, scaled according to need. Now we've got all those files from the Agency, all we need to do is label them up so they can be delivered to the anchor properties when the time comes. Sam's staff helped put them together—I just gave them a list—and Des has put the names and addresses into a database for me so all the labels are printed. We just need to check each box and stick them on."

The gargoyle sniffed at a couple. "So do the men get the smallest ones because they're evil bastards who don't deserve anything?"

Cathy smirked. "They have the least need. Practically all of them have substantial mundane wealth. But their wives won't have anything. In their boxes I've put in ways to get to a safe house if they want to leave their husbands. Sam has apartments that are protected from the Fae already. If a woman leaves her husband and is in danger of being pursued, I'll ward her apartment against him. If I work out how to, that is. I'm not sure Beatrice will be very helpful with that, or even if she's coming back here to teach me again."

"These books I've brought you from Petra will help," Max said, putting the suitcase down.

"Yeah, I do appreciate that, thanks. It's all early days, and there's still a lot to do, but it's a start." She had to be positive. Otherwise the sheer scale of what they were involved in would overwhelm her.

The gargoyle found a spot under the billiard table to curl up in whilst Cathy handed a sheet of printed labels to Max and showed him the list of items to check in each box.

"Beatrice hasn't been around for days," Cathy said after a little while, uncomfortable with the silence. "I wonder what she's up to."

"Lord Iron gave her the information she wanted," Max said. "If that was all she needed, I suspect she returned to the tower."

"What tower? Where?"

"The Kingdom of Essex," Max replied. "It belonged to the former Sorcerer. Her brother, we think. The only route to it that I know of is through the Camden Chapter Master's office."

"I wonder if that's where Sam went," Cathy said. "It's not like him to go somewhere without—" The floor pitched beneath her and she slapped her hand against the wall to steady herself. All thoughts were pushed aside by a single dominant thought: *Beatrice is going to kill me.* She knew it, with as much certainty as if Beatrice were standing there about to plunge a knife into her heart.

"Cathy?"

"Beatrice is going to kill me," she whispered. "The oath… she said I'd know when she was going to betray me. I don't know how she's planning to do it, but she's started working the magic, whatever it is."

"We'll find her before she finishes it," the gargoyle growled.

She thought of the day Max and the gargoyle first arrived, asking for Beatrice to be handed over. She'd decided to not tell Beatrice that one of the Sorcerers was still alive. Was that enough to constitute betrayal in Beatrice's eyes? Was it because she'd placed

Max and the gargoyle's safety above that of her tutor? Cathy had been so caught up in her father's death and getting to Tom as soon as she could, then going to the Agency and exposing the Irises, that she hadn't really stopped to think about the consequences. Besides, hadn't she brought Max onside? Maybe that wasn't enough for Beatrice. Or maybe it had nothing to do with that at all. Beatrice had everything she needed, and a fledgling Sorcerer was not one of them. Killing her might simply be a matter of tying up loose ends.

Pulling out her mobile with shaking hands, she tried to call Sam but it went straight to answerphone again. Was he with Beatrice? Did he know what she was doing? Max called Des, but he didn't know where Sam was either. "I'm not going to sit around waiting to die!" she said to Max, tossing the phone onto one of the boxes in frustration. "Can you take me to that tower?" She looked under the billiard table, wondering why the gargoyle hadn't said anything, but it was gone. "Where's the gargoyle?"

"It's by the gatehouse," he said, looking distant. "Looking in the hedge." He frowned. "I was paying attention to you; I didn't notice."

They went out into the hall to find the front door open and his coat in a heap on the floor. Max picked it up and checked the pockets. "The gargoyle took the Opener."

"What? Where is he going?"

Max's frown deepened. "The gargoyle has found the tracker, the one Rupert made. It's going to kill Beatrice before she kills you."

24

Will looked down at his former patron, seeing the top of the Fae's head for the first time as Iris was knelt before him. It was a petty thing, an indulgence, but Will savoured the moment. He was at the top of the ladder he'd talked to Cathy about on the night of their marriage.

Was Iris frightened, as he had once been?

He hoped so.

"Where is Sophia?"

"In my domain, your majesty. Unharmed."

"Did you take her memory of me?"

"No, your majesty. I made it more powerful."

Will gripped the arms of the throne. "To make her suffer?"

"To make her talk about you and draw pictures of you. And to miss you all the more. A gentle suffering."

"Bring her to me, unharmed, as she was when she arrived with my father."

"As you wish, your majesty." Iris snapped his fingers and one of his faeries popped into existence at his shoulder. He whispered to it and it flew out of one of the open windows. Will had opened all of them, needing to feel the breeze to push away the sense of being closed in. Lord Dianthus, the previous king, seemed to understand and a look had passed between him and Lady Orchid. They knew what it was like to wear the crown. How it pressed him into the throne.

Will shrugged the sensation off. If he dwelt upon it, it worsened. There were better things to focus upon. He tried not to think of how happy Dianthus and Orchid were when they left the castle.

Iris kept his head bowed, still on one knee, and Will knew he was literally unable to look up at him without permission. Delight and disgust warred within him. He didn't want to be like the Fae, having seen the horrors they were capable of. He had to rise above it and be a true king, as he'd always daydreamed about when he was a boy. The charming prince had held no interest for him in the stories. They did nothing but marry princesses and know that one day, they would be king. And the kings in those stories were just as dissatisfying: portly fathers who either loved their daughters too much or ate too much or set impossible tasks for lovers. Were there no young kings in these tales? Why were there no dynamic princes that took the throne for themselves while they had youth enough to enjoy it? He smiled. He was that king now. And once Sophia was safe, he would forge the rest of his court in the way he saw fit, once his queen was at his side.

There was a shower of iris petals and Sophia appeared. She was sitting cross-legged next to Iris surrounded by a circle of iris flowers that withered and faded to sparkling dust in moments. She looked tired but healthy. "Will-yum!"

He opened his arms to her and she ran into his embrace as Iris's faerie returned to its master. Will scooped her up, held her close, and silently vowed that he would never let another person take her from him again. Once she'd covered his cheeks in kisses, she wriggled until she was sitting on his lap with his arms wrapped around her, which she held tight. She looked down at Iris and then up at Will. "Are you the King now, Will-yum?"

"I am."

"So am I a princess?"

"If you want to be, once you've grown up," he said, but he had no intention of placing that crown on her head until she was older, and perhaps never at all. He saw no reason to imprison her in Exilium.

"I do want to be. Does that mean I can shoot lasers from my eyes now?"

"No, darling."

"But I can still be an ark-leagist—"

"Archaeologist, darling."

"But I can still be an archaeologist and build bridges for people's cars?"

"If that's what you want to do, my darling, you can. It's all rather new, so we'll have to see. Now, tell me, was Iris there kind to you?"

She frowned at Iris. "He wouldn't let me see you. He was a poopy pants and I don't like him."

"Did he hurt you?"

She shook her head. "He gave me magic paper and pencils. And cakes that tasted like clouds. And when I cried, he sent the faerie and it made me laugh. But he didn't cuddle me. Nobody did. It was horrible. Where's Uncle Vincent?"

"Do you want to see him?"

She nodded. "Yes. I want to go home. And I want Cathy too."

"Cathy will be here soon, darling. I have something else I need to do first."

"Is this your castle?" When he nodded, she grinned. "Can I explore it? I want to be an explorer too. I could make a map!"

He was glad that he'd already had a quick look around the ground floor to check that it was safe for Sophia and also to keep Iris waiting. He'd freed the slaves, though he had no idea what to do with the poor souls. They'd been there so long they had no homes or family to return to in Mundanus. At least Sophia wouldn't see them. "Are you happy for the faerie to go with you? The one that made you laugh?" When she nodded and smiled at Iris's faerie, Will pointed at it. "You'll give her pencils and paper, and stay with her as she explores. You will make sure no harm comes to her." The faerie nodded. Satisfied, Will kissed Sophia's forehead. "Darling, can you make me a map of the ground floor? There are so many rooms we might get lost without one."

Filled with purpose, Sophia slid from his lap, gave him a last kiss on the cheek, and ran out of the throne room, the faerie flying at her shoulder. Once the door was closed and he was alone with Iris, Will took a moment to let his relief subside so he could think clearly. Before he decided what to do about his former patron, he needed some answers.

"Why did you make the Patroon marry me to Cathy?"

"Because she is rebellious, your majesty."

"And that…substance you pulled from my mother, when she confessed in your domain, was that…rebellion?"

"Yes. Extracted in a form I could consume."

"And you thought our child would make more, somehow?"

Iris shook his head, still bowed, still looking at the floor. "I expected nothing from the child, your majesty, aside from the possibility that having such a mother could create an interesting rebel in time. I wasn't prepared to wait that long."

Will struggled to manage his anger. All of the pressure, all of the conflict between him and Cathy, all the terrible things he'd done to try to make her acquiesce to his patron's desire for them to have a child and Iris wasn't even interested in it? "Then why make the demand?" he shouted, and Iris visibly flinched.

"Because I knew you would love the child so much that when I asked you to give it to me so I could kill it, you would finally rebel against me."

The soaring rush of power caused by that flinch evaporated. "Are you seriously telling me that you put all that pressure on us just to force me into disobedience?"

"Yes. You were the first Iris child in so long that showed the potential to give me what I needed. You hid it well, always the dutiful son, but I saw moments of doubt and glimpses of anger. Insisting on a union with the Poppy woman was my plan to…infect you with her ideals and give you a taste of standing up to those who control you, as she had. I pressured her to be the antithesis of her true self in the hope she would try to turn you. Then she left, so I could only pressure you. Then when your father produced the bastard, I hoped to use her instead, but your self-control was too strong."

"My self-control is the only thing stopping me from smearing you across this floor!" Will yelled, and Iris twitched with fear. "And the way you've always treated my family…the way you controlled us…that was just to make us rebel?"

"Yes. But they were all too weak."

"They were terrified of you!" Will's voice rang off the walls and windows. "You…disgusting creature! You made so many suffer, kept us in fear…made me do terrible things. I killed a man for you! More than one for the sake of the family. And it was all just… meaningless?"

"No, your majesty, your actions when you were mine pleased me greatly!"

"And yet you cast me out and did nothing to defend my family when we needed you."

"There was nothing to be done in Aquae Sulis. Your father failed. As for you, I decided that a few months of suffering out in the cold might give you some of the fire your wife has. Then when I brought you back, helped you rise again, you might have been strong enough to—"

"Enough!" Will shouted. He closed his eyes, imagining so many ways to make Iris suffer, all so easy with the power he now had. But he wasn't satisfied yet. "Why did you need me to rebel? Why did you take that from my mother?"

"I needed it to resist the Prince, your majesty. It was the only way I could fortify my will enough to challenge him. Your father has been bringing me rebellious mortals, giving me enough to plot and remember my plan. I needed something pure, something from one of mine, something potent enough to demand he give back my love's heart so I might find her again, and restore her."

All of that suffering, the mortals stolen, his own family terrorised…all for love? Will shook his head, appalled. "You selfish bastard," he spat. He reached into his pocket and pulled out the lock of hair he'd taken from Petra. Perhaps "taking her heart" was only a figurative expression of stealing her love and her memory of herself. "Look at this. Is it familiar?"

Iris looked up for the first time since he'd arrived at the palace. "It could be hers, your majesty, but I need to touch it, to be certain."

Will tossed it to him and Iris sniffed the lock of hair. Then with an expression of frantic hope he pulled out a strand and sucked it like spaghetti. "It's hers!" he cried, with such joy Will barely recognised his voice. "Where is she? How did you get this?"

"Do you forget your place?" Will said in a low voice, and Iris dropped to both knees and lowered his forehead to the floor. Words alone did that to Iris, such was the power he now had. It made Will shudder with both apprehension and delight. He wasn't sure the words had been entirely his, but he was so angry, he wasn't exactly watching what he said. Then he realised how much of his life he'd spent worrying about what he was going to say and how he said it. All because of the creature cowering before him. "Why didn't you tell me about her? Why torment so many when I could have found her for you?"

"I was cursed," Iris said, an unfamiliar quiver in his voice. "I could not speak her name. I could not tell another soul about her, let alone ask for her to be found."

Will leaned forwards. "Why did the Prince take her from you?"

"When the worlds were split, we were forced to abandon the mortals we favoured. Several of us did not. The Prince was forced to give up his favourites when he took the crown and it made him bitter. There was nowhere for him to hide them, not as Prince. When he discovered I had hidden my love and still enjoyed her company, his jealousy was unbridled. He came to my domain and stole her heart, forcing me to watch as she forgot me. He took her away and then returned without her, gloating that I'd never find her. He cursed me and for the hundreds of years since that day he took every opportunity to remind me of my loss."

Will looked out of the window at the blue sky and fluffy white clouds. Always a perfect summer's day here, always beautiful. Always lonely. He had Sophia, soon he would have Cathy. The thought of being trapped in Exilium with no one to love—and be loved by— made him shiver. But did Petra feel the same way about Iris? If he reunited them, would he be repeating the same mistakes he was trying to put behind him?

"Where is her heart?"

"In this very palace, your majesty. In the former Prince's chambers, I imagine."

Will thought of Petra, lost and alone in that hotel. He had to restore her and make something good come of this mess. He didn't know which room it was, and wasn't prepared to admit that in front of Iris. Then he remembered the faerie that had spoken to him before, the one dressed in oak leaves. Could he command one of them, even though he wasn't a Fae?

Experimentally he snapped his fingers, wishing one would come to him. With a small pop, one appeared. "Take us to the former Prince's chamber," he said, and the faerie bowed and flitted off towards the doors. "Come with me, Iris," Will said.

The faerie led them up the wide staircase and Will remembered the first day at Lancaster House, climbing the stairs with Cathy, trying to see the grand property as his home. Iris walked behind him in silence, several steps back.

The Prince's chambers were larger than several of the rooms in Lancaster House put together. The bed was huge and yet Will had the distinct impression it had never been slept in. Did the Fae sleep? Why have a bed if they didn't? There was so much he didn't know about the creatures he now ruled over. He'd have time enough to learn. "Leave us," Will said to the faerie, and it flew off.

Iris was staring at the far side of the room and Will followed his gaze. There was a stone pedestal with a small glass case resting on top. Something inside glittered in the sunlight streaming through the windows. As Will approached it, he could see it looked like an actual heart, something he'd only ever seen in a mundane book. It seemed to be made of pure ruby covered in something that reminded him of frost on a winter's morning.

Iris followed him and Will appreciated the power of the crown. Surely Iris wanted to rush over there and smash the case?

"Is that actually her heart?"

"Yes, your majesty. It's a very powerful curse."

"Can you restore her, now the Prince is no longer here?"

"I can, if you permit it, your majesty. I would be able to summon her, as I once summoned you, and restore her fully when she is here."

"Do it."

Iris moved over to the case and smashed it so swiftly that Will didn't realise what he'd done until he heard the glass break. Iris moved close to the heart and for a moment Will thought he was going to kiss it, but instead the Fae whispered into it. The frost didn't melt, but Will was certain he saw a faint glow coming from inside the ruby heart.

Iris moved to stand in front of a huge mirror set in a gilded frame. It shimmered and Will saw Petra touching the glass from the other side, her cheeks flushed. Iris reached through and took her hand, guiding her into Exilium.

"You're familiar," she whispered. "But I can't...I can't remember." She noticed Will and curtsied. "I don't understand. Is this Exilium?"

Will nodded. "My circumstances have changed since I last saw you. There's no need to be afraid."

She smiled at him and then Iris, her hand still resting in his. "I'm not."

"Allow me to restore you," Iris said to Petra with uncharacteristic reverence and warmth. As he guided her across the room, Will marvelled at how gently Iris held her hand. The Fae didn't take his eyes off her.

Petra gasped at the sight of the heart and her free hand flew to her chest, as if somehow she knew it belonged to her.

"Take it from the pedestal," Iris said, letting go of her hand.

Approaching the heart, Petra frowned. "This is the reason why her magic didn't kill me when she attacked Ekstrand..." she whispered to herself. "My heart was elsewhere."

She picked it up and instinctively held it close. Iris moved closer to her and then breathed over the heart, whispering a Charm as he did so, and the frost covering the ruby started to melt. Iris cupped his hands over Petra's and gently pushed the heart towards her chest, whispering all the while. The heart, still appearing to be made of ruby, started to glow, and Will even thought he saw it beat, before it started to disappear. It was as if it were being pushed into her, somehow able to pass through her dress and skin.

A moment after her hands and his were pressed flat against her chest Petra convulsed, her back arching and her eyes and mouth wide open as she cried out. Iris stepped forwards, gathering her into his arms as she suddenly relaxed and seemed to melt against him. They kissed and a rich dark blond colour swept through Iris's white hair from roots to tip, a streak of dark blue appearing moments later.

"Iris! Iris, my love, my darling!" Petra wept, stroking his hair.

Concerned she'd been Charmed, Will said "Iris, wait outside, I want to speak to Petra." Iris looked at him as if Will had tried to stab him, tears glittering on his cheeks, but then he separated himself from Petra and bowed.

"No! Please, no, we've been apart for so long!" Petra said, reaching for Iris. The Fae stepped away from her and left the room at a quick march.

"I need to know you aren't being controlled by him," Will said. "I want you to be truthful with me."

Petra sighed. "Only as much as he is controlled by me. We love each other. Deeply."

"Forgive me, but I don't trust the Fae." Will snapped his fingers again and when the faerie appeared, he pointed at Petra. "Tell me if she is under the influence of any magic."

The faerie flew over, looked into Petra's eyes, licked her hand, and sucked on a strand of her hair. "No, your majesty. Would you like her to be?"

"No," Will said, and waved it away. "I don't understand," he muttered. "How could you love Iris? He's…monstrous."

Petra pulled a chair away from the nearby dressing table and sat down. "Not the Iris I know and love. He's gentle and loving and loyal. We've been kept apart; perhaps…"

"He ruined my life!" Will yelled. "His demands destroyed my marriage!"

"Your majesty?" Petra said softly. "I can only imagine our separation did this to him. And you must understand, our love was forged before Exilium ever was. I thought he was an angel the first time I met him. The second time I thought he was a demon, the third, a Sorcerer. He was cold and frightening but he saved me, a mere miller's daughter, from marriage to a stupid king who thought I could spin gold out of straw."

"Out of kindness?"

Petra laughed. "Oh, no, not out of kindness. He got my firstborn in return. Your great-great-great-great-grandfather or thereabouts, fathered by a better king that Iris gave to me. Then Iris and I fell in love and the king…well, he was a tiresome man and died on the battlefield. Iris promised to favour my descendants if I loved only him, and I agreed. It was all my choice. And I want nothing more. I've suffered years of service to my love's enemy, been denied my memory, my will, even my own heart. Please, whatever he's done, please forgive him."

Will sat on the edge of the bed, tired of all the broken lives. For the first time he was able to mend something, to heal a wound instead of inflict one, but the one who'd done the most damage to him would be the one who benefitted most. It felt so unjust.

But if he punished Iris and banished Petra to Mundanus, what would be achieved? He thought of Margritte and the moment she forgave him for killing her husband. She put a stop to a cycle of revenge that had done nothing more than spread violence and misery. He'd done a lot of that himself. The Rosas, Bartholomew, that poor Tulipa…so many lives damaged or destroyed by his own petty needs. Iris might have been the one who drove him to it, but he'd made many of those choices himself. Perhaps if he'd listened to Cathy sooner, found a way out of that system as she had, Bartholomew would still be alive now, Duke of Londinium, Margritte happy by his side.

He wanted Cathy back. He had to prove to her that he wasn't the same man who'd hurt her. And there was no other way to do that than act. He stood and called for Iris, who came back inside.

"Go, be together, be happy," Will said. "All I ask is that you end your tyranny over my family, Iris. Support them, but don't use them. Don't hurt them or do anything to them that makes them unhappy."

Iris came and knelt before him. "Thank you, your majesty. May your merciful reign be long and bring you happiness. I am your faithful servant."

Petra curtsied to him. "Thank you, your majesty. We will never forget your kindness."

Will dismissed them, waiting for the moment when he felt good about what he'd just done. It didn't come. And that sense of imperfection in his court rose once more. He summoned the faerie. "Go to Lord Poppy. Tell him to bring me Thomas Rhoeas-Papaver. Immediately."

25

"Where's the gargoyle now?" Cathy asked Max. As she paced up and down in the living room, he directed his attention elsewhere as he had before, seeing through the gargoyle's eyes even though it was in the Nether as he and Cathy remained in Sam's house.

"Outside the Sorceress's tower. Do you feel any different?"

She shook her head. "I can't stop shaking and I feel sick, but I think that's just fear."

Through the gargoyle's eyes, Max looked up at the tower, seeing light coming from the topmost room. It sniffed around the door at the base, both of them uncertain whether any wards would be a problem. They'd been able to enter the tower before. Caution and the desire for the most direct route made the gargoyle start to climb the outer wall instead.

Max wondered if he should try harder to pull the gargoyle back into Mundanus. So many times he'd condemned the Sorcerers for being murderers and yet there was his own soul, going to kill someone. He looked at Cathy, at how pale and terrified she looked. He felt nothing towards her except an intellectual loyalty. They protected each other. Helped each other, when the Sorcerers had threatened their lives. Was this…friendship? He knew the gargoyle was very fond of her. So he was too, technically speaking. Fond enough to kill another to keep her safe.

Killing the Sorceress would put an end to their plans, though. "Cathy, which do you value more: your life or seeing the worlds rejoined?" Her eyes became huge, shining with tears. She opened her mouth but no answer came. "That is what this amounts to," he said. "I've tried to pull the gargoyle back, several times, but it's been getting more independent of late. It started with Kay. I don't think I can stop it from killing Beatrice, but I could try harder."

"I don't want to die." She covered her face with her hands, her shoulders rounded with shame.

The gargoyle started to climb the outside of the tower, its sharp stone claws finding handholds easily.

"But," Cathy said, "I'm just one person. Millions of lives would be saved if the Fae balanced the Elemental Court."

The gargoyle reached the stone sill of the uppermost window of the tower. It peered over the top, seeing the Sorceress inside standing in front of the glass and lenses as she had the last time they'd seen her there, painting the formula to kill again. The gargoyle took the tracker from between its jaws and after the briefest pause, threw it at the glass.

"No, stop him!" Cathy said as the glass shattered. "We can't kill her; she's the only one who knows how to unsplit the worlds! That's more important than me."

"It's too late," Max said, seeing the flash of the tracker's activation before the gargoyle looked away. "She's dying."

The gargoyle cowered under the sill as a horrific scream cut through the air and then ended abruptly. Max was concerned that Beatrice had somehow escaped, and willed the gargoyle to look. After considerable resistance, the gargoyle finally peeped over the sill again.

There were bones lying in the middle of the room, an entire skeleton, by the look of it, and a stain on the floorboards below them. Nothing more of the Sorceress remained. The tracker was nowhere to be seen, but as Rupert had told Kay it would, it had indeed destroyed all the flesh in its proximity. After a few moments of staring at the skeleton, the gargoyle spotted a rectangular pile of black dust about the size of the device. It made sense: Rupert would have designed it to be harmless once it had done its job, so he'd be able to go and examine the damage afterwards.

"She's dead," Max said, and Cathy dropped into the armchair to bury her face in one of the cushions.

There was a book lying open on the floor of the tower room and Max thought of the ones he'd obtained for Cathy. The gargoyle broke the rest of the glass of the window and very slowly reached in with one paw. When nothing terrible happened, it climbed inside cautiously. If there had been a ward protecting the Sorceress from intruders, it certainly wasn't working now.

The gargoyle went over to the book, saw a few lines of sorcerous symbols written down, and picked it up. An Opener lay next to it, which surprised both of them. The gargoyle picked that up too, and, avoiding the stain and the bones, pushed it into the wall. It opened a Way into a room that looked very similar to the bedroom Max had been given in Lord Iron's house. When the gargoyle stepped through and the floorboards creaked above, Max knew it was a shortcut created by the Sorceress between her two residences. Useful.

His mobile rang. *Rupert* was displayed on the screen. "Is it Sam?" Cathy said hopefully.

"No. Rupert." Max accepted the call and put it on speakerphone.

"Max! Hey, how's it going?" The voice was cheerful.

"How can I help you, sir?" Max said in his usual deadpan.

"So you tracked that bitch down in the end and avoided the side effects. That's awesome! Come to Oxenford. I wanna thank you in person. And we need to make plans."

"It may take me some time to reach you, sir. Where should I go?" Max said as Cathy frantically shook her head.

"The Bodleian. Come to the Nether quadrangle. I got some cleaning up to do. See ya soon!"

Max ended the call.

"Is he some sort of psychopath?" Cathy asked. "He must know that you heard him kill Kay. Why the hell did you say you'd go?"

"I need to understand what he is going to do next," Max replied. "He really is the last Sorcerer in Albion now. Now that Beatrice is dead, he may be the only one who can help us to protect innocents."

She nodded. "Just be careful. Call me when you can, okay?

And Max," she rested a hand on his shoulder, "for what it's worth, thank you."

"For what?"

"For caring about me."

Uncertain how best to reply, he erred on the side of silence and joined the gargoyle in the hallway. "Keep hold of that Opener," he said to it. "But give the book to Cathy. We have to go to Oxenford."

• • •

Cathy went over to the fire in Sam's living room, poked it back into life, and leaned against the mantelpiece, reeling. She'd gone from fearing she'd drop dead at any moment to an uncomfortable mix of relief, guilt, and despair. Although it felt nothing like the death of her father, Beatrice's death still prodded the same wound. She hadn't known her well—far from it—and she'd done a lot of things Cathy couldn't stand. But she'd also been strangely admirable. All that knowledge and skill she'd acquired through sheer bloody-mindedness…if only she hadn't been so quick to murder people with it.

But there was another loss that she felt more keenly: the hope of real change. Without Beatrice, the plan to rejoin the worlds was dead in the water. The Nether would go on forever and all of her dreams of true freedom—for herself as well as for the women trapped there—were lost.

She opened the suitcase Max had brought her and looked at the books recovered from Ekstrand's library. Could she rejoin the worlds? Cathy groaned. How could she possibly do that? Beatrice had been practising sorcery for hundreds of years and had even developed her own hybrid discipline, whereas she was only just starting to get a grip on fairly basic wards.

But surely she had to at least try? When she'd first started to plan her original escape from life in the Nether the obstacles had seemed insurmountable, but she'd figured out a way to do it. Cathy cringed. They were incomparable, and she knew it.

EMMA NEWMAN

"Cathy, love," Mrs M said from the door, making her jump. "I've just had a call from the gatehouse. They said a bloke called Thomas was there, asking to see you." She came over, holding out an iPad showing a picture of Tom, standing awkwardly at the gates. "Do you recognise him? Only he said he were yer brother, and I didn't know if it were true."

What was Tom doing here? Had something gone wrong at the ball? Why not phone? "It's him. Can you tell them to let him in, please?"

"Jared will escort him over. I'll put the kettle on."

Cathy lurked in the hallway until there was a knock at the front door. "What are you doing here, Tom? Thanks, Jared. Come in, it's freezing. What's wrong? You look terrible. Oh God, has someone else died?"

Tom stepped inside, shivering despite his coat. "You need to come with me to Exilium."

"What?"

"Cat...I don't know how to say this..."

"Come to the fire. You look freezing."

"Hello, love," Mrs M smiled at him. "You're a tall one. You look like you need a bit of apple crumble and custard. I'll get some for both of you."

"That's Mrs M and she makes the best pies in all the worlds." She led him to the living room and stoked the fire. "I was expecting you to phone me. What happened at the ball?"

"Oh. Yes, I suppose I should have phoned ahead," he said. "The ball...yes...I seem to have become Duke of Londinium and—"

"Holy shit! What happened to Will?"

Tom blinked. If she didn't know better, she'd say he was in shock. "He was disowned by the Irises when I exposed your separation. I thought I'd won, Cat. We destroyed them, Aquae Sulis belongs to our aunt and uncle again, and the Irises are banned from the city. Then I became Duke and Lucy impressed Lord Poppy and won independence for the Californicas, and potentially the entirety of the Colonies."

248

"What? Sit down, tell me everything."

"But I'm not here to tell you about any of that," he said as she gently pulled him down to sit next to her on the sofa. "Oh, Cat, something dreadful has happened. It's Will…"

"Is he dead?"

"No! He's King of the Fae."

For a few moments, there were no words in her head. Then, bubbling up like the times she'd been forced to try and sing at recitals as a child, she started to laugh. It was a horrible, brittle, slightly hysterical sound. "What are you talking about?"

"He made Lord Poppy summon me there. I've seen Will on the Exilium throne, Cat, wearing a crown of oak leaves. I don't know how it happened—not even Lord Poppy did—but I swear it's true."

The laughter died. "He wants you to take me to him, doesn't he?"

Tom nodded. "Immediately." He gathered her hands in his. "I'm so sorry, Cat. I thought I'd freed you from him. I saw him humiliated and disowned. He left the Guildhall with nothing, not even his name. But now…I don't know how to protect you. I couldn't say no to him. I tried. I simply…couldn't. Even Lord Poppy bowed to him. I don't know what to do."

"I can't go to him." Her gaze drifted back to the books. All that knowledge. All that power. All within her reach. If she could just be left alone for a little while, perhaps—

"If I don't do this," Tom said, "I dread to think what Lord Poppy will do. He said he was going to fetch Lucy. Please, Cat, we have to go."

Could she ward herself against Will? Was it a matter of simply replacing that clause for the Irises with something meaning the King? She didn't know how to express that in either Fae or sorcerous magic, though, and her thoughts were woolly with panic.

Surely there was something she could do to protect herself? She'd given the Opener she'd used in Aquae Sulis back to Max, and she had the awful feeling that if the King of the Fae didn't want her to leave Exilium, a simple Charm of Openings wouldn't work. If only she could take Sam with her. Where the hell was he? If only he was at the forge and—"That's it!" she said, jumping to her feet. "I'll go with you, but we need to get something first. It'll be very quick."

"Aren't you going to put smarter clothes on and brush your hair?"

"For Will? No way."

"But he's the King, Cat."

"No. I'll listen to what he has to say and then I'm coming back here as soon as I can. Do you need a mirror? Because it won't work in this house. We'll have to take one to the gatehouse or something."

"Poppy gave me a powerful Charm to take you straight through to Exilium. It can be used on any old tree, apparently."

"Let's get this over with."

She almost bumped into Mrs M at the door, carrying a tray with two generous servings of apple crumble and custard. "Don't tell me you're off out?" she asked as Cathy put on her coat and boots.

"Sorry, Mrs M," she said. "We'll have it later." Mrs M didn't hear the "hopefully" Cathy added beneath her breath as she bustled back to the kitchen, muttering.

When Cathy put her hand on the door handle she almost burst into tears. How could this be happening? How could Will be forcing her to do something yet again?

"I'll be with you, Cat," Tom said. "This won't be like before. You won't be alone."

She thought of Lucy, not wanting to give Poppy a reason to torment her, and opened the front door. "I have to make a call while we walk," she said, and dialled Sam's number to reach his voicemail. "Sam…Bad news. Will is now King of the Fae and is using my family to force me to go to him in Exilium. I'm calling to ask you to come and get me, if I'm not back home by the time you get back. Don't leave me there with him." She breathed in deep after her voice wavered. "I'm going to take some iron with me. It's the only thing I can think of. I'll call as soon as I'm back."

"We need to stop off there," she said to Tom, pointing at the forge. "You mustn't mention this to anyone, okay?"

Cathy found a small piece of pure iron on top of the anvil,

more than she'd hoped for. It looked like a silver arrowhead and was very sharp. She wrapped it in one of the leather gloves draped over the anvil before putting it in her pocket. It was small enough to hold in the palm of her hand, which reassured her. She led Tom through the estate by the light of the moon, thankful that she'd walked it during the day and knew the fastest route to the boundary. He helped her over the fence, climbed over himself, and then doubled over, crying out.

"Poppy's summoning you," Cathy said. "Iris did it to me once. Cast the Charm and it'll stop."

He staggered to a nearby oak tree and pressed his hands against it, whispering. The bark seemed to sink inwards, as if the trunk of the tree had become soft, and then he toppled forwards, disappearing from sight as a shaft of sunlight burst from the tree. Pausing to take a deep breath, Cathy threw herself at the same spot with her eyes squeezed shut.

She landed on soft grass, bathed in warm sunshine, the scent of flowers on the breeze. With a groan she sat up and saw Lord Poppy walking towards her, holding Lucy's hand. Her sister-in-law was wearing her nightdress with a satin dressing gown over the top and silk slippers, as if she'd been plucked from her bedchamber. Knowing Poppy, she probably had been. Tom scrabbled to his feet, bowed deeply to the Fae, and helped Cathy up.

"Ah, my favourite! How I have missed you! You must have missed me."

"Indeed, Lord Poppy. Just this morning, I was thinking about how long it had been since I last saw you." She neglected to mention the genuine smile that had been on her face at the time.

Poppy released Lucy's hand and watched her run to embrace Tom. "So sweet," he said, striding over to Cathy as he smiled at them. "They're Duke and Duchess of Londinium now, I believe. Does that upset you?"

"Not in the slightest, Lord Poppy."

"What an interesting day it's been," he said, closing the distance. "Your brother and your sister-in-law have been magnificent, and then for a few scant hours you were mine again and I was so happy, and then…" he sighed. "From Duchess to Queen in one day. And Queen of Exilium, no less."

Cathy shivered. "I am not Queen, Lord Poppy."

"Not yet." He smiled and extended his arm for her to take as if they were to go promenading. When he scowled at her hesitation she slipped her hand into the crook of his elbow and he drew his arm in tight, crushing her hand against him. "You always were my favourite. I will have to content myself with what time we have now, I suppose."

"Tom and Lucy can go home now, can't they?" she said as Tom shook his head at her.

"No, I'm going to keep them with me for a little while. I know how clever you are, my little sunlit one. Imagine if you managed to slip from my grasp before we reached the King. I would hate to have to go through the trouble of having to go and find them again, to make you come back. This way we can all enjoy a stroll to the palace together, can't we?"

He started walking and Cathy had to hurry to keep up with his long strides. She glanced back to see Tom and Lucy following, both looking as nervous as she surely did. Lucy tried to give her a brave nod, but her reassurance wasn't convincing.

She picked up the pace and Poppy laughed. "Why, my dear, it's almost as if you want to see the King. Have you missed your husband?"

"Not one bit," she said. "I want to get this over with so we can all go home."

Poppy laughed. "But you are home, my little bird. You'll never leave that palace. I can see how much he loves you now. It seems that he only realised it after he'd lost everything, but that's often the way, is it not? We don't realise how much we want to keep something until it is no longer ours."

He tightened his grip on her hand, gazing at her as he said it. Could she use Poppy's possessiveness to her advantage? "But surely you don't want me to be his again, Lord Poppy?"

"I want my King to be happy and pleased with me," he sighed. "No matter how unhappy it makes me."

"But it's only Will! He's mortal."

"Not anymore. He wears the crown. And when you are his Queen, you'll be immortal too. And we'll all live here together for eternity."

Eternity? Here? With Will? Without thinking, she stopped and started to pull back, shaking her head, breathless. She could feel that choker around her throat again, and the thought of being his, to do with as he wanted, sent her spiralling into panic. As the grip on her hand tightened, she remembered the arrowhead and promised herself that if Will made her feel anything for him again, she'd stick it right in his eye. Then Poppy was there, stroking her face as if she were a child. "I know, my little bird, I know you only want to be with me…"

Cathy almost palmed the iron to stab Poppy, but she held back, getting her fear under control again as she endured his attention. She had to stay calm, think clearly, and pick her moment. If she revealed her secret weapon now, it could be taken from her.

"I'm sorry," she said. "I don't want to be his, Lord Poppy. I forgot myself, for a moment."

Lord Poppy tucked her hand back into place and pulled her on again. "This is what happens when you insist upon being relentlessly interesting, my little sunlit one. They want to keep you. But, alas, we can't keep the King waiting…"

26

Rupert wasn't in the quadrangle when they'd arrived in Oxenford, so Max and the gargoyle decided to stake the place out covertly instead. The Sorcerer knew that Beatrice was dead, as soon as his bomb went off. The call might simply have been to check if he'd survived and the invitation quick thinking. What Rupert wanted to do to "celebrate" was difficult to predict, but he shared the gargoyle's lack of faith in the man.

Max lurked in Catte Street, keeping an eye on one side of the Bodleian Library, as the gargoyle staked out Broad Street. The city's architecture provided many opportunities for a gargoyle to remain unnoticed, and the streets were empty of people. As far as Max knew, the city was still under the control of the Irises. He knew Rupert would be keen to reclaim his home. Max suspected that the Nether reflection of the Bodleian contained Rupert's sorcerous library.

The gargoyle pulled his attention to several Fae-touched it could see approaching the Sheldonian Theatre, dressed in academic gowns. Where were they going so late at night?

Max agreed with the gargoyle's instinct to investigate further, so he left his nook and headed down Catte Street. Turning left and passing through the wrought iron gates and along the path to the east side of the Sheldonian, Max ducked behind one of the stone columns of the university admissions office when he saw the academics heading into the theatre through the east door.

When he was certain it was clear, both around him and through the gargoyle's eyes, Max hurried as quickly as he could to the Sheldonian. He worked his way round the D-shaped building to find a place where he could use a Peeper without being seen. He settled on a spot just to the right of the doors at the back of the building, along its only straight wall, and twisted the lenses of the Peeper in the correct orientation to see inside the Nether building, rather than through to the mundane anchor property.

There was a semicircle of about twenty chairs just in front of him. A larger chair in the middle was flanked by two large gilded stands, each with a metal basket on the top. The men in the robes were heading towards the seats, looking confused and uneasy. "Do you have any idea what this is about?" one whispered to his neighbour as they sat down.

"No, but we haven't been summoned like this since Iris—"

"Shush! Be careful what you say!"

Both men straightened as a man who looked like he could be a Wisteria sat down to the right of the largest chair. He didn't seem very popular.

There was a long pause once all of the chairs, save the largest one, were filled. "Does anyone know why the meeting was called?" asked one man, and everyone looked at the Wisteria, who squirmed in his seat.

Something contained within the baskets on either side of the largest chair burst into flames and they stayed lit, like torches. The men all cried out in shock; it evidently had significance to them, but Max had no idea what it was supposed to mean.

All of them were looking at the Wisteria, who had started to shake visibly. Before he could say anything, the doors of the theatre opened and Rupert walked in, dressed in the same scruffy jeans and hoodie as he had been the last time Max saw him. A strangled gasp came from the Wisteria, and the men sitting near him leaned away, distancing themselves as much as possible.

"Hey! I'm back!" Rupert cheered. "Had to deal with some sorcerous bullshit for a while there and—" He stopped halfway down the aisle, staring at the Wisteria. "Why are you in Alexander's chair? Wait a minute...what the fuck is going on here? Where's my Vice-Chancellor?" When none of the men answered, Rupert walked the rest of the aisle until he was standing right in front of them. "Where is he?"

A man who had the look of a Buttercup about him cleared his throat. "He's been exiled, Chancellor. By...the...um...Chancellor of Oxenford."

Rupert laughed. "Okay, very funny. So where's the real council? Why are you wearing Brasenose colours, Buttercup? Why are you even here?"

The Wisteria stood up. "Chancellor," he stammered, "we thought you were dead. The torches went out for the first time in hundreds of years and you told us that if they did, you had died. And...and so—"

"And so Wisteria sided with Nathaniel Reticulata-Iris," said one of the men at the edge of the semicircle, "who abused Margritte Tulipa in our presence, threatened us all with the Iris Patroon's sword, and bullied his way into power. Wisteria gave him the one rule that could be exploited so he could force his way in."

"I had to end the stand-off somehow!" the Wisteria said as Rupert stared at him. "He was threatening everyone, not just Alexander's mother! You're an Iris and you didn't have the courage to say anything! He would have killed—"

"Oh, shut the fuck up, Wisteria!" Rupert shouted. "Some streak of piss Iris has taken my city? No offence, Theo, you're solid, but the Reticulata-Irises are a bunch of fucking gangsters. For the love of—shit, I'm away for like five fucking minutes and this happens?"

"We thought you were dead," the Wisteria mumbled.

"You're not the Vice-Chancellor," Rupert said. "Take that gown off. And you, Buttercup. Shit, you couldn't even organise a decent party, let alone run a college."

"I had no idea the punch was alcohol-free, Chancellor!"

"Oh, the fact that everyone there was bored out of their fucking minds didn't give you a clue? Take the gown off." He looked at Theo. "What happened to Alex's mum?"

"She was taken prisoner by Nathaniel and put in the tower at Oxford Castle. That's been the seat of power in your absence, sir.

The last we heard, Margritte was prosecuted by the Patroons and exiled to the Colonies."

The doors of the theatre banged open a second time and Nathaniel Iris stormed in. "Why are you holding a meeting without me? Who called it?"

"I did," Rupert said, turning to face him.

"I take it by your attire that you've been sleeping rough in Mundanus. Who are you?"

"The Chancellor of Oxenford. The real one. Didn't this bunch of reprobates tell you about me? How I've run this city for hundreds of years?" He laughed. "So they managed to keep that secret at least."

"You were such a secret, sir, you did not exist when I arrived. I was voted in by the Hebdomadal Council. If you weren't responsible enough to care for your city, you have no right to claim it now."

From his viewpoint, Max could see the Wisteria shaking his head at Nathaniel, trying to signal a warning to him now that Rupert's back was turned.

"Are you related to William, by any chance?" Rupert asked.

"He's my brother."

"Yeah, I thought I could see the same arsehole streak running through the two of you."

"How dare you!" Nathaniel reached for his sword.

"Don't bother," Rupert said. "You can't hurt me with that. So, Oxford Castle, eh? I always hated that place. Can see why it suits you, though. You should go back there and think about what you've done."

"I'm no child, sir, I am the Chancellor of Oxenford, a Duke of Albion, and this is my city now. Get out or face the consequences."

Rupert pulled his yo-yo out of his pocket as Nathaniel drew his sword. Rupert laughed. "Fancy yourself as a swordsman, do you?"

"I've already killed several men who dared challenge me," Nathaniel said, readying his stance. "I can easily add you to the list."

Rupert jerked the yo-yo up the string and then held it in his palm, whispering something to it. "If you like being the king of the castle so much, you should go back and stay there."

He crouched as Nathaniel lunged, ducking below the blade to tap the floor with the yo-yo at full extension. Nathaniel fell through a hole that opened below him where the yo-yo had touched. Rupert yanked it back into his palm and walked to the edge of what Max assumed was some sort of pit, judging by the echo of Nathaniel's shouts. He spat into it and then with a second tap of the yo-yo at its edge, the hole closed and the shouting was cut off.

Rupert strolled back to the Council, the Wisteria and Buttercup now just wearing plain suits, the robes draped over the chairs. "I've got a couple of things to sort out. I'm gonna go and seal that prick into that fucking castle permanently and destroy the road to it. If any of you try to help him to get out, I'll kill you. Capisce?"

They all nodded.

"Theo, get a message to Alex, wherever he is; tell him to come back and do his fucking job. By the time I get back, I want this Council back to what it was before I left. Buttercup, piss off until you're competent. Wisteria…your job is to figure out what to say to me to stop me from burning you at the stake as a traitor to this city. Got it? Right."

Rupert left the building and Max detached the Peeper, moving round to see the Sorcerer heading for the Bodleian instead of Broad Street. Why wasn't he going to seal Nathaniel into the castle, as he'd said? As he walked into the quadrangle, Rupert put his fingers to his lips and whistled. Benson or Hedges—Max had no way to tell between Rupert's golems—rolled out of Convocation House and went up to the Sorcerer.

Rupert leaned his head against the golem's chest, looking exhausted. Max pulled a Listener from his pocket and tucked it into his ear, staying as far back as he could.

He could hear Rupert breathing clearly and a soft clanking sound as he banged his head against the golem's metal casing. "Benson. Thank fuck. Add in an entry about Nathaniel Iris taking the city; I'll fill in the details later. Bring me notes on how to sever a Nether road made by the Fae. And Margritte Tulipa… Rings a bell, just can't place her."

"Margritte Semper-Augustus Tulipa has extensive entries in the archive," Benson replied in its flat, artificial voice. "She is the only mortal who has been brought into the stacks. She still has clearance. Should that be amended?"

"Why the fuck would I take someone into the stacks? That's madness."

"She almost died when Ekstrand attacked Convocation House. She was removed with you and brought round. You requested that she not be disposed of, despite the security breach. I brought her tea at your command."

Max remembered that day of Ekstrand's attack very clearly. It was only a few weeks ago. Had Rupert already forgotten? Then Max remembered the way Ekstrand had to be constantly reminded of even the most important issues, sometimes getting so distracted he was hopelessly inefficient. Now Max was starting to suspect that Ekstrand's eccentricities were as much to do with an appalling memory problem as anything else. He made a mental note to mention it to Cathy at his earliest convenience. If she wanted to learn more about sorcery, she needed to know the risks involved.

"Right," Rupert said quietly. "I'll read up on that later. What was the last thing I said about Max?"

"That he should be killed."

"Reasons?"

A series of whirrs and clicks came from the golem. "The gargoyle is insubordinate and was attached to Kay. It knows you killed her. Probability of retribution: 80 per cent."

Rupert nodded. "Shit, yeah. Damn. He's the only Arbiter I've got. Ah, well, I'll just have to make some more. No biggie. Go get that other info for me. I'm gonna get a kebab. I won't be long."

He opened a Way with his yo-yo and stepped through into the shadowy mundane quadrangle. Max watched Benson roll away as the gargoyle climbed down the wall next to him and took the Sorceress's Opener out of its jaws.

"He's going to kill us," the gargoyle whispered, and Max nodded. "I don't want to make a habit of this, but…" It didn't finish the sentence, but Max knew it was considering harming Rupert. "I don't want to kill him," the gargoyle added. "I can't stop thinking about that screaming…but we can't just ignore this."

"We can't attack Rupert; he'll be warded," Max whispered to it. "We need to find a weakness. Follow the golem. See if you can get into the stacks. I think we'll find what we need there. If you get into trouble, go back to the tower." The gargoyle put the Opener back in its mouth, holding it between its stone jaws as it scampered off.

Max went back to Catte Street, finding a better nook to hide in so he could focus on what the gargoyle saw. By the time he was settled and able to properly watch through the gargoyle's eyes it was underground, having gone through a door in the Bodleian quadrangle and down a shallow slope.

It was lit with bright electric bulbs, something Max had never seen in the Nether. The walls were plain stone, all grey and featureless, but at the bottom of the slope there was a stone arch standing proud from the walls and ceiling. As the gargoyle approached silently, several paces behind Benson, it became clear that the arch was covered in wards that stretched across the floor beneath it too. The gargoyle hesitated as Benson rolled through without pausing.

Max knew it was scared to go through the arch, and that was understandable, given Rupert's skill. It crept as close as it dared, sniffing at the stone, but then the familiar noise of Benson's trundling along the flagstones stopped. The gargoyle pressed itself against the wall, still watching, as Benson swivelled around. But instead of turning a full 180 degrees to look behind it, Benson pulled out a book from the shelf next to it, only to set it aside. It extended its arm attachment to the back of the shelf and pulled out a small tin. After shaking it a couple of times, Benson prised off the lid, looked at the contents, and shook the tin gently again. It sounded like buttons or other very small hard objects were inside. After a few moments of staring at it, Benson closed the tin, put it back in its hiding place, and replaced the book.

It was such a human act. Why would a golem do such a thing? Then Max considered the complexity of speech and tasks that both

Benson and Hedges were capable of. Far too sophisticated for a simple animated assistant. What if they were more than simply golems? What if they were more like the gargoyle, a soul trapped inside something animated? Perhaps a soul split in two between them?

The gargoyle looked at the arch again, thinking the same as Max: if Benson and Hedges were really fragments of a soul trapped in inorganic animated constructs, surely the gargoyle would be just as safe from the wards that let them through? The gargoyle dashed through the arch, as if to get it done before courage faltered, and all was well on the other side.

Curiosity getting the better of it, the gargoyle found the tin and peeped inside. It was filled with multi-coloured beads, a couple of earrings and a pearl, looking for all the world like a magpie's hoard. The gargoyle put it back where it was found and pressed on.

It followed Benson deeper into the tunnel, past shelves of books running down the left-hand side that were all bound identically in red leather, with strings of numbers embossed in gold on the spines. After a minute or so of passing through the pools of yellow light cast by the regularly spaced bulbs above, Benson finally paused outside a door, opened it with a special key attachment, and rolled inside. The gargoyle crept up to the door which had been left open, seeing a room filled with piles of the same books—only these copies had no numbers embossed on the spines. Benson went over to one that was on a stand and opened it, flicking the pages until the first blank one was reached, right at the end of the volume. It switched the arm attachment to something that looked like a plastic rolling pin and then ran it across the blank page, leaving words in its wake. It turned the page and did the same again to the other side and the opposite page and then the very last page of the book before turning it on its side, making some sort of adjustment to the attachment before rolling it down the spine. The embossed numbers in place, it picked the book up, and started to turn, sending the gargoyle running to hide.

Cautiously, the gargoyle peeped round the corner at the sound of Benson rolling along again as the door to the small room closed behind it. Down more long tunnels, a few turns along the way, Max estimated that there were thousands of books on the shelves. Eventually Benson reached a partially filled section of shelving and placed the book on a shelf. It rolled a little way back, plucked two other books out and rolled off again.

Max wanted to see inside the latest book to confirm a growing suspicion about the nature of this underground library. Once the gargoyle was certain that Benson had gone round a couple of corners, it hurried over to the last book placed on the shelf and opened it.

The text was tiny and it was mostly bullet points and snippets of conversation. It was difficult to read, even when the gargoyle moved beneath one of the lights, a mixture of English and some sort of shorthand. Max focused on some of the transcribed dialogue and recognised the last thing Rupert said to Kay: *What the fuck? I fucking trusted you!*

How had Benson known what he said? Was there something connecting them? Could the golems be animated with slivers of Rupert's soul? However it worked, it was clear that the books were as he suspected: a record of what Rupert had done and said. Hence his need for Benson to look something up for him, probably in the books Benson removed.

The gargoyle picked another book from the shelf and flipped back a few pages, scanning the shorthand until other snippets of conversation were recognised, things he'd said in the office a few weeks ago. It was like reading a diary, with certain lines and illegible entries highlighted with gold. As the gargoyle looked through the rest of the book, they could see how it detailed not only the conversations but also activities when he was away from the office. Most of it was written in the code, and Max assumed that was his sorcerous research into killing Beatrice. After sampling two other books and picking out memorable conversations, it seemed that each book covered a week.

Max considered the sheer number of books they'd seen. How many of them were there in total? Thousands upon thousands, storing not only sorcerous knowledge but also conversations that were hardly monumental in the life of a Sorcerer. He recalled how Rupert had forgotten Margritte, a woman who'd been in the stacks, someone who must have meant a great deal to him if he'd trusted her so. How could she have been forgotten so swiftly?

This underground repository was more than an aide-mémoire. It held his thoughts and memories, like a paper reproduction of Rupert's brain. No wonder he'd been so keen to get back. Perhaps all of this was the reason he spent so long away from the office. Was he spending time with Benson and Hedges, recording entries and struggling to remember things without the need for secret trips back into the stacks?

Max set off for the entrance to the quadrangle as a plan fell into place. If he could destroy those books, he could destroy Rupert's memories. If the Sorcerer couldn't remember him or the gargoyle, he'd never pose a threat; they would simply be forgotten. As he hobbled back across Catte Street, the gargoyle tried to tear out the page, but no matter how hard he tried, the paper remained intact.

The gargoyle tried to scratch out the words with his claws, but even though the page felt like it was made of normal paper, his claws left no marks. Max suspected the books were warded against damage; of course they would be. The shelves were undoubtedly protected too, probably against fire and water as well. But Max was willing to bet that an Opener would still work in there.

Frustrated by the wards, the gargoyle replaced the book and heeded Max's desire for him to test the Opener by pressing the pin into the floor. The gargoyle turned the doorknob and the Way opened to Beatrice's tower. With a grin, the gargoyle swept an entire section of books straight off the shelf to fall into the room below.

A movement nearby made Max look up, focusing on his own surroundings instead. He saw Rupert toss a half-eaten kebab away at the end of the street and start sprinting towards the Bodleian. There must have been some sort of alarm. Max mentally telegraphed the warning to the gargoyle before he used his Opener to create a Way to London, with the aim of heading the long way round to Beatrice's tower. He could only hope the gargoyle would send enough books through—and manage to escape—before Rupert put a stop to it.

27

One glance at the Fae palace was enough to make Cathy tremble. It was an amalgam of every single fairytale castle she'd seen at the end of childhood storybooks, with green fields all around it and the promise of happily ever afters. She thought of the arrowhead and Tom and Lucy and keeping them safe. She had to make sure she didn't anger Poppy, otherwise he'd take it out on them.

"Wait here," Poppy said to Tom and Lucy. The large oak doors swung open ahead and his grip on her hand tightened. He didn't want to let her go. As if she were his to keep.

Cathy stole one last glance at Tom, who looked devastated at having to let her go on without him. She tried her best to look brave for him, to assure him that she would get through this, but it didn't seem to make much difference. Lucy looked tearful, her arms wrapped around Tom as he held her close. Then Cathy was pulled forward and the doors slammed shut, cutting her off from them.

She was escorted through an entrance hall beneath dozens of sprites, unable to stop herself from gawping at the beauty of the decorated pillars and vaulted ceiling, then down a long corridor to another set of doors that opened before them too.

There was a man on the throne but she couldn't look directly at him.

"Let her go, Poppy."

She twitched at the sound of Will's voice and the panic surged again.

"I was simply escorting her, your majesty." As he removed his arm from hers, Poppy whispered, "I do so hope I will see you reach your full potential." Then, after a deep bow to the throne, Poppy left and the doors closed behind him, leaving her alone with the one man she never wanted to see again.

"Cathy," Will said, so tenderly. "Cathy, look at me, please."

Even though Cathy tried to resist, she couldn't stop herself from doing as he asked. He sat on a throne, a crown of oak leaves resting on his hair, wearing an exquisite green frock coat with black trousers. His waistcoat was embroidered with golden oak leaves, his cravat was perfectly tied, and he looked even more handsome than she remembered. He was smiling at her and she pressed her lips together, biting down on them inside, to stop herself reciprocating it.

"Won't you even greet me, my love?"

"I am *not* your love!" she said, and lowered her gaze again, unable to look at him a moment more.

"I wanted to say I'm sorry," Will said.

"What for, exactly? Forcing my brother to bring me here? Putting that dog collar on me? Raping me? Which one?"

"I never raped you!"

"You did. You gave me that Charm to make me lustful and pliable when you knew I wasn't ready to consummate our marriage. Making me incapable of fighting you off doesn't stop it being rape. And I will never fucking forgive you for that."

"You're right."

She looked up in shock, hearing the sincerity in his voice and needing to see if it matched his face. But it was so hard to maintain her stare, not just because of the anger, but the sheer majesty of him. Of the crown, no doubt. She lowered her head again.

"I never should have done that," he said. "I am so sorry. And the choker...it was despicable. I regret it more than I can express. I was so caught up in keeping Iris happy, and keeping us safe from his anger, I didn't think. I didn't think about you, that is. I thought I was protecting you. When I saw what he did to Dame Iris...I was terrified he'd do the same to you."

"So you made me a slave. Well done. What brilliant protection. I suppose this kidnapping by the back door is actually protecting me too? Terrorising my brother is still okay, obviously."

"You wouldn't speak to me! You just ran and—"

"Of course I fucking ran, you bastard! I never wanted to see you again!"

"You didn't give me the chance to explain. To apologise."

"Jesus, Will. Even when you're trying to say sorry, it still seems like it's my fault."

Cathy listened to the sound of his shoes on the stone floor, getting closer. She wanted to take a step back—she wanted to run—but she could do neither. At the back of her mind was the constant worry that she wasn't kneeling to him, but her rage was enough to keep that from swamping her. She'd never kneel to him. She'd rather die.

The tips of his black leather shoes came into view. She flinched away when he reached towards her, so he clasped his hands behind his back. She could smell him, the sweet muskiness of his skin, tangling her in memories of lust and shame.

"How can I make this right between us? How can I show you how sorry I am?"

"You can leave me alone. Forever."

His sigh was deep. "But I love you."

She laughed. She didn't even find it funny, but once she started, it wouldn't stop.

"Don't laugh at me," he said, hurt, and the laughter died in her throat.

"You don't love me. You just can't stand the fact that I don't want you. I will never give myself to you willingly and that makes you want me more. It's pride, Will. Not love."

He almost reached out to touch her again and she flinched, just like before. He walked away a few paces, as if to remove the temptation. "You're wrong. Everything's changed now. There's no pressure on us anymore. I rule over Iris now. He'll never force us to do anything again! All the reasons why I did those things have gone now. We can start again."

"Start again?" She clenched her fists, wanting nothing more

than to just turn and leave, but she felt rooted to the spot. "This isn't like burning a pie and deciding to make another one."

"I know that! What I mean is that we were forced together, and you tried so hard to make me a better man and I was just too trapped in that world to even try. But now there's no external pressure to do anything. We can start again. Take our time. No Patroon breathing down our necks, no Lord Iris threatening us. Just me and you. I got to the top of the ladder, Cathy. We can be free."

She knuckled her temples, struggling to understand. "You force me to come here by threatening my brother and setting one of the Fae upon me, to tell me we can be free? Are you even listening to yourself?"

"Goddamn it, Cathy, why are you making this so difficult?" he shouted, and she shrank back from his anger, her right leg buckling until she realised what she was about to do. She gritted her teeth and dug her fingernails into her palms, fighting the urge to kneel and supplicate herself before him.

"It's difficult because I can't trust you. You cast magic upon my heart and forced yourself upon me. You said you believed in my cause and then systematically blocked any attempts to achieve change. You collared me like a dog to make me obedient and told your father something I shared in confidence, that led to *my* father's suicide. That's why this is so fucking difficult, William. Because I'm not a machine or a doll or a pet. I'm a woman that you have raped and abused and hurt."

There was a long silence between them, long enough for Cathy to worry about Tom and Lucy.

"I need to earn your forgiveness and your trust, I understand that," Will said.

"No, you don't need to do that at all. You just have to let me go back to Mundanus and leave me alone."

He came close again, took hold of her hands before she could pull them away. "But we're married."

"Our marriage is as real as the night we consummated it," she said, pulling her hands away with a supreme effort. "If Iris doesn't need a child from us anymore, he doesn't need us to be married anymore."

"Look at me."

She did, without thinking. His eyes were so beautiful, large and brown and filled with sincerity. "I did all of those things and I regret every single one. And I know how angry you are with me and I understand why you wouldn't want to be with me. But I'm not just asking for the chance to earn your forgiveness and your trust. I'm offering you a place at the top of the ladder with me. I don't just want to stay married to you. I want you to be my Queen. I want you to rule Exilium with me."

"But why me?"

"Because I love you." He pressed his lips to her hands. "Because I know you will make me a better person. And I know you will be an incredible Queen when you can make the Kingdom whatever you want. There are no Patroons here, no rules, no stuffy men to keep happy for the sake of safety and stability. You can make it your own, in the way I should have let you in Londinium."

It still made no sense to her. Why was he persisting like this? Was his ego so fragile that he had to win her back? Why did he even care? She tried to remember any sign of his love before she left him, but every single moment of kindness or tenderness was clouded by the thought of being under the Charm's thrall at the time. He'd simply acted that way to keep her sweet so she wouldn't rock the boat. So she'd give him a child.

Now he said he didn't need anything like that from her. So why wouldn't he let her go? It couldn't be love, not after all the things he'd done.

But what if he really did love her? Shouldn't she forgive him, to please him? No! That wasn't her own thought, it couldn't be. He was doing something to her again.

"It's not my job to make you a better person," she said, desperate to pick holes in what he said to keep herself from temptation. "Haven't you heard anything I've said? And you can stop making me feel…strange."

He frowned. "It's the crown, I swear. You don't have to kneel to me, or look down all the time. I don't want that. I want the *real* you."

The pressure to be deferent eased. "Let go of me. Please."

He did as she asked and took a step back. "I'll never force you to do anything again. But this is the only way I can give you what I couldn't before. We wouldn't just rule Exilium, Cathy, we'd rule the Nether too. Don't you see? The Fae have to obey me, and as the Queen, they'd have to obey you too. You could tell them to remove the Patroons if you wanted to. You could tell them to make the reforms you've wanted all this time. You could shape the Nether and give the women there all the rights you want them to have. And no one could stop us."

She dug her nails into her palms again, her resolve wavering. True change in the Nether? The end of the Patroons and their patriarchy? It was all she had ever wanted. It was the only reason she'd even listened to Beatrice in the first place and now that she was gone, this was the only way to change anything. The thought of destroying the Nether herself seemed ridiculous. It was like asking a schoolchild to finish building a nuclear power station. Surely becoming Queen was the only way to achieve her goals now?

But what about Sam? If she stayed and made a life with Will to make those changes, he'd never understand. He'd come for her and what would happen then? War? And she couldn't leave him to deal with the Elemental Court alone. She couldn't reform the Nether whilst damning Mundanus.

"No one could stop you, Cathy," Will said, pulling her thoughts back to him. "Not if you were Queen."

"Could you stop me?"

"There would be no need. I only held you back in Londinium because of the Patroon, not because I disagreed with your ideals. On the contrary, I support them."

Cathy looked at the crown to avoid looking into those beautiful eyes of his. She had the vaguest memory of Beatrice saying something about crowns. What was it? "How did you become King?"

"I took the crowns."

"And the Fae royalty didn't stop you. Why? Didn't they want to be in charge of everyone else?"

"It's different for the Fae, ruling over their own. They'd grown to hate it."

"Then why didn't they pass it on to another Fae?"

"Because I was strong enough to take the throne for myself," Will said, a harsh edge to his voice.

"But you're just a man. You weren't even an Iris when you took it."

"Do you have so little respect for my ability? I took Londinium, didn't I?"

"Yeah, but you had Iris's help to do that."

He turned his back on her to walk back to the throne. She'd touched a nerve. Interesting. This was more than his pride, this had something to do with the crowns, something that made him tense.

She expected him to sit, so he could look down on her, but instead he went to the other throne. She hadn't noticed the circlet there, the one he now held as he came back to her. "This is yours, Cathy," he said when he reached her. "You have so much potential, and with the power this crown gives you, you could realise it."

Potential. Sam had told her that Poppy believed her potential was to destroy everything, even though she'd been led to believe it was something to do with painting. Why did Poppy say he wanted to see her reach it?

The crown in Will's hands sparkled in the sun and sprite light. The leaves were such a vibrant green, the gold such a rich colour. It reminded her of Beatrice again. *The crowns made sure of that.* What had Beatrice been talking about when she said those words? Something about stopping the Fae…that was it! The Sorcerers made the crowns—the very crown Will was wearing now and the one he held out to her—as part of the prison they stood in. The crowns gave the Sorcerers the power to stop the Fae from doing anything and made the royalty here the jailers. That was what Will was now, a glorified jailer of a beautiful prison.

"Can you leave Exilium, now you are King?"

His open, hopeful smile faded. "I have no need to leave it. Why would I? Look at what I have here. Look at what you could have too."

"But what about Sophia? She needs to be in Mundanus until she comes of age, otherwise she'll never grow up. Won't you want to visit her?"

"She likes it here. She'll visit us. She's missed you so much, Cathy."

"Just answer the question. Please. Can you leave?" He looked away, answering the question for her. "So that's the price, is it? I can change the Nether, but will be imprisoned here with you and the Fae, forever."

"You always knew there would be sacrifices to make the changes you wanted." He took a step closer, raising the Queen's crown ever so slightly.

"And when were you planning to tell me that the crown is just like that damn choker?"

"It's nothing like it! You will still be you, fully you, in control."

"But unable to leave. You know how much I love Mundanus."

"I know how much you love equality and fairness and rights for women too. Which is more important to you? Getting rained on or seeing the Nether change?"

Cathy tucked her hands in her pockets, feeling for the arrowhead. "This has nothing to do with what is more important to *me*. This is all about you controlling me again. I'd be willing to bet that even if I were Queen, you'd still be able to veto me." She couldn't imagine the Sorcerers creating a prison with equal jailers. In their minds, women were lesser, and she was certain they would have seen to it that the Queen was lesser than the King, even in Exilium.

"I don't want to control you," Will said. "If I wanted a pet, I could have one. What do I have to say to convince you? I want to give you the worlds, Cathy. I want to give you the power to achieve your dream. And yet you keep throwing it back at me."

The crown raised another inch. He was close enough to put it on her head. She wriggled her fingers into the leather glove, trying to find the arrowhead buried in its folds.

"You've apologised," she said, trying hard to keep her voice steady as her heart galloped. "Thank you. I'm glad you understand now. And I thank you for the offer to be made Queen; however, I decline."

His shock was beautiful. "But…but how else will you change the Nether? How else will you get what you want?"

"I don't know." *But I'll learn,* she promised herself. *I'll shut myself away and learn all the sorcery I need to destroy this place before I'll be yours again.* "I want to find my own way, rather than have it handed to me on a plate as the cell door is being closed. You stay here, be King, be happy. We're no longer married, because you're no longer an Iris. Make whoever you want your Queen. It won't be me."

"But I need you."

"You need to let me go. You don't really want me, Will. You just want to win." She saw the Queen's crown move another inch, the anger flare in his eyes. "If you put that on my head, you'll prove that everything you've just said to me is total bullshit. You'll be the man you say you don't want to be."

"You don't know what's best for you," he said. "You never have. Catherine, you are my Queen and you will accept this crown."

Of course she was. He was her King. She had to accept. Her knees buckled just as her fingers grasped the arrowhead. It felt like she was plunged into cold water, the weight of his expectation upon her suddenly washed away.

She pulled her hand from her pocket, fist closed around the iron, to block him with her arms as he moved the crown above her head. The arrowhead's sharp point scratched his hand on the way up and he cried out as if he'd been stabbed with a sabre, dropping the Queen's crown in shock. The clatter of metal on stone rang out, filling the throne room.

The doors behind her burst inwards and dozens of sprites and faeries dressed in oak leaves flew in, screeching, circling above them. Will clutched his bleeding hand and staggered back, shaken, as Cathy moved towards the open doorway slowly, putting distance between them. All of the tiny creatures above them were glaring at her and she had the sense they were just waiting for the command to shred her to pieces.

There were footsteps, light and fast, coming down the corridor behind her. Cathy braced herself for whatever was about to hit, unwilling to take her eyes off Will and the horde above them.

"Cathy!" Sophia cheered, and wrapped her arms around her legs. "You're here! Will-yum said you would be. I missed you! Are you Queen now? Look! I made a map!"

"Hello, darling," Cathy said, nervously watching Will. "That's a beautiful map."

"You didn't even look."

"Well, I'm just leaving now and—"

"Aww. Can't you stay and play with me? You were gone for millions of years."

"I'm sorry, I can't," Cathy said, still watching Will as she gently untangled herself from Sophia's embrace. "Lord Poppy needs to take me and my brother and sister-in-law home now."

"But why?"

"Because I don't live here, and I have my own things to do. And you know how kind Will is. He wouldn't keep me here when I need to be somewhere else, would he?"

"I suppose not. Are you going to come back?"

"No."

"Yes," Will said as his blood dripped onto the stone floor. "Yes, she will be coming back. In the meantime, Cathy has something very important to think about. I'm sure she'll realise the best way to keep all of her friends and family safe is to be Queen."

"Good," Sophia said. "When you're Queen, Cathy, can we make a rocket for my dollies?"

"We'll see," Cathy said. She had to get out now—she knew Will wasn't willing to do something ugly in front of the child. "Now you go and give Will a big cuddle. He looks like he needs one."

Sophia gasped at the sight of the blood. "Oh, Will-yum! You've got a boo! We need a bandage. I can be your doctor."

Cathy backed out the doorway as Sophia went to Will. "I'll see you again," Will said as one of the faeries laid a sparkling bandage across Sophia's outstretched hands so she could wrap it around the wound. "You'll be much happier here with me. I'm certain of it."

Cathy turned and ran, expecting to be dragged back any moment, but she wasn't. She heaved the outermost doors open to find Lord Poppy, Tom, and Lucy all sitting a little way away, Poppy sunning himself as if it were a lazy Sunday afternoon in a park whilst Tom and Lucy clung to each other.

"Cat!" Tom said, embracing her when she ran to them.

"Take us all back to Mundanus, Lord Poppy, to the place—and time—we came through from."

Poppy tilted his head as he regarded her. "You order me as if you are Queen, yet I see no crown on your head, my sunlit one."

She'd had enough of his bullshit. "Do you see the blood on this?" She brandished the arrowhead in front of her. "Want some of yours to join it? I'm sure Lord Iron will be very interested to know if you don't do what I ask."

Poppy got up, his eyes twinkling. "You don't need to threaten me. You are the queen of my heart, after all."

"Urgh." Cathy cringed.

"The only mortal in the worlds who would be appalled by my affection," Poppy laughed. "Shall we go?"

28

Lucy was shivering by the time they got to the house Cathy had been hiding in since leaving her husband. She wished she was dressed properly, but when Poppy took her from the Nether, she'd only just got ready for bed and was wearing a nightdress and dressing gown. Her slippers were sodden and even with Tom's jacket draped over her shoulders she felt like she was going to die from the cold.

Cathy had run ahead and was talking to a plump housekeeper in the entrance hall. "Oh, hello again," the woman said as she smiled at Tom.

"This is Lucy," Cathy said as Tom managed a nod. "My sister-in-law. Lucy, this is Mrs M."

"You all look frozen. Shall I go and make some hot chocolate?" They nodded, and as she went off to the kitchen Cathy raced up the stairs and came back with a thicker dressing gown and huge fluffy socks. Lucy accepted them gratefully and soon she was wrapped up and in front of the fire with a hot chocolate.

All three of them hunched over their mugs, worrying over what was to come. Unable to bear the silence any longer, Lucy said, "So what happened with Will? Did you stab him or something?"

"No. It was just a scratch," Cathy said, staring at the arrowhead. "He was forcing me to accept the crown and be trapped there forever. With him." She shuddered.

"I'm just glad you walked out of the palace a free woman," Tom said. "Poppy was convinced you'd be crowned. I don't understand any of it."

"The crowns are part of a massive magical ritual created by the Sorcerers," Cathy said. "There are four of them: King, Queen,

Prince, Princess. They're part of the magic that makes Exilium a prison for the Fae. He's their jailer now, effectively. He was trying to sell it to me, saying I'd be able to change the Nether because I'd be able to order the Fae to remove the Patroons. But I'd be trapped in Exilium forever if I did that."

"You could really change the Nether? Forever?" Lucy asked.

"Yeah, but I'd be Will's forever too. And I don't exactly trust him to let me change anything there, even if I was Queen."

Sipping her hot chocolate, Lucy tried to reconcile the irritation simmering within. Cathy's response was perfectly understandable; Will had done some terrible things to her. But having all that power to remove the Patroons and shape Albion into something truly decent...that was one hell of an opportunity to pass up.

"We know that Will isn't trustworthy," Tom said to her. "He might have promised that, but once Cathy was his again, who knows what he would have permitted her to do?" He kissed Cathy's cheek. "You did the right thing."

"Did I? He pretty much threatened everyone I love and care about as I was leaving. If Sophia hadn't been there, I think it would have gone very differently. Shit, why won't he let me go? This is a fucking nightmare."

"We're never going to be safe," Lucy said. "Especially you, Tom. He knows how much you love each other."

"Yes, but Cathy giving up her freedom for us is not an acceptable solution."

Lucy stared down at her mug, remembering her own father saying something very similar when the family had gathered to discuss the plan for independence. The letter from the Patroon about Tom had rested on the table they sat around and she'd stared at it, trying to weigh up what was more important: the struggle for freedom from colonial rule or her right to lead the life she'd planned. When she considered the sheer number of people who would benefit from her sacrifice, it wasn't a hard choice.

She looked at Cathy, pale-faced and scowling into the fire. Lucy tried to tell herself that this wasn't the same. Will wasn't an unknown man in a foreign land. Cathy was terrified of being abused again. But considering what was at stake, Lucy still couldn't shake off the feeling that Cathy had always been selfish, wrapped up in her own struggles without being aware of others around her.

"I think there's a solution," Cathy said. "It's something that's been on the cards for a while. I'm not sure how long it would take me to figure out, but there is a way to destroy his power. And Exilium." She chewed her lip, looking at Tom nervously. "And the Nether too."

"I beg your pardon?"

"What about the people who live there?" Lucy asked, appalled.

"They'd live in Mundanus. As would the Fae. Listen, I know this sounds insane, but this is something my friend Sam and I have been tangled up in for a while now. The Sorcerers split the worlds and we were told they did that to keep people safe from the Fae. And that's really easy to believe, given how awful they are to people, but I really do think it's more complex than that. And there's the Elemental Court, and that's fucked and the environment is being destroyed by them and…" She let out a long sigh. "This must sound like total bobbins, but you have to believe me—I think there is a case for reversing that ritual and re-integrating the Fae. We need them to balance against the Elemental Court. And we need to take down Will. If I destroy that magic, I'm certain it will destroy the crowns too. It's all interlinked."

"Could you really do that?" Tom asked. "You're not a Sorcerer."

"Not yet, but I've had some lessons and I have books and a brain. It'll be hard, but not impossible."

"But if you do this, all the people who live in the Nether will age and die!" Lucy said. "Our families and friends! Us!"

Cathy shrugged. "I think that's the way it's supposed to be. Don't you?"

Lucy stood, spilling the hot chocolate in her anger. "No, I don't! I know Albion sucks, but things are starting to change! Just because it didn't happen quickly enough for you, doesn't mean it won't. And I've just won independence for my family, and maybe all the other families in America! The Nether is great over there; it's nothing like Albion! We do so much for the mundanes and…and you just want to trash all of that because of your ex? That's…that's so fucking selfish!"

Horrified, Tom set his mug down and put his arm around Cathy. "Lucy, I know this is a difficult time, but we must remain civil!"

"Civil? Cathy's talking about condemning every single person I love to death. I didn't give up everything to have our lives trashed by someone who won't step up!"

"Step up?" Cathy shook her head. "If you think that life in the Nether will get better with Will as King, you're an idiot. What do you think will happen when the rest of his family find out? They'll be back in power before you can say 'Nepotism is bullshit' and they sure as hell won't be progressive."

"But Poppy said Iris has changed," Lucy said. "Didn't he, Tom?"

"He said Iris has been reunited with his love and didn't care about being cruel to his family anymore," Tom said. "But they're rotten to the core. Besides, if Will remains King, he'll see us destroyed, regardless of what Cathy does. He'll never forgive me for taking them down in Aquae Sulis and I dread to think what he'll order the Fae to do to my aunt and uncle."

"If Cathy gave herself up, she could protect all of us!"

"Yeah, right up until he changes his mind," Cathy said, slamming her mug down. "This isn't some noble sacrifice. This is putting myself in chains and giving a pathological liar the fucking key! I refuse to have that man holding power over me again. And even if I did go and be Queen, and even if he turned out not to be a raging arsehole—which I don't believe for a moment—it doesn't solve the wider problem. The Elemental Court is sucking the life out of this planet. They need to be rebalanced. It won't matter if there's a Nether or not when Mundanus falls apart."

Lucy had no idea what this Elemental Court was, but wasn't convinced. Cathy was simply saving her own neck. She had no parents to worry about, she hated her sister and obviously didn't care if her own brother got old and died. She wasn't prepared to listen to this any longer. Lucy dumped the mug on the coffee table and left the room, fearing she would say something she'd regret if she didn't.

"Lucy!" Tom said, following her out. "Where are you going?"

"I can't believe you're listening to that crap and not challenging her, Tom! Will is a terrible man, I'm not denying that, but we have to find a better solution. Either Cathy has lost it or she's dangerous, and either way, we shouldn't enable her. We need to appease Will and protect the Nether, not trash it!"

"Cathy is no fool. We should hear her out. And appeasing Will is little more than rolling over for the devil. There's no solution to be found when a man is as evil and corrupt as he is."

"You got along fine with him before."

"Before I knew what he did to my sister! Good grief, Lucy, what has got into you?"

"I'm not going to stand back and watch your damn sister destroy everything and condemn me and my family to a slow death."

He watched her unlock the front door. "We're in the middle of nowhere! Where will you go?"

"Home. California," she lied. "I wasn't going to go back. I thought that finally, I had something worth staying for. But if you're more interested in pandering to her madness, there's no reason for me to stay in Albion."

He looked like a lost puppy. "Don't make me choose between you, Lucy. Cathy's been through so much and I should have been there for her. I'm not going to let her down now. Stay and talk it through with us. We can find a solution together!"

"Do you think she can do it? Destroy the Nether and Exilium?"

He nodded. "She mentioned some things when she came to me before the funeral. Some ward thing or other. And this is Lord Iron's house; he's one of the Elemental Court. I think she knows what she's talking about."

"And you don't want to stop her from destroying our way of life?"

"I don't want Will to be the King of the Fae. We'll never be safe. That's what this is about, Lucy."

"So you're willing to burn down an entire house—and the people in it—to kill a spider?"

"That's hardly an accurate analogy."

She opened the door.

"Lucy, wait!" He came closer. "I know I haven't been the best husband. I should have been more loving and...more... Well, the simple fact is that I love you. I love you and I need you to stay here and support us, because I love my sister too and I owe her a debt and I won't leave her to face this crisis alone."

Shivering in the cold air that rushed into the house, Lucy squared her shoulders and sacrificed another dream for the sake of her family. She had hoped for love between them once. But her family came first, and she wasn't prepared to let anyone threaten them. She reached up, as if to cup his cheek affectionately, so the Sleep Charm would take effect more swiftly.

As he fell back she dashed out of the door and ran, heading back the way they'd come before. She had to make it to the boundary, she knew that much from what Tom had told her on the way back, and she had the feeling Lord Poppy would be alert for any signs of drama.

Feet drenched and freezing cold once more, Lucy sprinted past the strange little outhouse they'd passed earlier. A gap in the dark hedgerow ahead reassured her that she was going the right way. After a few stumbles whilst negotiating the ditch, she made it to the fence, resorting to getting onto her front and wriggling under without Tom there to lift her over the top.

Her bottom lip wobbled at the thought of him but she pushed on to the oak tree and slapped her hands against the bark. "Lord Poppy, Lord Poppy, Lord Poppy! I need to come to Exilium! Please!"

The wind cut through the dressing gown and she felt like an idiot. She'd acted without thinking. She had no Charms on her, no money, and for all she knew, she was just pressing against an average tree. She rested her forehead against the bark, thinking of her mother and father, her siblings, Edwin, all of them getting old and dying just because of Cathy's self-centredness. Starting to weep, she whispered Lord Poppy's name into the tiny crevices, wishing with everything in her that he could hear.

Then she was tumbling forwards and landed on her back beneath a blue sky.

Lord Poppy looked down at her, his long hair tickling her cheeks. "What a surprise! You do look upset." He licked the tears from her cheeks as she squeezed her eyes shut. "Ah, the tang of desperation. Such a spicy flavour. Why did you call me? Did you realise I should keep your hair?"

"I need to see the King, Lord Poppy, most urgently."

"Does this have something to do with my favourite?"

She wasn't sure if Poppy would be an ally or not in this situation. "Yes, my Lord," she said. "I have a message for the King about Cathy. I need to see him."

Poppy twisted a lock of his hair around his fingers as she got to her feet. She was wet and filthy and couldn't stop shivering, despite the warmth of the sun.

Before he'd decided what to say a faerie dressed in oak leaves appeared. "Come this way," it said to Lucy, and flitted off in the direction of a gentle hill as Poppy scowled.

It escorted her to the palace, Poppy following a few paces behind. When they reached the doors, the faerie cast a shower of sparkling dust over her and the filthy dressing gown was transformed into a simple white dress in the Regency style, edged with tiny embroidered poppies around the neckline. The doors opened for her but closed as Poppy approached. She didn't need to look at him to know how frustrated he was.

Lucy barely noticed the beautiful interior as she struggled to get a grip on her emotions. She regretted leaving Tom slumped asleep in the hallway. She'd as good as walked out on the marriage, too. Had she overreacted? Her breath caught in her chest as she thought of him waking up, confused, knowing she'd gone.

But then she rallied herself. Tom was too guilt-ridden to see sense when it came to Cathy. He was so scared of letting her down again that he wasn't prepared to stand up to her when she spouted nonsense. Will was far from her first choice for King, but she'd rather see his reign endure than see the Nether destroyed.

Doors opened in front of her and she was guided into a throne room. Without thinking, she curtsied deeply, awestruck by the sheer power that radiated from the man on the throne.

"Lucy? Please, come closer. You have news of Cathy?"

She did as he asked, thankful he didn't seem to care about what had happened at the ball mere hours before. "I know things didn't go well between you. I understand why she reacted the way she did, but I don't agree with what she's planning to do about it. That's why I'm here. I think you need to know, because I can't think of anyone else who could stop her."

"Stop her from doing what?"

"She's going to destroy the Nether, and Exilium, and your crown, your majesty," Lucy said. "She's going to kill us all."

29

Tom woke in the hallway with a blanket draped over him and a pillow beneath his head. A hideous gargoyle's face stared at him, mere inches from his nose, and he yelped in surprise. When the gargoyle also leaped back with its own cry, Tom yelled again.

"Sorry," the gargoyle said. "I was checking you weren't dead."

Tom was only able to blink at it in surprise.

"Is he awake?" Cathy's voice called through from a nearby room.

"Yeah," the gargoyle called back, and then offered a stone paw to help him up.

Tom scrabbled to his feet, the gargoyle's presence doing nothing to help with the disorientation. "Cat?" he called.

"In the library," she called back.

Tom stumbled in to find an Arbiter standing in front of the fire, warming his hands as Cathy made notes from a huge book open on a desk. It was all too surreal. Perhaps he was still asleep. "Where's Lucy?"

"No idea," Cathy mumbled, disinterested.

"We have to find her! She was upset."

"Busy right now," Cathy said.

"And there's a monster in the hallway."

"That's just the gargoyle, he's lovely," Cathy said. "Tom, I need some space here. Oh, that's Max, by the way. He's the Arbiter who confirmed the forgery for us."

"That was you? Ah, thank you," Tom said. "Cat, help me to find Lucy, please."

"She's studying," Max said. "Sorcery requires concentration."

Frustrated, Tom went back out into the hallway, frowning at the pillow and blanket. "Cathy said you'd been Charmed to sleep," the gargoyle said. "You can close your mouth now."

Tom hadn't realised it had dropped open again. It seemed just like a person, only in the shape of a gargoyle. "I'm going to look for my wife," he said. "She was upset."

"Okay." The gargoyle nodded. "Want me to come and help?"

Shrugging on his coat, Tom declined and went outside, hoping the bitterly cold night would make more sense.

The moon was full and bright enough to cast shadows. He scanned the driveway and garden but couldn't see any sign of Lucy. He had no idea how long he'd been asleep. She couldn't have gone far on foot, though.

"Lucy?" he called, the wind stealing the sound. He buttoned his coat and headed towards the forge Cathy had stopped off at before. Perhaps Lucy had taken shelter there to calm down.

Once he was past the sculpted formal gardens and into the huge expanse of lawn, the forge came into view and his heart leaped when he saw a light on inside. "Lucy?" he called, and ran over.

He could hear her crying before he opened the door. Pushing it open, he found her huddled in a corner, wrapped in a grotty coat she must have found in there, shivering violently as she wept. At the sight of him she turned her face away to cry into the coat's collar.

"Lucy," he said softly. "What are you doing in here? You'll catch your death of cold!"

"I couldn't come back to the house, not after what I said," she sniffled. "Not after I made you sleep."

"Don't be silly. You were upset and you panicked, that's all."

"You're not mad at me?"

"I'm not angry," he said. "Do you still feel the same as you did?"

"I don't know," she replied, wiping her cheeks with the cuff of the coat. "But I regret what I said to Cathy. That wasn't right."

Flooded with relief, Tom took off his coat. He pulled away the horrible old thing Lucy was shivering under and helped her to her feet so he could wrap his coat around her. Her dressing gown was filthy and her slippers and socks were soaked. "Come back to the house," he said, embracing her and kissing her hair. "I'm sure Cathy will understand."

"All right," she said, and he picked her up, cradling her to him as they crossed the garden, the wind slicing through his shirt.

Cathy was in the entrance hall when they got back and gave Lucy a wary look as Tom set her down. "Are you all right?"

"I'm sorry for what I said." Lucy approached her slowly. "I was upset, but that's no excuse. This is hard, especially for you. I should have been more understanding."

With a relieved smile, Cathy embraced her. "You need a hot bath. I'll run one for you."

Tom escorted her back to the living room and a hurried set of introductions were made between the Arbiter, the gargoyle, and his wife. Cathy came back with a towel and gave it to Lucy, who peeled the sopping socks and slippers off her feet to rub them dry. Tom smiled at Cathy as she steered Lucy towards the bathroom, glad that she'd been quick to forgive, and she gave a tired smile back.

Before long, Lucy returned from her bath looking much better, wearing a clean dressing gown that dragged on the floor. Cathy fetched the Arbiter and gargoyle and they all gathered together.

"This is what I propose," Cathy said. "We go to the tower where Beatrice was setting up everything to undo the Sorcerer's ritual. I'll see if I can make head or tail of it and if I think I can complete her work, I say we get everything set up ready to prepare Mundanus for a world with the Fae in it. It's going to be horrible and messy, but I don't think there's any other way to handle it. We do it as quick as we can, before Rupert works out what we're doing and causes problems, and before Will drags me back to Exilium. Then when we're ready, I unsplit the worlds, taking Will down and setting things in motion to rebalance the Elemental Court."

"Rupert won't be a problem," said Max. "Not in the short term. We've scrubbed about two years of memories from his brain."

"Long story," the gargoyle said at the sight of their shocked faces. "It's not a long-term solution, but we should be okay to sort all this out."

Lucy was silent. Tom brushed the back of her hand with his fingertips and she looked at him with tear-filled eyes. "What about the people in the Nether?" he asked for her, seeing her worry. "What can we do to protect them?"

"Beatrice—the one who started training me in sorcery—said that they'll just be in Mundanus. Or rather, there won't be a Nether anymore and they'll all get shunted into the single reality that will be restored."

"There's no chance people will just be lost forever in the mists?"

"As far as I understand it, no. They'll just be in the Nether property one minute and then in the anchor property the next. I reckon the worst we'd see is collisions with carriages in the street. I will warn everyone first, though, okay? I've drafted a letter to send out if we go ahead with the plan. I've already been making up emergency survival packs for everyone, including the staff. Sam will help, too. We're not going to do this and then abandon them all."

Lucy just nodded. Tom wasn't sure if it was because she was so clearly outnumbered or because she'd made her peace with it. Either way, he could see how hard it was for her.

"I'm going to get all the books and my notes together. Tom, Lucy, I'm going to make the tower safe and then you should come with us. It's going to have the best wards and Sam will soon be with us, I'm sure."

"Once all of you are through, I'll wait here until he gets back," said the gargoyle. "Then I can take him straight to the tower."

Cathy nodded. "Even if Will sends one of the Fae after you to get to me, they won't be able to get past Sam," she said to Lucy. "It'll be the safest place in all the worlds until this is done."

"Thanks," Lucy said. "That's good to know. We'll keep out of your way."

• • •

Sam went to check his watch and remembered he'd left it at home, following Beatrice's instructions. It felt like he'd been waiting in the forge near Bath for hours. At least there was a fire. He just wished he'd brought a book to read.

Just as he was about to go back to the car and make some phone calls, a burning line appeared in the wall, describing a doorway that shimmered in the centre. Within moments, he could see a strange room on the other side and then Cathy stepped into view, a paintbrush in her hand. She looked just as surprised to see him as he was to see her.

"Sam! What are you doing there? We've been trying to call you. Come through."

"But Beatrice told me I needed to wait here for her."

Cathy bit her lip and after a pause said, "Change of plan. Come through and I'll explain."

He stepped into the room and embraced her. It was much colder and he already missed the fire. He took in the smashed window and the curved walls. "Is this a tower? Where's Beatrice?"

She rested the paintbrush against a pot after making a single stroke on a pane of glass held in a frame in front of her. The Way to the forge closed behind him. "You'd better sit down. There's a lot to tell you."

He found a wooden stool to sit on nearby and listened as Cathy told him what had happened since they last spoke.

"...Fuck."

Cathy nodded. "Yeah. So, I've been trying to work out what Beatrice was doing. We have a book of hers, which was open when the gargoyle..." She looked down at a stain on the floorboards, swallowed, and carried on, "When she died. Seven lines of notation, and I thought they might be the seven forges. So I picked the top one and worked out how to open a Way and there you were."

"That was lucky!"

Cathy smirked. "Not really. Beatrice sent you there, didn't she? It makes sense that the first on the list would be where she sent you to keep you out of the way until you were needed."

He nodded. "Right. And you did that door thing with sorcery?"

"Yeah."

"So you're, like, a proper Sorcerer now?"

She laughed. "Hardly! It took me hours and I reckon she'd have done it without thinking." She pointed to a table covered in books and scraps of paper. "Those books Max got me are awesome, but it's like trying to translate a story written in a foreign language using a few chaotic dictionaries. I think I'm more a code-breaker than a Sorcerer."

He went over to her. She looked so tired and strung out. He could see how heavily it all weighed upon her. "You look exhausted," he said. "Have you got any sleep?"

She yawned. "No. How can I sleep with that bastard on the throne? It's just a matter of time before he fucks with me again. I know it."

"If you don't sleep, you'll make mistakes. I reckon that's dangerous in sorcery. And Will can't find you here, can he? And if he does, I'm here now. It doesn't matter what he throws at you. He might be King of the Fae but I'm Lord Fucking Iron, and he can jog on if he thinks he can get through me."

Cathy laughed. "Is 'Lord Fucking Iron' your new title? With added badassitude?"

He grinned. "Check it out. I am the ultimate badass!"

"State of the badass art!" Cathy said, and then kissed him.

He was so shocked he didn't respond at first, and then he was pulling her closer and deepening the kiss. An electric thrill ran through him as her hands moved across his back.

But then she pulled back. "Whoa. I'm sorry."

"No need to be sorry," Sam whispered.

"I'm just tired," she said, blushing. "My brain isn't in gear. You're right, I should get some sleep."

"I liked it," he said. "Maybe we should do it again."

She got up, her blush deepening to an impressive scarlet. "I'm going to get some sleep." She stepped over the books and then turned back towards him. "I liked it too," she said with a shy smile. "But I need to focus on all of this. If I sleep in Beatrice's old room, will you be close by?"

"I won't leave this tower."

"Thanks. I sleep better when you're nearby," she said, and headed off, leaving him and his pounding heart alone.

• • •

Lucy woke with the same headache she'd gone to sleep with and it was still there by the evening. If anything, it was getting worse.

At least she had some actual clothes to wear, which were fine as long as she didn't think too hard about the fact that they belonged to a woman murdered in the very tower they'd slept in. That thought alone would have been enough to keep her wide awake, without the churning guilt and torn loyalties. Somehow she'd slept, despite the fact they were sleeping on a mattress on the floor that she and Tom had dragged over from the nearby abandoned mansion.

She kept to herself as she dithered over when to betray them. And even now, even when it was certain they were all working to destroy the Nether and condemn everyone there to death, she still felt reluctant. She couldn't stand how she was helping Will after all the things he'd done. She hated how Tom was merrily getting involved with the sorcery, treating it like one of those damn crossword puzzles he did late at night to help him wind down. He seemed incapable of thinking it all through. How would they all survive when thrust into the masses with the rest of the mundanes? Perhaps he was depending on her family's great wealth to sustain them.

It wasn't much consolation when she considered that they'd never have to face up to that anyway. Once this was all over, Will would owe her a great debt and she would see to it that the entirety of America would be given independence, not just her family. She would go back home, as she'd always planned to, and try her best to forget about Tom. Cathy would be Queen of the Fae, but Lucy was certain Will would protect her from any revenge.

He couldn't protect her from her own feelings, though. Was this the kind of person she wanted to be? But then every time she wavered, thinking she couldn't possibly do this, she remembered her parents and siblings and all the good they did back home. She imagined them getting old and frail and watching them die.

There was no way she was going to let that happen.

"Lucy?"

Tom found her staring out of the arrow-slit window at the silver sky beyond. "How's it going?"

"We've made good progress, actually. Cat's a natural. She thinks she can do it. There are some details to work out, but it's feasible." He pulled a blanket from their makeshift bed and came over to drape it around her shoulders. "I haven't seen you for a few hours. I wanted to make sure you were all right. I know you're upset."

"What have you been doing?" She didn't want to talk about herself. She was too scared of giving something away.

"Helping Cat decipher some of the symbols. Some of them have similarities to the Coptic alphabet. I have a passable knowledge of that."

Lucy couldn't help but smile at his modesty. When Tom said he had a "passable knowledge" of something, it usually meant he'd be able to give a university professor a run for their money. "Is she close to figuring it all out?"

He nodded. "I need to get back, but I was worried you'd been left alone to stew about it all. Would you like to come and join in?"

"I have a terrible headache," she said. "And I don't think I have much to contribute. You go ahead."

"I've been thinking," Tom said. "I know you're worried about your family, but we'd still be special to Lord Poppy, I'm sure of it. Even if we don't have the Nether anymore, I'm sure he'd be able to prolong life and protect us from disease, in the way the magic in the property anchors does. What I'm trying to say is that I'm sure there will be a solution."

She mustered a smile for him, but he had no idea its root was a sudden, bitter appreciation of his imperial sense of superiority. Only an Albion man, privileged to the extent he was, would be certain the Fae would even remember they existed when the potential pool of entertaining mortals opened up to several billion.

"We're just at the top of the tower if you need us," he said. "Press the dome on the bottom of the painting's frame to open the Way."

She watched him leave. It was time.

After checking that everyone was occupied, she went down the stairs and out the tower and hurried across to the mansion, hoping that everyone was too busy to look out of the arrow slits as she ran.

Once she was inside, Lucy pressed herself against the wall, catching her breath as she argued with herself. It had to be done. She headed straight for the bedroom they'd taken the mattress from, knowing there was a mirror there. After closing the bedroom door, she cleaned off the dust until she could see her reflection. White-lipped and wearing the billowing white dress, she looked like a ghost in the drab room. Lucy pulled the pendant out from under the fabric, grateful that the long chain it was strung onto was so thin that no one had noticed it. She took one last look at the sparkling oak leaf and then pressed it against the glass. It rippled for a moment, distorting her reflection, until the throne room came into view with the King walking towards her. She bowed her head, awestruck once more, despite everything else she felt about him. "Your majesty."

"I've been waiting."

"It's been difficult to find an opportunity to slip away. I'm in an abandoned mansion in the Nether. A few hundred metres away there's a tower that used to belong to a Sorcerer. Cathy and all the others are there now, and Tom says she's close to working out how to destroy the Nether."

"And Lord Iron?"

"He's there with an Arbiter and a weird gargoyle thing, too."

The King frowned. "Tell me about the tower."

"It's warded against practically everything," Lucy said. "Cathy fixed it so we could all go inside, but it's still warded against the Fae and any other Arbiters. I don't think you'll be able to send anyone in there."

"I don't need to," the King said. "She will come to me."

"Well, it has to be quick. She's taken to sorcery and they're all gunning for this."

"Leave this Way open and go back to the tower. Make sure they think you're supporting their plan. I may have need of you later."

Lucy felt sick. She'd gone through so much to free herself and her family from men like this and now she was following orders from one. A King, no less. What bitter irony. She nodded, hating herself, trying so hard to remember that this was for the greater good.

"Lucy, I know this is difficult for you," he said. "You're doing the right thing. And when this is all done and Cathy is my Queen and her passions redirected, I won't forget what you've done."

Neither will I, she thought. *I'll have to live with this for the rest of my life.*

30

Cathy rubbed her eyes. Four hours of sleep wasn't enough, but as soon as she'd woken up, she'd been unable to drift back off. There was too much to do, and she feared there wasn't enough time to do it before Will made his next move.

Sam had come to the top of the tower to see how she was getting on. Cathy welcomed the chance to talk her work through, finding it easier to spot errors in her reasoning if she explained it to someone else. She'd shown him how the lenses were set up to enable Beatrice to inscribe formulae onto different places without having to leave the tower, drawing upon the same magic as opening a Way. Then she pointed out the different parts of the formula that Beatrice had partially written out before she died.

"And...all this makes sense to you?" Sam asked, incredulous.

"Yeah," Cathy said. "At least, I think I know what it all means, but there's no one to ask if I've got it right. Which is scary." She paused as her chest tightened with the thought of what she was trying to do. How many ways it could go wrong. And how many ways it could still go wrong, even if she got the sorcery part right.

"Talk me through it," Sam said.

He knew how stressed she was. He wasn't mollycoddling her, or giving her platitudes, or trying to muscle in. She wanted to hug him for it but then she might want to kiss him again, so she stayed focused on the formula, trying to ignore how his proximity was making her feel.

"Okay, so it's made of several parts, and references things in the negative, which I was confused by at first but I think I've got it now. I think it's two phases, one in which things are broken, and then the

293

second phase in which the descriptions of those broken states are placed in the final formula. Basically, this really big formula here," she ran her finger along Beatrice's elegant script painted across the largest pane of glass, "is based on the…um…the expression of the Split Worlds. I don't know what it should be called. I think the original contains references to the seven forges, a very specific place in each one. Because I know where yours is, and where the one near Bath is, thanks to Max, I've cracked the code used to express them. That's important, because sorcery needs a mind and will behind it. If a random person off the street wrote this out, nothing would happen. Now, because I know how all these work, I can open a way to each of the forges. As far as I can tell, the first phase involves going to each of the forges and breaking the connection to Exilium there. Then describing each one as broken and inserting them into the bigger formula here. That clause is the one that would have killed me once the ritual was done."

"Shit! Are you sure?"

"Yeah. I recognise this bit here, from the warded formula she taught me. It's an expression of me, bracketed by this part here, which means broken or ended. It was really useful, actually, it helped me figure out the different phases and needing to break those seven points of contact."

Sam shook his head. "I don't get it. Surely she'd have realised you'd call me as soon as you knew she was going to kill you and that I'd pull out?"

Cathy shrugged. "She sent you to the forge so you wouldn't have known until after it was all finished. I should have seen it coming. Of course she wouldn't want me to be a proper Sorcerer. Why make more of the people who caused all this mess in the first place? She was just keeping us sweet whilst it was convenient."

"You can take that clause out without screwing it all up, though, right?"

She nodded. "Yeah."

"So why did Beatrice send me to the forge in Bath?"

"Ah! Yes, so, going back to the different phases…there's a

specific place in each forge which I need to work a formula on. As far as I can tell, it's to break a ward against…you."

"Eh?"

Cathy grinned. "Yeah, it threw me at first, but reading around it, I think what must have happened is that the first Lord or Lady Iron—or at least, the one who was around when the world was split—helped the Sorcerers set it up. Then once that bit was done, the Sorcerers warded the point where the iron meets Mundanus. Not to keep you away, just to stop you from changing it, so you can't break those roads you told me about."

Sam nodded. "That makes sense. I bet it's the seal I saw under the anvil. So you'll break that and then I'll add some carbon to the iron and do whatever I can to make it impure. I'll just need some charcoal for that; it should be easy if we start with my forge or the one in Bath. Will the worlds start going cockeyed when we break the first cable?"

"No. The Sorcerers were massively overcautious. Only one of these separation points needs to exist to keep the worlds apart, but they built in six redundancies. It's clever, I suppose; if one Sorcerer became corrupted, that one man couldn't unsplit the worlds. That's why Beatrice had to kill all of them. Max has removed enough of Rupert's recent memories that he won't know to keep watch over the Mercia forge until it's too late. So we need to destroy all of them, but things won't really kick off until the last one is gone."

"So we're sorted then."

"Nearly. There are two problems. The first is that the final formula is incomplete and I need to work out the right way to close it, once all the rest of the ritual is done. I've narrowed it down to three possibilities, but I'm already punching above my weight here. The second is that the only way to warn people in the Nether—that I can think of, anyway—isn't perfect. I thought we'd have more time. I'm scared it won't work at all, and I'm scared that even if it does, people will still get hurt."

"This is the Letterboxer plan?"

She nodded. The letter told people to stay at home over the next twenty-four hours and thanks to the addresses they'd found in the Agency files, she knew where every household within an anchor property was, and had worked out a formula to send the letters to all of them at once. The plan was horribly flawed. Only those at home would receive it, and there was no way to tell if it would cause panic or be written off as a prank without actually going to one of the Nether cities to see. Those away from home wouldn't even get the warning. "I can't think of a better solution."

"Neither can I," Sam said. "I don't think there's a way to do something this big and this fundamental without putting some people at risk. That sounds horrible but…"

Cathy sighed, feeling exhausted. "Yeah. It's all horrible, when you think about it. How Arbiters are made. What happens in the Nether. The insanity of the Elemental Court. The Fae…shit, are we really doing the right thing?"

"We know doing nothing is just as bad," Sam said. "Worse, when it comes to Mundanus. So I guess you're going to be working on closing the formula for a while?"

She nodded. "And practising what I need to write over the seals in the forges. We work through them systematically until the last anchor road cable thing is broken, then I finish it all off. Then… then it's done."

"Can King Fuckwit fight any of this, once it's started? Do I need to go and kick his ass first?"

She smirked. "I know you want an excuse, but no, I don't think so, because his crown is part of this magic. The Sorcerers were top of this food chain. If anything, I think it will be easier for us, because the other three crowns aren't in use. I reckon that works against Will. They wouldn't have made four unless four were needed." A piece of the puzzle suddenly clicked into place. "That's why he's so obsessed with me being the Queen! The crown must be making him fixate on it, to strengthen the magic."

Sam shook his head. "That's not the only reason."

Cathy frowned. "He doesn't love me."

Sam looked into her eyes. "It's not hard, you know. Even a twat like him would be able to do something as easy as that. And if this doesn't go to plan, it isn't all on you. We're just doing the best we can with a shitty situation. For what it's worth, though, I think you can pull this off."

She could feel a sense of strength and security radiating from him. When she found out what Will had done to her, she'd been certain she'd never be able to trust a man again. But Sam was different. He wouldn't do anything like that to her, and, critically, he was literally incapable of it. With him, everything was straightforward and simple in a way it never could be with a man from the Nether.

What was she doing, thinking about her friend this way, now of all times? But then he was moving closer to her and she was reaching across to close the embrace.

"Catherine!"

At first Cathy thought the female voice had come up from the room below. Both she and Sam froze.

"Catherine, are you in there?"

The voice was all too familiar. A shiver ran down her back. "That's my sister, I'm sure of it," she said, scrabbling to her feet to go to the broken window.

Elizabeth was standing on the path between the mansion and the tower, dressed in a black mourning gown. "Catherine, you must come and speak to me immediately!"

Cathy stepped back before Elizabeth spotted her, bumping into Sam, who'd come over to look. "How can she be here? No one else knows where this place is!"

"I know you're in there, Catherine. I have a message for you. It's very important."

Sam went to the window and peered down. "Tom's going out to talk to her."

"Shit!" Terrified that Elizabeth was going to cast a Doll Charm on Tom and use him against her, Cathy opened the hatch to the room below, jumped down, and hammered down the stairs, almost colliding with the gargoyle on the way up.

"Don't go out there," it said.

"I'm not going to," she replied. "I have to make Tom come

back." She pushed past and reached the bottom of the tower. Max had followed Tom out, thankfully, so he would be safe.

"I cannot believe you've taken her side," Elizabeth was saying to Tom in a horribly shrill voice. "Don't you realise what she's planning to do?" Cathy couldn't make out Tom's reply but it was clear Elizabeth wasn't impressed by it. "I have a message for Catherine from the King of Exilium. And if you have any love for me or loyalty to our kind, Thomas, you will help me."

"I'm not interested in anything Will has to say," Cathy called from the doorway.

Elizabeth peered round Tom, looking like a child next to his height. Max moved to stand next to her, ready to intervene. "So you do have the decency to speak to me."

"I would have thought that playing messenger for an Iris would be beneath you, especially considering what they did to our family."

"Since when did you have a care for our family? You didn't even bother to pay your respects to Father. You always were the most selfish wretch."

Elizabeth's hateful glare was enough to make Cathy fold her arms protectively. Even now, Elizabeth still got under her skin. "How did you get here?"

"Oh, the King knows exactly where you are." She looked down her nose at Max. "It isn't against the Treaty to open a Way into the Nether, after all."

Cathy pinched the skin across the bridge of her nose. "Then just say what you have to say and piss off."

Elizabeth's shocked expression would have been funny in any other circumstances. "You always were uncouth." She held up a silk bag and pulled out something that looked like a skein of brown embroidery silk. "The King requires that you return to Exilium and honour the marriage between you. He is currently entertaining Miss Rainer, who will remain at his pleasure until you accept the crown. Quite why he insists upon you being the Queen is beyond my understanding."

"So much is beyond your understanding, Elizabeth, that's hardly a surprise." It was a cheap shot and Cathy said it without thinking; she was too busy panicking. Of course holding Miss Rainer was within his power. He could demand anyone be brought to him and the Fae would obey without question.

Elizabeth's eyes narrowed. "He said you would be difficult, not that I needed to be reminded of how awful you are."

"Elizabeth," Tom said, putting his hand on her shoulder. "Please, don't—"

She shrugged him off. "Unlike you," she said to him, "I can see what's best for our family and the Nether." She held up the skein. "In case you don't believe me, this is a lock of Miss Rainer's hair."

Cathy gripped the doorframe, forcing herself to not run out there and swipe it from Elizabeth's hand. She couldn't stop the tears welling, though.

"That's disgusting!" Tom said. "How can you do this, Elizabeth?"

She shot Tom a foul glare. "Because I know what's best for all of us. Catherine, the King said that for every minute that you fail to go to him, he will cut another lock from her head. When he runs out of hair, he will start taking fingers." Cathy tried to blink, to stop herself from showing her hateful sister how upset she was, but it only sent the tears running down her cheeks. "He's sent for Margritte Tulipa, too," Elizabeth said with a smile. "So if he runs out of ways to hurt that horrible governess, he'll still have—"

"Shut up!" Cathy yelled. "You evil little shit!"

Elizabeth flung the lock of hair towards her. It landed on the path a few feet away. "Anyone would think you were being asked to go to the gallows. You're being made a queen and you're the last woman in the worlds who deserves it! If you're too selfish to do as he wishes, that's your problem. And Miss Rainer's."

Cathy moved forwards, not sure whether she was going to retrieve the hair or hit her sister first. Arms wrapped around her waist and she felt Sam's breath on her ear. "No, Cathy," he whispered. "Don't let her bait you, it's what they want."

"But my friend…" Cathy tried not to break down as the tears splashed onto his sleeves.

"You've delivered his message," Sam shouted at Elizabeth. "Go back to wherever you came from."

Elizabeth's eyes took in the way Sam held Cathy. "You whore," she hissed, and then marched off towards the mansion.

Tom followed for a few steps until Max said something to him that made him turn around and head back to the tower as the Arbiter followed Elizabeth. Sam tightened his embrace as Cathy pulled herself back together, the initial shock and fear for her friend shifting into anger at Will. "That fucking bastard." She wept. "I knew he was going to do something, but this? Fuck!"

Tom came over, the hair in his hand. "Could he be lying, Cat?"

It was certainly the right shade of brown. "Why would he need to? Miss Rainer could easily have been brought to him. And if I do go, he'll need her there to pressure me into wearing the crown."

"He's a disgusting man," Tom said. "What are we going to do?"

"You're not going to him," Sam said. "I'll go. I'll bring her back."

"And then what?" Cathy asked. "Kill him?"

"I couldn't do that," Sam said, letting her go so she could face him. "I'll take the crown."

"No," Cathy said. "If you take the crown, nothing changes. Someone else will have to wear it and if it's one of the Fae we're back to square one, and there's no human being decent enough to be the King who deserves to be trapped there."

"Then I'll take a load of iron with me and seal him in a fucking box."

"I think that would be unwise, Lord Iron," Tom said. "William is devious and I think there's every chance this has been designed to lure you in, rather than Cat. He knows how stubborn she is— no offence, darling, but you are. And he knows that you are close friends. I know that iron breaks Fae magic, but he has Miss Rainer. He could easily manipulate you, without recourse to magic. Then Cathy would be even more at risk, without your protection."

"Tom's right," Cathy said. "Fuck Will. Fuck all of this! We have to restore the worlds. And we have to do it before he hurts my friend."

31

Sam followed Cathy and Tom to the topmost room. A space had already been cleared around the glass that Beatrice had written on before. It was cleaned, ready for the new working to be started.

"Are you sure you're ready?" Tom said as Cathy hurriedly checked her notes. When she nodded, he said, "Really? Are you absolutely certain?"

"Shit, Tom, you're not helping!" She picked up the paintbrush and it quivered in her hand. "Give me some space." She noticed Sam. "Get ready to go through. I'm going to send the Letterboxer first."

They moved to stand near the mirror to the right of Cathy. "Ready," he said. It all felt too rushed. He didn't know what was going to happen when they started breaking the cables between the worlds. He still wasn't certain if he should just go to Exilium and wrap William Iris in a coil of iron and throw him off a cliff or something.

"But you don't know how to complete the formula," Tom said. "Are you sure you should start something you can't finish?"

"I need you to take another look at the notes," Cathy said. "I'm hoping that when I work the rest of the formula, I'll have a better feel for the right answer."

Tom shared a worried look with Sam, but they both knew there was no stopping her, so they remained silent as she worked.

"That's the Letterboxer done," Cathy said. "Opening the Way to the first forge now. Tom, make sure no one comes in here. That Way has to stay open. I don't know how to open them without the lenses here, so if the Way closes when we're on the other side, it'll be a pain in the arse."

Sam focused on the mirror, watching his reflection distort and then disappear, to be replaced by the interior of his forge at home. He stepped through and turned to see a portion of the wall replaced by the view of the tower room. The Way seemed stable. Cathy was finishing off a brushstroke, then picked up the pot of paint and stepped through into the forge with him. He went to the anvil and dragged it from its usual place, dusting off the dirt to reveal the core of iron and the slivers of copper in cross-section.

"Okay," he said. "That's where this cable joins Mundanus. When I found it before, and just concentrated on it, I ended up in the Nether."

Cathy knelt down, pulled out a pouch from her pocket, and blew a pinch of sparkling dust over the top of the seal. Symbols that Sam had never seen before seemed to catch the dust and glow. Muttering to herself, she dabbed the paintbrush once in the pot and then started to work.

Sam watched her paint over the formulae in deep concentration. The paint seemed to seep into the metal, leaving an etched impression of the new symbols she was leaving there instead. After a couple of minutes, she pulled back. "I think it's done."

Somehow, the seal looked less solid to Sam, more like a foil lid on a yoghurt pot than something embedded into the ground. He picked at the edge, unsurprised when it peeled upwards, away from the iron core beneath. "Whatever you did, it worked," he said with a grin, tossing the old seal aside to grab a handful of charcoal from the nearby ashes of the fire.

He crumbled the black chunks into dust and smoothed it over the surface, thinking back to when Beatrice taught him how to purify iron. Would this simply be a matter of reversing that? He grabbed the knife from the box on the other side of the room and cut the outer edge of his thumb. At Cathy's sharp intake of breath, he said, "It's okay. I heal really quickly these days."

After a few drops had spattered onto the dust, Sam focused his mind on the iron beneath it. Initially there was the tug to think of the entire length of it and he could feel the misty detachment starting that had landed him in the Nether before. Forcing his mind to think of only the top two inches, he imagined the iron opening up, being receptive, as an opposite to the working of pure iron in which he focused on a sense of pushing out impurities.

The dust on the top seemed to seep into the iron, almost like sugar melting on the top of Mrs M's apple pie. There was a terrific shudder that ran through the floor of the forge. "Did you feel that?" he asked Cathy.

"Yeah. I reckon they felt it in Exilium, too. Get some more charcoal and don't forget the knife. One down, six to go."

• • •

Max followed Elizabeth back to the mansion, his steady pursuit making her glance over her shoulder and quicken her pace. He had no interest in stopping her; he simply wanted to see where the Way was and close it.

Once they were in the house, Elizabeth went up the stairs and Max followed, unconcerned when she started to run. He noted the bedroom she went into and by the time he'd limped there, she was gone.

The mirror she must have used remained even though the Way had closed. He approached it, noting how it had been recently polished, before spotting a small oak leaf that seemed to be stuck to the glass. He pulled it off, seeing that it was in fact a pendant that could be worn around the neck. Someone at the tower must have smuggled it here. Not Cathy; there was no way she'd be interested in any communication with her ex-husband. Nor could it be Lord Iron, as he would break it. Obviously it hadn't been the gargoyle, which left only Thomas or Lucy Papaver.

He'd seen Thomas helping Cathy with the unknown symbols in the Sorceress's work and he'd seemed appalled at his youngest sister's behaviour. That could not guarantee his innocence, however. It was possible that he could have been deliberately misleading Cathy in her work and acting out a plan with Elizabeth. It was unlikely that

EMMA NEWMAN

Thomas would be able to support William Iris, however, considering how he'd worked with Cathy to destroy his family in Aquae Sulis.

It had to be Lucy. She'd been utterly disengaged from any of the work in the tower that day, and seemed withdrawn even from her own husband. Max didn't have the greatest faith in his ability to read people's emotions, but even he could see she'd been struggling. Then he remembered how she'd Charmed her husband to sleep at Lord Iron's house and how Tom had found her. That was ample time for her to open a Way to Exilium and appeal to William.

He put the oak leaf into his pocket and then smashed the mirror. He was sure it wouldn't keep Will at bay for long, but smashing all the mirrors in the house seemed to be a wise precaution. If Cathy decided to go there, she was more than able to open a Way with her own knowledge now.

Methodically, Max went to each of the rooms on the top floor and smashed any mirrors he found within, no matter how small. Once he was certain the top floor was clear, he went downstairs and started at the kitchen at the far end of the house. Just as he was heading for the dining room, its door opened and Petra came out. She was wearing a medieval-style gown with her blonde hair loosely braided, looking very different to the last time he saw her at the hotel.

"Max!" she smiled, came over and kissed him on the cheek. "Where's the gargoyle?"

"Nearby," he said. "What are you doing here? Has King William sent you?" He couldn't understand why, but it was the only explanation—how else would Petra be able to open a Way, let alone know where to find them?

"Lord Iris did," she said. "The King has no idea I'm here. I don't have a lot of time. I've been restored. The Prince of the Fae stole me from Iris hundreds of years ago, took my heart and cursed me to serve Ekstrand. William worked out who I was and then somehow he became King and reunited me with my heart and my love. It was a genuine act of kindness."

"He's holding a woman hostage and threatening to harm her unless Cathy goes to be his Queen. Hardly kind."

"He's obsessed," Petra said. "Iris is convinced it's the crown's work. He needs a queen and Cathy is his wife."

"That's not how she sees it."

Petra nodded. "I know. Poppy has told us that one of his own has betrayed Cathy, and is helping the King to try and get her back. We must stop this from happening!"

Max felt like he'd missed something. "Are you telling me that Lord Iris and Lord Poppy are in support of Cathy's desire to remain free? That doesn't seem to be in keeping with their previous behaviour."

"Everything has changed, Max, now that Iris and I are reunited. I need your help to protect Cathy from the King. She is the only one who can put an end to all this misery and madness."

It made sense now. "Of course—the Fae want her to release them from Exilium."

"They aren't the monsters you think they are," Petra said. "Their confinement makes them cruel. Iris has told me the things he did to try and bring me back to him and I was so shocked. The Treaty harms everyone, Max: innocents, Fae, and those in the Nether. Poppy says Cathy has the potential to destroy Exilium and free them. Help us to help her!"

Max sighed. Whom to trust? Whom to support?

"Cathy's already started," said the gargoyle. Max had been paying such close attention to Petra he hadn't noticed its arrival. "And because of that bag-of-cat-sick husband of hers, she's not ready."

"We can't stop the King," Petra said. "But we can slow him down. Iris has been working on a way to resist the power of the crown, and with Cathy's help he can make Poppy strong enough to stop the King from hurting that woman, giving Cathy more time."

"She needs it," the gargoyle said. "We've got to do this," it said to Max. "We're committed. Anything half-arsed here isn't going to work. This is one of the few times when we know the Fae want the same as we do."

"If we work together now," Petra added, "it makes it easier for us all to work together once the world is restored."

Max nodded and Petra produced a poppy in full bloom from behind her back. "Cathy doesn't know me well, so you'll be better to get this from her. Make her express her desire to fight the King, as forcefully as you can, then bring it back to me."

The gargoyle took the bloom and raced off. "Do you think we're doing the right thing?" Max asked Petra. "Iris had people stolen from Mundanus, without giving a second thought to the pain he caused their families. What will they do if they have free rein?"

"I was born before the worlds were split," Petra said. "People knew how to protect themselves from magic. The old ways will need to be brought back. Iron scissors over cribs, horseshoes on doors, the rule of hospitality…these are not difficult ideas. There will be places the Fae will favour and humanity will have to learn to avoid them or suffer the consequences. It worked well in the past."

"Did Iris steal you away?"

She shook her head. "He saved me from the idiocy of my father and the then-king. Without him I would have died. The Sorcerers made sure that everyone hated the Fae as much as they did. They learned the language of the world and still couldn't bring the Fae fully under their control. They were too chaotic for the minds of men. So they tricked them and imprisoned them. And Mundanus has suffered for it."

Max had a sudden image of Thomas in his mind, blocking the gargoyle's way into the topmost room of the tower. "No one can go in there!" he was saying.

"But I have to speak to Cathy," the gargoyle said. "It's about Will."

"You mustn't disturb her. She's just got back from the first forge. They're right in the middle of it all."

"Cathy!" the gargoyle shouted. "We think you need to go and be Queen. It's the best thing to do. Maybe then the King will settle down and stop being such a—"

"Are you fucking joking?" Cathy yelled, and the gargoyle shoved

Thomas aside with ease. "I'd rather eat my own intestines than give in to that festering shitbag, and if you and Max think I'm just going to give in because this is hard, then you can fuck off too. I'll never go back to that bastard!"

"Right you are," said the gargoyle, seeing the poppy petals close up tight and start glowing slightly. "My mistake, sorry, carry on."

Thomas pushed him back through the Way that was still open to the bedroom. "Stay away!" he hissed, and then noticed the poppy. He followed the gargoyle into the bedroom. "What is that? What are you up to?"

"Lord Poppy and Lord Iris are going to help us slow the King down, to buy Cathy and her friend some time. If there's a good moment to tell her, let her know. I doubt it will be long, though."

Thomas nodded. "I will."

"Oh," the gargoyle said as it headed for the door. "You'd better not let your wife in there."

"I wasn't planning to; Cathy needs space. Why would you…" The gargoyle had already started to bound down the stairs before he finished the sentence.

"We have what you need," Max said to Petra. "But I have a question. Why does Poppy think Cathy is capable of this?" He couldn't imagine that Cathy would have bragged about her newfound skills to the Fae she so despised. Did Lucy already know about it, back at Lord Iron's house?

Petra smiled. "He saw the potential to destroy anything that confines her written across her soul. It's one of the things he loves most about her."

The gargoyle arrived, the closed poppy in its jaws. Petra took it from him and smiled. "Thank you. I wish you both the very best."

She went into the dining room and Max followed to see her step through a mirror mounted on the wall. Once she was through, he smashed it.

"What if Petra needs to come back?" asked the gargoyle.

"If she needs to come back, Cathy has already failed," Max

replied. "Now, let's find the rest of the mirrors and smash them before anyone else comes to interfere."

. . .

After the second tremor rippled through Exilium, Will sent for his uncle. He'd barely noticed the first, thinking that it was just the pressure he was under playing tricks on him. He'd hoped it was something to do with the fact that the other three crowns were still in want of a bearer, but when it happened again he knew it was Cathy. By the time he'd given his uncle a concise briefing on what Cathy was trying to do, a third tremor made them pause.

"There was a letter," Uncle Vincent said. "Saying we should all stay at home. Everyone got one."

"Take Sophia back to the nursery wing and stay in Mundanus," Will told him. "Don't let her out of your sight."

"Do you think Cathy can actually do this?"

Will didn't want to admit his fear that she could. "I'm doing everything I can to stop her." He sent for Sophia, embraced her, and watched them leave. At least Sophia would be safe. But what would happen to him if Cathy succeeded?

Pacing the throne room, Will considered his options. All the easy routes to Cathy's tower had been cut off, but he knew any one of the Fae could break through there, now he knew where it was. The threat of hurting the governess had evidently not been enough. He'd hoped that Lord Iron would take the bait and come for him, falling into his carefully prepared trap. No magic, no metal, all of the things that would have been used to restrain and imprison him were in place. But no, Cathy had obviously gone ahead with her plan anyway.

He had to escalate faster than he wanted to and show Cathy it hadn't been an empty threat. And if Rainer's suffering wasn't sufficient to bring Cathy in, her brother's would be.

With a snap of his fingers, one of his faeries appeared. "Tell Lord Poppy to bring the woman to me," he said. Moments after it had left, the doors opened and Lord Poppy strode in, dragging Rainer behind him. She was crying and looking back towards the door she'd been brought through.

Will sucked in air between his teeth, uncertain of whether he could do this. It was one thing to duel a man, but to mutilate a woman? What had he been thinking?

He knew the answer: he'd thought that Iron would come to rescue the hostage. Now it hadn't gone to plan, Will wasn't sure how to handle it.

Poppy threw Rainer forwards so she landed on her knees before the throne. "Your prisoner, your majesty."

Will looked down at the top of Rainer's head and the stubby patch of recently cut hair. "Do you have a knife, Poppy?"

Poppy's smile was chilling as he drew a blade from his cane. "I do indeed, your majesty." He offered it to Will with a bent head and then withdrew. It was light and not particularly well balanced, but it would do the job. If Will could bring himself to use it.

"Poppy, can you force a Way to the house Elizabeth went to?"

"Yes, your majesty, my favourite's sister has recently returned from there. I can use her."

"Do it. Summon Tom. If he doesn't come, send Elizabeth to get him."

Poppy bowed deeply. "At once, your majesty." He spun round on his heel to leave.

"Wait," Will said, and the Fae froze. "You'll need to take something with you." He rose from the throne and went down the steps.

At the sound of his movement, Rainer started sobbing. "Please, don't do this! It won't work! It will just make her hate you even more!"

"Your majesty, may I suggest I prepare the Way? It may take me longer than usual, as I'll have to depend on my pet's memory. As soon as I have succeeded, I will return to collect any…package you wish to send."

Will didn't trust Poppy, but he didn't want an audience, either.

Besides, Poppy had no choice but to obey him, and he could summon him back in an instant. He gave a curt nod and Poppy left the throne room.

His hand gripping the sword cane, Will stood in front of Rainer. He felt sick. It wasn't the right thing to do; Cathy would never forgive him if he hurt this poor woman. But how else could he stop her? She was so single-minded. Had she not believed his threat? He looked at the cut on his hand. It stung with each movement. Perhaps he had to find another Queen. But as soon as he had the thought, he knew it was impossible. No one else would do. He and Cathy were married, regardless of his change of status. She belonged to him.

There was another tremor, this one more prolonged than before. It wasn't simply what he felt through the floor, it was a deeper sense of instability. He reached up to touch the crown, feeling for one panicked moment that it wasn't there anymore. He felt the hard oak leaves and breathed again. He had to stop her. One act of cruelty, to protect hundreds in the Nether. Cathy would forgive him. No Queen of Exilium would remain angry with the King.

Just one, swift cut. Just one and it would be done. Will ignored the sweat running down his collar, gripped the sword tighter, and grabbed Rainer's wrist.

His fist closed around poppy petals and in the next blink there was no woman there at all, just a flurry of more petals settling into a heap at his feet. He crushed those in his hand as the sword disintegrated. Poppy had betrayed him? But how? He was the King! "Poppy!" he roared, his shout ringing off the windows. "You will come to me now!"

32

Tom sat on the floor of the tower bedroom beneath the painting, staring at the notes he'd made alongside Cathy's. It didn't help that as he tried to solve the problem of how to end the formula, he was constantly worrying about whether he should be in the room above with her. But they'd agreed it was best for him to make sure no one used the Way to get into that room.

He agreed with her shortlist of three closing concepts. They all seemed plausible. Too plausible to settle on one over the others, alas. He didn't understand how they were written, which frustrated him, as these were composed of several other symbols put together—"sigils," as Cathy had described them. If only the Sorceress had stuck to the pure Coptic alphabet throughout the formula. Then he could be more use.

"How's it going up there?" Lucy's voice was quiet, timid, almost. She'd come up the stairs so quietly he hadn't noticed her arrival.

He put the notes down and got to his feet as she came over. "Quite well, I think."

"Tom, can you…could you hold me?" She looked so lost and vulnerable. He opened his arms to her and she settled into an embrace, her head pressed against his heart. He closed his arms around her, resting a hand on her hair, thinking of how she'd carried him through the days after his father's suicide. He couldn't imagine how he would have coped without her. That was why, when she whispered the Sleep Charm as he'd expected, his heart broke.

He felt her go rigid with panic when the Charm had no effect. "I know it was you, Lucy," he said softly. "You opened the Way so William could send Elizabeth through. We knew you'd try something else, so Cathy warded me against the Sleep Charm." She'd done it in moments, just before going to the second forge, once he'd told her what the gargoyle had said.

Lucy stepped back away from him, breaking the embrace. Her eyes were bloodshot, her lips pale. "I had to."

"You betrayed us."

"Did you expect me to just stand back while she kills my family? How can you support this?"

"Lucy, I—" She darted forwards and kneed him in the groin, making him double over and gasp for breath. She reached over his back to slap the glass dome on the painting and light streamed into the room as the Way opened behind him.

When Lucy pushed past, Tom grabbed her just before she went through, spinning around with her momentum. She stamped back with her right foot, scraping his shin and making him bellow in pain. Through the Way he could see Cat and Sam returning from another forge, his sister so focused on what she was doing that she didn't even see them. Sam frowned and then Tom was distracted as Lucy stamped on his left foot, making him cry out and fumble his grip on her.

She lurched forwards but there was no way he was going to let her get to Cat. Tom stretched with desperation, catching hold of Lucy's hair and yanking it hard. She screamed and staggered back, giving him the opportunity to grab her in a tight bear hug and lift her into the air.

Through the Way he could see Cat and Sam staring in horror. Tom swung Lucy away from its threshold, crossing the bedroom in long strides as Lucy kicked and struggled like a wild animal. "Cathy! Don't do it!" Lucy screamed. "You're going to kill everyone!"

He had to get her away from them and give Cat the chance to continue uninterrupted. Gritting his teeth as Lucy bit his arm, he managed to get to the stairs, pressing his back against the wall and stepping down sideways so she didn't make them fall. Lucy screamed in frustration, knocking her head back to hammer his chest with several blows that must have hurt her as much as him. He just had to keep calm, he told himself, as Lucy yelled at Cat again. Just keep calm, get her out of the tower, then fall apart.

The gargoyle was coming up from the room below and got out of their way, choosing instead to follow Tom down the second segment of the spiral staircase. Lucy had stopped yelling at Cat, instead unleashing a torrent of expletives at Tom as he manhandled her down to the bottom floor. He went outside, but then Lucy started calling up to Cat again in the hope her pleas would be heard through the broken window. Surely she knew it wouldn't stop Cat? When Lucy screamed as loud as she could, as if he were murdering her, Tom realised her goal was to distract. Lucy probably thought that if Cat made an error, the Nether would be saved. This far into the process, Tom was certain it would only lead to disaster.

He adjusted his grip and threw her over his shoulder, as he had with Cat back in Manchester, but this time there was no doubt in his mind that he was doing the right thing. As she clawed at his back he sprinted to the house, the gargoyle close behind him. Once they were all inside, he went to the dining room on the other side of the property, as far away from the tower as possible.

Max came to the doorway as Tom put Lucy down, the gargoyle hanging back. "You bastard," she sobbed. "You stupid, stupid bastard. I'll never forgive you for this." She dropped into one of the dusty chairs, covered her face with her hands, and wept into them.

Tom looked down at her, his body aching but nothing hurting as much as his heart. "I don't think we can come back from this," he said quietly.

"You're damn right!"

He tried to swallow down the lump in his throat. "I think when this is all done, you should go back to your family."

"That was always the plan!" she said, giving him a furious glare. "I don't need your goddamn permission to leave your sorry ass!"

He clenched his teeth, breathing in deep enough to suck the urge to weep inwards. "Thank you for helping me after my father died," he said with as much dignity as he could muster. "I...I wish you well, Lucy."

"We'll keep an eye on her," the gargoyle said. "Just until it's all done."

After a confirmation from Max, Tom left the room, feeling like he'd been keelhauled. He wanted to go and find a corner to huddle in, but Cat needed his help. He'd have to grieve for his marriage later.

• • •

The palace shook with another tremor, sending Will staggering. He clutched the crown, checking it was still there, certain it didn't feel as heavy as it did before. He stared at the doors, expecting Poppy to enter and beg for forgiveness any moment, but they remained shut.

He snapped his fingers. "Bring me Poppy!" he said to the faerie which appeared and flitted nervously in front of him. It disappeared with a pop.

Will stormed towards the doors, but as he reached them, he saw green tendrils creeping through the gap beneath them, sprouting shoots that ended in poppies bursting into bloom. Enraged, he tore them away from the handles and flung the doors open, ripping the poppies apart.

Lord Poppy was at the far end of the corridor, legs rigid, heels scraping the floor as a cloud of sprites and oak-leaf-clad faeries pushed and pulled him towards Will. The Fae was obviously doing all he could to resist.

Will pointed to one of the royal faeries. "Give me a sword, now!" he shouted. The tiny creature abandoned Poppy and flew over, scattering a line of sparkling dust across Will's outstretched hands that formed a glittering sword. This one was properly balanced, at least. "Come here, Poppy," he said, adjusting his grip, ready to strike. "And explain why you have disobeyed your King."

"I imagine you're far more interested in *how* I did it," Poppy said, still leaning back as far as he could as his boots scraped the stone. "Will it be upsetting to discover that your former patron showed me how? Not even he wants to support your rule."

Will tightened his grip on the sword. "Iris, you will come to me too," he hissed through his teeth.

"You never deserved my favourite," Poppy said, now halfway to the throne room. "And you don't deserve that crown. Soon my favourite will take it from you. And then what will you do, little man?"

"I'll be glad I dealt with you whilst I still had the chance," Will said, stepping out of the throne room just as Lord Iris entered the hallway behind Poppy.

Iris walked past Poppy, giving his resistance a disdainful glance before reaching Will. "Your majesty," he said with a bow.

Standing in the corridor, sword in hand, suddenly felt undignified in the presence of his former patron. It was all spiralling out of control. He'd been so swept up in his rage at Poppy's disobedience that he'd lost sight of the true problem. But what could he do? The crown felt light on him, but not, he feared, because he'd become accustomed to it or strong enough to bear it with ease. The tremors had been getting worse. With a quiver in his chest, Will caught a glimpse of his own defeat. "How do I stop Cathy?" he said to Iris.

"I think that is the wrong question to ask," Iris replied. "Perhaps a better one would be 'What should be my last act as King?'"

Will's chest felt as if it were about to burst, unable to contain the rage and panic boiling within. He'd finally got everything he'd wanted and now it was being taken from him. No. Almost everything. He looked past Iris to Poppy, who was trying to bat away the horde dragging him forwards, clinging onto his rebellion for every last moment that he could. Will looked down at the sword that he in turn was clinging to, felt the crown he was desperate to wear for every last moment he could. If the crown was taken and his rule was ended, who would he be then?

His last act? Was it inevitable? Was Cathy really going to win?

"I'd bind you to a promise, Lord Iris," he said, forcing his voice to be level. "To protect me, regardless of whether I am a king, your servant, or a free man."

"Stay your hand against Poppy, and I will promise to protect you."

Will tossed the sword aside and gave a nod. The faeries and sprites abandoned their struggle and flew off. Poppy tidied his frock coat and adjusted his cuffs before coming to Iris's side. "It was nothing personal, your majesty," Poppy said with a mere incline of his head. "I am a slave to the needs of my favourite. She would have been so sad if her friend had been hurt."

Will couldn't be bothered to challenge the lie. Poppy had revelled in upsetting Cathy in the past. They simply didn't want him to be King. He turned and went back to the dais, running through his dwindling options. Poppy's rebellion had delayed him too much. There was no point in harming that woman now. "Poppy, return Miss Rainer to wherever you took her from. Restore her and offer my apologies. Worthless as they are."

"I will," Poppy said, and left.

Lord Iris came into the throne room, closing the doors behind him. "You know it's inevitable," he said. "You feel it too."

Iris was right. Will did feel different. Less powerful, less assured of his own majesty. He looked at the Queen's crown resting on the other throne, waiting for Cathy. It would never be worn again. "What was it like for mortals, before the worlds were split?"

Iris smiled. "Dangerous. Magical. There were so many more possibilities. The knowledgeable could do extraordinary things, even without the Fae. Witches were powerful. Blacksmiths were feared. Both were revered. It was very different."

"And if Cathy succeeds, and the worlds are rejoined, what then? What will the Fae do?"

"We shall revel in our freedom! Nothing ever changes here, in our prison. When this place is gone, we will plunge ourselves into the chaos of humanity. Mortals are always creating things. We shall feast ourselves upon the sheer novelty of it all."

"And then you'll enslave them?"

"Some, probably," Iris said with a shrug. "But we have had many slaves, during our confinement. The free will fascinate us far more, I should imagine."

"And your 'pets'? They'll age and die like the rest of the mundanes?"

"The ones we've lost interest in, yes."

"Have you lost interest in me, Iris?"

The Fae's smile was horribly enigmatic.

A trembling, felt first through the floor and then the throne, distracted Will. It built steadily until a terrific shudder ran through the entire palace, shattering the windows and making the throne rock. He gripped the arms and looked out the window to see faeries and sprites bursting out of the castle as the sun itself seemed to dim.

Will felt suddenly tired and heavy-limbed, and in the next moment his crown cracked and tumbled from his head. He watched, dumbstruck, as the oak leaves lost their lustre and fell from the gold circlet. The same was happening to the Queen's crown, and even the decoration on the thrones was beginning to crumble. The oak leaves on the pillars were peeling from the stone, collapsing to the floor in plumes of dust as the gilded stars on the ceiling fell away.

Iris laughed, scooping up the remnants of the crumbling leaves to toss them into the air like a child playing in an autumnal park. He gave Will one last glance before running out of the throne room calling for Petra.

Will went to the window, his shoes crunching over the glass. It was over. He was merely a man again. He'd reached the top of the ladder, only to have Cathy pull it away from under him.

But there was no anger. It was as if all his emotions were spent, having peaked in his rage against Poppy. Now? He felt tired. How long had he been lurching from one crisis to the next? How long had it been since he felt truly secure? He looked back at the throne. Had he really felt in control wearing that crown? No. He had felt like a prisoner. How long could he realistically have kept pushing that sensation aside? He'd been distracted by the overwhelming need to bring Cathy so they could suffer luxurious imprisonment together. Why? What madness was that? How could he have believed that it was the right thing to do—for either of them? Yet again, what he had perceived as power—and the desperation to retain it—had merely driven him to commit more horrific acts. All in the hope that he would finally feel safe and powerful and free of vulnerability.

Tabula rasa. He was no one now. Not an Iris. Not a king. Not a Fae-touched. Not a mundane. There was a hollowness he'd never dared to face before and now he realised it had always been there, covered up by the desire to please his family, his Patroon, his patron. It had been beneath the surface long before Iris took his name in Aquae Sulis. Perhaps if he'd stopped and faced it earlier, none of this would have happened. But then again, what could he have done differently? How can the pawn abandon the game by choice and leave the board of its own volition? To think he had once believed that he controlled some of the pieces. He laughed, bitterly. Now there was no game to play.

Sophia was safe, at least, but he had no way to get back to her. At least she wasn't alone, and now that everything was changing, Uncle Vincent wouldn't be under pressure to take Jorvic. Soon that place wouldn't even exist.

He swept the shards of glass from the windowsill and sat there, staring out at the horizon. Was all of this simply going to disappear? Was it going to fracture, like the crowns, and kill him in the process? He couldn't even muster any concern about that. He was too tired, too ashamed of himself to care what would happen to him.

"There you are."

Will didn't recognise the woman's voice, so he turned to face the doorway it came from. All the exhaustion was pushed from his body at the sight of Lady Rose and the murderous glee on her ethereal face.

"I've waited so long for this," she said. "You didn't really think I'd forget what you did to my family, did you?"

33

Cathy stepped through the Way, back into the tower room for the last time, shaking with fatigue. The last of the iron cables had been destroyed.

"Did you do it?" Tom asked, rushing over to her and Sam. When she nodded, he pointed out the window at the silver sky. "Well, it didn't work! Look, we're still in the Nether!"

She waved him to one side so she could put the paint pot down and stand in front of the glass again. "It has worked, it just isn't finished," she said as she tried to flex the cramp from her fingers. "We've broken the bonds that keep Exilium stable and separate from Mundanus."

"So Exilium is just…floating somewhere?" Tom asked.

She nodded. Exilium felt like a world contained in a helium balloon and she'd just cut the strings that held it tethered to the earth. Now that she was stopping to think about the magnitude of what she'd done, it seemed too big, too important for her to finish. For the briefest moment, she imagined letting it just float off, no longer her concern. She dismissed the fantasy. If she did that the Nether would still be there, and anyway, the Fae had a right to exist. She wasn't sure if they'd survive indefinitely without the whole ritual being intact. She hadn't broken those cables to commit magical genocide. "Where are my notes?"

Tom grabbed them from a nearby table and put them in her hands. "I haven't been able to make any progress. All three concepts seem appropriate. I think it comes down to which one you wish to emphasise: completion, unification, or stability. Alone, none of them seems enough."

Cathy scoured her workings, double- and triple-checking her deciphering of Beatrice's formula and the logical endings she and Tom had pieced together. They fit with the shape of the working as a whole. All were plausible. But there was no way to tell whether any of them were what Beatrice had in mind. It was like trying to predict the final sentence of a political speech. They'd analysed the content, could see the structure, and knew the argument. But predicting what the final note should be—which aspect of rhetoric or statement of fact should be used—was more difficult than she'd appreciated.

The notes read like gibberish and the symbols blurred on the page. How could she work out how to finish this formula? Why had she started it all without knowing how to finish it?

"Cathy." Sam was standing there, on the other side of the notebook, pressing it down so he could look into her eyes. "Breathe." She tried, but it seemed to snag in her throat. "Breathe," he repeated, and she slapped his hand away.

"Don't just stand there and tell me to breathe! What fucking use is that?" Both he and Tom stared at her, making her feel wretched. "I'm sorry," she whispered, determined not to cry. "It's just…it's really hard."

"Why don't you talk me through it," Sam said gently.

"I need to close the formula. Beatrice wrote everything I've used so far and I understand it, but the way it's closed is important and she didn't get that far because she had to break all the cables first, just like we have. There aren't any notes. I think she just knew what to write. I don't. I don't have that kind of knowledge."

"Okay. So there are three options, that's what you said. How have you got those?"

"Logical progression, using the same techniques that made the rest of the formula. Some of it is drawn from the Coptic alphabet. Some of it is drawn from sorcerous symbols, luckily the ones I've learned; it's like an inversion of warding. And she made sigils, pretty basic ones, really, drawing upon those sources. It opens with sigils, so I think it should be closed with them. Thing is, I don't know which one. I could use any of them—I drew them up using the same base sources as her—and I just need to work it with some will behind it."

"And what do the opening sigils do?"

"They define Mundanus and Exilium and express the connections between them. Then the middle section involves the seven locations we went to, breaking them from the definition of the part that expresses the connections one by one. The first part of the closing clause defines Mundanus and Exilium at the start, with no connections between them. Which is fundamentally unstable for Exilium."

"Didn't you say one was for stability?" Sam asked Tom, who nodded. "Well, maybe that's the closer."

Cathy shook her head. "No. I see it now; if I closed it with the concept of stability, they'd remain as they are but separate, and the Nether would be unaffected. Okay, that's that one out."

"What was the second one?" Sam asked.

"Completion," Tom said. "For obvious reasons."

"That's wrong, too," Cathy said confidently. Now that she'd written the rest of the formula out and immersed herself in the meaning behind all the formulae she'd written, she knew it wasn't right. "How can we say it's completed when the purpose of the formula itself can't be? We're still in the Nether, so we're not done. Dump that one too."

"It's unification, then," Tom said firmly. "That's the one you should use. The worlds are separate and they need to be unified once more."

Cathy focused on the idea and felt a shadow of doubt. She recalled saying something along the lines of dumping Exilium into Mundanus to Beatrice, who'd rejected that. *Shit, what did she say?* Cathy closed her eyes, pressing her thumb and forefinger against her forehead, dredging it back from memory. *I am trying to restore something that was broken* was what she'd said, or something very close to it.

"I'm so stupid," Cathy muttered. "It's bloody obvious."

Tom nodded. "Good, yes, unification! I'll hold the page so it's easier for you to—"

"No," Cathy said, dashing over to the desk to grab a pencil. "Unification is wrong too. It's not unifying two separate things to form one."

"Yes it is," Tom said, following her. "You said it yourself, Exilium is separate from Mundanus."

"No. That's the effect of what the Sorcerers did. Beatrice said she was trying to restore something that was broken, and she didn't talk about it like sticking two halves of a broken jug back together again. This is sorcery! This is redefining reality. The Sorcerers imposed their own definition upon the world and she wrote that definition out to start the formula and then it systematically breaks each of the things that makes it true. I don't need 'unify.' I need to define a *single world*, encapsulating both, within the concept of restoration. Nothing is actively holding them apart any more. There should be nothing that can stop it from being true."

"From what being true?" Sam asked. "You lost me."

"That there is no Mundanus and Exilium. There is only the world, and it can hold what used to be Mundanus and the Fae and their magic too. If I conceptualise a distinction between the two—even if it's just to express unification—I'd be reinforcing the idea of them being separate. I mustn't do that at all."

"I don't know, Cat," Tom said as she rifled through the pile of books on the floor. "That's quite an assumption. Did she say anything else?" He interpreted her silence as a negative. "So you're basing this on one comment in one conversation that you may have misremembered?"

"Tom," Sam said quietly. "Are you a Sorcerer?"

"No, but—"

"Have you had any lessons from a Sorcerer?"

Tom folded his arms. "No, of course not, I just—"

"Have you just managed to work a tonne of kickass sorcery, under pressure, with minimal assistance?"

"No."

"Then, no offence, but I think you should let the one person who can answer yes to all of those get on with it."

Tom nodded. "Sorry, Cat."

"It's okay," Cathy said, and got back to work.

It didn't take long for her to look up the base symbols that would make a good sigil to express the concept, and as she worked, Cathy started to feel more confident about her decision. Tom suggested a couple of symbols from the Coptic alphabet and then, thankfully, backed off. She could tell he was desperate to do more, but appreciated that he wasn't the one to do it.

She designed the sigil in pencil first, layering the ancient letters along with a couple of symbols that Beatrice had used in the first part of the formula, reduced to the purest concept of "world" rather than "world without Fae magic" that had been used to express Mundanus. As the sigil took shape, Cathy started to realise that it was only the way they focused her mind that was important, rather than the actual form itself. After all, by the time the sigil was designed, it was hard to make out the individual components, layered as they were, one on top of the other. Only now, right at the end of the complex formula, did she appreciate that it was probably the point; constructing the sigil made her consider the nuances and complexity of the concept she wanted to work into the magic, but when it came to writing the actual sigil itself, it was little more than shorthand for the will behind it. She suspected that the way she concentrated on the intent behind it was far more important than the shape of what she painted. The only doubt now was whether her concentration and intent were strong enough.

• • •

"The Irises are like weeds," Lady Rose hissed as she approached Will, her auburn hair almost glowing against the room's decaying decorations. "You spread and choke and want everything for yourselves."

Will stood up and went to straighten his frock coat, only to realise he was wearing the mundane clothes he'd arrived in before taking the crowns. "I am no longer an Iris."

"That offers no protection. You were an Iris when you ruined everything."

"Your pets did that all on their own," Will replied, planning to leap out of the window if she got any closer.

"Where are my brothers?"

"I've no idea."

"Then there's no reason to let you live!"

• • •

"Okay. I'm ready."

Cathy pushed away the other books, clearing a space around the glass, leaving her notebook open at the correct page by her feet. She grabbed the brush, dipped the tip in the pot, and stared at the sigil, seeing it as something new, rather than a composite thing. That was good; the meaning was more important and prominent in her mind than anything else. It was time.

But as Cathy held the brush poised, ready to undo the work of the Sorcerers and restore the world to what it used to be, crippling doubts kept her hand inches from the glass. Lucy's words echoed: *You're going to kill everyone!* And she was right. She was going to condemn everyone in the Nether to mortality. To ageing and disease. Did she have the right to do that?

And what if Beatrice was wrong? What if the Fae simply made things worse without balancing out the Elemental Court? What if they were just as cruel as they'd always been, only with the technology and tools of modern society?

What if she'd interpreted the formula incorrectly? What if she wasn't about to simply restore the world to its original state? What if this sigil was in fact going to make all three planes of existence collide together in a fatal, chaotic crash of realities?

The tip of the brush trembled over the glass. Poppy had told Sam that her potential was to destroy. She'd already helped Sam to destroy the connections between the worlds; now she was trying to destroy the Nether, and Exilium too. Her vision blurred as her confidence crumbled and tears welled. She was only doing this because she had failed to change the Nether. Should she have stuck it out? If she'd been a better diplomat, a better politician, would she have made enough progress instead of just running away and deciding to blow it up instead?

"Cat?" Tom whispered. "Is something wrong?"

Cathy sniffed and blinked away the tears. "Just making sure I'm doing the right thing," she said, trying to sound brave and in control. She looked back down at the sigil. The only thing she didn't have any doubts about was its construction.

But then she remembered life in the Nether. How it crushed people and forced them to lead miserable lives. She remembered her mother, forced to hide her sexuality for so many years in a loveless, violent marriage. How many other men and women were hiding theirs? How could they ever hope to be happy in that stifling hell? She couldn't imagine anyone diplomatic enough to be able to persuade the Patroons that everyone had the right to live their lives as they wished.

She had failed. But she couldn't see how it would ever change. How many times had she thought of the Nether as a gilded cage? Why was she so concerned about breaking those bars? What was the point of living forever in a place like that?

Sometimes something had to be destroyed, so that something better could be built.

Besides, she'd come too far to run away now. She'd broken the chains holding the worlds apart, forged by men unwilling to live in a world they could not fully control, and now that she considered it, something already felt different. There was a sense of danger, yes, but also potential. The Sorcerers had pushed magic out of reality, condemning it to myth and folklore and reducing Mundanus to a sterile shadow of itself. Now something that had been wrenched away from humanity was poised to return and somehow she could feel that. She had grown up in worlds shaped by misogynistic, cruel, selfish men. Now that she was smashing the reality that they had imposed upon everyone, not just the Nether, perhaps there would be other ripples through the world, other balances restored along with magic. And somehow it felt right that she, a woman who never fitted in anywhere, who had constantly struggled and railed against a twilight world created by their magic, was the one undoing their work.

With a deep breath, Cathy fixed the sigil in her mind, willing the world to be restored to a place of both magic and mundanity with each movement of the brush. As she focused on the magical intent, the doubts receded and her hand steadied. She could do this. With the last stroke she held her breath.

It felt like she'd been trapped in an airtight room and someone had opened all the windows as a wave of fresh, cold air crashed over her. As she breathed in sharply, reality warped around her, rippling out from the glass she'd painted the formula onto so quickly she couldn't follow its progress. One moment she was in the topmost room of the Nether tower and the next she was standing out in the bitter cold at the top of a crumbling tower with no roof. The sky was the grey blue of pre-dawn, with blushes of red just starting to appear on the horizon, and she could hear birds calling.

There was an almighty crash below her and she looked down to see rough wooden boards instead of the polished floorboards of the tower. All of her books and the magical equipment were still there, so she assumed the crash was all the other furniture falling to the bottom of the tower. The anchor property seemed a lot less intact than the Nether reflection.

It felt as if they were in Mundanus. The fact that the tower had changed around them proved that couldn't be true, though. They hadn't moved from one world to another. It had collapsed into one around them at the completion of the formula.

Cathy looked up at the sky, at the reddening clouds, and realised it was over. She'd done it. She had restored the world to what it once was, and for the first time in a thousand years, everybody would wake in the same reality. She started shivering, feeling tearful and somehow hollow, as Tom wrapped his arms around her. She had destroyed the Nether, fulfilling her potential at last. It was over. It was done.

• • •

Lady Rose stretched out her hands and, looking past his shoulder, seemed to beckon to someone outside the castle. Will turned to see a wall of greenery surging in through the window, and then there were thorns, everywhere. He covered his face as they enveloped him, tearing through his clothes and making him cry out as they pierced his skin. He fell, trying to curl into a ball as the thorns rent his flesh. Where was Iris? Did that promise mean nothing?

Then something changed. The air was suddenly bitterly cold and he could feel a sharp breeze through the tendrils. They stopped constricting, leaving him trapped in thorny bonds, too scared to try to move his arms in case the thorns reached his eyes.

"Mundanus!" Lady Rose gasped. "No…no, this feels different…"

Will heard a car smash into something and shouts and screams nearby. He was lying on cold ground, outside somewhere.

"You there, what is that?" Lady Rose shouted at someone.

"It's a car, you silly cow, call an ambulance!" Whoever shouted it soon cried out in pain.

"I'm free!" Lady Rose laughed. She squeaked with delight and then there was the sense that she'd gone.

Will strained experimentally at the thorns and they snapped, not without tearing at him more. He winced with each movement, feeling every one of the dozens of puncture wounds as he moved. The thought of Sophia having suffered this made him curse the Rosas with renewed vigour, then look around fearfully in case Lady Rose was closer than he thought.

She was gone, having left him where they had arrived in Mundanus. Was that the right name for it now? Peeling the last of the thorny tendrils away as carefully as he could, Will got his bearings. He was sitting on some sort of village green, by the look of it, on a frosty morning shortly after dawn. Next to him was a stone monument, worn with age, with a pale metal plaque riveted to a stone plinth. One phrase stood out in particular: ...*and by tradition it marks the centre of England*. The monument was apparently five hundred years old. It looked like Will felt.

"You all right, mate?" a man said, jogging over with a pug dog on a lead. "You're bleeding. Come and sit down, there's an ambulance on the way for that crash."

Will followed the man's pointed finger to a car that had ploughed into a fence across the road. There were people in dressing gowns and coats clustered around it. "What happened?"

"That weirdo in the ball gown freaked them out, I suppose. I didn't see it myself, but Jim said she just jumped out from behind the monument, like some sort of bloody prank. Honestly, there are some real cockwombles around."

The pug was sniffing at Will's shoes. He shuffled them away from it. "Where am I?"

With a raised eyebrow, the man said, "Meriden. Near Coventry. You must be in shock. Here." The man took off his coat and draped it around Will's shoulders. A siren in the distance made him smile. "That's the ambulance now. It's all going to be all right, see? I live just over there," and he pointed at a house on the edge of the green. "I'll make you a cuppa once they're here. You'll be right as rain in no time."

34

Sam went to the edge of the tower room, shivering. The roof and windows were gone and everything from Beatrice's room lay in disarray around them. The sun was rising and the clouds were a brilliant red. If he weren't freezing cold, he'd have thought it looked lovely. He went as close to the crumbling wall as he dared and looked out, seeing nothing but marshland all around. "Where the bloody hell are we?"

Tom came to his side. "Well, I'll be damned. I'd wager that this is Hadleigh Castle, or rather, what's left of it. Those are the Essex marshes. Lucky for us, they've been doing restoration work." He pointed out the scaffolding and Sam realised they were actually on a large temporary platform. "Without all this, we'd have fallen right to the bottom."

Restoration work in the winter? Sam wondered if Beatrice had set all this up to make sure she didn't die when she'd reached the same point. He didn't agree with her methods, but he had to admire her ability to plan ahead.

"It worked," Cathy said. She was still standing with the brush in her hand, even though the glass she'd painted the last clause of the formula onto had smashed. "It really worked."

"You did it," Sam said, going over to her. "You're bloody brilliant."

"I'm bloody cold," she said, and he embraced her. "Can you see the mansion?" she asked Tom.

"No. There's something over there, but it's a modern building, nothing like the one in the Nether."

"It must have been anchored to a different property," Cathy

said. "I hope Max and the gargoyle are all right." She pulled her phone from her pocket. "No signal here."

"Shit, what about Lucy?" Sam said, trying to peer down to the bottom of the tower through the gaps between the rough wooden boards.

"She was with Max in the mansion," Tom said, still looking out over the marshes. "I doubt we'll see her again."

Sam didn't feel he knew Tom well enough to say anything about that, so he just shared an awkward glance with Cathy before going to look over the edge of the parapet. He noticed the corner of a book caught in the long grasses below. "Are you missing a red book, Cathy?"

Cathy scanned the pile. "No, not that I know of." After a quick rummage, she held up a doorknob. "This will take us back to your place, Sam! We'll open a Way, chuck all of this stuff through, and then I need to sleep for about a week. After some apple crumble."

Sam nodded. "Crumble, custard, bath, booze, bed. In that order." He looked over at Cathy, who was looking for the best place to use the gadget. There were dark circles under her eyes, she looked almost ill with fatigue, and her hair was a tangled lump of a messy ponytail, but he'd never wanted to kiss her more. She settled on a portion of the wall that was higher than her waist and pushed the pin into the crumbly mortar. They all watched the Opener burn a line into the stone, then in the air, and he breathed in relief.

It didn't take them long to chuck everything through into Beatrice's old bedroom, leaving the tower's platform clear of any sorcerous materials. Tom volunteered to climb down the ladder and reopen the Way at the bottom to clear out everything that had fallen through from the lower floors, aside from the largest pieces of furniture. Sam had the feeling that Tom wanted to keep busy, so he left him to it.

Mrs M was on the upstairs landing in her dressing gown when Sam opened the door. "I thought it were you," she said, her arms folded, looking tired. "Look at the state of you. Max just called. He's in London, he's going to go to York and wants help to get back 'ere. I told him to call when he gets there."

Sam whipped out his phone and sent a text to Ben to have a car sent to York. There were so many messages that his phone had stopped displaying them after fifty and just added a plus sign. He sighed. No doubt all hell was breaking loose, but he was just too wiped to deal with it. He texted Des, asking him to come over that afternoon with a prioritised list of fires he needed to fight and then switched his phone to silent.

They ate a full English breakfast, Tom joining them as it was being served, all too tired to chat. Then everyone went off to bathe and change. It all helped, but Sam knew he needed to crash for a few hours. He flopped onto the bed and lay there, so tired yet unable to drop off. He waited a little while, swore, and then went to Cathy's room. He tapped lightly on the door. "Cathy, are you asleep?" he whispered through the wood.

"No. Come in."

She was dressed in one of his hoodies and a pair of jeans that were too big for her, lying on the bed, watching the rain fall outside. He came in and she patted the empty half of the bed. He went and sat down next to her. "I'd thought I'd go straight off," he said. "I'm knackered."

"Same," she replied. "I can't stop thinking about how close I was to fucking it all up. I'm still not sure I haven't. I had a quick look at the news and there are a few breaking stories that could be Fae stuff, but it's not obvious."

"That's a good thing, though, right?" he said. "If something really catastrophic happened, we'd know. Maybe it's just like you said it would be, the Fae-touched just appearing in their anchor properties and scaring the staff."

"I think we'll hear a lot more over the next day or so," Cathy replied.

He reached across and brushed the back of her hand with his fingertips. "You don't seem very happy about it."

She sighed, looking up at the ceiling. "I think I'm just wrecked.

I keep waiting for something really awful to happen. I've no idea where Miss Rainer is, or if she's okay. I don't even know if we did the right thing."

"We did the best we could at the time," Sam said, feeling her thumb hook around his fingers. "It's gonna take a few days for it all to settle down and to get a sense of what things will be like now."

"Don't you think we should be in London or something? Somewhere there were Fae-touched?"

"I think we need to rest. The boxes are being delivered to their houses. We're still wired right now, but I reckon in half an hour we'll be conked out."

"But they'll be freaking out. Maybe I should send a Letterboxer. But I'm not sure I can now…I'd have to change the formula to account for it not being the Nether anymore, and—"

"Cathy, they'll sort themselves out."

"But we're responsible! Some of them won't even know what cars are!"

"And they'll be the ones staying indoors while they get their bearings. And we're not responsible for every single person affected. We didn't split the worlds and lie to people for hundreds of years. We haven't dislocated souls or murdered people or made the Elemental Court into twats. We didn't do any of that. We take a breath, we rest, and then we release the information we prepared before and we figure out how to sort it in the long term, okay?"

Still staring at the ceiling, she let out a long breath. "Yeah. Okay."

They were holding hands now. "Is it okay if I lie down?" he asked.

"Yeah."

Their arms were touching now as they lay side by side. He wanted to kiss her. He wanted more than that, but he'd forgotten how to initiate that sort of thing. He'd only had two girlfriends before Leanne, one he'd only kissed, the second he'd been dumped by after they'd had a fumbling attempt at sex. Leanne had led everything and had always joked that she'd had to seduce him because if she'd waited for him she would have died a spinster.

He felt a pang in his chest, a sudden longing for her and a crushing guilt that he was even considering moving things forward with Cathy. But as it receded, he remembered that it had been a long time since he and Leanne had really been together. And that she'd wanted him to find someone else and be happy. She'd said so in her letters.

Turning his head made Cathy look at him. Slowly, tentatively, he closed the gap between them and kissed her. She kissed him back and then broke away to prop herself up on one elbow. "That's the third time you've done that."

"Sorry?"

She smirked. "That wasn't an accusation."

"I really like you," he said. "Like, really, a lot. I was wondering if you wanted to stay here and...if you wanted to, um...be my girlfriend. Oh God, that sounds so lame."

She flicked a strand of damp hair from her eyes. "I really like you too. But I'm not going to stay here and I'm not ready to commit to anything. I think it's going to be a really long time before I could do that again."

"Oh, yeah, of course." Sam silently berated himself for his selfishness. He should have known it was too soon.

"Can we take it really slow? I need to get my life sorted out. And I want you to be in it. I really do. I just need you to be patient. Is that okay?"

He felt like a pillock. "Yeah, of course it is. I should have thought about it. It's fine."

She lay back down, shuffling closer until their arms were touching again. She squeezed his hand. "If you want to get all mushy, I do love you, Sam. I just need to do this at my own pace."

"Okay," he said, grinning at the ceiling. "I love you too. In a totally non-pressured, non-shit way."

"Good. That's that settled, then." She wriggled closer and rested her head against his shoulder. "Urgh, I'm so tired."

In moments her breathing slowed and her hand relaxed. He breathed in the scent of her freshly washed hair and looked out of the window at the anvil-coloured sky. He wasn't looking forward to the fall-out from the return of the Fae, but as they lay there, rain pelting the window, he knew they were going to be okay.

• • •

Sitting outside the cottage, the wind howling and the rain beating on the car roof, Will considered that following the advice of a five-year-old was probably not the most sensible thing he'd ever done. But then, he'd done so many stupid things, it was hard to tell if it was the worst.

Carter sat silently in the driver's seat in front, waiting patiently. At least he'd decided to stay in his employ, unlike the majority of the staff. Not even his valet could be persuaded to stay in service, now that the worlds had collapsed into one. Will had expected Carter to leave, too, knowing his loyalty towards Cathy, but it seemed the huge man needed to feel rooted somewhere. When Will had gone back to Lancaster House to pay off the staff and ensure they'd remain silent about their life before, Carter was the only one who'd stayed when given the chance to leave. Will couldn't bring himself to explain that Cathy hadn't been kidnapped—it was too shameful a lie to admit to—leaving him wondering whether Carter had stayed out of pity. They would never speak of it, of course. Whereas Cathy was happy to blur the boundaries of the relationship with staff, Will never would.

Sophia had fallen asleep in the last hour of the drive and he didn't have the heart to wake her. She was curled up against him, arms wrapped around his, head resting against his chest. She'd barely let him out of her sight over the past two weeks.

The first week after Exilium's destruction had been an exercise in logistics. Thankfully his room was still being kept at the hotel, as he'd given no check-out date. The bill was horrendous, but all his belongings, including all the assets he'd taken from his house, were still in the safe. He wasn't going to be destitute, but he was still homeless. He'd found his family at Oxford Castle, all of whom were rather traumatised by having fallen afoul of the newly returned Sorcerer and being sealed in, and installed them in a rental property just outside the city. Despite Nathaniel being convinced they were still favoured, Lord Iris never came. Watching his family struggle to come to terms with the fact that they were just average people now was simply too miserable, so he'd left them to adjust and went back to London.

Uncle Vincent's small Hampstead anchor property was cosy and easy to care for, giving him a base to work out his next steps. Will couldn't quite admit to himself that he couldn't bear to be around his mother, a mere shadow of the woman she'd been before Iris took what he had from her. He didn't like the way it made him reflect upon how much of her warmth towards him was evidently rooted in her disobedience to the family. Her love for Sophia, as weak as it had been, had also died. Without any need for an excruciating family debate, everyone accepted that Sophia would be better off staying with Will and Uncle Vincent. Will suspected his father never wanted to see the poor girl again.

Once he'd seen his immediate family safe, Will found himself unable to do anything of note. He drifted through the days, initially scouring the newspapers for coverage about the Fae. But soon he started dreading finding the stories about Iris and Poppy, and the rest of them, plucking new people out of the masses to favour. He really was nothing now. He stopped reading the papers.

Then he stopped leaving the house.

"Will-yum," Sophia had said to him a couple of days ago. "Why are you still in bed? Are you poorly?"

"No."

"Can you take me to the park? Uncle Vincent went out and I'm bored."

"No."

Instead of leaving him alone, as he'd hoped she would, she came in and bounced on the bed. "Bored. Bored. Bored." She sniffed. "It's smelly in here. It smells better at the park. We can feed the duckies."

He'd groaned and pulled the duvet higher. She'd pulled it down. Then she'd tickled him. When he didn't laugh, she'd wormed her way into a cuddle and said, "Why do you have a sad, Will-yum?"

"Because I used to be someone important and now I'm not."

"You are still imported. You are to me."

"Important, darling, not imported."

"That's what I said. Is anything else making you sad?"

"I hurt some people. I feel bad about it."

"Oh! Well, that's easy to fix! You just need to say sorry to them!"

"It's not that easy."

"Yes it is. When I hurt someone I have to say sorry. Even when it's a snail I stepped on. If you don't, you're a bad person."

"Sophia…I love you, but can you just leave me alone?"

She'd pulled the duvet off him then. "No. We're going to find the people you hurt so you can say sorry."

By the time Vincent had returned, she'd almost worn him down with a combination of logic, emotional blackmail, and nagging. When his uncle agreed that it would be good for him to sort his life out, there was no point arguing.

Now he was sitting outside of the cottage he'd sent Amelia to. She'd be heavily pregnant with his child by now. He sighed so deeply that Sophia's head rose up with his chest and she woke up. After a huge yawn, she looked out of the window. "Are we there?"

He nodded. "I think you should wait in the car. I won't be long." He didn't want Amelia to know about her.

Settling her with a teddy bear and colouring books, Will left her with Carter and ran up the path. He was soaked by the time he reached the door. His knock was swiftly answered by a housemaid who let him in as soon as she heard his name.

"She's in the living room, sir," she said, and hurried away after bobbing a curtsy.

The cottage was pleasant enough, with country charm and homeliness. Just the sort of place Amelia would hate. That's why he'd sent her there for her confinement, of course. The scent of rosewater made him feel nauseous as he was bombarded by memories of Amelia ensnaring his affections in the hallway at the Peonias' soiree, of countless kisses, of their first night together. All lies. All exactly what he'd done to Cathy. Did she suffer the same at the scent or sight of Irises? He shuddered and, steeling himself, entered the living room.

Amelia was sitting in a rocking chair near the fire, her belly round, her face softened by pregnancy. She didn't turn when he came in, keeping her gaze firmly fixed on the fire. "So you finally decided to visit."

"I wanted to see how you were."

"Fat. There," she waved a hand over the bump, "now you've seen it, you can go."

"Do you know about the Nether?"

She nodded. "I know all about it. Half of the servants have left. The other half are too scared to go. They've told me everything. And I know about Cornelius."

He sat down on one of the overstuffed armchairs, pulling off his scarf and gloves. The room was stuffy and the fire was banked far too high. "I came to talk to you about the future. And about what we did to each other."

She looked at him then, and even now, even after everything, she looked beautiful. "I assume you're going to leave me here until I've borne your child and then you'll dispose of me, like all of the others who have wronged or inconvenienced you."

He shrugged off his coat. "There was a time when I did plan to do just that. No more. I've come to realise some difficult truths. I'm not proud of what I've done, regardless of the reasons. At the time, I could justify all of it, even murdering your brother. But it doesn't change the fact that I've harmed too many people. I don't want to harm you more than I already have."

"You'll want the child, I take it?"

"Yes, of course."

"And what would you propose for me?"

"Amelia…that feels like jumping ahead to the end of a very long conversation. We don't trust each other. You hate me. I hate what you did to me. I don't know whether we'll be able to forgive each other, but I would like to try and make things right between us."

"Now your wife has abandoned you, you come sniffing around me again."

"It isn't like that. Everything has changed. Literally everything, Amelia. Our patrons care nothing for us now, not when there are so many new people to torment. We're on our own. If I throw you out after you've given birth, where will you go? How will you support yourself?"

She gave him the most disdainful glare. "I would not need your assistance. I can assure you of that."

He balled up the scarf, squeezing it in his fists. What had he expected? Tears and gratitude? "Would you like to come back to London? Not to live with me, but to an apartment there. You may enjoy it more closer to civilisation."

"And what would be the price? I can't imagine this being a genuine act of kindness."

"All I'd ask is that we dine together twice a week. That we try and find a way to forgive each other. Or at least, stop trying to hurt each other any more than we have already."

After a long pause, she stood, revealing the bump even more. He resisted the urge to touch it in the hope of feeling his child. "You really have changed."

He nodded. "We don't have to play the game anymore. And when there's nothing to win, it makes you consider what else there is to life."

"I'd like to come back to London. I'll never forgive you for Cornelius. He was the other half of me. But I think you and I should try to be civil. For the sake of the child."

Standing, he gave a short bow and made his way to the door.

"It's a boy, by the way," she said as he headed out. He paused and turned to look at her, resting her hand on the bump. "I'm certain."

"I know," Will said, thinking of Iris's faerie and the Charm it had placed upon him. That felt like a lifetime ago. "I'll be in touch with arrangements for your relocation."

As he shut the front door behind him, his mobile phone rang. *Nathaniel* was displayed on the screen.

"Will, are you in London?"

"No, but I will be tonight."

"Excellent. Keep tomorrow free. An opportunity has come up, one that could serve us very well indeed. I'll call later with details."

The call ended. Nathaniel had sounded excited, hopeful even. What foul scheme had he cooked up now?

He got into the car and Sophia beamed at him. "Do you feel better now, Will-yum?"

"I do, actually."

She grinned as she put the cap back onto a felt-tip pen. "Good. And now are we going to see Cathy?"

He looked back at the cottage, seeing Amelia at the window. "No, darling. I already said sorry to Cathy, in Exilium. We won't be seeing her again." He settled Sophia and did up her seat belt before seeing to his own.

"Not even for tea?"

"No, darling, not even for tea. I don't make Cathy happy. And I think she deserves to be happy, don't you?"

Sophia nodded and cuddled his arm. "And you do too, Will-yum." She kissed him on the cheek.

"Maybe one day," he said, watching Amelia as the car pulled away.

35

Max accepted the cup of tea from his great-nephew, David, and sipped it as his elderly niece accepted hers with thanks. He cast his eyes over the flock wallpaper and ceramic ducks flying in formation over the fireplace. The semi-detached house at the end of a cul-de-sac was as average as they came.

"I still can't get over it," Joy said in a croaky Lancashire accent. "How can you be so young when you were Mum's brother? You don't look a day over fifty!"

"How old are you, Uncle Max?" David asked, returning with a biscuit tin.

"One hundred and six years old," Max said. "But you must understand, I spent a lot of time in the Nether, where people didn't age."

"There was a woman on the telly the other day who said she were born in 1781 and she looked like she were all of twenty! David, I said, that can't be right. It's all a big joke."

"It's true," Max said. "Some were born before that. But they lived in the Nether too."

"And all the stories about the 'Fae,' are they true?" David asked. "There was one about the newspaper editor who disappeared. The news this morning said his wife has been put in hospital, saying he was turned into a frog. I mean, we don't know what to believe anymore!"

Max pulled out his notebook and wrote *Newspaper editor— frog?* before putting it back in his pocket. "I'll look into that. It's a possibility. I know of a case a few years ago where a man was turned into a frog and accidentally killed by his children."

"Oh, give over!" Joy said with a crackly laugh.

David wasn't laughing, though. He leaned forwards. "How common is this going to be?"

"Not very," Max said. "Unless you have a specific connection to the Fae, as the people from the Nether did, or you're remarkable in some way or in the public eye, the odds of you being targeted are incredibly low. Far worse odds than winning the lottery, I'm given to understand."

David didn't look reassured. "And that Mr Ferran. Can we trust him?"

Max nodded. "Mr Ferran is a personal friend of mine. He's a genuinely good man and is working very hard to make things better."

Sitting back and folding his arms, David said, "I bet you a tenner he runs for Parliament next year."

"I doubt that very much."

"The *Mail* was saying it's all a stunt to drive up the price of iron. And then the editor who wrote it disappeared. Looks a bit fishy to me."

"It isn't a stunt, and that newspaper has printed nothing but lies since the worlds were rejoined. It's as if they want people to be terrified. Mr Ferran could not have turned the editor into a frog; that would have been one of the Fae, and they will not go near him, let alone do his bidding."

"Then why isn't anyone saying anything about that?"

"They are," Max said. "Numerous press releases have been sent out containing details of the websites that contain real advice. Have you not seen them?"

David shrugged. "It's so hard to know who to believe these days."

"No it isn't," Max said. "Mr Ferran's organisation is trustworthy and gives sound advice. I suggest you go direct to their website and follow it, and tell everyone you know, too."

"You look like Mum," Joy said, squinting at him. "Same chin and mouth. She was prettier than you, though."

Max noted David's embarrassment. "I look like this because

my soul was dislocated. As I explained in the letter." Joy frowned but didn't question his words. Max wasn't convinced she fully understood. He looked at the clock. "The others are late."

David pulled a mobile phone from his pocket, tapped on it, and got an instant reply. "They're only five minutes away," he said. "They got caught in traffic. It's been murder since that stretch of the M5 was turned into a meadow. And that's another thing—"

"Go get the photo albums, David," Joy said. "Max will want to see the pictures. And bring the tin that's with them." Leaving his next complaint unfinished, David dutifully went off to find them.

Max was aware of the gargoyle's increasing impatience. It was currently curled up in the boot of his car. They'd agreed that it would be best for him to meet all of the family at once, but most of them had been delayed.

"That bureau over there was my mother's," Joy said. "What was she like when you knew her?"

"She fussed about whether I'd washed behind my ears," Max said, making Joy laugh. "She helped our mother a great deal. She sang a lot."

"She never talked about you," Joy said. "Whenever it came up, she'd get all teary and change the subject. Hurt too much, I suppose. Couldn't you have sent her a note, just to let her know you were alive?"

"No. I wasn't allowed. And then later, after the dislocation, I could only do my job."

Joy pushed her cup of tea to one side and reached across the table, taking hold of Max's hand. Her hands had prominent veins, easy to see through her papery skin, but they still had strength in them. "I am so glad I got to meet you. And you take no notice of David. He's a grumpy bugger and he doesn't trust people easily."

The sound of a car drawing up outside brought David back down the stairs with an armful of photo albums and a tin balanced precariously on the top. He left them on the sofa and went to answer the door.

"I love my family," Joy said. "But they're a noisy bunch and the twins can be an 'andful.'"

There was a flurry of introductions, Max meeting no less than four generations of his family in one go. They'd arrived in a minibus that was now parked next to his estate car and while the adults exchanged travel horror stories, the four-year-old twins took one look at Max and ran upstairs screaming.

"It happens a lot," Max said, as the parents apologised. "I have some things in the car; I'll be right back."

He went outside and opened the boot. The gargoyle sat up, looking excited. "Can I come in now?"

Max hefted out the two heavy bags on either side of it. "Yes, just let me go in first, so I can prepare them. Shut the boot when you come in." He staggered back into the hallway and dropped the bags inside, making a loud clanking sound. The hum of conversation coming from the living room stopped.

David peeped his head round the door. "Can I give you a hand with anything?"

Max declined and carried just one of the bags inside. "Can I talk to all of you about something important? Then we can do... family things." He had no idea what those were, but he knew they would all have something in mind, even if it was just looking at photos. "I explained in my letter that I'm an Arbiter and how that's a sort of policeman."

They all nodded, starting to settle on the sofa and chairs brought through from the dining room.

"You've been seeing reports on the news and in the papers about magic and the Fae and it's all very confusing. I want to brief you all on what's true, what's hearsay, and how you can protect yourselves and your children. I'd like you to pass on this information to everyone you know." He opened the bag. "You've probably heard about advice to nail iron horseshoes on doors. I have two bags of them, made of pure iron by Mr Ferran himself. Nail these to your front and back doors or any other doors into your house. It doesn't matter which way up. It will stop the Fae from interfering with your household by indicating that you are under the protection of Lord Iron. These shoes in particular are very potent. Don't tell anyone else about how special these are, otherwise they could be stolen and we cannot keep up with demand. There's another bag of them in the hallway."

"So is that where the old tradition comes from?" his great-great-niece asked. "About protecting from evil? Was the evil the Fae?"

"It's a dilution of the real reason," Max replied. "It was always to protect the home from evil spirits. More often than not, those evil spirits were the Fae. But there was a lot of misinformation and misattribution of events at the time. We're only just starting to appreciate how much humanity's view of magic has been distorted. The fact that they're horseshoes isn't important in itself, it's just that the Fae will recognise the shape from a distance."

He went on to describe Charms, how to recognise the Fae, how to protect themselves outside of the home, and all of the other facts that he, Cathy, and Sam had agreed upon. The family listened quietly, asking occasional questions, some even making notes on their phones.

As Max finished, there was a fake cough from the hallway. "Is that one of the twins?" Joy asked.

"No, that's someone I want to introduce to you," Max said. "I explained in my letter that as an Arbiter, my soul was put somewhere else, to make me more effective in the policing of Fae magic. Due to an accident, mine ended up in a gargoyle." At the sight of all their blank faces, Max realised the best way was to show them. "Come in and meet everyone," he called.

The gargoyle padded in and everyone yelled and leaned back, apart from Joy, who started to laugh and clap. "Oh, look at that!" Her rasping laugh, at stark odds with everyone else's reactions, made the gargoyle laugh too.

"Hi, everyone," it said, making Joy laugh all the louder.

"And you talk!"

"Of course I do," it said. "We're two halves of the same person. I do all the feeling for him, all the emotions, you know."

"Mummy…" One of the twins was at the doorway, drawn down by all the noise.

"Hey there," said the gargoyle. "Could you scratch just behind my ear? My claws are too big to do it properly." The boy looked uncertainly towards the adults for an indication of what to do.

When none of them gave any guidance, Joy got up and went over to the gargoyle to scratch his head. "Don't be such a great Bertie," she said. "Come on, Jason, show yer brother there's nothing to be afraid of."

The child approached cautiously and the gargoyle lowered its head further so he could reach it. The boy scratched. "It feels like stone."

"That's what I'm made of. Stone with a soul inside."

The other twin came over and after the gargoyle's head was sufficiently scratched, one of them said, "Do you like swings?"

"I don't know."

"Great Nanna has a swing in her garden. Come and see."

The gargoyle was led out and soon all three of them were in the garden running around, the gargoyle chasing the twins, who were screaming in delight. Max gave a satisfied nod as Joy came over and kissed him on the cheek.

"I know it's all a bit strange," she said to the adults, who were still in varying states of shock. "But Max and that there gargoyle are family. And in this family, we accept that we're all different and a bit strange and that's okay as long as we're kind to each other. Now, someone go and put the kettle on. There's a cake in the tin, freshly made, and bring over the biscuit tin, too. I want Max to see the photos."

He was steered to the sofa, where the matriarch took her place in the middle, Max to her left, and the rest of the family either sitting with them or fetching tea. She started with the most recent album, showing him the birth of the twins and various other birthdays. When she started the second one, the gargoyle and the twins came back inside. After suffering the indignity of having its paws wiped free of mud and grass, the gargoyle came and sat on the floor next to Max, resting its head on his knee as Joy talked about the weddings in the pictures.

It was harder to keep up with the names and dates, now that Max was inundated by the rush of emotions that contact with the gargoyle had unleashed. Such relief, to have finally made contact with the only people who rooted him to the real world. Happiness at how Joy had accepted both halves of him so readily and how the rest of the family were starting to relax around them too. Sheer delight at the way the twins came in after having a drink to climb onto the gargoyle's back, one wrapping his arms around his neck, the other sitting high and proud, like he was riding a horse. The novelty of being welcomed and accepted, of feeling part of something greater than himself. He looked down at the gargoyle, who looked up at him with one eye, not wanting to move so the twins could stay in place, smiling.

"Now this is what I wanted," Joy said. "We can look at them other albums after." She picked the tin off the pile and prised it open. Dozens of sepia photos were inside, and, rummaging through them, she plucked one out. "There's my Mum and Dad, on their wedding day."

Max looked at his sister, older than he remembered her, but still familiar. Her hair was in a 1930s curled bob, her husband handsome enough, both wearing their best clothes and standing rather awkwardly outside a church.

"It rained after they took that," Joy said. "They went to the village hall and had beer and pork pies with their friends."

"Beer and pork pies?" David sounded unimpressed.

"Well, beer was Mum's favourite and pork pies were Dad's favourite. Though Mum went on to stout when she got older. Now, there's another one in here…oh! I forgot about this one! This is me when I were born." Max and the gargoyle looked at the chubby-faced child in a frilly cap and dress before it was passed round.

"This is the one I were lookin' for!" Joy handed Max a picture with a very familiar background: the foundry his father had worked at. But instead of the men all lined up, there was his father, mother,

Jane, and him. Jane's arm was around the young Max's shoulders, squeezing him protectively, whilst their mother and father stood formally behind them. They were all in their Sunday best, Max not yet old enough to be wearing long trousers, his knobbly knees in plain view between his short breeches and long socks.

"I remember this!" Max said, the memory returning bright and clear, like a coin buried in a muddy river bed suddenly revealed. "My knees were cold and I was shivering, that's why Jane put her arm around me. But I can't remember why it was taken."

"Mum said it were because grandad had just been made foreman and the foundry wanted a picture of him. He gave the photographer a shilling on the side to take a family portrait, because they couldn't afford to get one done proper like. It used to be framed over the fire, but when you and grandad disappeared, it were taken down and put away. My Mum only found it when Granny died."

Max stared at his own young face. How thin he and Jane were! He could remember the scratchy wool of that jumper pressing against his skin under the jacket, how he was bending his arms slightly to hide the fact that its sleeves weren't long enough anymore.

It couldn't have been long after that when he was taken by the Arbiter. Looking at himself as a child, and thinking of how he was taken from his family and forced to be part of the Chapter made a rush of tearful anger sweep through him. He'd lost so much. His mother and sister had suffered so. All because he'd seen something that could have been easily explained away to a child.

"Oh!" Joy saw the tears break free and run down his cheeks. "Oh, there, there. Oh, I didn't mean to make you cry!"

"I lost so much," Max said as the gargoyle's face crumpled too.

"But look what you have now!" Joy said, taking his hand. "Look! A family! And we're so glad to know you now. You're like a little piece of my mum come back to me after all this time." And then she was crying and they held onto each other as the rest of the family sniffed and resolved to make more tea and struck up conversations about the cake, all of them trying hard to make everything seem normal.

Max held his niece tight, the gargoyle nuzzling her arm with its nose, and for the first time in over a hundred years, he felt loved.

• • •

"Yes!"

Glimpsing the ceramic surface through the gap in the newspaper, Cathy pulled the mug from the box and unwrapped it on the way to the kitchen of her new flat. She'd found the kettle first, had bought teabags and milk on the way to picking the keys up, but it had taken over three hours to find something to make the tea in. She'd packed everything in such a hurry, months before, when the Seeker Charm was bringing her brother to her door and her dreams of freedom were lost. None of the boxes were labelled and all of the contents were randomly packed, but thankfully, nothing had been found broken. Yet. She rinsed the mug in the sink as the kettle boiled, grinning at the old-fashioned lady's face on the side against a lurid pink background. *Tea! Crisis management since 1652!* said the words below it. She nodded in agreement.

At least she'd had the wherewithal to ask one of her most reliable university friends to take care of things when Tom was on his way to drag her back to the Nether. After a phone call and a happy reunion over coffee, Cathy had all the details she needed to get back on her feet again. With luck worthy of something she'd bought in an egg, it turned out that her friend's brother was looking to break his tenancy early and was happy to have her move in at short notice. She took over the bills, too, meaning everything was already set up when she moved in. It was a nice place, very small, but close enough to the centre of Manchester to walk in whenever she felt like it.

It felt like a palace.

The first sip of tea in her new flat was a happy milestone, and not the first one that day. When she'd unlocked the door for the first time, she realised that she was going to live somewhere she had chosen, that she was paying for herself (admittedly with the proceeds from the jewellery she was supposed to pass on to her children but sod that), without the fear of being discovered. Before, in her old place, the constant fear that her family would find her and that the Fae would ruin everything, had tainted every single day. And they had found her. And the Fae had ruined everything.

But she had survived. And more than that, she had destroyed the box they tried to keep her in.

It was also the first home that she had warded against the Fae. She'd scratched the formulae into the very top edge of the door and window frames, balanced precariously on a dodgy stepladder she'd borrowed from the building manager.

Taking the steaming mug back through to the tiny living room, she surveyed the chaos. Han Solo was propped up in the corner in his cardboard glory, her scarf draped around his neck. Her TV was plugged in and still worked, which amazed her considering that she'd dropped it when carrying it from the storage centre's trolley to the hire van. That had been the only moment she'd regretted not accepting Sam's offer of help.

"Just give me the details and I'll have my people sort it all out for you," Sam had said when he'd found her searching for van hire companies online.

"No, thanks." She'd smiled at him. "I'm going to do all of it. I've got all my finances sorted again and I've put down the deposit. I got this."

"I've got loads of property in Manchester. Salford Quays is nice. I own a whole bloody building there, much bigger than that place and better security, too."

She'd got up from the desk, gone over and taken his hands. "Sam. I know you mean well. And I'm really grateful for your help. But I don't want to be dependent on anyone. Not even you. And paying the rent on a flat you own just doesn't feel right to me. It all has to be totally mine. Okay?"

He'd nodded. "Okay. Sorry. I get it. I just…"

"Want to take care of me?" He'd nodded again. "Like the nice rich man taking care of his favourite lady?"

His earnest expression distorted into one of disgust. "Urgh, no! Not fair."

She'd kissed him on the cheek. "Are you saying I'm not your favourite lady?" It had quickly unravelled into tickling and taunts until Mrs M had come in to ask if they wanted dinner yet. She was going to miss Mrs M's cooking. There were three of her pies in the freezer and she wasn't sure how long they'd last.

Cathy leaned against the window frame, looking out at the other red-bricked buildings and the tram rattling past below. She couldn't remember the last time she'd felt this happy. There were background worries about how she and Sam still had so much to do in the effort to educate the public about the Fae, and a nebulous concern that Will would hunt her down, but it all felt distant right now. Will hadn't been in touch for over two weeks, and he'd have had ample opportunity. She hoped his behaviour really had been caused by the crown and that he had no interest in her now.

It was tempting to resume her studies. She had the feeling that human rights law was going to go through some interesting changes over the next few years, and regardless of the addition of the Fae, there were still many people who needed passionate advocates. But she also wanted to continue to study sorcery. Rupert was still in Oxford and there was always the chance he'd try to split the worlds again. She didn't think it would be possible for him to do it alone, but nevertheless, having someone to counterbalance the man was surely useful. Besides, she could already see how many useful applications her skills would have in everyday life. If only she'd known how to ward herself against drunk men when she'd been a student before. She tried not to think about the hushed warning Max had given her before going to seek his family. He seemed to think that learning sorcery created memory problems, but Beatrice hadn't shown any sign of them. Maybe it had been something to do with being just a pure Sorcerer. Max only knew two of them anyway. Hardly a representative sample. Still, the worry remained. She'd be careful.

The front door rattled with the familiar sound of a Letterboxer and Cathy was glad she'd put that exclusion clause into her ward.

It was too useful to block. A postcard and two letters rested on the mat.

The postcard was one of the Roman Colosseum and she recognised Tom's handwriting as soon as she flipped it over.

> *Dearest Cat,*
>
> *Rome is more splendid than I could have possibly imagined and the winter sunshine has been most welcome. Saw the Trevi Fountain the other day, larger than I thought it would be. Coffee terrible, no tea to speak of, ice cream excellent. On to Milan tomorrow. Ciao!*
>
> *Your loving brother,*
>
> *Tom*

Smiling, she rested it on the kitchen counter, ready for when she found her fridge magnets. She was glad Tom had finally gone to Europe. He'd been such a rock for the people in Aquae Sulis in the week following the restoration, helping the oldest of them to come to terms with the modern world enough to stop panicking every time they went outside. They'd spoken on the phone every day, checking in every lunchtime as they both did all they could to stabilise and reassure those they could influence. When the worst of the transition was done, and the Lavandulas were able to host a soiree to reassure previous residents of Aquae Sulis that civilised behaviour would continue, Tom had started to grow restless. Cathy knew he had always wanted to travel and had managed to persuade him that it was his time to do as he wished. It was almost as if he'd needed permission to be selfish. There was no better way to get over the grief about his failed marriage.

The first of the letters was from Natasha.

> *Dear Cathy,*
>
> *I do hope you are well and that you have managed to find a flat. I am writing to pass on my new address which you will find enclosed. If you decide to remain in the north-west, I hope we will be able to meet, as I have decided to take employment at the library in Manchester. They were impressed by my knowledge of the Dewey*

Decimal System, coupled with my passion for local history and my experience with the Fae. I start there on Monday and I am most excited.

With love,
Natasha

Cathy looked up the address on her phone. An hour's walk or ten minutes on the tram. She beamed at the thought of living so close to her. She'd make sure her house was warded too. Cathy was determined to make sure that nothing horrible ever happened to Natasha again as a result of their friendship.

The last letter was from Charlotte.

Dear Cathy,

I write to reassure you that Margritte is back in England and is currently lodging with myself and Emmeline whilst she considers her options. She has asked me to pass on her thanks to you and Lord Iron for arranging her passage back from the Americas. We are all rather shocked by the recent events and rumours abound that the Patroons are currently informing the residents of Londinium that they are in negotiations to secure a new "Nether" for the Great Families and that they should not consider leaving the city. Have you heard anything about this?

Margritte says that Alexander was reinstated as Vice-Chancellor but barely had time to return before the collapse. Apparently there's a Sorcerer in Oxford, have you heard? I think it's one of those silly rumours that people like to spread to feel important. Margritte and I scour the newspapers daily for any mention of it, and indeed of any of our old friends and rivals. Did you see what happened to poor Harold? Knocked down by a bus in Oxford Street, apparently. How is your sister? What will she do now she is widowed?

Do you have any idea what caused the collapse? The Fae are most definitely at large, did you see the picture of Lord Poppy in the newspaper? He seems to be having a lot of fun. Do you think he could have been responsible for that arms shipment being turned into poppy seeds, or could that have been a rogue faerie? We've heard rumours about those too.

When you have a moment, let me know how you are. I'm sorry William wasn't who we thought he was. Is it true that you've been staying at Mr Ferran's house? I saw him in the newspaper too. He is quite handsome, isn't he?

Oh, I almost forgot! Emmeline has been accepted into Cambridge and will be studying Human, Social and Political Sciences. We are so thrilled. I am considering the pursuit of higher education myself, and Margritte and I have been discussing the possibility of setting up an organisation to aid women of the Nether to access the education denied to them before the collapse. Is this something you'd be interested in? I thought Natasha might like to be involved too. I shall pen her a letter after this. Benedict has decided to continue his Grand Tour as planned, which I think is very wise.

I miss you, Cathy. Let's arrange a day soon when we can all meet in happier circumstances and make our plans to help fellow ladies take advantage of all the opportunities now available to them.

With love and affection,
Charlotte

A new Nether? Cathy sighed. Those Patroons would say anything to try and keep their clutches on the ignorant few. As soon as she was settled, she'd make sure those rumours were put to death. As for Elizabeth being a widow, she was sure she was very happy. She wouldn't put it past her sister to have pushed the poor man under the bus herself. She made a note in her phone to write back about the organisation to help women gain the education they'd been deprived of. Her heart started to race at the thought of the four of them, together again, making plans without Will's obstruction.

She still had to unpack, though, so the letters were left to one side as Cathy went back to the front room. She turned on the TV, needing some background noise while she ploughed through the chaos.

"I have no interest in a political career."

Cathy nearly dropped a mug at the sound of Sam's voice on the lunchtime news. He was outside the Manchester office, not that far away, nabbed by the small crowd of journalists that always seemed to be camped outside.

"How would you respond to accusations that these outlandish claims about the return of magic is a plot to drive up the price of iron?"

Sam laughed at the man who'd asked the question. "Seriously?" he laughed again. "That's just bloody bonkers. I haven't got time to waste on conspiracy theories."

"Isn't the rejuvenation of the UK steel industry at odds with your radical environmental activism?"

Cathy held her breath. They'd discussed this question coming up just yesterday, and had drafted an ideal response to it. Had he had a chance to learn it?

"I'm not some hippie who thinks we should all return to nature," Sam replied. "It's possible to have a steel industry that meets the very best environmental protection guidelines and create thousands of jobs in the process. There's a bigger picture here, and not just the increased demand. The politicians have ignored swathes of the population who just want solid, reliable jobs that create tangible things. I'm hoping that my vision for our steel industry will restore the pride and self-respect of people like my father and grandfather who lost their jobs in industry years ago."

She grinned. Word perfect.

"And what about rumours that you've bought government permission to do this?"

Sam smiled right into the camera. "All of the paperwork is in place and available to be scrutinised by anyone who feels they need to. The government should have been driving this a long time ago, but it doesn't have the will to make these improvements. This is a better solution than austerity."

"And what would you say to your fellow billionaires, Mr Ferran? Are you putting the pressure on them to start a golden age of philanthropy?"

Sam shrugged. "I don't know about any golden age. I'd say to them...pay some bloody taxes for a change."

Cathy laughed as she unwrapped the mugs and carried them through to the kitchen. When she came back into the front room, another man was being interviewed, grey-haired and jowly, standing outside the Houses of Parliament. "We're very concerned, of course we are. Rumours of the 'Letterboxer' alone have caused a crash across all postal company shares. Free, instantaneous postage? It's...it's appalling. I mean unregulated. And dangerous. I'd urge the public to avoid any offers to be taught this dark art. How can we stop bombs being posted directly into an office with magic? I can't believe we even have to have this conversation."

It cut abruptly to a government minister running the gamut into Downing Street. "A full statement will be made shortly," she said. "I cannot confirm or deny the rumours that weapons have been turned into poppies in areas of active engagement."

A cluster of advisors were being ushered through with her and Cathy barely registered their faces until one leaped out from the crowd.

Surely she'd imagined it?

Cathy scrabbled around the clumps of discarded newspaper looking for the remote. With a shaking hand, she rewound the footage.

"...in areas of active engagement."

There. Standing mere paces away from the foreign secretary, was Nathaniel Reticulata-Iris, dressed in a smart modern suit, behaving like he had every right to be there. Sickened, she watched him move into Downing Street, only to notice Will following at the back.

"Fuck."

She turned off the TV and chucked the remote onto the sofa. She was shaking, just at the sight of them. "Okay, breathe," she whispered. "He's not here. He won't do anything to me."

The buzzer rang, making her jump. She had to clamber over boxes to reach the entry phone and its screen in her hallway. There was a courier on the doorstep. "Hello?"

He pressed the intercom button. "Delivery for Catherine Papaver."

"I'll be right down."

"It's heavy, love, buzz me in and I'll bring it up to you." Cathy released the intercom button, resting her head against the wall next to it as she shivered. Was this Will, starting a new round of harassment? Or Lord Poppy, sending her something awful to remind her of his affection?

"Hello?"

She jumped at the sound of the courier's voice. "I'll buzz you in," she said, and pressed the button.

Fidgeting with nervous energy as she waited for him to come up to her floor, Cathy fretted over whether she'd made the right decision. But she refused to be ruled by fear. She had to move on.

And she had to add wards to the building entrances.

The knock on her flat's door made her jolt. She looked through the spy hole. It wasn't Poppy. She put on the chain and opened it as far as it would go. There was a large flat parcel resting against the wall, the courier catching his breath beside it. "Miss Papaver?"

"Yeah."

"Can you sign for it?"

He passed the handheld device through and she scribbled her signature with the stylus before passing it back. He smiled and jogged down the corridor to the lift.

Once she was sure he'd gone, she undid the security chain and looked at the parcel's address label. *Sam Ferran* was listed as the sender.

She laughed with relief, feeling like a paranoid fool as she dragged it into the flat and locked the door.

A framed picture was inside, covered with bubble wrap, which she peeled off in excitement. It was one of the promotional pictures of Ripley from *Aliens*, standing in her khaki jumpsuit, arms folded, rifle slung over her shoulder. There was an envelope taped to it with *Cathy* written in Sam's handwriting.

I'm here if you need anything. Here's to the future, whatever it may bring.

Sam xxx

Grinning, Cathy found her phone and shot him a text. *OMG love it! Thanks so much. She can watch over my stuff and remind me to not take any shit from anyone.*

A moment later she got a reply. *Glad you like it. Wanna meet up tonight? Missing you.*

Cathy tapped the phone against her lips, feeling torn. She'd planned to not see him for a few days, to make sure she was fully settled first. *How about a housewarming drink? Bring some booze, I've only got tea!*

The reply was swift: *I'll bring booze and pizza xx.*

Still grinning, she went back into the living room and turned the television back on. The news had finished and the weather forecast was on. Rain for Manchester. No surprise there.

Cathy went back to the window and looked out on the street again, then up to the sky heavy with rainclouds. She'd get the living room straight, then go for a walk in the rain. The days stretched ahead of her, filled with half-formed plans, fears, and worries, but above all else, hope. Everything was changing. At long last, the cloying stagnancy of the Nether was gone. She had destroyed it. She had fulfilled her potential, in Poppy's eyes.

"Nah," Cathy said to herself, reaching for her tea. She hadn't reached her potential yet. She was just getting started.

acknowledgements

This Split Worlds novel was written after the Masked Ball LARP that took place in Bath on May 7th, 2016, and I want to thank each and every player and member of the immensely wonderful crew— and of course Katie Logan who was in charge of them and who basically made it all happen—for bringing this world to life in a way I never believed possible. I also want to thank you all for being so vibrant in my mind as I wrote the majority of the characters in this book, and for being so very supportive since the ball. I feel so blessed and so lucky to have you all in my life.

I also want to say sorry to a few players who might have felt... emotional when reading this! (Sorry not sorry, of course. Love you!)

But seriously, I want to draw attention to Amy Green and Russell Smith in particular, who played Lucy Rhoeas-Papaver and Edwin Californica-Papaver at the Masked Ball LARP (and played them perfectly, I might add!), for the solution to the problem of how to impress Lord Poppy at a ball. This challenge was presented to them that night and the solution they cooked up, with help from Hannah Earnshaw, is the one you have read in this novel. I hope I did it justice! Russell, I will never forget the sight of you in that dress, reading those words, nor the look on Lord Poppy's face as you did so!

There were so many amazing moments from that night that I was desperate to put into this novel, but there simply wasn't room. But each and every one of you made writing this book even more exciting and enjoyable, so thank you.

Moving away from the ball, I'd like to thank my agent Jennifer Udden and my editor Jaime Levine for helping me to make this book better. I won't lie, it was hard wrapping up a long series like this, but you both had my back, and I am grateful.

Big thanks, of course, to my husband, Peter, for all the chats, the knot untangling, the hours of listening to me reading the first draft aloud. I couldn't have done this without you.

A hearty thanks to you, the reader, and all the people who have showered love upon this series. I'd also like to thank Arran Dutton and Dave Perry for all the help when recording the audiobook versions of this series. I love working with you guys!

I realise now that these are the last words I am writing for this series, and it feels right that they be given to Kate. I have been haunted by the memory of a visit, years ago, when I read some of the first novels in the series to her. We were saying our goodbyes in the hallway of her flat and she hugged me fiercely and said, "Don't die before you have finished this series! I need to know what happens at the end!" and I promised her faithfully that not only would I not die, but I would also finish the series.

Sadly, Kate passed away before the fourth book was written and it still breaks my heart that she didn't get to hear the end of the story. But every moment I wrote these last two books she was in my thoughts, the memory of her yelling at Will and laughing at the gargoyle so bright in my mind. So here you are, darling, I finished the series for you and now I am releasing it into the world with love and gratitude for the time we had together. I think of you every day. I love you. Always.

EMMA NEWMAN writes dark short stories and science fiction and urban fantasy novels. She won the British Fantasy Society Best Short Story Award 2015 and *Between Two Thorns*, the first book in Emma's Split Worlds urban fantasy series, was shortlisted for the BFS Best Novel and Best Newcomer 2014 awards. Emma is an audiobook narrator and also co-writes and hosts the Hugo-nominated podcast 'Tea and Jeopardy' which involves tea, cake, mild peril and singing chickens. Her hobbies include dressmaking and playing RPGs. She blogs at **www.enewman.co.uk** and can be found as **@emapocalyptic** on Twitter.

If you want to go deeper into the Split Worlds, go to **www.splitworlds.com** where you can sign up to a newsletter and find over fifty short stories set in the Split Worlds!